SHADOW

AND

STORM

BOOK 2 OF THE MAREK SERIES

ALSO BY JULIET KEMP

THE DEEP AND SHINING DARK
BOOK 1 OF THE MAREK SERIES

JULIET KEMP

SHADOW
AND
STORM

BOOK 2 OF THE MAREK SERIES

Elsewhen Press

Shadow and Storm
First published in Great Britain by Elsewhen Press, 2020
An imprint of Alnpete Limited

Elsewhen Press, PO Box 757, Dartford, Kent DA2 7TQ
www.elsewhen.press
British Library Cataloguing in Publication Data.
A catalogue record for this book is available from the British Library.
ISBN 978-1-911409-49-6 Print edition
ISBN 978-1-911409-59-5 eBook edition

Printed and bound by CPI Group (UK) Ltd, Croydon, CR0 4YY

This book is a work of fiction. All names, characters, places, trading
organisations, governing councils and events are either a product of the
author's fertile imagination or are used fictitiously. Any resemblance to
actual events, governments, companies, places or people (living, dead, or
spirit) is purely coincidental. No angels or demons were harmed in the
making of this book.

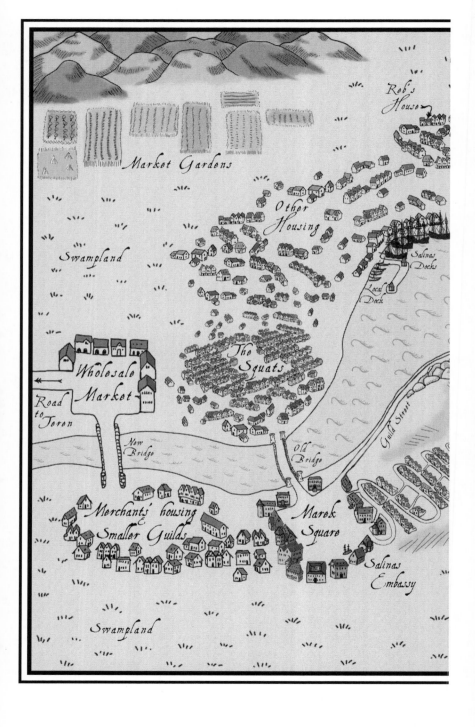

© Juliet Kemp and Alison Buck, 2018

ONE

When Jonas opened the door – cautiously, because he still felt far from comfortable with this room and what it represented – Cato was lying full length on his bed, propped up on a couple of pillows, hands behind his head. It was an unseasonably warm day for autumn, and one of the windows was open to catch the breeze. The room was, as usual, a mess, with clothes flung over the end of the bed, oddments piled on the dresser, and half-a-dozen books on the floor. The only neat area was the table and shelves containing Cato's magical equipment. The chaos grated on Jonas, brought up living in close quarters at sea, where stowing everything away when not in use was both necessity and habit strictly enforced by his sea-captain mother and his shipmates; and grated worse because Cato obviously could keep things neat if he chose. At least the open window meant the place smelt clean today.

Cato stretched a little and scrubbed a hand through his close-cropped brown hair, looking eminently at ease. Much more at ease than Jonas felt. This was the fourth of these practice sessions and it had been nearly two months since the whole debacle at the Salinas embassy, after which Jonas had chosen to miss his ship back home to Salina in favour of learning about what Cato maintained was 'his magic'.

Not that there was much magic going on, as far as Jonas could see. Flickers, yes, he was still having those, same as he had since he was a child, but actual deliberate magic? That, not so much.

And he'd stayed in Marek for this. He felt a familiar pang of homesickness.

"Hm. That whole foreign and interesting thing you have going on," Cato said, in apparent response to absolutely nothing. "You can definitely play that up."

Jonas stared at him. "Play it up?"

Foreign? Interesting? He supposed that his fair hair did stand out among mostly dark-haired Marekers, although his

skin was much the same light brown as Cato and his sister
Marcia. Cato in particular was distinctly pale for a Mareker,
possibly because he rarely bothered to leave his room in
daylight.

Cato shrugged. "You need a thing, right? If you want to get
work. A reputation. Sulky, immoral, mysterious past isn't
going to work for you, not with that honest face. Anyway,
that's my thing."

"So you're just making it up?" Jonas said. "It's all a
pretence?"

He wasn't sure how he would feel about that. On the one
hand, Cato's behaviour in the embassy – working for the
rogue sorcerer Urso in his attempt to overthrow Marek's
government and forcibly replace Marek's cityangel – had
suggested that he did, once you got right down to it, have a
small quantity of moral backbone. Cato had backed out, after
all; had, with Jonas' help, disrupted Urso's magic. Beckett,
Marek's cityangel, was back in their proper place. On the
other hand, Cato had been willing to work with Urso and his
fellow plotter Daril b'Leandra in the first place, mostly
because they'd paid him and without troubling himself overmuch about what their plans were. On the other *other* hand,
he'd offered to teach Jonas how to use magic. Which would
be more of a mark in his favour if Jonas had been wholly sure
that he wanted to be able to use magic. He'd stayed in Marek
to do it, right enough, but...

"Well. I am immoral," Cato said, with a shrug. "And often
sulky. My past – anyone's past – is only as mysterious as
people try to make it, but they seem to like making it more
mysterious, who knows why. The lure of the dramatic, I
suppose. It's a good image, in any case. It works, you
know?" He paused. "Debonaire. I missed out debonaire."

Jonas found himself doubting, again, whether all this had
really been a good idea. The magic, to start with; but also
working with Cato, rather than, say, Reb. Reb was certainly
more irritable than Cato and Jonas was slightly scared of her,
but she was straightforward.

Cato was looking at him narrowly. "Look. You're my
apprentice, right? I'm not going to be dishonest with you.
And that includes the, ah, trimmings of this as a profession,
not just the mechanics of it as sorcery. You can't do sorcery

part-time. It's a full-time endeavour, and that means you need to make a damn living at it, unless you've got a private income you've not yet mentioned, and that means you need clients. And sometimes, maybe, you need to be a little bit economical with the truth when you're dealing with them. They're hiring a sorcerer. Not Cato, nor yet Jonas. Nor Reb, come to that, though I'm not sure she'd see things quite this way. They want a sorcerer of a particular type. And that means you need to make sure you're giving them that. So's to be sure they fuckin' pay you, you understand me?" His Marekhill drawl had dropped for a moment into the tones of the squats that both he and Jonas now lived in. "Because magic can do some interesting things, but it can't put bread on the table nor yet be exchanged for a flask of wine."

"You can't create things," Jonas said, finally on slightly firmer ground. Cato had given him a brief theoretical run-down at his first lesson.

"That's it. No concrete effects, more's the pity."

"But look." Jonas' frustration erupted. "It doesn't matter if I can't create things, because I'm not doing any magic. It's not happening."

"Patience, dear boy," Cato started, then he caught Jonas' eye, and sat up with a sigh. "Fine, I know. It's frustrating. But honestly, I'm sure you have it in you. I'm not sure what it is that's blocking it."

He tilted his head on one side and looked Jonas up and down, assessing.

"Not sure I do have it in me," Jonas said.

"You were contributing to that shitshow of Urso's at the embassy," Cato said, with absolute conviction. "I would stake my worldly fortune on it."

"For what that's worth," Jonas muttered.

Cato beamed cheerfully at him. "What's money for if not for spending?"

Cato had only collected half of the money that Urso and Daril had promised him, but he'd blown through almost all of it within three weeks. "And I needed all those ingredients."

"And the wine?" Jonas asked.

"You are a most impolite apprentice," Cato complained.

"A magical apprentice who can't do magic." Jonas folded his arms.

"You can," Cato insisted. "Look. Have you had any more of those flickers of yours lately?"

Jonas absolutely hated talking about the tiny snippets of future-vision that he referred to, when he had to refer to them at all, as his flickers. He looked away.

"Have you?" Cato demanded. "I'm not asking for the fun of it. If you want to do this, I do need a little honesty. Or openness, if you prefer."

"Two," Jonas said, still staring at the shelf of ingredient-jars.

One had been the very-near-future sort, where the flicker barely ended before the thing it predicted. They made Jonas dizzy, but they were handy when playing dice, and they weren't too bothersome. This one had shown him paying for his beer a second or two before he handed over the money, and had led to him dropping coins all over the bar, but that was nothing worth fussing about. The other, though, had shown Cato and someone Jonas didn't recognise, talking quietly in the corner of a bathhouse, Cato looking almost affectionate; and it had come with the ringing in his ears which usually meant something important.

"Oh yes?" Cato said. He leant forwards a little, his eyes alight. "What about, then?"

"None of your business," Jonas said. He wouldn't have told Cato about his flickers at all, for choice. He certainly wasn't providing any detail. And he felt a bone-deep reluctance to tell Cato that he'd seen anything of Cato's own future. His flickers didn't seem like the sort of thing he should share with their subjects.

"Oh, come on," Cato said. "Surely as a good apprentice…"

"I said no," Jonas said, more loudly than he'd intended.

Cato's eyebrows went up, as if he were genuinely startled, then he gave a more theatrical eyeroll and shrugged gracefully. "Well, if it's that sore of a subject, then by all means, keep your strange secrets. It might help me to work out what's going on here," Jonas didn't believe that for a second, "but I have no intention of insisting. In any case, if they're still happening, then you can't have burnt yourself out with that farradiddle of Urso's."

"Could that happen?" Jonas asked. "Could it have happened, I mean?" He had a horrible feeling that he sounded hopeful. He had an even more horrible feeling that he didn't know whether he was hopeful or not.

"I have no idea," Cato said. "The flickers mean that you're coming at this from an unusual angle. Lacking previous data of that specific type, I can't be sure. But there's no records of any other Marek sorcerer burning themself out, so I think no, it's not likely."

Jonas nodded slowly. His own people, the sea-faring Salinas, didn't hold with magic of any sort. Originally, Jonas had come to Marek to look for a sorcerer who could take his flickers away, so he would be able to join a ship. Cato had convinced him – no, that wasn't fair; Jonas had chosen – to stay in Marek and try to work with his magic instead. He'd second-guessed that decision *at least* once a day since, but there wouldn't be another Salinas ship in the harbour now until the storm season was over.

Another couple of weeks, and he could hop a ship, if he wanted. Any Salinas ship would take him on for the rest of their voyage and then home. As long as they didn't know about the flickers, that was.

"I can still try to take it away, if you want," Cato said, sounding surprisingly gentle.

"Thought you said it wouldn't work," Jonas said.

"Well, it most likely wouldn't. Not entirely. I could probably teach you to suppress it, but if you're going to do that, you might as well learn to use it first. It's all much the same skill." He looked slightly shifty. "Arguably," he added. "So. If you're not going to tell me about these flickers," he paused very slightly, and Jonas glared at him, "we may as well try the summoning spell again."

Jonas sighed and picked up a pigeon-feather from the desk. He didn't see why it was likely to work now if it hadn't before, but Cato was right; if he was here, he might as well keep trying. He took a pinch of ground ginger, placed it into his cupped left hand, and mixed it with a pinch of wood-shavings.

"Now," Cato said, peaceably, lying back down on the bed. "Focusing your mind on what you wish to achieve. And holding the charming Beckett in mind as you make your request."

With the tip of the feather, Jonas began to flick the ginger and wood mixture, a little at a time, out of his hand, changing the direction he swept it in each time. He thought of the pigeons outside the window, going about their business; thought of the squats as they looked from the roof, as the pigeons must see them. He thought of Cato's window frame, and where it was in the building, and where the building was in Marek, imagining the city as a pigeon would see it from on high, the river winding through the middle of it, to the south of where he currently stood. He envisaged one of the pigeons flying down towards the building, in towards Cato's windowsill. He placed Beckett, the cityangel, the spirit that looked to Marek and made its magic work, in the Marek of his imagination, permeating the city as a half-real half-imagined presence; and for a fraction of a second, he could have sworn he felt Beckett's grave unmoving regard, saw Beckett in his mind's eye as Jonas had first met them, confused and part-human in a pub.

And at the back of it, he felt a great frustration boiling in his skull. A frustration with his flickers, and with his apparent inability to do this thing that Cato had said he could. It wasn't *fair* to have one and not the other, not when Cato kept telling him that they were connected. A frustration with Beckett, who had brought him to the attention of sorcerers and dragged him into a magical and political confusion that he was still surprised he'd come out of in one piece. A frustration with Cato, lying on the bed watching him with a faint and unconcerned smile. A frustration with this whole damn city, and with the Salinas ships whose welcome would sour if they knew what he could do. He clenched his teeth as it built, still thinking of the squats and the city and the pigeons, and flicked the last little bit of the mixture out of the palm of his hand.

There was a great fluttering of wings, and pigeons began to pour into the room through the open window. Five, ten, dozens of them crowding into the room, as Jonas stared open-mouthed. Cato, shocked out of his lethargy, sat up just a little and mouthed what was undoubtedly a swearword. Pigeons were flapping around his head, feathers everywhere, a claw tangling in his hair then ripping away, and he felt the beginnings of panic. He'd done this, hadn't he? How had he done it? How could he undo it?

There was a roaring in his head, a tightening across his skull, and then…

… someone tall, and travel-stained, climbing out of a window, a Marek window, Jonas knew with inescapable certainty, with a bag over their back, anxiety around them like a cloud, and the scent of danger…

He staggered and almost fell with the dizziness that always accompanied a flicker, just as Cato stood up on the bed, batting pigeons aside with his hands. Through the storm of wings, Jonas saw him make a gesture with one hand, then the other, saying something that Jonas couldn't hear through the noise of the birds. The fluttering died down even as he was saying it, the birds funnelling back out through the window as quickly as they'd come in, until the room was silent again.

"I thought you needed ingredients to do sorcery," Jonas said, inanely, the first thing that came to mind.

"*You* do," Cato said, sitting back down again, cross-legged. "At least for now. And I generally find them helpful. They provide a focus, and a certain amount of energy, or power, or what-have-you. But – well, in an emergency, yes?" He took a deep breath. "Takes it out of you, though." And, indeed, he did look a trifle worn, beneath his mask of casual unconcern.

"What happened?" Jonas asked.

Had the flicker had anything to do with the magic? With the pigeons? He almost opened his mouth to tell Cato about the flicker, then thought better of it.

"We-ll," Cato drawled. "At a guess, I'd say that you did some magic. Perhaps slightly more magic than we had quite intended. I did say that Beckett might still be quite fond of you."

"Fond of me? To send all those birds here?"

"You asked for birds, no? Birds were sent." Cato beamed at him. "Now, Jonas, do tell me. Just how annoyed were you – at me, perhaps? People often are annoyed at me, I have noticed this in the past – when you did that? I'm thinking, perhaps, very annoyed."

Jonas looked at him, sitting cross-legged in the middle of his rumpled bed, feathers still drifting down around him, the bedcover and the floor of the room spattered with bird-shit. There was an expression of polite inquiry on his face.

Jonas started to laugh. Cato's lips twitched, and then he

was laughing too.

"Don't worry," Jonas choked through his laughter. "I'm sure I'll be able to get annoyed again."

"Happy to help," Cato said, and cackled once more.

☺ ☺

Tait stared down the side of the mountain, and shivered. They really didn't like heights; which made joining an expedition through a mountain a bloody stupid idea, except that none of the other options had been any better.

It was cold, and Tait's feet had been wet inside their ageing boots for days now. In an ideal world, they'd have bought good-quality new boots, maybe with sheepskin lining, before they started out on this trip. In an ideal world, they wouldn't have been in quite the hurry that they had been. In an ideal world, they would never have decided to train as a sorcerer and they would still be living happily in Ameten. Somewhere warm. With a fire, and a nice stack of books to read in front of it.

Below them, here in this very non-ideal world, the rest of the expedition were strung out along the absurdly narrow path that wound its way sinuously down the mountainside, snaking between boulders and stunted gnarled mountain trees. Captain Anna had directed Tait to keep to the rear, on the grounds both that Tait was slower than anyone else, and that Tait's job was to be prepared to perform sorcery at a moment's notice should something require it. Which Tait strenuously hoped it would not.

Bracken, just behind Tait's shoulder, made a huffing noise, indicative of his wish for Tait to get a bloody move on. Bracken's job was to protect Tait should they need to do sorcery, and also to get Tait down the mountainside safely without freezing up at any point along the terrifying path. Bracken quite clearly thought that Tait should have mentioned a fear of heights when persuading Captain Anna to take them on for the journey. Captain Anna most likely thought the same, even if she hadn't said it. Though Bracken had become less visibly irritated after the expedition was attacked by a dragon-bear − only a small one, but still big enough to have ripped them all to pieces – and Tait had opened a vein and translocated it straight across a ravine, to roar at them, baffled, from the other side.

Dragon-bears didn't worry Tait. Well, that wasn't wholly true. Tait had no desire to be ripped to pieces either. But the dragon-bear, in itself, hadn't been Tait's main concern right then. Tait's main concern had been not attracting spirit attention that they really, really didn't want. Which was why they'd risked bleeding out rather than do what any other Teren sorcerer would have done and summon a spirit. It was well worth the cost of a pint of so of blood and several stitches afterwards courtesy of the expedition medic not to become visible on the spirit plane. Happily, everyone else on the expedition was from Marek and knew sod all about Teren sorcery, so no one asked awkward questions.

And once Tait got down this damn mountain and into the swamps at its foot, they would be nearly at Marek, and once they got to Marek, they would be able to avoid spirit attention altogether. Or that was the theory. Maybe they could even work out how to be a sorcerer again safely…

It was a thought warming enough to get them moving down the absurd goat-track of a path.

"'Bout time," Bracken muttered under his breath, stomping down behind Tait.

Bracken was shorter than Tait but about twice Tait's weight, which surely should have meant he would find the narrow paths harder going, but apparently it didn't work that way; Bracken seemed to have endless endurance and no fear at all. And he was carrying a significantly heavier pack, too, containing a share of the money and trading goods that the expedition was bringing back for its sponsor, House Fereno, one of Marek's ruling Thirteen Houses. Captain Anna seemed to think quite highly of House Fereno, and in particular of whoever had organised this expedition. Personally, Tait couldn't give a shit about Marek politics. What Tait cared about was that Marek only had the one spirit, and didn't let any others in. And that meant Tait would be safe.

Hopefully.

"How much longer?" Tait asked Bracken, as the path widened out enough for them to walk side by side.

A certain amount of shouting was drifting up from below them. Tait looked down to see the rest of the expedition gathered by the side of a stream – well, a waterfall – that cut across the path. It looked like they were trying to bridge it. Great. Crossing a slippery tree-trunk across a raging torrent was exactly what this day needed.

"'Til camp? Think Captain wanted to get right out of the mountains," Bracken said. He nodded downhill. "See them trees down there? Reckon that'll be where we camp tonight."

As far as Tait could see, the land kept on going downhill beyond the forested bit that Bracken indicated. They said as much.

"Nah, but, that's not mountains, right? That's just hills."

"Right," Tait said doubtfully, peering downhill again, then wishing they hadn't.

"Much easier going," Bracken said, obviously trying to sound reassuring.

A shower of stones slid out under Tait's foot and bounced down the rocky mountainside, and they flailed, before Bracken grabbed their shoulder and steadied them.

"Proper paths, not stony like this," Bracken added, as Tait regained their balance and tried to pretend it hadn't happened.

"Well," Tait said. "Good. And then, how long after that to Marek?"

Bracken made a thoughtful *tch* noise in the back of his throat. "Well now. Camp tonight. Another day to the river. Quicker, in the hills. Maybe a day and a half on the boats through the delta. Nice and easy, with the current. No trouble at all. So not tomorrow, nor yet the next day, but midday of the day after, should be." He nodded, happy with his assessment. "And I'll be glad enough to get home, and with a nice healthy lump of cash for our efforts, too." He grinned cheerfully at Tait, and clapped them on the back. "And not eaten by dragon-bears either, eh?"

Tait did their best to grin back at him. On the path below, the rest of the expedition had crossed the waterfall, had their packs back on, and were heading onwards down the mountain, leaving a single person by the bridge to wait for Tait and Bracken. Two and a half more days. And then Tait could stop looking over their shoulder. Hopefully.

Of course, what they were going to do in Marek was another matter, but Tait could work that out once they were no longer at risk of being pulled apart by an angry demon. For now, the prospect of reaching Marek was enough to get them heading down towards the bridge with a glad heart. Well. Glad-ish.

TWO

Someone was calling Jonas' name from the upper balcony of the Dog's Tail. He looked up to see Asa waving down at him.

"I have a seat," they called, then held up a nearly-empty glass. "Get us a beer?"

Waiting at the bar, Jonas' glance fell on the charms hung over the barrels to keep the beer sweet; he still found that strange to look at. The Salinas dockside pub he'd been in last night with Tam wouldn't have dreamt of having anything of the sort; but then, their beer wasn't the best anyway. Their berith was nicer, and he'd bought Tam one, so as to try it, but that was too expensive to drink all evening. That pub hadn't been this crowded; the docks were empty of Salinas ships at the moment, and the Mareker dock-workers not so inclined to spend money on drink while they had less work.

He paid for two mugs of beer, then made his way up the stairs and through the crowded upper room. The pub was on a street corner, and once he was out on the balcony he could see down towards the river, a little sliver of water just visible at the end of the street between the closely-packed houses. Lemon-bark torches burnt on the corners of the railings to ward off the mosquitos; Asa had assured him that the season for them was nearly over. You didn't get them out at sea, either, nor yet in Salina, but Marek was surrounded by swamp. He'd never been here at this time of year before.

He put the beer glasses down, slid onto the bench beside Asa, and leaned into them a little before backing away again. Salinas didn't go in for physical affection in public, but Marekers did, and he was trying to make allowance for Asa's preferences.

"Good day?" Asa asked him. The low sun shone off their smooth brown cheekbone as they turned towards him. They'd untied their red messenger's armband; Jonas could see it peeking out of their shirt pocket.

Jonas shrugged a shoulder. "Morning running messages. With Cato in the afternoon."

"How was it?"

Jonas really didn't want to talk about it. He shrugged again. "Fine." *I summoned half the pigeons in the city. It's possible that I need to get annoyed to do magic. I had a flicker.* Asa didn't know about his flickers. "Just, you know. Fine."

"Trade secrets, eh?" Asa said. "Fair enough. Well, *I* got a whole series of runs through the merchants' quarter." They sounded deeply satisfied. "Right along Guildstreet, three in a row, then back to some jeweller at the foot of Marekhill, and she tipped me very generously indeed. I'll get the next round in."

"I'd appreciate it," Jonas said a bit ruefully. Working with Cato was really cutting down his time for paid work.

"Weirdest thing happened, though," Asa said. "I was coming along Guildstreet, second message of the run, and all of a sudden every pigeon in the street just up and took off, all at once. Strangest thing I ever saw. Nothing to account for it – just this huge cloud of pigeons, all flying over the river. Towards the squats, far as I could tell."

"Goodness," Jonas said, feeling very self-conscious, and hoping that his surprise sounded convincing. "How peculiar. What happened after that?"

Asa shook their head. "Just as suddenly as they started up, they all just stopped again. They didn't just stop flying, I don't mean. But it was like they'd all had an idea, and then the idea disappeared, and they all flew off their separate ways." They laughed. "Strange birds."

"I suppose they just forgot what they were doing," Jonas said. "Not the brightest, are they?"

"No indeed, but I wonder what set it off? The only time I've seen anything like was once when someone was flying a hawk in Marek Square, and every bird in the place took off and away. But I didn't see a hawk this time."

"A mystery," Jonas said, and changed the subject as quickly as he decently could.

Asa, as promised, went to fetch the next round. Leaning back into the corner of the rail behind him, Jonas started to wonder if he could, reasonably, share with Asa some of what he was doing. It wasn't fair, surely, to expect him to keep silence and speak only to Cato. But then again, Asa was right – all trades had their secrets. It wouldn't do for him to tell Asa something that Cato would think he should have kept quiet.

In any case, it wasn't the sorcery he really wanted to talk about. He could talk to Cato about sorcery. If he really wanted to, even, he could find Reb and talk to her – though he'd been avoiding her. And he'd have to admit to the whole business of learning sorcery from Cato. He was a little surprised that she hadn't come chasing him down, after she'd seen him apparently performing sorcery in the embassy, but perhaps she had enough on her plate.

Either way. It wasn't the sorcery. It was the flickers. He wanted to be able to tell Asa about his flickers. And he never did that. He'd told Urso, when he'd just thought Urso was a trader with an interest in magic, before he'd discovered that the man was, illicitly, a sorcerer himself. He remembered the relief of that moment, of mentioning it and of Urso's reaction – interested, fascinated, but not in any way disapproving. And then, on the other side, he remembered telling his mother. The sinking feeling when she'd flinched and turned away from him, told him to *deal with* this problem. By which she meant: get rid of it.

That difference was why he'd listened to Urso, more fool him. Urso hadn't told him to get rid of it, hadn't flinched from him. Urso had just accepted the truth of it. Granted, then Urso had moved straight on to trying to use Jonas for his own purposes, and Jonas had been an idiot to allow that to happen, but still.

He wasn't sure what had happened to Urso, after the embassy. He'd been arrested, Jonas thought, but he'd not heard anything of a trial. Maybe sorcerers didn't get trials.

His mother would be even more upset by the sorcery than she had been by the flickers. Like everyone else at home. He could walk away from the sorcery, though, if he wanted to. He'd never wanted to be a sorcerer. He barely even believed in it. But Cato said that the flickers and the sorcery were the same thing, and… and he didn't want the flickers, either, but Cato had said "It's yours, and you can learn to use it," and…

Jonas sighed, and rubbed at his eyes. He didn't want the flickers or the sorcery, but that didn't stop both of them from tugging at him in some deep part of his soul. He'd have to get rid of them eventually, if he wanted to go home. When he wanted to go home. But surely that would be *easier* if he understood more first. Then he could get rid of it with an easy mind.

But how was he to understand his flickers without anyone to talk to? Cato was interested, and unlike Urso, he didn't seem to have his own purposes in mind, but with Cato one could never be sure.

And in any case, he couldn't say anything to Cato of how he *felt* about them. Theirs wasn't that sort of relationship. And he sorely felt the need of someone to have that conversation with. It was absurd, really; he'd gotten through his entire childhood holding it secret. He was used to it. And yet somehow, now there was someone else who knew, it felt almost impossible to continue.

Asa wasn't Salinas; didn't have that automatic distrust and dislike of anything remotely magical. Asa wasn't bothered about him apprenticing to Cato. Surely, that meant he could tell them about the flickers? If they were just a form of magic?

Maybe they weren't. Reb, when he'd asked her, months ago, without mentioning that he was asking about himself, had never heard of such a thing. Cato was convinced that they were a form of magic, but hadn't any idea beyond that. Marek magic was supposed to be all about the cityangel, and Beckett had told Jonas that the flickers were not of Beckett's doing. Could they really be magic of a different kind?

"You're quiet tonight," Asa observed, sitting down next to him and startling him badly. He hadn't been paying attention. That wasn't a great habit, round here, though the Dog's Tail itself was safe enough. "What's on your mind?"

Jonas looked into Asa's warm dark eyes. Surely Asa would be fine with the flickers.

But… what if they weren't? What if those warm dark eyes would turn cold and doubtful; would turn away from him the way his mother had?

"Oh, nothing much," he said, and felt his insides shrivel slightly. "Hey, you haven't caught me up on the gossip yet."

"Well then," Asa said, laughing. "So, Tam, right…"

Maybe tomorrow he could tell Asa about it. Or the day after, even. Maybe when he understood it himself a little more. And once he understood it, he could decide what he was going to do with himself.

☺ ☺

Cato was lying flat on his bed, staring at the ceiling as the reflected red of the sunset gradually dimmed, when he heard the knock on the door. Well; less of a knock, more of a highly irritated pounding. He glanced over at the clock that Marcia had given him. Reb was exactly when he'd expected her.

The pounding intensified, and he smirked up at the ceiling.

"Do come in," he called.

"You want me just to take them down?" Reb demanded from outside the door.

Cato considered it – it wasn't like they didn't both already know that Reb could take his wards down if she wanted to, and it might as well be her that did the work – but he suspected that she was annoyed enough to make a deliberate mess, and that meant more hassle putting them back up again.

"One moment."

He rolled over to take a pinch from the pot of wards-mixture under the bed, and threw it towards the door, focusing his attention onto it and muttering a couple of words. A pleasurable shiver ran down his spine, and the wards around the door sparked then disappeared into – the spirit-world, Cato supposed, though his theory on these things was shaky. He'd like to ask Beckett some questions, except for the bit where that would involve talking to Beckett. Cato's magic might depend on the cityangel, but he was just as happy for that to happen from a distance. Beckett saw too much.

Reb barged the door open and Cato smirked over at her from his prone position. Her short brown curls were untidy, and her skin shone with sweat. It had been too warm today to be storming around Marek at Reb's customary speed.

"I was expecting to see you," she said, glaring at him. "This afternoon."

Yes, she did seem quite annoyed. But he hadn't seen any particular reason to reply to her message, so she shouldn't have expected him to show up. He'd guessed that it would take her a while after his non-appearance to come round and yell at him.

"I don't really respond well to demands," Cato drawled. "For the love of the angel, sit up, you lazy sot." Cato didn't move. "Still not responding well to demands." "I didn't send you a demand," Reb said. "I sent you a request. To discuss something that you must agree is important. To both of us. To Marek. To Beckett." Cato winced a little. He preferred not to name Beckett out loud too often. Names had power. "Sounded like a demand to me." "It was a request. And if it didn't suit you, you should have replied to tell me so." "Not many reliable messengers round here," Cato said. Not at his end of the squats. Not many reliable people of any sort, form, or description, in fact; though that depended on your definition of 'reliable'. If you paid the right rates, people could be surprisingly 'reliable', in that they mostly stayed bought; and of course, very few people were prepared to risk crossing a sorcerer, which was handy.

"You could have got off your damn arse and walked two minutes down the road," Reb said. "Where there are a great many perfectly reliable messengers."

This was also true. Lots of messengers lived in the rest of the squats. But Cato didn't see why he should walk down the road purely to make Reb's life easier.

He shrugged, which was surprisingly hard when lying down.

Reb appeared to be searching for something especially cutting to say. Cato was quite looking forward to it for the entertainment value. She opened her mouth, then shut it again as the air in the room shuddered. She looked over at Cato, alarmed, and Cato pulled an expressive face back at her, experiencing a sudden surge of fellow-feeling. The air shuddered again, glittering in spirit-side colours that didn't belong on this plane. A soundless thump reverberated through Cato's bones, and suddenly Beckett was standing between them.

Cato sat up in a hurry. He was happy to piss Reb off. Not so much Beckett. He had no idea what exactly would piss Beckett off, but starting with basic good manners seemed wise.

The cityangel still looked the way they had during their

brief time on the human plane: paper-pale skin, a white fuzz of hair, wearing a long tunic in nondescript grey-brown cloth over their tall, angular body, and nothing else. They didn't look like a human body fit naturally. Cato wasn't sure why they were keeping to it, but perhaps it was for the same reason they had kept the name they'd acquired on the human plane. Which was to say, Cato had no damn idea why, and didn't particularly want to enquire.

Had Reb arranged this? Her wide eyes as she looked across at Beckett suggested not. That implied Beckett had decided to barge in of their own accord, which was not an idea Cato liked in the slightest.

"You waste time arguing about the past," Beckett said. "You are both here now."

Cato chose not to contemplate how Beckett could know the content of their conversation thus far. What theory he was familiar with suggested that the cityangel had, in some sense, access to the city as a whole. Presumably Beckett couldn't actually engage with that all the time; it was a spirit, but it wasn't a god, since there were no such beings, and it didn't have godlike powers. Cato's best conceptualisation of the matter was that Beckett could somehow treat the city and its history as a library of sorts.

Or the cityangel had already been deliberately watching him and Reb, which was more than possible and also something Cato had no wish to think about.

He caught Reb's eye, and got the strong impression that she felt similarly. Which, given that she undoubtedly had a better relationship with Beckett than Cato did, was either reassuring or entirely the opposite.

"We are indeed both here now," he agreed. "Reb, I apologise for my terrible lack of manners." Beckett might or might not pick up on his tone, but Reb certainly would. It cheered Cato up a bit when her eyes narrowed. "I fully agree with Beckett that we should move onwards with... uh, whatever it was you were after me to talk about."

Reb glanced over at Beckett, who did something with their face that looked like it was supposed to be a smile. It was, frankly, creepy.

"We need to reorganise magic in Marek," Reb said.

"In what way?" Cato asked politely. "I personally have not

felt any lack of organisation."

"The Group no longer exists," Reb said.

The Group – which Reb had once been part of, and Cato most certainly had not – had been responsible for, in a very loose sense, overseeing the practice of magic in Marek. It examined apprentices, placed some very loose limits on what sorcerers might do within city limits, kept the ban on blood magic, and dealt with any nasty little awkwardnesses that might arise in the magical realm. Like that business his sister had been involved with, a bit over a decade ago. Until the plague, when all its members except Reb herself had died; and Reb hadn't been in the mood to return to the job all by herself. She'd barely kept working her own magic, come to that.

Cato approved, in a detached kind of way, of the last part of the Group's responsibilities, owing as how he didn't want the fabric of reality ripped apart, or demons rampaging through the city, any more than the next person. Back when teenage Marcia and that idiot Daril and his friends had got themselves into trouble, there was no way they could have controlled that thing if Reb and Zareth hadn't stepped in to send it back spirit-side. Cato's regret for Zareth's death had been real. Cato had only been a teenager himself, but Zareth's reputation was impeccable.

Cato was less convinced about the matter of blood magic – wasn't it up to a sorcerer to make their own decision about that? Doing blood magic in Marek was damn stupid, if you asked him, given that the whole point of Marek magic, of Beckett's commitment to the city, was that you didn't need to. But if someone would rather open a vein than appeal to Beckett, surely that was their own business.

He wasn't convinced at all by the need to certify sorcerers and oversee them thereafter. He didn't care to be overseen.

And more pertinently, they'd been without the Group for two years now, and nothing much had come of it. Cato would quite happily see that situation continue.

"Good thing too," he said, affably. "Your point?"

"If the Group had still been operational, we could have avoided everything that happened this summer," Reb said. "Urso would have been spotted."

By 'everything that happened this summer', Reb

presumably meant the attempt by Urso Leanvit and Daril b'Leandra to instigate their coup by removing Beckett and inviting in a spirit who would lack Beckett's restrictions. One that would, in particular, not be bound from interfering with politics as Beckett was. Daril b'Leandra – who had form on this kind of thing – had been driving the political side but had no sorcery whatsoever. Urso, on the other hand, had been a decent sorcerer, and Reb wasn't wrong that he should have been spotted.

Cato himself had been involved with 'everything that happened this summer', albeit only after the most disastrous part had already happened and strictly for financial return, so the comment was more than a little pointy. Perhaps, after all, it wasn't quite accurate that 'nothing much' had come of the Group's absence.

"But it was all resolved," Cato said, determined nonetheless to hold his corner.

"More by luck than good judgement," Reb said, which must have cost her a bit to admit since she'd been the one trying to resolve it. "We can't rely on luck to keep Marek magic running."

"So what are you envisaging?" Cato demanded. "An emergency reaction group? An oversight committee? Is your new Group going to come barging in demanding information about every sorcerer in the damn city?" All two of them, right now – three if you included Jonas, which Reb wouldn't because she didn't know about him currently – but that wasn't the point.

"We need some kind of oversight," Reb said. "We need to know that there aren't more Ursos out there creating chaos."

"It's none of anyone else's business what a sorcerer is up to," Cato said, more fervently than he'd expected. "Or what their apprentices do, come to that. Why should one set of sorcerers have power over another set? Who decides which is who?"

"Well, I had in mind yourself and me," Reb said. "Given that there's not really any other option."

Cato's mouth dropped open. He'd assumed that Reb meant to be the new Group all by herself, and find more sorcerers to join it over time, presumably by training them up herself. He hadn't thought for a moment that she would be prepared to work with him; or would consider him a suitable person to be pronouncing on the activities of other sorcerers.

He didn't consider himself a suitable person to be pronouncing on the activities of other sorcerers, although obviously his judgement was excellent in all regards.

Reb was waiting for a response. Her toe was tapping, even. Reb had very little patience.

"My objections don't disappear if I'm the one with the power," he said with his best attempt at dignity. It even had the advantage of being the truth.

Beckett was still watching both of them. Their presence didn't help Cato think clearly. Or perhaps it helped him think far too clearly. One or the other.

"What exactly are your objections?" Reb asked. As far as he could tell, it was a genuine question.

"Well…" Cato said, drawing the word out to buy himself thinking time.

"Is there a form of the Group that you could subscribe to?" Reb prompted. "Because I wouldn't wish to simply enforce it over your objections."

Cato blinked, surprised yet again. Reb was being remarkably… sensible about this. Reasonable, almost, behind the tapping toe and the irritable expression.

"I could," Beckett said, and both Cato and Reb jumped.

"You could," Reb agreed, "but I'd rather you didn't. Cato, we both know we've never got on, and that if there were anyone else I wouldn't be here. But you are a very competent sorcerer," she grimaced slightly as she said it, but Cato could see she was sincere, "and there isn't anyone else. I don't want to be at odds with you."

"So if I don't agree to this, you won't do it?" Cato asked.

"If you don't agree to this, I'll do it alone, I suppose. If you're actively against it – well. I would like to find a solution that we can both agree to."

"You'd do it alone?" Cato said. "So, you'd be, ah, judge, jury, and executioner? Over me, specifically, in the absence of anyone else." He wasn't about to mention Jonas. Jonas wasn't really a sorcerer yet, and whilst revealing his apprenticeship would muddy up the waters of the current discussion in a very entertaining fashion, it would be more trouble than it was worth. "That doesn't sound like a *group* to me."

"What do you want me to do?" Reb demanded. "If you won't do it, that only leaves me."

Cato shrugged. "Or not doing it at all."

"And wait for another Urso to come along, but more successfully this time?" Reb demanded through her teeth. "I will not…"

"I could withdraw my co-operation," Beckett said. Their voice fell into the conversation like a stone. "If that would help."

Cato's stomach lurched. 'Withdraw their co-operation'. That was a disingenuous way of putting it. Without Beckett, Cato couldn't do magic; at least, not Mareker magic. He swallowed, and tried to keep his face calm.

Reb was staring at Beckett. She didn't look enthusiastic either. That was something.

"*Could* you?" Reb asked. "Within your compact?"

Rufus Marek and Eli Beckett, the original finders – founders – of Marek the city, had made the deal that bound the cityangel to the city and vice versa, thereby creating Marek's unique form of magic. Cato wasn't wholly sure of the details of the deal, but it worked, so he wasn't going to pry.

"If I believe it best for the city," Beckett said. After a moment, and with visible reluctance, they added, "Perhaps."

"And then what, he starts in on the blood magic? Or drags other spirits in to mediate for him?" Reb demanded.

"I will not tolerate other spirits here," Beckett said, seeming to grow slightly.

"Cato works with other spirits," Reb said, irritably. "As we all know fine well."

"Not here I don't," Cato pointed out, trying to sound relaxed.

It was a tricky point; he did indeed work with other spirits, always had, but he did it by creating a space partway between this plane and the spirit plane, so the other spirits never set foot into Marek, meaning the cityangel didn't have to be bothered. He'd always assumed that Beckett knew about it, inasmuch as he'd thought in quite those terms prior to Beckett's enforced sojourn on this plane.

"I could close that loophole," Beckett said. "If I so wished."

Well, at least his assumption that Beckett knew had been correct. On the other hand: he'd really rather Beckett didn't keep thinking along these lines. Not that he had, as a matter of fact, done anything that way lately.

"I'd rather you didn't mess around with Cato's magic," Reb said, and the statement had more weight behind it than her careful words indicated. "In any way."

"Ditto," Cato agreed. "Though while we're on the matter – blood magic? No, thank you all the same."

The bare idea of losing his magic had bile rising at the back of his throat. Magic was – he was a sorcerer; that was what he did. He was a *good* sorcerer. He'd chosen this.

"I don't think it is suitable for you to be treating sorcerers differently," Reb said. "The cityangel should not be enforcing anything on sorcerers in Marek. That is a job for sorcerers themselves. Which is why we need the Group." She turned back to Cato. "Look. I don't think either of us want to see Beckett dragged into this, do we?"

Cato licked his lips. "No. Indeed not. No offence," he nodded politely at Beckett.

"So," Reb said. "The easiest way to prevent that would be to come to our own agreement."

"You're sure you really can bring yourself to work with me?" Cato asked, genuinely curious. He and Reb had never got along. Among other disagreements, Reb thought that one should be bound by mundane law. Cato didn't, in part because when he'd been disowned at sixteen with only a stack of magic books to fall back on, his options for keeping himself fed had been limited; and in part because he didn't see why he should bother about mundane law when no one was going to enforce it on him or any other sorcerer.

Reb scowled. "I can't say I'm madly enthusiastic. But yes, I am willing."

"Marcia will be pleased," Beckett observed.

Cato and Reb both winced at the same time. Cato, of course, knew about his sister's burgeoning relationship with Reb; he'd spotted it almost before either of the participants noticed, in fact. But he preferred not to think about it or acknowledge it, and he greatly doubted that Reb wished to discuss it with him either.

"So what I want," Reb said, ignoring the interjection, "is to find a description of the Group, and its duties, that we can agree on. For example: let's not have any spirits invited into the city."

Cato nodded reluctantly.

"And if you can't bring yourself to agree to oversight, at least to the Group making sure they're aware of who is performing sorcery in the city?"

"Ugh. Fine," Cato said. He could see the wisdom of the idea.

"I will leave you to the details," Beckett said, and disappeared with another thump.

Cato exhaled, and dropped his head into his hands.

"I have paper," Reb said, pulling it out of the bag attached to her belt. "Let's write down what we can agree on. And a time to meet."

"Ugh," Cato said again.

"Or I can call Beckett back?" Reb suggested.

He didn't want to do this at all, and he deeply resented Reb pushing him into it; but if the alternative was Beckett coming back and threatening his magic again…

Cato bared his teeth. "I am absolutely confident we are both going to regret this. Very well. Write."

THREE

Selene was woken by one of the Guesthouse Emilia's servants knocking on the door with her breakfast. If one could call it 'breakfast' when it arrived close on midday. Very shortly after her arrival in Marek, Selene had realised the wisdom of minimising morning appointments. The Houses were keen to ensure that they entertained the Lord Lieutenant of Teren suitably, and that meant late evenings; although Selene had noted that other than the host of any given evening, most of the Heads and some of the Heirs tended to imbibe with caution, and excuse themselves at a reasonable hour. The Houses were prosperous because they traded; and they worked for that prosperity.

Selene, of course, hadn't seen that part of Marek. Her role, as far as the Houses were concerned, was simply to exist in public as the Lord Lieutenant, visible symbol of Teren in Marek. She wasn't welcome to interfere in the real work of the city.

However, the early disappearance every evening of the most responsible House members gave Selene a freer hand in talking to the more dissatisfied ones. And enabled more private conversation with the hosts of any given event, in a setting where their guard might be a little down.

Last night had been less official: a late-night show at the theatre with some of the younger House members, who had taken full advantage of the refreshments. She imagined she felt better on waking than most of them would. They might or might not remember the detail of the conversations; but they would feel better about Teren than they had before she came, and that was her goal.

One goal, at least. She had other goals.

Selene wrapped herself in her crisp linen robe, and sat at the table by the window to address herself to her breakfast. Rolls, goat-butter, and the Teren mountain mint infusion that she allowed herself as a concession to being away from home. At home, she had cow-butter from one of the few, expensive, herds that grazed the flatlands around Ameten; here it seemed it was an article of Marek pride to rely on the goats on the far side of Marekhill. She couldn't, however, bring herself to replace mint infusion with rosemary, Salinas lemon (cheaper here than in Teren), or green-leaf the way Marekers preferred. One had to allow oneself some comforts.

Not that the Guesthouse Emilia was without comforts. Her room looked out over the river, which the proprietor evidently expected to please her. Today the river was dull under an overcast sky, with no sign of the sun. It was a nice enough view, but it reminded her, every time, of the Houses built on the two streets that rose up the hill above her. Of course the Lord Lieutenant could not show preference by staying at one of the Houses. Of course the Guesthouse Emilia was the only option, the most prestigious guesthouse in the city, and very nice it was too. And yet it felt uncomfortably symbolic. Marek was supposed to be part of Teren. A subordinate part. She should not be a *guest* here; she should be a ruler. She was the Lord Lieutenant of Marek; she held authority here. And yet, she did not. The Houses ran Marek, and the Houses saw Teren as a distant connection. No Lord Lieutenant had exercised real power, real influence, over any Marek decision for a good couple of centuries.

Selene, and Teren, had had enough of that.

Increasing Teren influence was not an easy task. She had spoken gently to Heads about the sad withering of the links with Teren. With some of the weaker, poorer, Houses, she had mentioned the advantages of their lands in Teren, and how making stronger links with Teren might empower them in Marek. There were one or two who, she thought, had been interested by that.

And then there were the younger House members. The ones who were bored, or dissatisfied, or both. Gently, she was planting seeds in their minds. If Marek couldn't be brought wholly into line, perhaps bringing some of the members of its governing families back to Teren would boost those links. Perhaps that would pay off more further along the line, if Teren found the need to be more... forceful.

She buttered a piece of roll, and chewed it thoughtfully.

The Council opening was only a couple of days hence; and she was expected to leave shortly afterwards. She was seeing results, but she would be in a far better position back in Ameten if she had something more solid. Perhaps it was time to push a little harder, when she had the opportunity. Perhaps.

There was another knock on the door and Selene turned, frowning. "Yes?"

"Message for you, Lord Lieutenant."

Her heart sank when she saw, underneath the scrawled charcoal mark of a Marek messenger, the Teren Archion's seal. The seal didn't mean it came directly from the Archion; but anything from Ameten was unlikely to be good news.

It wasn't a long message. She read it, glowering.

Apparently, they still hadn't found that wretched sorcerer, the one who'd summoned a demon, lost their nerve and banished it without doing what they were supposed to, and fled. The last Selene had heard, a week or so after coming to Marek, another sorcerer had retrieved the demon, done the job, and then set it to tracking the runaway, Tait. Selene had assumed it would be quick enough. Retrieve Tait or eat it; either would do to instil the requisite dread in the other Academy sorcerers.

But no. Tait hadn't been found; and now the sorcerer tracking them – Hira, and the Archion's office giving the name was an annoying indication that Selene should expect to hear from him – had reason to believe that this Tait was heading for Marek.

"Reason to believe," Selene muttered under her breath. She could wish that the Archion's office had shared more detail with her; she wasn't sure how far to trust the assessment.

She came to the kick in the tail of the message, and swore. She'd assumed that all they wanted was for her to assist this Hira, if necessary; after all, she wasn't a sorcerer. But no. They wanted her to seek support from Marek's magic. From the… cityangel. Marek's cityangel.

Selene strongly preferred to keep her distance from magic, especially of the sort practised in Teren. But Marek's magic was different, wasn't it? In some way? The Houses disliked magic to the point of ignoring its existence, and Selene had comfortably chosen to ignore it too. She pressed her lips together. She had less than no desire to find out more about magic, Marek's or any other, but an order was an order. She wasn't about to deal directly with a spirit, though. That was the job of a sorcerer.

Perhaps the sorcerers of Marek could be convinced that it was in their interest, or in the interest of this cityangel, to interfere... with what, though? They wouldn't interfere with something they saw as a Teren matter. A sorcerer who'd run away from the Academy; why would that be their problem?

Selene took another sip of mint infusion, her mind working. This Tait had banished the demon before they ran away. But what if they hadn't? What if... they'd run and left it unbound? What if a rampaging demon were chasing Tait to Marek. And, indeed, the demon *was* chasing Tait to Marek. Selene didn't need to tell the Marek sorcerers that it was under someone else's control now. A rogue uncontrolled demon, and a sorcerer running from their responsibilities; that story might buy her some cooperation.

Selene tapped the table thoughtfully. House Fereno was her afternoon appointment. House Fereno had a link with a sorcerer, as she recalled. A child of the House, disowned for their magic. Rarely spoken of – it had been a while, hadn't it? And of course Fereno-Head wouldn't wish to speak of it, or of magic at all. But Selene could pretend not to know that, could ask from an innocent curiosity. She might get something useful. And she might, as well, get useful information from how Fereno-Head reacted to her inappropriate question: whether she was treated as an impertinent underling, an equal to be tolerated, or someone to be placated.

She glanced over at the clock. Time to prepare for this meeting; and more carefully than she might otherwise have done.

☺ ☺

Marcia looked at the pile of papers on her desk and sighed. She liked her new office, now she had more House responsibility. It was next to the library, and had a window that looked out over the mouth of the river. But however nice the view, the downside of having a desk was the tendency of work to pile up on it.

She had a nasty suspicion that Madeleine was deliberately

offloading the more tedious aspects of House management onto her. To put her off? Or, more charitably, to make sure she understood the reality of what she would, eventually, be taking on, at whatever point Madeleine finally chose to fully hand over.

She wasn't in a particularly charitable mood today. Grimly, she started in on the pile of bills, authorisations, and bills-of-lading marked with queries for her attention, matching them against the House's account books.

She wrote a note to the agent telling them to compensate the captain of the Dolphin for the cargo they hadn't been able to load, and to bill the Broderers Guild for the failure to supply said cargo, put her pen down, and rubbed at her forehead.

Bills and discrepancies might be tedious, and occasionally involve some quite irritable disputes, but they were fundamentally tractable. There was a truth to track down, or a decision to make if it couldn't be tracked down.

Changing the basis of Marek's political system was rather less so.

The problem with 'winning' that showdown with Daril was that, while Daril's plan had been terrible, she'd been forced to realise that the problems he wanted to fix were real. The Guilds were treated badly. The younger offshoots of the Houses weren't dealt with well. The Heads were, all of them, hanging onto their power in a way that (as Gavin and Madeleine had demonstrated) allowed their thinking to stultify and made them vulnerable.

Some of that she could have, should have, seen sooner. Some of it she had seen. She'd known the Guilds were being badly treated, that they didn't have in practice the power that they had in theory. They were outvoted by the Houses, and the Houses stuck together. Not only that, but over recent years the House-only Small Council had been used more often. Notionally it was only for matters which affected only and exclusively the Houses; but that scope had been creeping wider.

She'd seen that. She just hadn't done anything about it.

She couldn't keep ignoring it now. But she'd allowed the business of the last couple of months to let her... defer it. It wasn't that she hadn't been busy. Around six weeks ago,

Madeleine had taken her to their agent, Celeste, and told Celeste which parts of the House business Marcia would now be responsible for. Celeste had half-raised an eyebrow, then spent the rest of the morning with Marcia inducting her into the relevant detail. Before that, Marcia would have said that she had a reasonably good grasp on the House business. She'd left Celeste's office somewhat chastened.

And furious with Madeleine. She, Marcia, had believed that she was already involved in what the House was doing, that she understood what her role as Head would be. Instead? It was clear that Madeleine had been keeping a great deal from her. She might be glad now to be more included, but it had stung that what she'd been given thus far hadn't been what she'd thought it was.

Worse than that, it made her political aims seem even less achievable. And she'd let that put her off. The Council didn't convene for six weeks after Mid-Year, but that didn't mean she couldn't have been talking to people more privately.

She cleared the last of the pile, and glanced at the desk clock that the Horologists' Guild had just delivered for her. It was a beautiful thing, the result of the Horologists' latest breakthrough in reducing the size of their mechanisms. Once the Salinas ships were back in dock, she had a contract to ship a couple of crates of them across to the Crescent, and expected to turn a tidy profit.

Right now, what it told her was that there was half-a-chime until she was due to meet the Teren Lord Lieutenant. She unlocked the drawer of the desk, and pulled out her own small pile of papers, bound together with twine. The ones that held her political notes.

She and Cato, as children, had worked out a written code. It was years since they'd used it between them, but Marcia still used it for her own private notes, when she particularly valued secrecy.

There were two main problems that she needed to tackle, and she hadn't got very far on either. The first was the Guilds. The obvious way to fix the problem would be to limit the powers of Small Council, and to increase the seats of the Guilds in full Council. But the nature of the problem made it hard to fix, because the Houses voting as a block defeated the Guilds. To make any change, Marcia had to convince at least two Houses to change their votes; and, realistically, she needed at least one or two beyond that, not to cause more problems than she solved. Currently, she wasn't even sure she'd have her own House vote; she hadn't begun to broach this with Madeleine.

She'd been talking – a little, and very cautiously, not wanting to be responsible herself for unsettling anything – to the Guilds about their experience of being in the Council, and she was starting to come to some alarming conclusions. It wasn't just that balancing the power better between Guilds and Houses was the right thing to do. Given the rising discontent between Guilds and Houses, and the increased tension both in Council and in private trading negotiations, the Guilds were eventually going to rebel. Custom and Marek's trading rules prevented the Guilds from doing their own deals with Salinas captains. But if the Guilds, unilaterally, decided to break the rules, could the Houses really enforce them? Without the Guilds, the Houses had nothing to trade. The Houses made good trades, certainly, and there were practical advantages to the Houses arranging shared shipments. But if it came right down to it... the Houses needed the Guilds more than vice versa, and Marcia had a suspicion that the Guilds were beginning to realise that. Unlike, it seemed, the Thirteen Houses.

She wanted to believe that she'd be able to talk them round just by pointing all of this out to them, but she knew the Heads well enough to know better. She'd begun to raise the matter, casually, at dinners and events over the last weeks, just to see where the wind lay. It hadn't been at all promising. She'd expected resistance to any idea of more Guild involvement in Council; but the Heads and Heirs that she'd brought it up with had been more scathing than she'd expected.

Four Houses to convince. Well. Apparently she would need to think of something better than just pointing out the injustice, or even the future risk.

The other problem was the flagrant waste of talent among the Houses themselves. Marcia was in a better position than most of the other Heirs; anyone further down the rankings had very little to do at all. Which suited some of them perfectly well, but others were chafing at the restrictions. More so since the Guilds, who were supposed to have agreed to take House members as apprentices or journeymen, were not, in fact, doing so, as part of their more subtle resistance to the Houses refusing the Guilds powers in Council. Solving the Council problem might solve that, but what of those younger House members who didn't have a Guild-suitable interest? How could Marcia convince other Houses to give their younger members more responsibility when even most Heirs didn't have any?

And then there were the sorcerers. There was a strict ruling that the Council, and the Thirteen Houses, were not allowed to have anything to do with magic. But since meeting the cityangel Beckett, Marcia had begun to wonder how appropriate that ban was.

Beckett's ban on political involvement was absolute, part of the contract that they had made with the founders of Marek. And it certainly made sense to ban magic in the Council itself, to make sure there was no risk of tampering. But should the sorcerers be kept out of the running of the city? Weren't they important to Marek?

She had to talk to Reb about it; and she wished she didn't feel quite so nervous about that. She and Reb had been slowly, gently, pursuing their incipient relationship, and it was going well – but they largely avoided politics. Reb tended to be scathing about the Council. Marcia wasn't at all sure that her lover would appreciate the idea of being represented on it; especially since Reb would have to be the representation. The only alternative was Marcia's brother Cato, which would be... provocative, to say the least. And Marcia *wanted* to make the offer to Reb, wanted to show Reb that Marcia was thinking about the whole of the city, not just her own limited part of it. It felt, sometimes, like Reb saw Marcia as out of touch with Marek, shut in a Marekhill bubble. Marcia wanted to demonstrate that that was untrue.

If Reb said yes, though... well, Marcia suspected that it would almost be easy to sell increased Guild representation to the Houses compared to persuading them to include the sorcerers. But that didn't mean it wouldn't be the right thing to do.

First things first, though; the Guilds, and the younger House members. Like Marcia's friend Nisha. Nisha was of House Kilzan, and high enough in it to make it difficult for her to do anything else with herself. But at the same time Nisha wasn't in line for Heir, nor likely to be, and was frustrated by the lack of meaningful work available to her, although Marcia had only recently seen past the facade Nisha presented to the world. Nisha was the sort of person who might have ideas about this stuff. Nisha was the sort of person who Marcia should be getting on board.

She shoved her notes back into the desk drawer and locked it, then scrawled a note to Nisha, inviting her to the baths later that afternoon, and sealed it. One of the servants would hand it off to a messenger. But if she was going to get changed and be on time to the meeting with the Teren Lord Lieutenant, she needed to be done now.

Thinking of Teren reminded her of the expedition which she'd sent off to see what profit could be made now that there was once again a foot-route across to Exuria, albeit one too small and narrow for carts or large baggage. Marcia had expected Captain Anna and her troop back at the start of the week. There was no reason to worry just yet, but she would be pleased to see them back. She'd longed to be able to go with them. She'd done the deal with the Jewellers' Guild, she'd overseen the outfitting of the expedition, she'd pored over the maps with Captain Anna – but it just hadn't been possible for her to take off for four weeks, out of Marek, right now. Or, very probably, ever. And there was a frustrating thought to take with her to this damn ceremonial meeting.

Marcia took the second staircase up to her room, to check herself over in the mirror. She wore her House Fereno tunic and trousers, and her hair was tidy. Her mother would doubtless think she should paint her face, but Marcia hated doing that other than for formal occasions. This was, explicitly, an informal afternoon tea, for the Teren Lord Lieutenant of Marek to have an equally informal chat with House Fereno. They'd already had a formal entertainment on her behalf, an informal morning meeting, and a formal meeting, and in none of them had anything of import been said. Doubtless today would be more of the same. Selene, the

Lieutenant, would be returning to the Teren capital Ameten shortly after the forthcoming Council Opening and, in Marcia's considered opinion, it was about time.

And if she wasn't down there on time, Madeleine would have her guts. Their relationship hadn't really recovered (yet? would it ever?) from Mid-Year; it didn't make sense to antagonise her mother further.

Madeleine was already sitting on one of the couches in the reception room when Marcia entered. Fabric from Teren, embroidered here in Marek; dark wood from Exuria, turned in Marek. Trade and manufacture, the engines of Marek's prosperity.

"Ah, Marcia," Madeleine said, looking up. She smiled, then frowned very slightly as she saw the absence of face paint. Madeleine herself had subtle loops around the sides of her forehead, extending onto her cheek, delicate against her brown skin and highlighting the blue of her eyes. Not the full formal paint of evening, but something suitable for afternoon tea. Marcia braced herself for comment, but Madeleine just tutted under her breath and looked away.

"Is there anything in particular we wish to bring up?" Marcia asked. "Or indeed to avoid?"

Madeleine shook her head. "Not to my knowledge. I do not believe there is any particular agenda here. I have had no warning from any of the other Heads."

She might not, of course, if the Lord Lieutenant was stirring something up. The Thirteen Houses worked together some of the time, and very much otherwise at other times. But House Fereno had allies, and if anything peculiar were happening, Madeleine would likely have heard. Not that Marcia thought it was likely. This was just more of the required diplomatic dance.

In theory, Marek was part of Teren, ruled on behalf of the Teren throne, from Teren, by the Lord Lieutenant of Marek. In practice, due to its location at the far end of a river that wound through extremely inhospitable swampland from landlocked Teren to the Oval Sea, Marek was largely an independent city-state, run by the Thirteen Houses and, in theory, for the last ten years, the Guilds. Without Marek, it was nearly impossible for Teren, surrounded by steep mountains, to trade with any of its neighbours. The only easy route across to Exuria had been destroyed in a winter of landslides some three hundred years previously; that had prompted Rufus Marek and Eli Beckett to undertake the expedition towards the sea which discovered, right where the Teren River gave into the Oval Sea, the island of solid land on which Marek now stood. The expedition had been considering the matter of turning their river boats into sea-going ones, when a Salinas trader had come by and offered them excellent terms for trading across the Oval Sea. Appended to the offer was the strong suggestion that any ships sailing without the permission and support of the Salina were unlikely to have a successful voyage. The Salinas had been carrying Marek goods, along with goods from everywhere else around the Oval Sea, ever since. The near-disastrous events of Mid-Year this year had involved Madeleine and Gavin Leandra-Head attempting to disrupt that relationship and send Marek's own ships out to trade directly; outright war had only just been averted.

So Teren relied on Marek, and the Teren Lord Lieutenant made an annual visit to both assert Teren's theoretical authority, and reassure the Houses that Teren did not intend to use it. The current Lord Lieutenant, Selene, was new; the previous one had retired. Unusual, as he hadn't been that elderly, and it was the sort of job that one held onto for life. Still. Doubtless Teren had its politics, the same as Marek; it hardly mattered.

There was a bustle of activity outside in the hall, signalling Selene's arrival. A footman showed her in, and Madeleine and Marcia both stood to greet her. She was a short woman, somewhere between Marcia's age and Madeleine's, with dark hair wound in a complicated plait around her head, and skin a shade or two darker than Marcia's own light brown. She wore a pale green dress, with elaborate embroidery of a type that Marcia recognised as originating in the Teren mountain villages – they traded it, occasionally, out to the Crescent cities, as decorative strips for fabric – and layers of flounces peeking out at the bottom.

"Fereno-Head," she greeted Madeleine, "and Fereno-Heir," turning to Marcia, touching the tips of her fingers to theirs in turn.

"Lord Lieutenant," Madeleine said. "I am pleased to

welcome you to our House."

"I am grateful for your hospitality," Selene said.

"Do come and sit down. Tea will be brought."

Marcia contributed little to the relatively superficial conversation over tea: the weather, the trading lull at this time of the year while storms raged on the Oval Sea, the entertainments that Selene had been enjoying during her stay.

"And how are things in Ameten?" Madeleine asked. "It is many years since I visited. I remember it as a most pleasant place."

"We are comfortable enough," Selene said. "Although there has been... some unrest, of late, among the lower orders."

Madeleine raised her eyebrows in polite enquiry.

"Radicals, you understand," Selene said. "Printing sedition, making trouble in the factories. You know the sort."

"Marek does not really have such difficulties," Madeleine said.

"No?" Selene sounded... disbelieving?

She wasn't entirely incorrect to disbelieve. Madeleine rarely – never, really – went over the other side of the river. Marcia did, and she saw the odd poster, or some of the more robust political newssheets hanging outside the stationers' shops. Not many, though, and hardly anything she'd describe as 'unrest'.

"The prosperity of Marek, the Houses and the Guilds," Madeleine was saying, "means that Marekers have no need to agitate." She waved a graceful hand. "The squats, for example. Housing for all. Food is plentiful. Marekers are content, and prosperous."

Selene smiled, but it didn't reach her eyes. "Marek is indeed fortunate. The Guilds, though..." She flicked a finger. "It is good of you to allow them to share in the success of the Houses, but surely it is the Houses, your good selves, who are the engine of this Marek prosperity? Who rightly, thus, hold the reins of Marek's power?"

Madeleine's face didn't shift, and her tone stayed smooth. "The Guilds and the Houses work together, of course," she said. "And the Guilds have their seats in the Council."

"Of course, of course," Selene said, in a tone that suggested that they were both conspiring in a public truth.

Had Selene been having this discussion with anyone else? Or, indeed, with Madeleine, in the quiet moments of one of those interminable evening dinners and entertainments?

"I do think," Selene went on, "that it is a shame that the links between the Houses and Teren have been pulled thin of late. You were saying, you spent time in Ameten in your youth? But Fereno-Heir here has never been?"

"No," Marcia agreed. "Perhaps one day." She had no intention of going to Ameten, or anywhere else in Teren; she had plenty to do here.

"It is a shame to see the Mareker Houses leaving their estates to paid managers, and staying away from Ameten. Once there was a stronger link between us. I would love to rebuild that." Selene paused, and took another cake, but didn't bite into it. "Another link we have been building, in Ameten, is that between the court and the sorcerers. I find myself curious, as a result, as to the ways in which Marker magic differs from Teren magic."

It was only with an effort that Marcia stilled her jerk.

"The Houses have nothing to do with that," Madeleine said dismissively. "We do not use magic on Marekhill, you understand."

A sore subject for Madeleine; she had disowned Marcia's brother Cato when he refused to abandon his magic. But even without that – the Houses did not engage with magic, nor, if they could possibly avoid it, so much as acknowledge its existence. Surely Selene knew that already?

"But I understood that one of your own children – Cato? – was a sorcerer."

This time Marcia saw Madeleine's jaw tense. "I have no sorcerer child," she said, flatly.

"Ah," Selene said. "I apologise. I must have misunderstood. But in any case – in Teren, sorcery is very risky, and operated only in service of the government, and at the sufferance of the government. Here, it seems, magic and politics do not mix? And yet magic is wholly safe. I am deeply curious about the difference."

Marcia knew quite a lot about the difference, as it happened, both from helping Marek's fallen cityangel during the events of Mid-Year, and from the fact that her girlfriend – if that was the right word to use – was a sorcerer. But

Madeleine would have a fit if she said anything about any of it here.

Madeleine looked caught between her desire to slap Selene down, her desire not to even think about magic, and her obligation to be polite to the Teren Lieutenant.

"As you say," Marcia said, taking over. "Magic and politics do not mix, here in Marek. The Houses, Marekhill – we do not engage with this superstition."

She sent up a silent apology to Reb, Cato, and, somewhat uncomfortably, to Beckett themself, at her dismissal.

"Superstition?" Selene asked. "But yet – surely, magic is very real."

Madeleine twitched.

"Magic does not occur on Marekhill," Marcia said. "I am aware that Teren uses it, but we do not. If magic occurs in the rest of the city, well, that is their own affair." She couldn't quite bring herself to explicitly dismiss the cityangel as superstition.

"Spirits and cityangels. Nonsense for the other side of the river," Madeleine said, waving a hand.

Madeleine's outright dismissal seemed – shortsighted, given that Selene had just been talking about Teren's use of spirit-magic. Madeleine was very close to calling Selene herself superstitious.

Selene tipped her head slightly to one side, evidently aware of the curious double-think that was going on here. It wasn't that Marekhill folk really thought that magic didn't exist. It was that as they couldn't, or wouldn't, use it, they had to dismiss it outright. Which was, of course, exactly what Marcia was going to have to overcome if she wanted Reb to join the Council.

Selene was about to say something. Marcia would have to jump in.

"As my mother says," she said, a little apologetically, "it is not something that is discussed on Marekhill. Would you like another biscuit? And I have been looking at the embroidery on your dress – one of the mountain villages, no? It is beautiful work."

Selene, thankfully, took the hint, and she and Marcia moved the conversation on to embroidery, the Broderers' Guild, and trade with the Crescent cities, while Madeleine recovered from her half-offence. After which she was deeply, almost excessively, gracious through the rest of the tea. But Marcia was certain that Selene hadn't just brought the matter up out of idle curiosity, and she wanted to know what was going on.

When Selene went to rise, Marcia contrived to escort her into the hallway, leaving Madeleine behind in the reception room.

"Sorcery is something of an unpleasant topic for my mother," she said, apologetically, as the footman helped Selene with her shawl. "And, indeed, most of Marekhill would consider it inappropriate. I do apologise. However, I would be happy to give you some information, if you would care to meet on another occasion?"

Madeleine would be furious, but then, there was no need for Madeleine to know.

"That would be most helpful," Selene said. "I would be delighted to have more opportunity to talk with you, in general."

"You may wish to know that most other Heads would react similarly, with regard to sorcery," Marcia warned her. Although surely she must know that already; could this really be the first time she'd mentioned it? In which case... why, and why now?

Selene nodded. "I see. I thank you for the information, and will endeavour not to cause further insult. But you are willing to discuss it? Excellent. I will send a note – a message, as you call them here – when I can consult my clerk about my availability."

"By all means," Marcia said, bowing. "It was a pleasure to meet you."

She wanted to know what it was that Selene hadn't said about magic in Teren; sharing what she knew about magic in Marek would be well worth the trade.

"Well, that was interesting," Madeleine said when Marcia walked back into the drawing room. "The Guilds, the links with Teren... Your thoughts, Marcia?"

Madeleine used to do this when Marcia was younger,

challenging her to draw her own conclusions about something they'd both seen. For her to do it once more felt like the beginnings of rebuilding their connection.

"Thinking about it, she's made those points before, but much more subtly," Marcia said, sitting back down opposite her mother. "So either she thinks we are open to less subtlety, or something has changed in Teren such that she feels the need to push harder." Marcia considered the matter. Her mother nodded without comment, encouraging her to go on. "Perhaps – she talked about unrest, didn't she? I wonder if perhaps it is a little more serious than she suggested."

"News-sheets and gutter radicals," Madeleine said, with a roll of her eyes. "Really?"

"Perhaps not," Marcia said. "But – she obviously seeks House support, and I think she was genuine in her desire to strengthen the links between Teren and Marek. There must be a reason for that."

"Teren relies on us for trade, and we are far more prosperous," Madeleine said. "Perhaps she simply wishes to secure better deals."

"She's new. Maybe it's not about Teren, or Ameten, or their Archion. Maybe she's just seeking to improve her own position."

"Possible," Madeleine conceded, "but that works only if those back in Ameten see a closer relationship as necessary, or desirable. Was there a reason for changing the Lord Lieutenant, or did the last one really just retire?" She paused. "Do they – does she – think that something might be about to change? Or wish to make a change?"

"You mean," Marcia said, "is she, or is Teren, worried that we want to pull more formally away from Teren? Or want us to come back under direct government?"

Madeleine shook her head, her eyes thoughtfully narrowed. "Direct government would be a stretch. It is a long time since that was the case. But... it is true that we are less close with Teren, with those ruling in Ameten, than we once were. Perhaps Teren has become uncomfortable about where that might be leading. Or perhaps Selene merely sees a change in that relationship as one which would enhance her reputation in Ameten. We will keep our minds open." She nodded slowly to herself, then sat back, and turned her gaze on

Marcia. "Now. Marcia. Selene mentioned the Guilds, which is convenient, as you have spent a great deal of time talking to the Guilds, of late."

"Yes?" Marcia said. She didn't really want to get into this unless she had to. "I have been liaising with the Jewellers' over this expedition, of course."

Madeleine frowned at her. "Not just the Jewellers, no. All of the Guilds. Please don't insult my intelligence, Marcia."

Marcia tried not to react. If Madeleine had noticed, had anyone else?

"I have put off any other enquiries into your behaviour," Madeleine said. So Marcia hadn't been as subtle as she'd thought, then. Dammit. "We have been seeking new contracts, you understand. But. As the price for my discretion, I wish to know what you are up to." For a moment, she sounded almost like she had when Marcia was a little girl, getting into trouble with Cato, back before he was Cato. Or, often, being got into trouble by him. It was simultaneously annoying – Marcia wasn't nine any more – and reassuring.

Marcia took a deep breath. "That thing you said. About the Guilds and the Houses working together."

"Go on."

"The Houses hold the power." She looked over at Madeleine, but Madeleine wasn't reacting. "Thirteen seats to ten, and the Small Chamber is being used more often."

"Mmm."

"The Guilds don't like it. I know that. We haven't spoken, I haven't spoken, directly of it, but… they say things. Imply things. And," Marcia paused. This was the crux. This was her committing herself to an opinion, an opinion that she very much doubted Madeleine shared. "I don't think it's fair, either."

"Fair," Madeleine said disdainfully.

Marcia grimaced. Of course Madeleine didn't care about 'fair', and wouldn't be impressed by Marcia worrying about it. "I don't think it makes for prosperity, then. For us, or for Marek."

"We've worked with the Guilds for centuries," Madeleine said. "And then we gave them Council seats. They should be pleased." Madeleine had been involved in bringing the

Guilds into the Council. She might well be taking this personally. "They should be *grateful*." Yes, she was definitely taking this personally.

"Yes, Mother, they have Council seats. But what they got is not what they expected," Marcia said. She could empathise. "Especially with the Small Council taking more and more power. It's not just that they're outvoted in anything touching on House matters, it's that they're not even being *consulted*. Nearly always, if someone proposes moving something to Small Council, the Houses all vote together."

"Nearly always," Madeleine scoffed. "Nonsense." But her eyes slid away from Marcia's.

Marcia cursed herself for not having accurate numbers to hand, but there was no point in getting caught up in that. She had to keep going. "There's unrest, Mother. Not the sort of unrest Selene was talking about in Teren, but dissatisfaction. And eventually, it will cause problems. Dissatisfied people are not open to good trades. Dissatisfaction with your partners poisons the well."

"And you have a solution."

"More seats on the Council for the Guilds," Marcia said.

"Hmm," Madeleine said. Which was better than the outright flat denial Marcia had expected at the start of this conversation. "How many seats?"

"It has to be three, if we're to do it at all," Marcia said.

"And a casting vote," Madeleine said. She tapped one finger on her knee. "Well. It is an interesting proposal, and I do see the outline of your point. But I disagree. The Guilds have plenty of power, and it has only been a very short while since they were brought onto the Council. I would not support another change so rapidly, and I very much doubt that any of the other Heads would. Bringing the Guilds in was hardly popular in the first place. But..." She stopped, and sighed. "But you will be Head in due course, and perhaps, in due course, this would be a suitable change, if you wish to champion it. But... slowly, you understand? Slowly and carefully. It might take years to win people gently over to your point of view. Just as when we brought the Guilds onto the Council in the first place."

Marcia noticed that Madeleine didn't mention the flat-out bribe they'd used to bring the Guilds in: the removal of the time limit on Headship of a House.

"Years," Marcia said, in dismay.

"Patience," Madeleine counselled. "Move slowly. For now, I would like to see a full report on your arguments, your aims, and your methods of approach. And any alliances you have gained so far."

"None from the Houses," Marcia admitted. "I've barely started to test support."

"And you haven't found any," Madeleine said. It was a statement, not a question. "Then you have even further to go. For this, you need a convincing House majority, not just two votes. We do not need a situation where the Houses defy the expressed wishes of the Council."

True enough. Marcia wished, fervently, that she did have more support; that she was able to tell Madeleine that she'd already been working on this, that she had already progressed on it. But she hadn't, and she couldn't.

"Would you vote for it?" She already knew the answer, but she wanted Madeleine to say it.

"No," Madeleine said. "The current situation has only been as it is for ten years, and we should allow it to settle for longer. And in all honesty, I do not see the Guilds as ready for more power. However, I am pleased that you are thinking about the future, and that you have a serious project. As long as your endeavours do not affect our House interests adversely. The House must come first, Marcia. I know you understand that." She paused. "I will, however, consider refusing a move to the Small Council the next time it comes up, depending on who moves it, and our relationship with their House. I do see your point there, and there is often no particular reason not to discuss things in full Council. If we can postpone or reduce the dissatisfaction you describe, that would be a reasonable goal."

It was more than Marcia might have expected, and less than she wanted. She nodded, and managed not to sigh. "Thank you, Mother. I would appreciate that. I think it will be good for our House relationship with the Guilds, too."

"Indeed," Madeleine agreed. She sat back, and waved a hand at Marcia in dismissal. "Now. Away with you. I am sure we both have plenty to do. Do not forget to send me that document on your plans."

FOUR

Reb was uncomfortably aware that she'd been procrastinating. She'd promised Beckett that she would start looking for more potential sorcerers and she hadn't, in the weeks since that promise, done a damn thing about it.

The trouble was, it was going to be so demanding of her time and energy. Once she'd found someone, and they'd agreed to an apprenticeship, it would be at least a year before they were at the point of semi-independent study and she could consider taking someone else on. She'd have to reduce her own practice to do it, too, and the assistance was unlikely to make up for it. Just thinking about it made her tired; so she'd been letting herself ignore the problem and practise her own skills, which she'd allowed, if not exactly to atrophy, then certainly to fall shy of her best, over the years since the plague had killed most of her colleagues.

Beckett, however, wasn't having any of it. The cityangel's new willingness to engage directly with humans, or at least with certain humans, was more than a little disconcerting. Not content with interfering about Cato and the Group, Beckett had appeared in the middle of her front room that morning to enquire sharply after the progress of her search for apprentices.

The Group. Reb would have much preferred to go on with the previous arrangement, whereby she and Cato ignored one another unless necessity absolutely required otherwise. But the absence of the Group was clearly dangerous, and that had to be fixed, whatever her personal preferences were. At least they had a functional proposal now, even if it had taken Beckett's somewhat worrying intervention to get there. But she couldn't put off the apprentice thing any further.

She sat back a little in her armchair, and sighed. Her front door stood slightly ajar, indicating that she was free for business enquiries. Today was unusually quiet. She'd put some effort into building up her customers in recent weeks, frustrating though it was to need to. She'd never had to look for customers, before. Marcia had assured her that it would be like that again, but in the meantime, she had to rebuild her reputation.

Her reputation, and Marek's magic. And Beckett was correct, when it really came down to it; she couldn't just continue to avoid the only other competent sorcerer in the city. And Cato was more than competent. That wasn't Reb's problem with him. Her first problem was his general lack of morals, and willingness to work with anyone who would pay him regardless of the job. In the last decade, she'd more than once had to solve problems that Cato's lack of care and forethought had created. In fact, she'd probably have had to do less of that if he were less able. He was also happy to promise things with no intention of doing them, for an easy life. He made a great many promises about his behaviour to the Group, back when there was a Group, over the years, and never once let that affect his decisions once he'd left their presence. And there never had been all that much one could do about a sorcerer who wasn't raising demons or risking the fabric of reality or anything like that; when they were just making a mess, breaking the law, and being a damn nuisance.

But that was old news; and until recently, she'd known that even Cato had some limits on what he was prepared to let happen. What she was more bothered by was the fact that she still didn't know exactly what his role had been in what had happened with Daril and Urso. She did know that Cato hadn't been involved with Beckett's initial removal. But he had been part of the arranging of a replacement, because "Daril offered me a very large sum of money". That was bloody typical.

On the other hand, whilst she didn't know how Jonas had wound up part of the final ritual, she was fairly certain that Cato had been behind Jonas' 'failure' at the critical moment. And also that Cato's own 'failure' immediately afterwards had been deliberate, leaving Urso to hold the thing up alone. Urso had almost managed it, too, until Jonas' friend Asa had, taking an entirely non-magical approach to the problem, hit him with a chair. The ritual had collapsed, Beckett had been restored, and all was well. Cato had steadfastly refused afterwards to say anything about what had happened, merely bemoaning the fact that he hadn't had the second half of his money. Reb strongly suspected that he'd thought better of the implications of linking a different spirit to Marek, one that wasn't bound by the same contract as Beckett; Cato wouldn't admit it. And much to her annoyance, Reb couldn't think of a way of making him talk about it. Not a way she was prepared to use, at least. Using sorcery on him would be unethical, unlikely to work, and disastrous for their already fraught professional relationship and she was annoyed at herself for even thinking of it.

In any case, that particular problem had been solved. The cityangel was still bound to the city, and vice versa; even if the cityangel now had themself a name for the first time and seemed to be taking a rather more *direct* interest in Marek than they ever had before. But the longer-term problem, the one resulting from the plague two years before, still existed: the fact that Marek, city of magic, had only two functional sorcerers.

In an ideal world, she and Cato would both be taking on apprentices, so they could both contribute to returning Marek's magical strength to its former levels. But it hardly seemed likely that Cato would do anything which didn't directly suit his own ends. She'd thought about talking to him about it, when they were coming to their agreement about the Group, but...

... But Reb hated arguing with Cato. He slid around her, always had, his words turned to perfection and dripping in multiple meanings. She hated how she always felt that he was laughing at her. Marcia insisted that it was just the world that Cato was laughing at, not anyone in particular, but Reb was unconvinced. Cato might not laugh at his sister; that didn't mean he wasn't laughing at Reb.

She scowled again, and got up to shut her door, finishing her working day. If she didn't want Beckett to be back again tomorrow morning, she should at least start seeking potential apprentices.

She went into her workroom, a tiny room off the main living area, and bolted the door. There were no windows in here; it was safer that way. Her ingredients were neatly lined up on shelves above her worktable, but most of the room was empty, the floor clear for sorcery.

She'd spent an absurd amount of money on a map of

Marek, showing the whole of the city, from the goat-villages on the other side of the Hill and the fishing-villages in the marshes east of the city proper, to the market square in the north-west where barges and carts from Teren unloaded, and the increasing sprawl in the south-west where builders kept trying to reclaim more of the marshland around the solid ground that Marek had been founded on. She was sincerely hoping that it would be undamaged by the sorcery. It was likely to be an expensive enough business training apprentices, without having to buy a new damn map just to find each one.

She spread it out on the floor and weighed it down with the scraps of street-stone she'd found from each corner of the city. She'd done the work herself rather than send messengers, to be certain it was correct. Over the map, she scattered the street-sweepings she'd collected from various shops across the city and mixed together; that had been a long day, but at Marcia's suggestion she'd also used the visits to remind people that Marek's sorcerers were still around and working, and she'd gotten a fair few commissions out of it. It had been reassuring to see Marekers' enthusiasm for their city's magic.

She had prevailed upon Marcia for some sweepings from House Fereno, although for the rest of Marekhill she'd had to ask at kitchen doors. Happily, Marekhill servants didn't share their employers' feelings about magic, and were perfectly happy to exchange charms for sweepings.

Once she'd spread the sweepings, Reb traced a quick rosemary-and-salt circle around the map. This working shouldn't generate any untoward energies, but some of the things that had happened during Beckett's absence from the city had left her cautious.

For scrying usually one might use a mirror, or water, but in this case the map itself was the scrying-tool, with the sweepings tying it to the city. To activate them, Reb needed something to direct the power. Soot was a good general mixer, earth and fire combined. She combined it with a little cinnamon for strength and some metal filings, into the open pouch at her waist, and tied a cats-cradle of string around the fingers of her right hand. Carefully, she stood up, standing across the map and within the circle. She muttered a few words under her breath, sought and caught the state of mind that permitted magic to happen – it seemed easier now that she'd met Beckett in person, and she wasn't sure if that was down to her or down to Beckett – and dumped a generous pinch of the mixture from the pouch across the string. The whole thing caught together and began to glow about her hand, and she nodded with satisfaction. She eased the string gently from her fingers, twisted the ends together, and let it float in mid-air. Once she was satisfied it was stable, she squatted down to take a closer look.

Dotted across the map were little glowing points, each reflecting the blue-green glow of the ball within the cats-cradle. Over in the squats she could see the bright round point that was Cato. Her own point glowed equally bright in her own street. Urso was no longer in the city; she knew that in any case, but it was nice to have it confirmed. He wouldn't have been as bright as either Cato or herself, but he'd been a surprisingly strong sorcerer (and she was still painfully aware that she should have realised he was there, but there was no point crying over that now). The remaining points of light – prospective sorcerers, those with possible ability – were all much dimmer. Ten or so, she counted, and she pulled a piece of paper and a pencil from her skirt pocket to note down the addresses. Not that she could be certain that they were permanently at the locations she'd seen them at – that was one of the downfalls of this method – but, if she visited, she'd be able to tell once she was at close range. A trained sorcerer was unmistakable to another sorcerer. An untrained one was easier to miss, but she would be looking, and she could take a scrying-tool.

As she finished her list, she saw one of the dots moving, heading along the docks. As she watched, whoever it was turned north again. Reb blinked. Could it be possible that this person was going to go straight past her front door? She tapped her thumb against her fingers, thinking quickly. The spell was stable enough, and she'd finished making her notes. If she took the cats-cradle back into her hand, and very gently broke the circle, the floor-sweepings would no longer be of use, but that was as expected. The map should be fine, and the cats-cradle would survive for as long as she held it. And it would flare if this potential sorcerer came close.

The dot was moving closer. She needed to act quickly. She gathered the cats-cradle up again, still softly glowing, broke the circle, and unbolted the workroom door with her spare hand, bolting it again (a long-established habit) behind her. She threw the front door open and stood in the doorway, watching the passers-by. The glowing ball in her right hand was drawing a great deal of attention. She suppressed a snort. Marcia would doubtless call this excellent advertising. Reb wasn't entirely comfortable with it, but she shouldn't need to stand here long.

Looking down the narrow street towards the Old Market and the alleys that came up to it from the docks, she saw someone coming towards her with the fast easy gait of a messenger. Well, that would make sense, someone moving at the speed she'd seen on the map could well be a messenger. She frowned. The messenger had Salinas-fair hair, and looked almost like…

"Jonas?" she said aloud. But hadn't he gone back to Salina?

The messenger looked up, and straight into her eyes, as the cats-cradle flared into brilliant life.

"Jonas!"

Reb. Jonas swore under his breath as he saw her standing in her doorway. And what in the hells was that thing she was holding? Something magical, for certain. He'd been avoiding Reb for a number of reasons, not least his deep desire not to have any kind of discussion about magic – especially one that might accidentally lead to talking about flickers – with her. But this street was the quickest route for the message he was running, and he'd thought he'd get away with it.

Idiot.

He tried to work out if there was any way that he could still just avoid her. Or… agree to come back later. (And then not do it, obviously, and hope that she didn't track him down some other way.)

"I want a word with you," Reb said, and moved towards him, that terrifying ball of light still balancing over her hand.

He shouldn't find it terrifying, by now; he'd seen enough magic. Perhaps it was Reb's expression that was alarming him. Reb was alarming all by herself; she exuded the solidity of someone who had power, and was comfortable in it.

"Reb," he said, trying for a smile. "If you'll excuse me, perhaps another time, I have a message to run…"

It was an inviolable law of Marek that one should not impede a messenger. It was equally an inviolable law of Marek that sorcerers were sacrosanct. Everyone within earshot immediately turned away and busied themselves with something, anything, else, having absolutely no desire to attempt to resolve these two competing principles.

Reb grabbed his arm with her free hand.

"We will pass the message on. I will compensate you accordingly. I need to speak with you. Immediately."

He could probably break away and run for it. But it wasn't like he could avoid her forever. Lots of people would happily do a favour for a sorcerer. Lots of people would happily hand him over to Reb, thinking they were doing entirely the right thing. He couldn't hide away and not run messages; he'd starve. Or have to throw himself on Cato's forbearance, which didn't appeal either.

He'd delayed for too long. The time for running was past.

"As you prefer," he said politely, attempting to salvage some dignity from this encounter.

Reb yanked him into the house and shut the door firmly. She indicated a chair for Jonas to sit in, then leant out of the window, collared a passing messenger, and negotiated the transfer of his message.

"Here," she said, handing him a couple of coins – twice what he'd expected for the run, he noticed.

She was still balancing that infernal light or whatever it was in one hand.

"Um," he said. "Does that – do you really need it?"

"Oh," Reb looked at it, as if she'd forgotten she was carrying it. "One moment."

She walked around him with it, backed off a little, came closer, studying the variations of light carefully as she did, then nodded to herself. She tossed it in the air, clapped her hands twice underneath it, and the light winked suddenly out. A scatter of dirt and string fell to the floor.

"Now then," she said, sitting herself down in an armchair. "This may or may not come as a surprise to you, but… how long have you known you were a sorcerer?"

Jonas could think of several things he could say, but not a single one that he actually wanted to. He stayed quiet.

"Since you spoke to Urso?" Reb suggested. "I saw you in the embassy, of course, but I could have sworn Urso and Cato were carrying most of that. I thought you must have a little talent – more than Daril, for example, who has none at all – but I imagined it was mostly about your being Salinas. A connection to the ground Urso was working on, which none of the rest of them had."

She stopped again, and looked enquiringly at Jonas. He still couldn't think of anything to say.

"Feel free to step in at any time," Reb said, her voice growing a little testy. "Or would direct questions help?"

Jonas shrugged a shoulder, very slightly.

"Well. Did Urso tell you you were a sorcerer?"

"No," Jonas said, unwillingly.

"Did you know you were a sorcerer? Before today?"

There was no way he was going to get of this, was there? And in any case, if he was a sorcerer – and he *had* done magic yesterday – then he couldn't avoid admitting that to Reb forever, could he? Unless he just gave up now and went back home, but he didn't *understand* any of this yet, and he wanted to.

Reb visibly fought her impatience, lips pursed, as he thought it through. Reluctantly, he concluded he'd have to admit it.

"Yes," he said, finally.

"Right. So. Urso didn't tell you. I didn't know until today. That leaves Beckett… ?"

Jonas shook his head. "I haven't seen Beckett since…" He tried out and rejected a number of ways of referring to that awful day. "Since Mid-Year." He regretted, as soon as he'd said it, using the Marek name and not the Salinas one. For Salinas, it was New-Year. And he was still Salinas.

"Right. So that means it was Cato," Reb said. "Unless there's another sorcerer kicking around Marek, in which case I really do need to know, Jonas." She sounded suddenly serious.

"It was Cato," Jonas said. "Before – things happened. It was him told Urso to include me in that – thing, and he got me to agree to drop it."

Reb nodded as if he were confirming something she'd already suspected.

"So. If you're a sorcerer, then you need to be learning what to do with your abilities."

"Why?" Jonas said, a little belligerently. Where did Reb get off, thinking that she could make decisions on his behalf like that? Even if he was, in fact, already learning what to do with his abilities. In theory, anyway. He remembered those pigeons, and Cato sitting covered in feathers, and his lips twitched slightly.

"Why? Because otherwise sooner or later you'll make something happen by accident, that's why. Which is bad news. You need to control your abilities, not just let them leak out willy-nilly." She nodded slightly. "So, I suppose we could start off a couple of times a week, perhaps."

"Could start off with what?" Jonas demanded.

Reb frowned. "With, well, it's an apprenticeship, I suppose, although we don't do it the way the Guilds do. But you need someone to learn from, like the Guild apprentices do."

"You want me to learn with you?"

"Well, yes." Reb was beginning to look slightly annoyed. "I told you, it's important that you learn how to use your abilities. I'm just sorry I didn't spot them before. I really wasn't… well, anyway."

"I'm learning with Cato," Jonas said, before she could go on any further. He hadn't meant to admit that, if he could avoid it, but he had to stop this. "I'm apprenticed to Cato."

Reb's look of shock was almost comical. "To Cato?"

"Yes. He said – after the embassy, he said he could help me." With his flickers, mostly, but he wasn't going to mention those to Reb.

"You're apprenticed to *Cato*?" Reb asked, as if she couldn't believe her ears.

"Yes," Jonas said impatiently. "Is that a problem?"

"Well, he's hardly reliable, is he?" Reb said, sitting back. She looked annoyed. "He does what he wants, when he wants, and damn anyone else around him. Honestly, Jonas, I can't think you're likely to be well-served by learning anything from Cato. You'd be much better off – I don't like to blow my own trumpet, but I promise I'd be a better teacher than Cato."

She sounded as though she expected Jonas just to fall in with whatever she was suggesting, and it infuriated him.

"I am quite happy learning from Cato," he said, letting a bit of his mother's shipboard voice slip in, the one she used when someone wasn't pulling their weight. "I have accepted apprenticeship with him. I do not intend to renege on that commitment."

Reb shook her head. "I'm sure Cato won't mind. I mean, he's never accepted any other responsibility since he came into his own abilities."

"And yet, he has accepted this one," Jonas said. Fine, Cato might not be the most responsible individual Jonas had ever met. But he'd told Jonas that he would help, and he had been helping. In his own way. In any case, Jonas wasn't sure he'd get on much better with Reb. She had a tendency to think that things should go just as she said. So did Cato, but Cato was more amenable to being argued with. Jonas could shout at Cato. He didn't think he could shout at Reb.

"Jonas, I don't want to be impolite, but I really think…"

"You appear not to be listening," Jonas said. He stood up. He was fed up with this. "I am a sorcerer." His legs shook slightly, as he said it out loud. A Salinas sorcerer? It wasn't forever. He was just finding things out. "I do indeed intend to learn to control my abilities." That was even true. Controlling them was the whole point. Once he could control them, he could maybe control his flickers too, and then he would be safe on board ship. "And I will learn from Cato. With whom I am already apprenticed. Now, if you will excuse me, I also have a living to make."

He swept out of the room past Reb before she could stop him or he could regret what he was saying. Then spent the rest of the early evening, on into the dark, running messages as fast as he could, from one side of the city to the other, up Marekhill and back down again, trying to use physical exertion to drown out the voice suggesting that Reb might have a point about Cato. Cato had been helping him. They were getting somewhere. It would all be fine.

FIVE

Smoke rose from the chimneys at the side of the bathhouse, signalling the hot water to be found inside, heated by an under-floor hypocaust system. The late-afternoon sun bounced off the smoke, echoing the clouds higher in the sky. Marcia was deliberately early, so she could soak and steam and clean herself a little before she had to talk to Nisha. She and Nisha had been friends since they'd attended little-school together, and then shared a tutor as teenagers. Nisha had disapproved of Marcia's teenage dalliance with Daril b'Leandra, but she hadn't said anything when it fell apart, nor asked about the bits that Marcia wasn't willing to talk about it; just let Marcia cry on her shoulder, and rebuilt their friendship as though it had never come under strain. Nisha had a justified reputation as being one for parties, pejo, and late nights, and she had a sarcastic tongue; but she was also sharp, thoughtful, and far more politically astute than she was generally given credit for. To Marcia's embarrassment, she herself had only fully realised that recently. If Marcia was going to make any of her ideas work, Nisha's support would be invaluable.

Marcia handed coins to the attendant at the door for her bath and a towel; changed, gave her clothes to another attendant, and hung the token she received around her neck. She scrubbed herself briskly under the cold showers, then moved through the steam-room for a couple of minutes, into the cold plunge-pool, and back into the steam room before another plunge. The sweat pouring off her and the shock of the cold water helped clear her mind, set her up for the intended discussion.

She moved to the smaller of the two warm pools, the grey tiles of the corridor smooth under her feet, and allowed herself to relax into the water. She stared up at the geometric patterns on the tiled walls – imported from the Crescent Alliance, the trader part of her mind remembered, not that House Fereno had been involved in that deal – and tried to run it all through in her mind.

The problem that Daril had made use of, earlier in the year, had been two-fold. Part of it was about – well, part of it was about the fact that he himself had not been named Heir, due to his long-running feud with his father. But he'd gained interest from others of the younger generation in Marekhill for two reasons. The first was that, at one time, a Head of House was obliged to retire after twenty-five years, meaning that Heirs tended to take over some time in their twenties. When the Guilds had been admitted to the Council, the cost of the votes from certain Houses had been the lifting of that restriction; which meant that the current crop of Heads could stay as long as they liked. They were taking full advantage of it; none of them seemed to have the slightest interest in handing over any time soon.

So the Heirs were annoyed, and kicking their heels. Those who were of a House but not Heirs had even less to do. Notionally, one could now join a Guild, but the Guilds, in practice, refused candidates with a tie to a House. The more distant cousins of a House, like Daril's co-conspirator Urso, could operate as a merchant or sole trader if they were prepared to accept mild social opprobrium, but for siblings and first cousins that was frowned upon.

And there were more of those than once there had been; more children surviving to adulthood, to be blunt about it. It was no longer the done thing for a younger sibling or cousin or two to go to Teren, to the court there, as Marek came to consider itself more independent, more cosmopolitan, more interesting, than Teren; and similarly, Teren agents rather than younger House members now routinely managed the Houses' Teren estates. Marcia had never even been to Fereno's estate.

All of which meant that there were a collection of Heirs and not-Heirs of roughly Daril and Marcia's age who would have been happy to support Daril's coup if they thought there was some scope for their own advancement in it. That alone suggested that there was an alarming instability, a weakness, in the system. Where Daril had failed, someone else might succeed.

Daril had been in it for himself, but his point was sound: the Houses represented themselves, the Guilds got little or no say in anything meaningful, and a generation was being lost to pointless dissipation. The Guilds had realised that power was moving away from them, not towards them. What happened when they decided to act?

Marcia's eyes narrowed as she lay back in the warm water and stared upwards. Marekers might not go to the Teren capital any more. But why should they not be going to the Crescent Alliance, or to Exuria, like the occasional independent trader did, taking a cabin on a Salinas ship? Would the Salinas accept that? It would give the Houses more information than relying on their local agents; with, of course, the risk of antagonising those local agents by looking like they were being checked upon.

Or was that just a sticking-plaster over a vulnerability, rather than a true fix?

"Marcia!"

Nisha slipped into the water beside her, dark hair plaited at the nape of her neck to corral it.

"How are you, darling? How's your secret romance?"

"There's no secret romance," Marcia said, awkwardly.

Reb wasn't exactly a secret. But neither were they rushing to share their relationship with the world. Marcia certainly wasn't about to mention it to Madeleine, for example. And she hadn't – yet – introduced Reb to her friends. It wasn't that she was embarrassed. Not at all. But it was true that there was a little discomfort in Fereno-Heir being involved with a sorcerer, when the Houses were forbidden to engage with magic. Not that Marcia *engaged* with magic. Reb did nothing on her behalf, and though she had once been present when Reb was performing sorcery, that had been an extreme case, not something that was likely to happen again.

Still. Marcia wasn't quite sure how she would pass the matter off, and she thought perhaps it would be better not to try that particular boat-race until she and Reb had been together a little longer.

"I don't believe you, darling," Nisha said. "You're clearly getting laid. I am just deeply curious who the lucky individual is. But," she gave a dramatic sigh, "if you don't want to share, I won't push you." This was an absolute lie, but Marcia let it slide.

"I'll order tea," Marcia said firmly, gesturing over the

bathhouse servant who waited at the side of the room.

"Lovely," Nisha said, leaning back in the water with a sigh once the man had returned with a pot of tea and two cups. Sun fell across her face in patches, broken by the shadows cast by the patterned leading of the domed skylight. "I needed this. It's been a busy week, card parties and what-all." She rolled her eyes. "All the important things, you know?"

Which was the ideal opening for Marcia to talk to her about her political ideas, half-formed though they might be. Nisha listened throughout with a half-raised eyebrow.

"You want me to swan off to the Crescent cities? Well, I suppose it would be more interesting than losing at dice and drinking too much; though doubtless there's that over there too. What would be the point of it, though, darling? Are you seriously suggesting that I'm going to come back and give my esteemed uncle a selection of new trading suggestions, and that he'll have the first idea of taking me seriously?" She shrugged a shoulder, but the bitterness in her tone was palpable. "Anyway, to be honest, I think you're rather missing the point. As did Daril, when he was flailing around preaching sedition before Mid-Year." She rolled her eyes. "I notice that since Gavin finally confirmed him, he's gone very quiet."

Marcia chose not to comment on any of that. Only a very few people knew what Daril had, in the end, attempted at Mid-Year, and Nisha wasn't among them.

"What point am I missing?" she asked instead.

"Houses, Guilds, whatever. It's all top-heavy, darling. All of us pissing around on our own side of the river, the Heads trying to keep their toys to themselves, the Guilds huffing and puffing about what they're being excluded from. What about the rest of the city? There's more of them than there is of us, in case you hadn't noticed."

Marcia sat up, splashing Nisha, who frowned at her.

"You think we should be representing – what, the squats?"

"The squats, by all means, but I was thinking of everyone who lives around the Old Market, and come to that, half of those on this side of the river who are neither apprenticed nor beholden to a House."

"Nisha. Where in the hell are you getting this from?"

"I read a rather interesting pamphlet," Nisha said, carelessly.

"Maybe that is what we should be doing," Marcia said, slowly. "Maybe… we should be making more of an attempt to talk to the rest of Marek. People like you should be."

"As if your mother and my father, or any of the rest of them, would have the slightest bit of interest. And in any case, what is this 'we'? You must be joking, darling, if you think that I'm going to go plunging through the squats talking to messengers and shop-girls."

Marcia bit back a flare of irritation.

"It would be interesting," she said. "The squats aren't that bad, anyway."

"Ah yes, you would know, wouldn't you? What with your fascinating brother," Nisha said. "Magical, bad, and dangerous to know."

Marcia knew fine well that Nisha hadn't seen Cato for a decade, but the tone hit her on the raw anyway. She bit her tongue, hard, and tried again.

"You were complaining that you've nothing to do and no political power. This could solve both. You're the one who brought it up."

"I'm criticising your ideas, darling, not proposing my own," Nisha said. "In any case. If I thought it was political power you were talking about, I might be interested. But as far as I can tell you're not talking about anything of the sort. You're talking about a position with no power at all, but where people will be expecting you to produce something from nothing. Because make no mistake, darling, if I were to go round Marek collecting grievances and requests, it would be me that would be thought of badly when my father and your mother and all the other Heads refused to consider the matter for a moment. Which is precisely what they would do."

"We need to demonstrate that it does matter," Marcia said.

"But why does it?" Nisha demanded. "Natural justice, yes, fine, but if you think natural justice is going to move the stony hearts of the collective Heads, you are deluded. They will say – and there is truth to it – that the system we have has worked thus far, that Marek prospers, that they themselves prosper, and that anyone who does not should ask the cityangel to better their luck, not come whining to the Council." She shrugged. "If you can give me a single reason that will convince one of them to take the matter seriously, then talk to me again then. Until then – I wish you luck of your quest, darling, but I will stick to card-parties and walking out."

"Well, what, then?" Marcia demanded. "What should I be doing, if it's not that?"

"You want me to come up with ideas for you?"

"I want you to come up with ideas with me," Marcia said.

At her tone, Nisha rolled over slightly in the water and looked at her hard. "You're serious," she said, flatly.

"Of course I'm serious. What the hell did you think all this was about?"

"I don't know," Nisha said, thoughtfully. "I suppose I thought you were flailing much the same way as Daril was. Like when you were a teenager and parroted everything he said."

"That was a long time ago," Marcia said through her teeth.

Nisha smirked, evidently pleased that the barb had hit home.

Marcia took a long breath. "You said some things to me, as well. I concluded that you were right. What you said about Aden, too, and the Broderers Guild. He can't be the only one."

Nisha's expression had sobered again, and there was something like surprise in her eyes. "He's not the only one," she agreed. "Look. Marcia. Are you serious about this?"

"About trying to broaden the Council, and about trying to find a better way of running things? Absolutely." She hesitated. "Trying to include the squats, though…"

"Oh, never mind that," Nisha said, waving a hand. "I mean, it was an interesting pamphlet, and it's not wrong, but one revolution at a time, darling. The Guilds, now, that is reasonable. Well. If you're serious… I'll speak to Aden." She sounded suddenly energised. Aden was another of Nisha and Marcia's group, though Marcia was less close to him than she was to Nisha. Marcia wouldn't have thought to involve him, but if Nisha thought it was a good idea… "Tomorrow, perhaps, we could meet? Morning tea, maybe. Petrior's has very discreet private rooms. I'll message you." She tilted her head slightly. "Convincing the Heads, though. I meant it. You're the closest to being able to solve that. You need to think it through."

She wasn't wrong. They agreed to meet at Petrior's, and moved on to other things – Nisha loved to gossip, and Marcia could always stand to know what was going on socially; it often came in handy politically – but the question churned at the back of her mind all the way through their leisurely tea and soak, and as she walked up the Hill back to House Fereno afterwards.

How could she convince the self-concerned Heads of the need for change?

"I saw your brother earlier," Reb said.

The two of them were lying on Reb's bed, legs entangled, quilt thrown to one side for now. The door through to the front room stood very slightly ajar, and through it, via the street window, came the faint noises of Marek in the evening; passer-by footsteps, the rumble of voices from the pub on the corner of the street, someone selling pastries.

Reb was lying on her side, facing Marcia, a little sweat glistening on her dark skin where the light fell on it. Her curls glowed in a shaft of sunset light.

"What, Cato was out and about?" Marcia asked, surprised. Cato tended to stay close to home, and his and Reb's taste in pubs hardly coincided.

"I went to his room," Reb said. "After he declined to come to mine." She grimaced. "Well, he didn't so much decline as not show up."

"You can't have been surprised," Marcia said. She had difficulty envisaging Cato sitting in Reb's neat, if down-at-heel, front room.

Reb scowled. "Pretty rude not to reply at all."

"You can't have been surprised," Marcia said again. "So you went to him? What on earth for?" She sat up a little. "Is there a problem? Is Beckett all right?" Surely Reb would have said something before this.

"Beckett's fine," Reb said. She rolled over onto her back and stared up at the ceiling. "We need to rebuild the Group."

"The Group?"

"Looks after sorcery in Marek," Reb said. "Keeps an eye on people, and magic. When Zareth and I..." She glanced over at Marcia, saw something on Marcia's face, and stopped. "Well. That time. We were acting as part of the Group."

Marcia had been a teenager back then, making damn stupid decisions, and she didn't really care to think about it. "Right," she said.

"But it hasn't existed since the plague," Reb said. "If it had, I'd have known about Urso, and maybe..." She scowled up at the ceiling. "Well. Maybe, maybe not. But I can't keep letting things slide."

Marcia slid herself under Reb's arm, which tightened around her.

"So what's that got to do with Cato?"

"I can't do it on my own," Reb said. "Which means..."

"He's the only other option," Marcia said, understanding dawning. "How did that go, then?"

"Badly. Until Beckett showed up and threatened him," Reb said. "Which I wasn't all that keen about either, to be honest."

"But he's agreed?" Marcia said, incredulous.

"Reluctantly," Reb said. "And to a radically more limited version than I had in mind. Major disasters and ensuring we know who's performing sorcery within Marek, that's all. No oversight, no centralised apprenticeship arrangements..." Her nose was wrinkled.

"So the Group used to act a bit like a Guild?" Marcia said.

"I suppose so. It seems – safer that way. Ensuring a basic standard."

"Cato didn't do an apprenticeship," Marcia said.

"Which is part of why he's against it, I assume," Reb said. "I remember it well. He did it all himself, against the Group's advice, and then hassled us into accepting that he was a competent practising sorcerer."

"Which he is," Marcia said, defending him automatically.

"Which he was and is," Reb agreed. "But he created an awful lot of grief for everyone else in getting to that point."

"But if he did it, why shouldn't other people?" Marcia asked.

"Cato was both competent and lucky," Reb said. "There's a

lot of things you can screw up. Admittedly, a lot of the time that solves the problem by removing the individual, one way or another, but... there's the Ursos of this world, too."

"Would an apprenticeship have meant that didn't happen?"

"No," Reb admitted, after a moment. "Probably not. It would at most have meant that someone was aware he was out there, and if you know a sorcerer is out there, then you can keep an eye on them, but then Cato doesn't want us to do that either, because he thinks it's an untoward interference with independent individuals, or something like that... I don't know. Maybe I'm wrong. I'd just prefer to deal with things before they become disasters."

Marcia kissed Reb's shoulder. "Maybe the two of you will work it out."

"Or maybe Beckett will feed us information," Reb said. "I mean, they're the one best placed to know what magic is going on in Marek, for certain, but their view of these things is a bit odd. And I didn't like it when they threatened to cut Cato's magic off."

Marcia's eyes widened. "Really?"

"Yes. I don't think that was appropriate. Even just as a threat." Reb chewed at a thumbnail. "So perhaps the Group needs to consider what our interactions with Beckett should be. Which is tough given that Beckett, when it comes down to it, has all the power." She sighed. "And then, after all of that, and Cato cutting up about apprentices – I assumed he was just making a point. But then I found out, this afternoon when I got home, that he's taken Jonas as an apprentice."

"Jonas? But he's..."

"Not magical? Salinas? All of the above?" Reb was scowling again. "Well, he's Salinas, right enough, but apparently he is magical as hell. And I didn't notice that either."

"He's Salinas," Marcia said, reasonably. "He wasn't exactly waving it around."

"And I wasn't looking. Which is part of the point."

"How did you find out?" Marcia asked, trying to move Reb away from more self-recrimination. She knew her lover felt badly about the last two years; but it didn't seem helpful to keep going over it.

"Did a spell to look for potential magic-users," Reb said.

"Found a few. Including one coming straight past my door, which turned out to be our Jonas."

"And he's apprenticed to Cato?"

"I tried to convince him it was a bad idea," Reb said.

"Cato's a decent sorcerer," Marcia said automatically.

Reb sat up a bit. "Fine, but do you think he should be supporting brand new sorcerers? Really?"

Marcia didn't say anything. She couldn't bring herself either to agree or to disagree.

"Anyway," Reb flopped back down. "He says he's happy enough with Cato. He – never mind. It was a bit of a rough day, that's all. What about you? What have you been up to?"

This was an ideal opportunity to introduce the idea of sorcerer representation on the Council – and this Group might be the right way to do it – except that Marcia felt hugely uncomfortable about it.

"Talking to the Teren Lord Lieutenant," she said, instead, putting the moment off. "Who was interested in Marek magic. My mother was not amused. I've agreed to talk to her tomorrow."

Reb frowned, evidently forgetting her own problems. "Wonder what she's after?"

Marcia shrugged. "Who knows? It sounds like she was interested in the differences between Marek and Teren magic."

"Well," Reb said. She looked away. "There are indeed differences, right enough."

Marcia had thought of asking Reb if she knew more about Teren magic, but something in Reb's voice dissuaded her.

"Hopefully the basics will satisfy her curiosity." She paused, then made herself go on. "And I was talking to Nisha, about reforming the Council. She might have some ideas. We're going to talk some more tomorrow."

Reb nodded, tension seeping out of her shoulders. "Right. Good luck."

"I thought," Marcia said, slowly. "I thought, if I'm trying to reform the Council anyway, give the Guilds more voice, I thought… maybe the sorcerers should have a voice, too."

Reb sat all the way up and stared at Marcia as if she'd grown a second head. "The sorcerers? Have you lost your mind? You know how the Hill feels about us."

"Yes, but, that's a problem, right? The Hill ignores magic – like my mother today, with Selene, that was exactly the issue, she just doesn't want to think about it – but magic is part of Marek, and Beckett…" Marcia ran out of words.

Reb was shaking her head, firmly. "We are perfectly fine without representation. As if we need representation. We've got magic, you know? We've got Beckett." She snorted. "If you want to give people representation, try looking to my neighbours. Try looking to the folks out in the streets south of the Square. Never mind your Houses and Guilds and certainly never mind Cato and me."

"Nisha said that too," Marcia said.

Reb's eyebrows went up. "She did, did she?"

"I don't think she was serious," Marcia said. "But you said, about the Group…"

"The Group doesn't want anything to do with city governance," Reb said. "And Beckett can't involve themself with politics, as well you know."

"Not using magic in Council, of course not," Marcia said. "But…"

"But nothing," Reb said. "Thanks and all that, but no."

It hurt more than Marcia would have expected. Of course Reb was entitled to decide what was best for her, and for Marek's sorcerers, but…

"Shouldn't you ask Cato?" she said. "Since you just said, you made him agree to join this Group of yours." Her tone was spikier than she meant it to be.

Reb's eyes narrowed just a little. "I suppose I should, yes," she said, and she in turn sounded borderline grudging.

Marcia shouldn't have said anything. Cato wouldn't want to be involved either, unless he decided to take the opposite view from Reb out of sheer contrariness, which was entirely possible.

"But I doubt he'll say anything different," Reb said. "I'll let you know if he does."

Marcia tried not to hear that as dismissive, patronising; and didn't quite succeed.

"Well," she said. "I'd better be going."

They both knew she couldn't stay overnight. It still felt like running away, even as Reb embraced her and they kissed one another goodbye.

☺ ☺

Insomnia wasn't a problem Reb usually had. But after Marcia left, sleep was unusually elusive. Things kept circling around her mind: Marcia and her bizarre suggestions about the Council; Marcia and what the hell Reb was doing being involved with her; Cato and Jonas; Beckett's insistence that Reb herself get an apprentice; the Group.

The Group had existed again for barely a day and already Cato was keeping things from her. Had been, even as they were talking about it. Hadn't they explicitly agreed that the Group should know who was performing magic in Marek? And yet Cato was teaching Jonas and hadn't bothered to tell her.

She was grinding her teeth. She deliberately relaxed her jaw muscles and took a couple of long breaths.

She'd have to talk to Cato about it. Sooner or later. For a moment she toyed with the idea of getting up now and going over there – Cato would doubtless be awake – but she was angry, and tired, and it wouldn't go well. She didn't need Cato to know how wound up she was. She needed to retain some kind of distance, or dignity, or something…

Superiority was what she wanted to retain, really, wasn't it? She laughed shortly at herself. The Group couldn't work that way. They had to be able to work together, if they were going to manage this at all. And Cato was as good a sorcerer as her. It was just that he did what he pleased, took clients that Reb wouldn't touch with a bargepole, and did absolutely nothing that didn't benefit him personally in some way. Hell, he'd only agreed to be part of the Group after Beckett had threatened him.

Which was part of her concern with Jonas. What was Cato's angle? What was he getting from this? And did Jonas know? Reb didn't believe for a second that Cato was apprenticing Jonas out of the goodness of his heart; but Jonas evidently didn't want to hear any warning. Which, when it came right down to it, meant that there was sod all she could do about it.

She turned over in bed and punched her pillow with a grunt of annoyance. Bloody Cato. She would have to mention it, at some point, but she was damned if she was going to go over there just to argue with him about it. It wasn't that important. It was just... annoying. Infuriating. And if she had to work directly with Cato for the next however-many years, this was hardly going to be the first infuriating thing she had to deal with. Bloody Cato. Bloody Beckett. Maybe she should just have resigned from magic after all.

As if she could. She'd considered it, a few times, in the aftermath of the plague. She'd certainly let herself retreat from anything at all difficult. But she couldn't possibly give up magic. It was part of her, all the way down to bone. That was, after all, why she'd come to Marek in the first place.

Marek, city of magic – apart from up on Marekhill, where they all pretended it didn't exist. The notable exceptions being Marcia, and the wretched Daril b'Leandra. Leandra-Heir now, and that left a sour taste in Reb's mouth. She understood why Marcia had done what she had, but... b'Leandra became Leandra-Heir; Urso, b'Leandra's distant relative, got disowned and shipped out of the city in a hurry rather than tried like he should have been; where was the justice in any of it?

Beckett had been returned to their place as cityangel. Marek's magic had been saved. The Council hadn't toppled. How much of that was justice, either? The first parts, yes. The Council... well. Reb was hardly a radical, but you couldn't live over this side of the city and care all that much about the Council and their preoccupations.

What was Marcia thinking, suggesting that sorcerers could be part of that? It was only ten years since the Guilds had won their Council seats, and everyone knew the Guilds hadn't got as much out of that deal as they'd expected. The Houses always would close ranks, if it came right down to it. Witness Marcia and b'Leandra.

That was unfair. Marcia was doing what she could, even if Reb doubted she'd get far.

Reb turned onto her back and grimaced up at the ceiling. The other thing about sorcery and Marekhill, the thing neither she nor Marcia were talking about, was that it meant that the two of them could never really go anywhere. Not that Reb wanted to get ahead of herself. They'd been seeing each other barely a couple of months. But she couldn't ignore the fact that Marcia, Fereno-Heir, couldn't be openly involved with a sorcerer. And they might not have talked about it, but both of them knew it.

So maybe that was what Marcia was thinking about. A future that could regularise their relationship – and Reb had thrown it straight back at her. But it was impossible, whatever Marcia might optimistically think. Sorcerers and the Hill didn't mix. That was all there was to it.

Sorcerers, the Hill, Cato, the Group...

It was a while before Reb finally slept.

SIX

House Berenaz was on Second Street, a couple of Houses along from the river end of the street. House Fereno sat at the river end of First Street, just before the road turned back on itself and became Second Street. A couple of hundred yards, at most; close enough that, especially for an informal meeting, Marcia was happy to walk, even if her mother would doubtless have taken the litter.

The street was relatively empty. Heads and Heirs might be up but were likely working; lesser House members tended to rise late and go out even later; and it was after early morning deliveries. In any case, messengers, porters, and tradespeople were strongly encouraged to come up via the alleys between the Houses, rather than clutter up the main streets.

House Berenaz was in a more modern style than most. The old building had burnt down back when Madeleine was a child, and Berenaz-Head of the time had taken the opportunity, not to put too fine a point on it, to show off. Marek wasn't well-provided with local building material in any case, so stone had to be shipped in; but cut marble from the quarries out near the Crescent cities, Marcia felt, might be imposing but was also somewhat ostentatious.

It was Piath, Berenaz-Heir that Marcia was due to meet this morning, hoping to discuss the Guilds with them. Despite what Madeleine had said, Marcia didn't think she needed to take things as slowly as all that; and she was less sanguine than Madeleine about whether the Guilds would sit still and wait for the Houses to come around. She had the itching feeling in her toes that something was coming, something big building up, and she didn't want to wait and be caught up in it.

Piath was some five years Marcia's senior, known as a quiet, studious type who was good with an account-book. Piath was rarely seen in Council, but House Berenaz had been doing very well of late, partly through some complicated trading which no one else, Marcia included, quite understood. Some aspects of it didn't seem even to *be* trading, not directly, but neither was it insurance as offered by the Crescent Alliance banks. Marcia had been wondering whether she should investigate. Though if it needed Piath's mathematical skills, she might not get very far.

In any case, although Piath wasn't a particular friend of hers, she got on well enough with them. Piath seemed like the sort of practical type to understand the value of working more closely with the Guilds, and building better relationships.

Her optimism sputtered out somewhere in the first few minutes of the meeting.

"Mm," Piath said. They wore their hair short, and were fiddling with a set of twist-beads as they listened to Marcia carefully outlining her wish – very lightly expressed – for the Houses to work more closely with the Guilds, and her wish to deal with the concerns the Guilds had begun to express more loudly. "Mm. I do see what you're saying. But – the Houses have been running Marek trading since the city was founded. Of course we need the Guilds. Of course we work with them. But… they simply do not have the experience that we do, in," they gestured with the beads, "pulling the entirety of the system together."

"I'm not suggesting that the Guilds should have *more* of a say than the Houses," Marcia said. "Merely that perhaps their inclusion in the Council has not gone far enough; that the Houses are perhaps too willing to ignore them."

"Well, well, only when that is appropriate," Piath said. "And I cannot think of an occasion when I would have disagreed with my Head on any matter in particular. The Guilds can, I fear, be short-sighted. Seeking their own individual profit rather than what is best for Marek as a whole." They nodded sagely, frowning.

"Are you suggesting that the Houses don't seek their own individual profit?" Marcia said incredulously, and, she realised after she'd said it, perhaps slightly less tactfully than she ought.

Piath frowned and began twisting the beads the other way. "The well-being of the Houses is the well-being of Marek, Marcia. We are the engine driving Marek's prosperity."

The words rang a faint bell in her head, but she couldn't

quite place them. Was it something Madeleine had said? It sounded like something Madeleine might have said.

"The Houses and the Guilds, together," Marcia said, though she was fairly certain by now that this was a lost cause.

"But with the far-sightedness of the Houses. Allowing the Guilds to overrule that – no, I can't see that it's wise," Piath said.

"But the Small Chamber," Marcia persisted. "That prevents the Guilds from even putting forward their opinion."

Piath pursed their lips. "The Small Chamber... I suppose perhaps that might be used with less alacrity. But there are many decisions where the Guilds' input is simply not needed. Why should we keep them from their own work, when the Houses could take the burden of these decisions on themselves?" They leant forward, resting their forearms on the table. "Marcia, I do not carry my House's vote."

"Nor do I," Marcia agreed. "But as Heirs, part of our job is to advise our Heads, and to prepare for the time when we will take that responsibility, no?"

"Indeed. Indeed. But I find, I am afraid, that I do agree with my Head's decisions. In fact." They shook their head with finality. "However. While you're here, I did wonder whether I could interest you in taking part in a venture I've been putting together." They took a piece of paper from the table, covered with small neat writing. "Now, in fact, this is precisely the sort of thing that the Guilds might not understand the value of. It is not so much a trading of items, you understand, as a trading of opportunities."

Marcia bit back on her frustration and undertook to consider the proposal, taking the paper away with her. She thought she could probably see what Piath was intending to do, but she wasn't about to commit to it without studying it more carefully.

Nothing there for the Guilds, even if she did potentially have something for House Fereno. At least the meeting hadn't been a total loss.

She couldn't shake the feeling that however in earnest Piath might have been, that they were echoing something they'd heard from someone else. That someone else was already seeking to keep the Houses from the Guilds. If not exactly to drive a wedge between them, then at least to prevent them joining together. She just wasn't sure who in Marek might have something to gain from that. And despite thinking it over all the way back up to House Fereno, she couldn't bring anyone, or any organisation, to mind.

Maybe she was just imagining things.

☺ ☺

The sun was up and it was a nice morning as Jonas trotted across the Old Bridge. A little brisk, maybe, and the streets were damp from overnight rain, but it was autumn. Jonas wasn't much looking forward to his first winter in Marek. At least here he could be inside some of the time. Out on the Oval Sea it didn't get as cold as Asa and Tam said it would here, but you were often very wet. Winter storms might not be impassable the way the late summer ones were, but they weren't exactly pleasant.

He had a message; the far side of Marek Square, to a jeweller, and he was to wait for the answer, which if he was lucky meant he might get offered a sit down and an infusion. Some folks were nice to messengers that way; some not so much.

The flicker, when it came, nearly drove him to his knees halfway through Marek Square, as he was passing the fountain. He staggered, and clung to the fountain's ledge. The worst part was that it wasn't even an image, the way they normally were. It was more like a bell clanging in his head, an urgent warning of alarm. Disaster. Dread. Something coming, getting nearer. Danger. Danger. His gorge rose, and he dry-heaved, just managing not to empty his stomach out in the middle of the square. He was vaguely aware, as the reverberations of the flicker died away, of people around him giving him a wide berth, or looking over at him disapprovingly.

Slowly, he straightened up. It was gone, now, leaving behind only the sense of unnamed advancing danger. To him? To Marek? He had no idea. He started walking again, ignoring the tremor he could still feel in his knees.

It had been dread, not just risk. If he'd seen just danger to himself, would it have felt that all-encompassing? He chewed at his lip. Unless it was some kind of warning about his sorcery. There were pretty unpleasant things that you could do with sorcery. But he didn't plan to do anything unpleasant at all. He wasn't even sure he wanted to do more than learn the basics so he could avoid doing anything he didn't intend.

Maybe that lack of commitment was itself the bad idea; maybe that was what he was being warned about. Maybe he was messing around with things that were really beyond him, and risking calling something down upon himself. Upon Marek? This flicker, happening so soon after he'd first managed to actually do sorcery – could that be coincidence?

Someone bumped into him from behind, and he took a step forward to regain his balance, realising that he'd slowed to a stop again.

"What you doing, just standing around lollygagging? Get out the road," a taller man said, scowling as he pushed past Jonas with a big bag strapped to his back.

The middle of Marek Square was not the place to stand around wondering about the details of what he'd just experienced. And he still had this message to deliver. He sighed and started walking again, towards the far side of the square.

He ought to tell someone about this. The obvious person would be Cato, who was his mentor, and who already knew about his flickers. And was curious about them, in a way that Jonas didn't entirely trust. What would Cato do, with a warning of danger? He'd protect himself, for certain, but would he have any interest in bothering to protect anyone else? Like, for example, Jonas?

Then there was Reb. Reb would try to help anyone she thought might be affected by whatever this was, without a doubt. But Reb didn't know about his flickers; and she didn't seem to trust his judgement, given the way she'd spoken to him yesterday. And he could just see how it would be if he told Reb: she'd be after him all the time, asking him questions, expecting him to drop the rest of his life to deal with whatever this turned out to be. She'd be as curious as Cato about the flickers, just in a different way.

Maybe, when it came down to it, he was overreacting. Taking himself too seriously. Maybe it wasn't anything he really needed to worry about.

He left Marek Square between two of the Guildhalls, and made his way into the neat streets that contained the houses of those not quite well enough off for Marekhill; artisans, Guildmembers, and so on. Coming out of the square seemed to take a weight off him; made it easier to brush away how the flicker had felt. It was just a flicker. There was no need to talk to Cato or to Reb. They'd overreact, and they'd pry, and they'd start expecting things of him. Better to leave it alone. It wasn't like worrying would do any good. He'd never yet been able to avoid anything he'd seen in a flicker.

He delivered the message, was given the answer immediately (so no infusion, and no chance to sit down, which was annoying), and retraced his steps towards Marek Square. He was sure, now, that he'd been overreacting. It would sort itself out, whatever it was. The flicker couldn't possibly have been as important as it had briefly felt. And he couldn't afford to take any more time away from earning money, given how much he was already losing to sorcery. It wasn't anything to worry about. It couldn't be.

"Hey! Jonas!" It was Tam, on his own way across the square, his cheerful round face creased in his customary smile.

"Hey there Tam. You busy?"

Tam shook his head. "Just started. Nothin' yet. Thought of breakfast though – fire the legs up, y'know? Want a pastry? My treat, pretty sure I'm owe you."

Jonas hesitated, tapping his belt pouch. "I've got a message..." But he wanted to sit with Tam, just for a few moments. He wanted to stop thinking about that flicker. "But – she thought the reply would take a while. So I can take a few minutes." He shouldn't, really; he should get it delivered and get onto the next message, the next coins. But a few minutes wouldn't hurt. And Tam wasn't wrong; he definitely owed Jonas a breakfast.

"Aw, grand. C'mon." Tam jogged over towards their favourite pastry-seller, at the pitch by the south side of the Old Bridge, and Jonas followed him.

The two of them sat on the river-wall in companionable mouth-full silence. The leaves of Jonas' pastry were as crunchy and sweet as ever, but it was the wrong time of year for his preferred berry filling; this one had goats-cheese instead. It was well enough, even if it wasn't berries; he could hardly complain.

"First of Sharf," Tam said. "Ships'll be back soon."

"Mm," Jonas agreed.

It was true enough. The late summer storms across the Oval Sea would be blowing themselves out, and his compatriots would be leaving their island villages and taking to the sea again. They usually started to arrive at ports around the quarter-year, by the Salinas calendar. Middle of Sharf, according to Marek.

He glanced out towards the mouth of the river. In fact…

"Oh hey! I summoned it," Tam beamed. "That's no fishing-skiff. The first Salinas ship. Me and my sisters used to think it was lucky to spot it, you know?"

"My mother used to say it was lucky to be the first one into a port," Jonas said. It had always been a good feeling, starting the season back up again, when he was sailing with his mother as a child. This ship was early, though, by a couple of weeks. Perhaps they had some urgent business; or the sea-storms had settled early this year.

In another world, he was one of the sailors on that ship, or some other at another port. It was early in the day to be coming in, though the tide was with her; idly, he wondered whether she'd lain-to outside the river mouth last night to make her way in in daylight, or whether she'd been sailing all night. She looked well, a neat sailor, like all Salinas ships…

His train of thought stopped dead as the ship came about and he saw her more clearly. That wasn't just any Salinas ship. That was the Lion t'Riseri. His mother's ship, *his* ship, the one he'd been brought up on.

And if that was the Lion, then his mother was on it. And there was no way he could even try to pretend that if his mother was coming to Marek, she wasn't looking for him.

"Jonas? You alright, there?"

"My mother," Jonas said, blankly.

"Your ma? That's her ship? And you can tell that all the way from here?" Tam squinted down the river. "Well, that's nice, then, spotting your ma…" He paused, and looked over at Jonas, more assessingly than Jonas expected from cheerful thoughtless Tam. "Is it nice?"

"She'll want to see me," Jonas said, which wasn't an answer.

He fought the urge to run away, and tried instead to think the matter through. He was known, a little, around the docks, because he went down there every so often to hear a familiar accent. And Kia, the Salinas ambassador, knew he was here, and knew roughly where he was to be found; he'd admitted to living in the squats. He couldn't realistically hide. And in any case, he did want to see her.

He just didn't want to be shouted at. And he had a horrible feeling that she was going to shout at him. He'd sent a letter with the last of the Salinas ships to leave after New-Year, Marek's Mid-Year. Just a couple of sentences: that he was well and that he was staying in Marek. He'd known at the time that it might not please her; he hadn't thought that it might bring her in search of him.

Well, it wouldn't just be in search of him. Marek was a prosperous place for a Salinas ship to put into, and most of them would stop here once or twice a year. His mother hadn't become Captain t'Riseri by doing things that didn't serve her trading needs. But it would be in search of him as well as in search of a trading bargain, he was mortally certain of that. And that she was this early...

An infusion-seller was passing in front of them, with her padded kettle in a basket slung from her shoulder and a net of disposable clay cups hanging from her belt. Tam handed her a coin, and passed Jonas a cup of something that smelt sweet.

"You look like you need it," Tam said. "Hey, Jonas. You don't have t'see her if you don't want." He sounded tentative.

He didn't have to; but he did want to, really. He was just nervous. And if she was going to find him anyway, she might be in a better mood if she didn't have to. If her loving and dutiful son was there to meet her at the docks when the ship came in. And he'd be pleased to see the Lion. A sudden gust of homesickness overtook him.

"I do want to see her," Jonas said. "And the Lion. It was just a bit of a surprise, you know?"

"Fair enough." Tam clapped him on the back.

The Lion had come about again, and was much closer now; she was coming in on the tide, barely needing the breeze she was tacking into. If he wanted to be there for her docking, he'd have to go now. But he had that message... if he ran, just for a moment...

"I should go see her," he said, half to himself, as he drained the infusion and threw the clay cup into the river.

"Hey, you want me to deliver that message?" Tam asked. "You c'n go straight there, that way."

"Would you?" Jonas fumbled for the penny to give Tam for the transfer, and Tam waved him off.

"No, don't worry. Buy your ma some flowers or something on your way over. My ma always likes flowers."

Jonas couldn't imagine flowers in his mother's neat, tidy cabin, but it was a kind thought. Jonas handed Tam the message, and the two of them jumped down from the parapet and crossed Old Bridge together.

Tam clapped him on the back again. "Go well, and my regards to your ma."

Jonas arrived at the docks just as the Lion did. The crew were busy, and Jonas stayed clear – no one would thank him for getting in the way. He recognised some of the crew on deck, not others; and he couldn't see his mother at the rail yet.

Then the ship was moored, and the accommodation ladder went down, and there was his mother at the top. Their eyes met, and she smiled at him briefly, before going rapidly down the ladder to greet the dock chief, there to welcome her. Captain t'Riseri had an excellent reputation; they'd be keen to keep her sweet here just like anywhere else the Lion sailed. Jonas resisted the urge to shift from foot to foot as he waited. Up on board the Lion, a couple of his old shipmates were waving; Jonas waved back, but shook his head at their gestured invitations to board. They looked down at his mother and nodded with over-dramatised sympathy. Jonas pulled a face, then hurriedly straightened his expression as his mother gave the dock chief a double handshake and turned towards him, moving with the slight unsteadiness of someone not used to solid ground under their feet. For a moment, Jonas felt a deep ache for a ship under him, for the lift of water rather than the unforgiving solidity of ground.

"Jonas," his mother said, and opened her arms to embrace him.

She smelled just as she always had, and a rush of emotions

overwhelmed Jonas. She was his mother; but she'd always been Captain t'Riseri too, and he'd been a child and then crew on the Lion, his relationship with her always complicated by those multiple roles. But she was his mother, and his earliest memory was of her arms round him. Holding him at the Lion's rail with the glittering sea spread in front of them, the Lion rising to meet the waves, and his mother's laugh in his ear.

"Mother," he said into her shoulder. "Well sailed, well met."

"And well met to you," she said, breaking the embrace and holding him at arms' length to look at him. "Are you well, Jonas? Have you lost your sea-legs entirely?"

"I'm sure they'd come back in a moment," he said, evading what he knew was the point of the question. But he wasn't about to discuss this standing on the dock with half the Lion's crew staring at them.

"I'm sure they will," she said.

Will, not would. He bit back his response.

"I would love nothing better than to catch up with you immediately," she said. "I would love to know what is it that has been keeping you here land bound, for example. Your letter was not wholly explicatory, Jonas."

Jonas winced. He hadn't explained anything in his letter, because he hadn't really wanted to, and in any case he didn't know where to start. And what she really wanted to hear was that he'd solved his little *problem*.

Cato didn't think his flickers were a problem. Urso hadn't either.

"I would love to catch up too, Mother. But you're just landed..."

"And I have much to arrange," she agreed.

Trading meetings, shore leave for the crew, messages to leave and to collect from the various dockside inns that doubled as mail-offices, all the other many and various things that a captain had to do. He knew all of that; had been brought up to it, following her through docks and trading towns right across the Oval Sea. She'd been bringing him up to take her place, in due course; and now here he was apprenticed to a landbound sorcerer.

He really, really didn't want to explain that. His mother

would be furious; more than furious, horrified. But how else could he explain why he was staying here?

Reb had been cross that he was apprenticed to Cato, but not about his sorcery. Asa wasn't bothered by either thing.

He was Salinas, though, and this was his family. His sorcery might not be welcome here, but he was. Wasn't he?

"Perhaps this evening?" his mother asked.

"I've to meet Asa this evening," Jonas said without thinking about it, too busy worrying about Cato and sorcery.

His mother's eyes narrowed speculatively, and he cursed himself.

"Asa? A – friend? A good friend?"

"Um," Jonas said, not wanting to confirm or deny, and his mother's eyebrows went up.

"Well. Perhaps you could bring Asa tonight?"

"It's fine," Jonas said. "They'll understand if I cancel. I mean, it's not every day my mother comes into port, is it? Perhaps another time? How long are you staying?"

"At least a week," his mother said, and his heart sank just a little. "Longer if need be." She was still looking speculative. "Never mind tonight, then. I need to meet with Kia, once I send a message; time enough to catch up then." Her eyes fell on his messenger's armband, and he saw her remembering its significance, remembering how Marek organised these things. "You're working as a messenger?"

"Yes," he said, raising his chin slightly.

"Oh, I don't disapprove at all, Jonas," his mother said. "It's a good enough job to be taking while you're here. I'm sure you know the city well now, then."

"That is an advantage," Jonas said. "And I'm my own employer, which I like too." He smiled at her, and she smiled back.

"Well then. If you'll wait a moment for me to write it, I'll send a message to Kia with you. And I'll tell her that I want you along to dinner. Old shipmates, hey? And you can bring this Asa." She counted on her knuckles. "Three days from now. That will work nicely."

Dinner with his mother and Kia. Kia who knew all about the whole mess with Daril and Urso and Cato a couple of months back, and at least something of Jonas's role in it. How delightful. And Asa too. Sea and spit. He had no desire to see Kia right now. Not before he had time to think.

"I'd love to, Mother," Jonas said, "but I'm on a message already," an outright lie, "and I really should be straight along. I've delayed already to meet you. But of course I'll be happy to have dinner with you and Kia. I'm sure Asa will be, too."

He could hardly say otherwise. But to say he wasn't looking forward to it was wildly to understate the case.

SEVEN

Marcia was thinking of Reb as she walked down the Hill the next morning, towards Petrior's. It was on Third Street, only two turns below her own House. She could shorten the route if she cut through the alleys between the Houses, but she'd regret it if she took a misstep into the rubbish that sometimes clogged them. It wasn't much further to go around the long way, and the streets were more frequently swept.

She was trying to talk herself out of feeling hurt by how dismissive Reb had been about the Council. Surely it wasn't that outrageous an idea? Though she had a sneaking suspicion that Cato would have been even more dismissive, and more likely to laugh in her face. She sighed. Reb didn't want the Council; best just to accept that, and not take it personally. Marcia had other things to think about. Such as what Nisha and Aden might have come up with.

Third Street was bustling with people wandering along it, peering into windows, and clustered into loudly chatting knots; but as soon as she stepped through the door of Petrior's sumptuous infusion-salon, nestled between a bookshop and a dressmaker's, the noise died away into a hushed quiet, aided by the richly dyed and embroidered fabric draped everywhere. Petrior had a fondness for purples and pinks which Marcia found a little overwhelming, but the infusions and the food were beyond criticism. A waiter appeared before the door had shut behind her, and showed her, with a bow and a murmured greeting, past the private curtained booths which lined the main room and up a half-flight of stairs to the private rooms. One of the doors stood a little open, and when the waiter showed her in, Nisha was already there, half-reclining on a grey velvet sofa.

"Marcia, darling," she said, gesturing at the waiter, who retreated and shut the door behind them. "They'll bring us an infusion in a moment. Do you have any preference? I find rosehip and lemon revitalising in the mornings." She sat up a little. "Do have a seat."

Marcia chose the equally comfy armchair opposite the sofa. The room was just about big enough for the two small sofas and armchair, with a table between them, its ornate inlay portraying the founding of Marek. There was no obvious reference to the cityangel, just Rufus Marek and Eli Beckett gazing off into the distance looking noble.

The door opened again revealing Aden – tall, thin, and red-haired, in his customary green – and another waiter with a tray of tea.

"Peppermint for me," Aden told the waiter. "Can't bear rosehip at any time of day."

"Your taste always was dubious, Aden darling," Nisha said, making room for him on her sofa as he pulled a face at her.

"So," Marcia said, pouring rosehip and lemon for herself and Nisha. "What has Nisha told you?"

"Convincing the Houses to let the Guilds actually do something in Council," Aden said promptly. "And as it happens, I do have an idea as to a deal that might work for at least a vote or two."

"Yes?" Marcia said. She tried not to raise her eyebrows. She had doubted that Aden would be interested in this; evidently she'd been wrong and Nisha right.

The door opened for the delivery of Aden's peppermint infusion, and they paused their conversation.

"The Guilds were supposed to raise their bar on House apprentices or journeyman, right? And they didn't," Aden said, once the waiter had gone again. "Well, they did, in theory, but not in practice." His cheek twitched. Aden himself had been one of those quietly rejected. "There's at least two Houses with close relatives affected by that. If the Guilds take those people on – it'll need to be real, though, not just a promise, not this time – then there's a chance of getting the House votes in exchange."

"Your House is one of them?" Marcia asked.

"I can talk to Tigero-Head," Aden said, referring to the Head of his own House. "We're friends, and – he owes me one, basically." Andreas, Tigero-Head, was rather younger than Marcia, Aden, and Nisha. His father had died a year previously, a bare month or so after Andreas had been confirmed as Heir at twenty-one. As far as Marcia could see,

Andreas was terrified of dealing with the other Heads, all a good twenty or thirty years older than him and far more experienced. Marcia had tried to reach out to him a couple of times but hadn't got anywhere. Maybe she should try again, via Aden. She hadn't been aware that they were friends.

"Enough of an owing to risk the enmity of the other Houses?" Marcia asked. She doubted it, unless Andreas had developed a backbone while she wasn't looking.

"Well, there's the thing, isn't it? It's going to depend very much on how it's handled. But," Aden tapped his teeth thoughtfully with the spoon from his infusion. "I do think Andreas knows the gulf between the Guilds and the Houses is growing, and that there might yet be consequences from that. A closer link for our House in particular, well, that might pay off, mightn't it?"

"You mean that if you're a journeyman you'll get a good deal on Broderers' Guild goods for your House," Marcia said. "You realise that that's exactly why there was a ban on House members joining Guilds in the first place?"

Aden shrugged. "But the ban's lifted. There's something to be had for both parties, is the point. And if I can remind Andreas that he's going to be dealing with all of this for a damn sight longer than the other Heads..." He sighed. "Marcia, if you think you're going to get this without a certain amount of, let's say, pragmatic dealing, then you're deluded."

"So that's one, maybe two votes," Nisha said. "If you, Marcia, can convince the Guilds to take on a couple of House members, as a show of goodwill."

"Risks strife between the Guilds," Marcia said. "They'll realise the trading advantage."

"Maybe they'll all go looking for House members," Nisha suggested. "Once the block is broken..."

"It's the breaking of the block in the first place, though," Marcia said. "You're not wrong, but... Fine. I'll give it some thought. I've got a contact at the Broderer's Guild." She was gloomily aware that installing Aden there would likely damage her own House advantage, but there it was. "That's still only two votes, at most."

"Three, with you."

With her, if she could talk Madeleine round; but she

couldn't say that. If Nisha and Aden thought her own House vote was in doubt, this whole thing would crumble under her.

"We need four, at least," Marcia said. Thirteen Houses, ten Guilds. Two for the majority, four for a solid result that wouldn't cause a dramatic rift between the Houses.

Nisha was wearing a slightly odd smile. Marcia frowned at her.

There was a gentle knock at the door, before the waiter put their head around it.

"We're fine with what we have…" Marcia began, and then the waiter opened the door a little further, and someone stepped in.

Daril. Daril Leandra-Heir.

After a frozen moment, Marcia opened her mouth – to say something like, *I think you must be mistaken* – but Nisha was standing up, greeting Daril warmly, offering him a choice of infusion. Marcia shut her mouth again.

"I don't think Marcia was expecting me," Daril said, once he had sat down on the spare sofa. "I certainly wasn't expecting her." He looked over at her, meeting her eyes for the first time. She couldn't read his expression. They hadn't seen one another other than across a formal function room since Mid-Year.

Suddenly, the armchair felt like it was sucking her in, suffocating her. She wanted to sit up straight, but she didn't want to reveal her discomfort. She forced her shoulders to relax, forced herself to sit back again.

"I thought it would be better as a surprise, given the strange antipathy the two of you have to one another," Nisha said, sitting back down as relaxed as ever.

Marcia met Daril's eyes again, and this time she could see him make exactly the same calculation that she did about whether or not to say anything about the 'strange antipathy'; and could see him realising that she too didn't want to give Nisha anything further to gossip about. For the first time, she swallowed a half-smile.

"Well," Daril said. "Perhaps you could explain why we're here."

"We're hoping for Leandra's vote," Nisha said, bluntly.

"Are you indeed. And on what? You are aware that I am Leandra-Heir, not Leandra-Head? At least – I haven't seen the old man yet this morning. You never know."

"Given you are Heir now," Aden said, "Nisha and I thought that you might have more influence than you... once... did."

Daril's eyes hardened slightly. "I see. Well, perhaps so, or perhaps not. Would you care to elaborate?"

Every bone in Marcia's body told her not to give herself away to Daril; but it was too late now. If she didn't tell him, he'd go looking, now he knew there was something to look for. And if he was watching, she wouldn't be able to hide it. The Guilds would happily hold private meetings, their content kept between those attending; they wouldn't tolerate out-and-out secrecy. And if Nisha and Aden thought that Daril could usefully be involved, they wouldn't be above recruiting him directly if Marcia refused.

"There is a gulf growing between the Houses and the Guilds," Marcia said, starting from the angle that might make most sense to Daril. "A gulf created by the fact that their apparent political power is in practice only theoretical. Created by the way in which the Houses have chosen to quite openly keep that power to themselves. And at the same time, the change in the way the Houses work has created – as you yourself are all too aware – a dissatisfied class of our peers. I would like to solve both of those problems; but to begin with the Guilds."

"You want to give the Guilds more power."

"I want to dissolve the Small Council, and elect a further two Guild seats."

"Goodness me," Daril said. He was silent for a while. "The rot goes a lot deeper than that, you know," he said, finally. He sounded almost chatty.

"I remember you arguing along similar lines earlier this year," Nisha said smoothly. "Which is why I thought of you."

Daril was looking at Marcia again, and ignoring Nisha.

"One thing at a time," Marcia said through her teeth.

Daril flicked an eyebrow upwards, then shrugged. "In any case. I fear I cannot be of assistance. My father... would most certainly not approve of your ideas."

"Your father?" Aden said incredulously. "Since when do you care about what your father wants?"

"Since he made me Heir," Daril said. "As the representatives of our House, we endeavour to remain on positive terms. And so – no. I wish you the best of luck, of course."

He stood up, and nodded affably to all of them.

Marcia wanted, desperately, to ask if he intended to mention it to anyone. From the tilt of his eyebrows, she thought Daril was waiting for the request. But she couldn't hand him that weapon; couldn't demonstrate that she cared whether this was secret or not. Couldn't, come to that, insult him by asking.

"See you at the card-tables," Nisha said cheerfully.

Daril shut the door behind him.

"Oh well," Nisha said. "Back to the drawing board, then, for the fourth vote."

Marcia fought not to shout at Nisha, to ask what the hell she had been thinking. It wasn't, on the face of it, a bad idea to speak to Daril, given what he'd been saying earlier in the year. It made sense. It wasn't Nisha's fault that Marcia didn't want anything to do with Daril, and it wasn't Nisha's fault that Daril had said no.

Even if she did, ever so slightly, suspect Nisha of stirring.

"I'll think over our allies," Marcia said, instead, striving for calmness of tone. "And perhaps you could consider whether there's anything Kilzan-Head might be in need of."

She was going to make this happen. Daril or no.

Selene, wrapped in a wool cloak against the breeze, stood next to Marcia at the top of Marekhill. Marcia, looking out over the city spread below them, felt her customary surge of affection and belonging. It occurred to her to wonder what Selene – as representative of the Teren crown, and thus notional overlord of the city – felt. A covert glance sideways at Selene's profile gave her no information.

"It is kind of you to agree to meet me," Selene said, without turning to look at Marcia. "And, indeed, to show me this view."

Marcia's main criteria for the choice of venue was that it offered little likelihood of being overheard and that it looked moderately unexceptionable, taking the Lord Lieutenant on a pleasant walk through Marekhill Park. The bathhouse worked well for discreet discussions, but Marcia hardly felt that she was at that level of casual friendly intimacy with Selene, and nor did she want to be. Taking a room at Petrior's or some other infusion-salon would make it all too obvious that they were seeking privacy. Marcia could get away with that with Nisha and Aden, even Daril; the Houses and their offshoot youth were constantly engaging in gossip and political chat. Not so the Lord Lieutenant. Marekhill was far safer. More obvious, and thus less obvious.

Of course, if all Selene wanted was information on magic, then only a small amount of decorum was warranted. One didn't speak of magic on Marekhill, but it wouldn't matter overmuch if Marcia was overheard doing so, beyond a few days of gossip among anyone looking to have a dig at her. It wasn't like everyone didn't remember Cato, however much they might pretend they didn't. Witness the fact that Selene had asked about him; she must have obtained that information somewhere.

Maybe it was only an excess of caution that meant Marcia wanted a little extra deniability.

"The Thirteen Houses are all at the top of the hill, just beneath us?" Selene asked.

"Yes, indeed," Marcia said. Selene had visited them all by now, of course, but probably in a litter, rather than walking on her own feet. "Along the first two tiers of the road that winds down the hill. The Council building, of course, you will remember – we passed it at the entrance to the park."

"And there are the docks," Selene gestured across the river.

"You can see the ferry there, leaving from the Old Market to come to the bottom of the cliff on this side of the river," Marcia said, pointing down at the boat in question.

"What does one buy at the Old Market?" Selene asked.

"Nearly anything," Marcia said. "The wholesale market is further to the west, you understand." She pointed. It was just visible to her eye, though Selene might not be able to spot it. "The Old Market sells on a smaller scale – food, cooked and uncooked, drink, some household goods and clothes. Most people on this side of the river buy from shops on Marekhill or over there in the merchants' quarter," she gestured southwest, towards an area at the foot of Marekhill, "but I

97

know our cook sends over to the Old Market for extras sometimes."

"And magic?" Selene asked.

"I beg your pardon?"

"Can one buy magic, in the Old Market?"

Reb's house was a couple of streets north of the Old Market, as it happened; but Marcia didn't want to use Reb's name to Selene.

"I believe there is a sorcerer on that side of the river, yes," she said.

"Your mother seemed unhappy at my talk of magic," Selene said.

"The Houses do not engage in magic," Marcia said. "May not, by law, engage in magic, either directly, or through a sorcerer, paid or gifted."

Of course, both she and Daril had broken that rule. She, at least, had only been helping Reb in an emergency; and, arguably, grounding Reb wasn't, technically, engaging directly in magic.

Cato had broken that rule very thoroughly, over a decade ago, and their mother had disowned him for it. In truth she couldn't have done otherwise, if he wouldn't stop. But she didn't have to do it as thoroughly as she did; not just expelling him from the House, but stopping all contact. She'd never even asked after him during the plague, though Marcia knew for a fact that Madeleine had known Marcia was nursing Cato through it.

"So that is why your mother said she did not have a sorcerer child," Selene said. "The sorcerer is no longer of the House."

Marcia was taken aback, both by the baldness of the statement, and by the correctness of Selene's deduction. Thus far she hadn't, to Marcia's knowledge, displayed any particular acuity; she'd just meandered around parties and social events making nice with everyone. But of course, Selene was presumably high in the Teren court, and one might suppose that that required just as much intelligence and social acumen as Marek politics within the Houses did. It might be perfectly reasonable that Selene had chosen not to demonstrate that until now; but it rang a warning bell in Marcia's mind.

She hesitated for a fraction of a second over how to respond, then chose frankness.

"My brother Cato was disowned, yes, when he chose magic over the House. He practises over in the squats, now."

"Ah yes, the famous free housing of Marek." Selene looked out over the city. "Can one see them from here?"

Marcia pointed over the river, slightly northwest of where they were now. "The streets over the other side of the river, closely-packed with fairly tall buildings? There." She reflected, not for the first time, on how seldom anyone from Marekhill went north of the river; Selene might have heard of the squats but no one would have taken her to visit them. Well, it wasn't like Marcia was about to offer either.

"Fascinating," Selene said, then hesitated. "Perhaps I could ask you about that some other time? If I may not speak of magic elsewhere in Marekhill company, I should like to remain with that subject."

She wouldn't find much conversation about the squats, either, in polite Marekhill society, but she was right that it was a question she could ask and expect an answer. Unlike magic. "Certainly," Marcia said.

"So. I take it you still know your brother?"

"He's my brother," Marcia said, flatly.

Selene nodded.

"How much do you know about how his magic is performed? I understand that it is not the same as happens in Teren."

"I don't know anything about Teren magic," Marcia admitted.

"In some cases it uses blood," Selene said. "The sorcerer's own blood, or animal blood, or the blood of other humans, which is most strictly forbidden."

"But using one's own blood has, I imagine, a, uh, practical limit."

"Just so," Selene agreed. "Which encourages the sorcerer to think about other sources of blood, whatever the law might say. And I gather that animal blood is not particularly powerful."

Marcia grimaced.

"That is not the case here?"

Marcia shook her head. "I've never seen Cato," or Reb,

"use blood in his magic."

"But my understanding was that the blood enables the passage of power between the spirit world and this world," Selene said.

"In Marek, we have the cityangel," Marcia said. This part she did know. "Who does that job, without the need for the blood."

"A spirit?"

"Yes, exactly. The cityangel acts as a channel between the two worlds, and the sorcerer uses a focus, or different sorts of focus, to direct the power in the right direction."

"A focus?"

Marcia shrugged. "Salt, or feathers, or, oh, various other things." Cato had shelves of this and that in his room; she'd only seen Reb's workroom once, but it was much the same. "I'm afraid, though, if you wish to know more detail, regarding sorcery or the cityangel, you will have to seek out a sorcerer to ask. We are coming to the end of my knowledge." That wasn't entirely true, but they were certainly reaching the end of the knowledge that Marcia cared to share with Selene.

Selene made a thoughtful noise, still looking out over Marek. The wind had picked up a little since they first walked up past the Council Chamber and through the park, and Marcia wrapped her shawl around her a bit more firmly. The trees had their autumn colours now, and the air had felt crisp this morning.

"The invocation of spirits is the other form of Teren magic. Invocation and binding." Selene sounded as though she had come to some kind of a decision. "It sounds as if your Marek magic, with the help of the cityangel, is – reliable?"

"Outcomes are not always guaranteed, if that is what you mean," Marcia said. "If you pay a sorcerer for a finding-spell, you most likely will find whatever you have lost, but sometimes the cityangel chooses not to assist." And sometimes you never lost it, or rather it wasn't yours to lose in the first place.

"Ah, no, that is not my meaning of reliable," Selene said. "The cityangel does not take payment or revenge?"

"Not that I've ever heard of," Marcia said. She turned and pointed to the statue that lay a few tens of feet behind them. "The cityangel came to an arrangement with Rufus Marek and Eli Beckett, when they founded the city; so goes the story." A story which Beckett, who had of course been there, although at the time unnamed, had confirmed. Beckett drew power from the city; sorcerers drew power via Beckett.

"Mm," Selene said. "It is not so in Teren. People – sorcerers – seek to do deals with a spirit, and the spirit may not always hold to the deal. Or may seek more payment than was promised. Or may otherwise exert their powers in a way that is – unwelcome. Sometimes dramatically so, involving many more people than the original sorcerer." She had the slightly pinched look of someone seeking not to remember – or not to remember in detail – something unpleasant.

"I see," Marcia said, and indeed, she was beginning to do so. She weighed up whether it was politic to enquire further. "I take it something of the sort has happened recently?"

"Something of the sort. Yes."

"How do you normally deal with such problems?" Marcia asked, after it seemed that Selene wasn't going to say anything more of her own accord. She knew Cato worked with spirits occasionally, in some form; but prior to the events of the summer, he'd never mentioned having any problems of that sort. Maybe he'd just been lucky.

"Sacrificing the one who called the spirit usually does the job," Selene said, and Marcia suppressed her instinctive recoil. Cato must be doing things some other way, when he dealt with spirits. Maybe things worked differently in Marek for that, as well as for the focus sort of magic. He was far too fond of his own skin to risk it that way.

"But in this case," Selene said heavily, "we could not do that, due to the fact that the sorcerer, ah, ran for it." The colloquialism sounded odd. She turned to face Marcia. "Our sorcerers sought instead to contain the demon, and that too was unsuccessful. We believe it is seeking the one who summoned it. When I first received word of this from Ameten, I assumed the summoner would be found relatively quickly. It seems now that… well, they are still being tracked, but they are coming towards Marek, and the demon is following. So far there is no other damage, but our experience is that demons do not mean well towards humans."

"And you think Marek is at risk?" Marcia asked.

Anxiety curdled in her stomach. But surely Beckett would protect Marek against another spirit?

"I hope not," Selene said. "I hope we will find the fool who summoned the thing. But should they come to Marek... I would seek to speak to a Marek sorcerer, to see if we can work together to solve this problem." She smiled without warmth. "I think we can agree that a rogue demon is everyone's problem."

"And you would like me to help you with that?" Marcia guessed.

Beckett had, or so they claimed, more or less eaten the fellow spirit that had tried to claim their place as Marek's cityangel at Mid-Year. That did not, of course, mean that Beckett either could or would assist Selene with this spirit, nor was Marcia about to reveal her own acquaintance with the cityangel. But she probably could, without harm, introduce Selene to Reb. With Reb's permission.

"If you are willing," Selene agreed.

"I may be able to introduce you to someone," Marcia said, slowly.

"Your brother?" Selene asked.

Marcia suppressed the automatic roll of her eyes. If Reb didn't want anything to do with it – and Reb, unlike Cato, didn't generally work with spirits – Cato was the only other option. Best not to prejudice Selene ahead of time.

"I'll make enquiries," she said instead. "He may not be the best fit."

"Marek has many sorcerers, then?" Selene said.

This time it was harder for Marcia not to react. If Selene didn't already know, she wasn't keen to reveal that the true number, at this time, was only two. It didn't do to give away information unnecessarily. And whilst Selene's story seemed believable enough, it was far from out of the question that her interest in Marek's magic had other sources, either as well as or instead of this business of a troublesome demon.

"Not so many since the plague," she said, with perfect truth. "But I am sure I will be able to find you someone. Please, leave it in my hands, and I will message you – let us say, within a couple of days?"

"Perfect," Selene said. "I appreciate your help, and that you have let me speak to you so candidly."

Marcia bowed politely in response.

"Now." Selene shivered again, trying to huddle further into the cloak. The unseasonable warmth of the last couple of weeks was definitely easing off, although Marcia wouldn't have said it was chilly yet; but then, wasn't Ameten warmer? Perhaps Selene felt the cold. "Perhaps we could walk back down the hill, and you could allow me to treat you to an infusion in one of the delightful salons close to my lodging?"

It occurred to Marcia, as they headed back towards the path, that she might be able to make an ally here. It would be a delicate matter – she didn't want to give Teren an in to Marek's affairs any more than anyone else did – but a subtle influence, perhaps... This little chat might yet be useful to both of them.

Jonas seriously considered skipping his scheduled meeting with Cato, but previous experience suggested that when he did that, Cato was much more irritating the next time he went round, whether deliberately or otherwise.

And he was still thinking about that flicker, even if he didn't intend to ask Cato about it directly.

Most pressingly, he really ought to tell Cato both that Reb had discovered that he, Jonas, was a proto-sorcerer – or whatever the hell he was – and that Reb now knew he was apprenticing – or whatever the hell he was doing – with Cato. If Reb came round to shout at Cato about that, and Cato hadn't been pre-warned when he could have been, he was liable to become sarcastic.

He nearly ran into someone on the stairs up to Cato's room. A narrow-faced, skinny woman, very carefully holding a small bag in front of her. She'd ducked her head forward to hide her face under her hood as soon as she saw Jonas. She must be one of Cato's clients; the other rooms on this corridor were rarely occupied. No one wanted to live near the sorcerer if they could help it.

It was none of his business what Cato was up to, and he most certainly wasn't going to ask. He had other things to worry about.

"Reb knows I'm a sorcerer," he blurted out, as soon as he got through the door. No point in putting it off. "And that I'm... learning stuff. From you."

Cato, today, was seated in the dilapidated armchair under the window. Its red brocade was threadbare, but never actually leaked any of its stuffing. Jonas suspected magic, but maybe it was just badly repaired. There was a faint singed smell in the air, which Jonas wasn't going to enquire about. Cato, leaning back with one ankle balanced on his knee, shrugged.

"Well, I wouldn't say you're a *sorcerer* yet, not exactly, but there we go. She was going to find out eventually."

"I know, but..."

"But she shouted at you?" Cato guessed. "She does that, Reb. It's the overdeveloped sense of responsibility. Doubtless she'll shout at me, too, whenever I next see her. Ah well." He eyed Jonas. "You did realise that this couldn't stay a secret for ever, yes?"

Jonas poked at a knot in the floorboard with his toe. "I... suppose so." He wasn't sure what he'd thought would happen eventually. It wasn't like he kept it secret, exactly. Asa knew. Tam – no, Tam didn't know, did he? Shit, he'd have to tell Asa not to tell his mother. The idea of his mother finding out anything about this made his skin prickle, even if he wasn't sure what else he could say to her to explain why he was staying.

So what was his end-goal? To be a secret sorcerer in Marek forever? Cato was right; that was hardly realistic. Cato seemed to think he would be taking it up as a job, in due course, and you couldn't exactly get clients in secret, could you? Well, the clients might be secret, but they wouldn't find you if you were...

Cato was looking at him, eyes narrowed.

"Uh," Jonas said, belatedly. "I suppose not. I just – I'm not a sorcerer yet, though, am I? I don't want to go round claiming something that I might be rubbish at." He felt quite proud of that, as an excuse. An explanation, even.

"Well," Cato said. "Shall we try some simple practice again? The light spell's always a nice one. And involves zero pigeons."

It was nice the way Cato did it, a tiny spark floating almost joyously through the air. Jonas, however, couldn't concentrate, and he couldn't make the spark happen at all.

"You're not thinking about what you're doing," Cato said, after a few fruitless minutes. "You know this is possible. It's a lot less draining than that finding-spell, especially the way you did it." He didn't sound irritable, but he sounded like he was avoiding frustration only by an effort of will. "Is there something else on your mind?"

Jonas stared at the floor. "M'mother. Came in this morning."

Cato's eyebrows shot up. "Your mother? Captain t'Riseri? Of the Lion? My goodness. I have to tell you, I would love to meet… her…" He trailed off, seeing Jonas' expression. "Of course. My apologies. The absurd Salinas feelings about magic."

"Not absurd," Jonas said, a bit sullenly. "It's – magic is dangerous, is what. Spirits too. It's all to be stayed away from."

"Like your flickers," Cato said. "That's why you wanted rid of them. Does your mother know?"

Jonas didn't say anything.

"She sent you here to lose them," Cato said. "Didn't she."

It didn't sound like a question, so Jonas didn't bother answering.

"Well, that's bloody ridiculous," Cato said, sounding deeply irritated. "It's not like you can just remove a thing that's part of you, that way."

"Thought you said you could, if I wanted to," Jonas said, looking up.

Cato grimaced. "You're right. I said that, and I meant it. If you wanted me to. But what I also said was, it would hurt like hell, and I'm not sure that there wouldn't be other consequences. I mean – you can't just take part of you out without it having any other effects."

"Maybe I should though, instead of sorcery," Jonas said. "Whatever the effects are. Maybe it would be better." It ought to be the obvious solution. It ought to have been the solution he chose, the first time Cato offered it. And yet, thinking of it, his stomach felt hollow, and his shoulders hunched.

"It is, as ever, your decision," Cato said. He had leant back in the chair again, and he was obviously trying for his habitual air of unconcern, but it wasn't quite sitting right.

Neither of them spoke for a moment. Cato sighed.

"Look. Jonas. The magic, your flickers. I think – they must be related, you understand? If you would tell me more about them, perhaps I could help you work out what's blocking you here. Because you have the power. We both know that." He paused. Jonas didn't look at him. "I'm interested on several levels, I admit that, but truly, a large part of it is because if I'm teaching you, then it's my job to damn well teach you. Here you are, tangled up about your mother and your magic and your flickers, and you can't so much as raise a spark. You see?"

"They're a pain in the arse," Jonas muttered. "That's all. Without them, I'd be…"

"Without them, you'd be someone else," Cato said.

"Maybe I'd rather be someone else," Jonas said, looking up, finally. He felt something hot inside him. "Maybe I'd rather not be stood here…" He waved his hands, something bursting inside his chest, as his fingers made, without thinking of it, the same movement he'd been practising for the last ten minutes.

A shower of sparks appeared between him and Cato, and he swore, and jumped back.

Cato calmly brushed out the one that had fallen on his trousers.

"Strong emotion, that'll do it," he said. "But Jonas, don't you see? This is you. Maybe you'd rather be someone else, maybe the whole thing is a pain in the arse, but you can say that until your breath runs out and it won't change anything."

Jonas sighed, and sat down, abruptly, on the end of the bed, half-facing Cato. He felt tired, and his knees were shaking, and he didn't want to have to deal with any of this.

"I tried to resist my magic, at first," Cato said, abruptly. He wasn't looking at Jonas.

"Really?" Jonas asked, surprised. "I thought you were all, 'go ahead and disown me', and all that." He regretted saying it almost as soon as it came out of his mouth – Cato never talked about his past, and Jonas knew it only through squats-gossip, and believed it only because he'd met Marcia – but Cato didn't react.

"Yes, well. I was, eventually. But before that, I wondered what I should do, and if I should just ignore it, and… I'd been through enough change, at that point, to be going on with. I didn't particularly want to have to deal with magic as well. But," he shrugged, "the magic carried on dealing with me, and in the end, there wasn't a decision to be made. Whatever my mother might have thought. It wasn't so much a choice as… I could have never used it, I suppose, but what the hell sort of a life is that?"

Jonas didn't say anything.

"So. I'm here to tell you. You can bung it up, if you like, like damming a river, and just let tiny bits leak out when you're safe alone. Or you can own it, and damn your bloody family if they won't let you make your own decisions."

Jonas' heart hurt. He couldn't bear to listen.

"Maybe my family aren't like your family," he snapped. "Maybe my mother's not like yours. Maybe I get to make a different decision from what you did, yeah?"

He stomped out of the room. Cato didn't say anything; and Jonas didn't dare turn around to see his expression.

Marcia walked up from the Old Market along the narrow street that led to Reb's house, half of it in shadow already as the afternoon sun dipped lower. In front of her, a man laden with packages was nagging at his child; behind her she could hear the infusion-seller who worked these streets with their padded kettle.

Reb's door was shut, but not locked. Reb never locked her front door; she relied on wards, and she'd set them to admit Marcia.

The front room was empty, but there were noises from the workroom, so Marcia shut the front door behind her and settled down to wait. She had no doubt that Reb knew of her arrival. It was nice, just to sit down for a moment. She sat back in the battered armchair, watched people going by the window, and did her best not to think about anything.

By the time Reb unbolted the workroom door and poked her head around it, the room was darkening, and Marcia, with a start, realised that she should have lit the lamps.

"Nearly done," Reb said. She looked satisfied, like she'd had a successful day. "Just tidying up now."

"I'll light the lamps," Marcia said. She'd meant to put the kettle on for an infusion, too.

Reb bolted the workroom door and came straight over to Marcia to put her arms around her. Reb wasn't usually all that demonstrative. Marcia felt a sudden surge of affection.

"How's your day been?" Marcia asked, after they'd shared a kiss. She was tempted to move things straight through to the bedroom; but she should probably tell Reb about Selene, first.

"Not too bad," Reb said. "Busy. Good busy."

"You need to get anything sent out this evening?"

Reb shook her head. "No, most of these I'll deliver in person, not by message, and I'd rather not do that at this time of night. Folks listen better in the daytime."

She went over to the window and looked out, rolling her shoulders to stretch them out.

"How about you?" she asked Marcia over her shoulder. "What've you been up to, over there?"

"Talking to the Teren Lord Lieutenant, most recently," Marcia said. She'd tried to think if there was a smooth way to raise this, and had come up with nothing. Blunt was the way to go, then. "You remember, she mentioned magic and my brother in front of my mother the other day? And I arranged to talk to her. As it happens, she's got something of a magical problem, and she wants to talk to a sorcerer."

Reb shifted round to stare at Marcia. "A magical problem?"

"Someone raised a demon, and now they – the Terens – can't get rid of it."

There was a twitch of something that Marcia couldn't quite read in Reb's face. "Usually they execute whoever raised it."

"Apparently the sorcerer took off. Before the problem was discovered, I suppose."

"And what does the Teren Lord Lieutenant want of a Marek sorcerer?"

"Help with getting rid of this demon, or spirit, or whatever it is, I believe. She wanted to talk to the cityangel."

Reb's eyebrows went up. "She knows of the cityangel?"

"Of course she does," Marcia said. "It's a well-known

story, and half the city – more than half – believes it entirely. It's only Marekhill idiots like me who think it's a myth. In Teren they deal with spirits all the time, don't they? Hence this demon, I assume."

Reb pulled a face, but didn't say anything.

"So of course Selene took it at face value. I said I might be able to find a sorcerer for her, but I didn't want to name you – or to reveal just how few sorcerers there are right now – before speaking to you."

Reb rubbed at her nose. "Ugh. I suppose, really, this should be a matter for the Group, since I'm trying to resurrect it."

"I have difficulty envisaging Cato being appropriately polite to the Lord Lieutenant."

"Me too," Reb agreed. "But I can't dragoon him into overseeing Marek-magic and then not bring him into this. It's Marek that's being asked, really, not an individual sorcerer, whatever the woman said. Especially if there's any possibility of needing to involve Beckett. Though I have to say, I can't see how there's much we could do. We can hardly send Beckett off to deal with it, and I've no sorcery outside of Marek, nor has Cato."

"And you wouldn't get Cato out of Marek with a winkle-pin," Marcia said.

"Or me, come to that."

"You grew up in Teren, didn't you?"

"Yes," Reb said, in a tone that didn't suggest that she wanted to discuss the matter any further.

"Do you want to talk to her, then? I mean, if you'd rather not…"

"I'm a Mareker now," Reb said, folding her arms. "It's not like where I was born is written on my forehead, and it's no business of hers anyway, Lord Lieutenant or not. In any case, what's the alternative? Leave Cato to do it alone? And then have to pick up the pieces anyway?"

"She seemed moderately – concerned. If you don't speak to her, there's a fighting chance she'll go looking for herself, which doesn't seem like the best of ideas."

"Angels and demons. No indeed. Well then." Reb sighed. "I'll speak to Cato." She rolled her eyes. "I should have thought twice about this, shouldn't I? Should have realised I'd have to be working with the bugger." Her voice was light again though, poking gentle fun at herself.

"Let me know if you want me to arrange a meeting, once you and Cato have talked it over," Marcia offered.

Reb shrugged a shoulder. "I'll send a messenger. If this ambassador wants to deal with a Marek sorcerer, she can deal directly. Or she can go without, I don't mind."

She came away from the window, towards Marcia, and smiled at her. "Now. I think we've got a little while longer before we should both be elsewhere. Had you any ideas how you might want to spend that time?"

"Oh, I'm sure I can think of a few," Marcia said, smiling back at her lover before pulling her in for a kiss. Sorcery and politics, and sorcerous politics, could all wait for a while.

EIGHT

What Jonas needed, he had eventually concluded, was to talk to Kia. Well, not so much *talk* to Kia, as convince her not to weigh in on his mother's side regarding his future. The trouble was, the only way he could think of to do that was – well. Not exactly honourable.

But then, was it honourable for his mother to turn up with no warning and the blithe assumption that she knew best? She was his mother, so maybe she had a right to an opinion, but turning up early and unannounced, that was unfair.

Unfair enough to justify threatening Kia?

Maybe not. He was going to do it anyway. There was no way he could stand against both his mother and Kia; and he was determined to make his own damn decision on this, not be driven by someone else. Whoever they might be.

He waited until the embassy's official opening hours were over before arriving on the doorstep. Xera, the embassy housekeeper and secretary, gave him a very hard stare when she opened the door, before she led him in and left him in the waiting room. How much did she know about what had happened at New-Year? Enough to be suspicious of him, evidently. He stared morosely at the Marek-style paintings and Salinas woven hangings that covered the walls. It was fair enough for Xera to be wary of him. Fair, but depressing.

"Jonas!" When Kia appeared in the waiting room door, she greeted him as he would expect of a former ship-mate – one who had looked after him as a child, even – but there was a wariness in her eyes too.

"My mother is here," he said without further preamble, once they were safely in Kia's office with the door shut.

Jonas usually liked Kia's office. It was a small room that resembled a captain's cabin; panelled, cramped, and tidy, but with Marek-style chairs and a table. Today, though, it reminded him uncomfortably of sailing with his mother; of sleeping on a hammock in a room very like this one.

"Yes," Kia said. "She visited me already. A delightful

surprise, ne?" She sounded truthful, but Jonas was moderately certain that she was as nervous as he was, albeit for a slightly different reason.

"She wants me to return to Salina," he said.

"No doubt," Kia said. "You are her child. Of course she wants you shipboard. To take over the Lion in due course, perhaps, if you are suited."

Once, that had been the pinnacle of his ambition. It was still tempting. But it would mean laying aside sorcery, forever. Perhaps it would be worth it. But here in Marek he'd found out that there might be other opportunities open to him. Maybe. If he wanted them.

"You support her, then?" Jonas asked.

Kia's eyes narrowed. "It's not my business, is it?"

Jonas sat back. "No. But Mother will put pressure on you to put pressure on me, and we both know it."

Kia didn't move or say anything, just looked at him. Jonas swallowed, and made himself go on. No point in easing around this, was there?

"What I think is, it would be a shame for Mother to find out that you let a Marek sorcerer into the embassy. To do magic right here."

Kia's head tilted. "Whereas I think it would be a shame if she learnt that you were staying here to study with a Marek sorcerer."

Jonas did his best not to react. How could she know that?

"I doubt Captain t'Riseri knows you're a sorcerer."

They stared at each other.

"So. We both have things we don't want to share with my mother, or with the rest of Salina," Jonas said, finally. "Perhaps we can come to some agreement."

Kia leant back in her chair, and regarded him narrowly. "Perhaps we can," she echoed.

"How about, neither of us will mention New-Year, and you will not mention that I am studying with Cato."

"Seems unbalanced," Kia said. "The matters of New-Year, well, they don't reflect on either of us very well, do they? It is in both of our interests not to mention them. Your association with the sorcerer Cato, on the other hand, is a separate matter."

Because Jonas couldn't reveal Kia's part in the matters of

New-Year without dropping himself in it at the same time. He controlled – just barely – an involuntary grimace.

"I was under pressure at New-Year," he tried. "I was acting under the impression, the correct impression, that you were happy with what was going on. I was following the lead of my elders."

"Your mother is hardly going to buy that," Kia said. "And I'm surprised you can even say it with a straight face. You were brought up to think for yourself, Jonas, and well you know it. If you try that on your mother she'll hang you out to dry."

He was brought up to think for himself, and yet his mother was here trying to push him to her preferences. It was unjust, was what it was.

"What then do you suggest, to balance the deal?" he asked, sullenly.

There was a pause. Kia tapped her fingers together.

"A favour," she said, eventually.

"What sort of favour?"

"An unspecified favour, to be collected at a later date."

"An open deal?" Jonas demanded. "And why should I agree to that?"

"To be mutually agreed at a later date," Kia said. "I will swear on the Lion t'Riseri to deal fairly with you, when it is needed, if you swear the same."

That was the most binding oath a Salinas could make; though neither of them truly had a ship, these days, the Lion was for both of them the closest they had. And that they shared a ship made the oath stronger.

And – when it came down to it, he did trust Kia.

"Very well," he agreed. "A mutually agreed debt, to be dealt fairly at your request, sworn by the Lion." He paused. "Within the year. I do not wish to be permanently bound by this."

Kia nodded, and put out both her hands, to shake on the arrangement.

"By the Lion," they both said, as they clasped hands.

Kia let go, then sat back and looked at him, her expression curious.

"Do you wish to stay here?" she asked, sounding genuinely interested. "In Marek?"

"For now," Jonas said, automatically evading the question. Kia shook her head. "For now, of course. For longer. Do you intend to become a sorcerer?"

Jonas winced. His study with Cato made it an obvious question, yet somehow it still stung, hearing it from another Salinas. "I don't know," he hedged.

Kia's eyebrows went up.

"I don't!" He hesitated; but Kia already knew most of this. He might as well let it out. "I have some kind of ability." He saw Kia's almost imperceptible wince. "I know. I am not so keen on the idea either," well, that held some truth, if not the whole truth, "but how am I not to find out what I can do? And how can I risk it emerging without any ability to control it?"

Kia nodded slowly. "Can you – burn it out?"

"Maybe," Jonas said. "Cato offered, but he warned me against it."

"You cannot sail if you are a sorcerer," Kia said, gently.

"I can learn to control it, and then I can *not* use it, and then I can sail," Jonas said, and wondered as he said it whether that was still what he wanted. And yet – he couldn't quite get himself around the idea of not sailing, either. That he would sail, once he was old enough, had been a truth of his life for his entire childhood. Even once his ability had got in the way; of course he would resolve that, and sail. And now?

"I suppose," Kia said, tapping her fingers against her lips. "And yet, an ability is a hard thing to abandon."

"The sea is hard to abandon," Jonas said, with absolute honesty.

Kia sighed. "Indeed so."

Of course. Kia no longer sailed, either.

"Would you prefer to go back?" he asked.

Kia pursed her lips. "I know Marek now better than any other Salinas. Yes, of course I would rather sail. But I am needed here."

"Someone is needed here. You learnt; someone else could, too, ne?" Jonas said.

"I don't see anyone else lining up for the job," Kia said, tartly.

"Well, why would they, when you're here?" Jonas said.

"You mean I should just resign? Well, it's an idea. But

what if no one came forward even then? What if there was no one here to negotiate with these damned Houses, and keep track of the independent traders, and to keep abreast of the politics of this wretched city?"

Kia's voice rose a little, and Jonas blinked. He felt a little insulted on Marek's behalf. There was nowhere else quite like Marek, he knew that, and… When did he start feeling that way?

Kia sighed, and let her voice drop again. "Well, I don't think about it so much. I am here, and I am needed, and I act for Salina. So it goes. But if your mother brought a replacement for me, I would be more than delighted. Hasn't happened yet."

Jonas wasn't sure what to say. Kia shook her head and flipped a hand at him. "In any case. It is, I think, time for you to go, ne? We have made our bargain. And I will see you again when Captain t'Riseri summons us both to dinner."

Underneath, as Jonas walked back down the steps and into the street, he wondered: if his mother thought he didn't want to leave Marek, and that Kia did, would she think of the alternative solution to that particular problem? He wasn't old enough, of course. Not to be the ambassador. But to learn…

He didn't want that, not at all. But could he avoid it, if his mother thought of it, without admitting the truth of his presence here?

Shit.

What with one thing and another, Reb hadn't yet got around to talking to Cato – shouting at Cato – about Jonas. Now she had this business of the Lord Lieutenant to deal with as well.

She'd much rather have still been spending time with Marcia this evening; but Marcia had left for some House responsibility or other. Cato kept late hours. Reb wasn't about to try sending a message again; he wouldn't respond, and she'd have to go over, and look like a fool into the bargain. She might as well just go there now.

Knowing it was the sensible choice didn't prevent her irritation rising as she made her way to Cato's door. That part of the squats wasn't, in the general way, entirely safe for people who didn't live there; but Reb was known to be a sorcerer, and no one would dream of messing with a sorcerer, for fear of ending up floating down the river with your insides tied in a knot. Reb, in general, didn't believe in using one's power against others unless absolutely necessary – and Beckett didn't much hold with it, come to that – but she had more sense than to make that widely known.

She was tempted to barge straight through Cato's door once she got there, but resisted the urge. Taking his wards down would be an unwarranted act of aggression, she told herself firmly, and wouldn't set them off on the right foot.

She contented herself with banging so hard on the door that she bruised a knuckle.

"What the hell?" she heard from inside.

There was a certain amount of clattering, and Cato opened the door a crack to peer through it.

"Oh. It's you." He stepped back and made a gesture, and Reb felt the wards fall. "Come in, I suppose."

"Nice to see you too," Reb said.

"Oh, come on, I can tell just from looking at you that you're here to complain about something," Cato said, rolling his eyes in disgust and closing the door behind her.

The room was untidy as ever, but the collection of things on his worktable suggested that he'd been in the middle of something. Cato might never pick up anything else, but he kept his magical things in perfect order.

"Sorry if I interrupted you," Reb said, grudging every word; but some magics were hard to set up.

"Oh, it doesn't matter," Cato said. "Nothing important." She couldn't tell from his tone whether or not he was telling the truth.

He flung himself down into the one armchair in the room, on top of the pile of clothes that already occupied it, and put his head back. "So. What can I do for you?"

There was nowhere for Reb to sit, unless she wanted to perch on the edge of Cato's bed, which she most certainly did not, or to use his workstool, which, given that he hadn't offered it, would be the height of rudeness. She wasn't about to stoop to his level. She settled for pacing.

"I've come for two things, as it happens. Firstly – why the

hell didn't you tell me that Jonas was apprenticed to you?" she demanded.

Cato's eyes narrowed. She could see the moment when he decided not to evade the question.

"Because it's none of your business," he said instead. "Like I said. This Group thing, if it's about keeping Marek safe, then very well. But it's not up to you who I apprentice, and I don't see the need to tell you."

"We should be keeping track of sorcerers," Reb said through her teeth.

Cato shrugged. "I know about him, and I'm part of your precious Group, so *we* were keeping track of him."

Reb ground her teeth together so hard that they squeaked. "And what am I to think, when I notice unidentified magic around the corner some day?"

"Is that what happened?" Cato asked. "Because I wouldn't have said Jonas was up to using magic alone yet."

"And yet there he is running around unsupervised," Reb said.

Cato sighed. "I mean, he can't do it half the time. In any case, he's not stupid. He's not going to go experimenting on his own."

"And if he does?" Reb demanded.

"Then it's my problem, not yours."

"Until he disagrees with you, or he does something accidentally," Reb said. "Then it becomes my problem too, and it's only happenstance that I know there's anything that could be a problem."

They glared at one another. Cato opened his mouth, then closed it again.

"I see your point," he said, sounding like it cost him something to say it.

"And quite apart from knowing about it," Reb said, "are you an appropriate person to be teaching him?"

She knew she'd mis-stepped as soon as she said it. Cato's jaw clenched, and the air in the room felt suddenly thick.

"And who the hell are you to judge that?" he demanded. "If you want to work with me, if you want me to work with you, it's time you bloody respected me. Stop looking down your nose because you think you're better, or more moral, or whatever it is. I'm not the one who barely cast a charm for two years. If it comes right down to it, which of us do you think, really, is the better sorcerer right now?"

Reb's anger blazed again, and she took a step towards Cato, who folded his arms and stared defiantly at her. Blood thumped in her ears, and she wondered what she had in her pockets, whether she could...

What the hell was she doing?

She closed her eyes for a second, took a step back, and made herself relax. When she opened her eyes again, Cato was looking very slightly sheepish, but she knew there was no way he would back down. Not when she'd been the first to escalate.

"That was over the line," she said. "I'm sorry. You're right, it's not on me to judge whether you're the right teacher for Jonas. That's between you and him."

Cato looked startled, then nodded. "Thank you. I..." His chin went up, just a little. "I overstepped too. I'm sorry."

"Right," Reb said. "Let's go back a little. Can we agree that both of us should let the other know if we discover a new sorcerer, or take an apprentice? But that it's not down to either of us to interfere with that."

"That it's not the business of the Group to interfere with that," Cato said. "Let's generalise."

"Unless one or the other – teacher or apprentice – requests intervention, or unless something happens that would otherwise be the business of the Group," Reb said. "Dangerous magic. Spirits. That kind of thing."

"Fine," Cato agreed. "I can live with that." He folded his arms. "That's not all, is it? You said, two things."

"Marcia's been speaking to the Teren Lord Lieutenant. She wants to meet with us."

"The Lord Lieutenant does?" Cato's eyebrows shot up. "Really?"

"Apparently so. She's interested in the differences between Teren and Marek magic. Marcia told her the basics, but thought it might be of use for her to talk to an actual sorcerer."

"Marcia got us into this?"

"She asked me, and I said we'd do it." She raised a hand as she saw Cato's expression change. "I'll do it, if you don't want to. But I thought it was perhaps a matter for the Group, and that I should see if you wanted to be involved as well."

"Fine. I suppose that's reasonable. I appreciate the thought." The last bit sounded slightly forced, but at least he was trying.

"Well? Do you?"

"Oh, why not." He flapped a hand. "It might be interesting. The Lord Lieutenant, hey? Well, there we go."

"She won't be coming here," Reb warned him.

"No, I would imagine she won't," Cato said drily. "Let me know where it is, and I'll come. As long as it's not Marekhill. I'll come as far as the Square and no further."

"I'll send a message," Reb said. She badly wanted to suggest that he dressed appropriately for the occasion, but that could surely only backfire.

"Well then," she said, instead. "I'll be leaving you to it, then."

"I always so appreciate your little visits," Cato said, closing his eyes. "Do feel free to see yourself out."

But despite the drawl in his voice, as she went back down the stairs, it felt like the two of them might have taken a step towards a working relationship.

NINE

Tait stood on the damp boards by the river, where the barge had tied up, and wondered whether they were in Marek yet. The giant unloading-yard was full of carts and people, shifting sacks off barges and moving crates around. The edge of Marek proper was a clutter of buildings maybe half a mile off. But surely this yard must be managed by Marek, given that the nearest part of Teren that wasn't swamp was eighty miles away. Did that mean it counted, or not? Was Tait safe yet?

"Out of the way," a porter snapped at them, pushing a huge trolley that seemed to Tait to be vastly and dangerously overladen. They hastily stepped backwards out of her way, and narrowly avoided going straight into the swamp-water.

The troop had spent the last two days poling their barges along the marked channel through the swamps between Teren and Marek. Not that Tait themself had done any poling, after nearly falling in on their first turn. Not wanting to shirk, they had assured Captain Anna they would do better with practice, but she felt it would be quicker for the experienced folk just to get on with it. She'd reminded Tait that they were supposed to be ready to solve any problems that might require sorcery. Since no such problems had arisen – thankfully – it had all left Tait feeling somewhat surplus to requirements.

But it was fine, because now they were – nearly – in Marek, which had been the point of the whole damn exercise. And Bracken had been accurate in his timing: it was just on noon.

Tait would feel a lot safer, though, once in Marek proper. Looking up the river, Tait could see where it curved and hid itself behind the dense buildings. Beyond that rose what must, from the maps they'd seen, be Marekhill, where the nobles lived. Closer at hand, a wide road led off from the far side of the square towards the city. Smaller carts trundled down it after loading up from the barges and the large carts that had come in from Teren; Marek streets must be narrow.

"Sorcerer Tait." Captain Anna came up to Tait, looking harassed.

"Captain Anna," they said, bowing politely.

"This is the formal end of our journey," she said. "I have found you a trader who is taking the road back to Teren, although only as far as Hareth. I know we agreed to pay for your return, so I've added a little to your pay to cover transport from Hareth to Ameten..."

"Ah," Tait interrupted. "In fact, I am intending to stay in Marek for a while."

Captain Anna blinked at them. "Oh." She looked down at the money-bag in her hand, obviously rethinking the matter of how much she'd put in there.

"But if my journey back was to be paid, I will save that money for when I do return," Tait said, plucking the bag out of Captain Anna's hand before she could recount it. It was only fair, really. That was the deal, after all. Not that Tait had ever intended to go back to Ameten, when they'd agreed the job, but it would have looked odd to admit that at the time. "Are you yourself going into Marek proper now? May I ride along with you?"

"We're walking," Captain Anna said, a little repressively.

Of course they were. Tait kept their smile on. "Then may I walk with you?"

"Of course," she said. "We will leave in half an hour."

Half an hour more to wonder whether they were yet under the protection of the cityangel. Still. It would look peculiar not to wait, having asked. Tait nodded politely, and found a bale to sit on.

Porters irritably moved them off that bale and various others a couple of times more before Captain Anna indicated it was time to go. The soldiers who weren't heading off to Teren formed up slightly raggedly, and Tait tagged on behind them as they walked along the side of the well-tended road towards the city proper.

The buildings on each side of the road grew denser as they went. Tait was paying so much attention to looking for some kind of indication that they were coming under the cityangel's power – a tingle? A figure appearing to bar Tait's way on the grounds that they were being chased? A fork of lightning? – that it was almost a surprise when they came to a halt in another large square. This one was obviously a market, and some of the carts were unloading here. People with hand-carts were haggling at various stalls. Unlit torches hung above the shops around the edge of the square, behind the stalls and barrows. The place was noisy, it smelt slightly of raw meat and rotting vegetables, and it was very definitely in Marek. Tait had made it.

"Well, here we are," Captain Anna said briskly. "We go now to the barracks, and I will report to House Fereno. Do you know Marek at all?"

Tait shook their head. Captain Anna looked like she was refraining from rolling her eyes.

"Well. If you wish somewhere free to stay, there are the squats." She gestured at a dense block of housing, built to three or four storeys, that rose into the sky a little way from the market. "I would recommend the areas nearest the river. If you prefer an inn, go over New Bridge here," she pointed at the bridge that rose from the middle of one end of the market square, "and, well, look for signs. That area is safe enough."

"The White Horse is good," Bracken put in over her shoulder. "Cheap. Clean. Good stew."

"Where is it?" Tait asked.

"Over the bridge, third left, second right," Bracken said.

"Thank you," Tait said. They had enough in that bag Captain Anna had handed over to pay for an inn room, rather than try to negotiate the squats. They'd heard of Marek's squats, and it sounded like an excellent idea which doubtless had a hugely complicated social context that Tait didn't feel up to wrangling right now.

Tait bid Captain Anna and Bracken and the rest goodbye, and they all disappeared off, presumably in the direction of the barracks. Tait shouldered their bag again, and set off to find the White Horse.

Bracken's instructions were excellent; the White Horse was easy to find with its very lifelike painted sign, the floor of the main taproom was clean and spread with fresh straw and herbs, and the landlady was friendly enough. Tait arranged a room – they would have to find something cheaper eventually, but it would do for a few nights, and maybe after that Tait would have some clue of what to do next – and ordered dinner for later, then closed the door of the room with a sigh of relief and collapsed backwards onto the bed. The beautiful, soft, comfortable bed. They kept their feet on the floor. Wouldn't do to get the counterpane – the lovely comfortable counterpane that smelt of soap – dirty, and Tait couldn't face taking their boots off just yet.

They stared up at the ceiling, revelling in the peace and solitude and reflecting that Bracken's standards for an inn were higher than Tait might have expected, and realised that they had no idea what to do next. Somehow, all of their planning had only gone as far as reaching Marek.

How certain was it that the demon the Academy would have sent after them couldn't get at them here? Tait chewed at the inside of their cheek. Moderately certain. They thought. Everything they had read about Marek's strange magical situation suggested that the cityangel would think very poorly of an interloper on its turf; but everything Tait had read about Marek's magical situation was written by non-Marek visitors. Who might have totally misunderstood everything, for all they knew. No one at the Academy of the Court had wanted to discuss Marek; they all dismissed it as a weird little oddity that wasn't worth bothering about.

Maybe the cityangel would keep the demon out, but would solve the problem by merrily handing over Tait to it. It wasn't like Tait belonged here, after all.

Really, the only reason Tait had come to Marek was because there was a possibility that here might be safe, whereas Teren very definitely wasn't. The Academy of the Court didn't take kindly to people running away from it.

If Tait had stood up to the Academy in the first place, instead of doing what they were told despite their increasing reservations, the Academy wouldn't have been able to raise a demon that could recognise Tait, and they'd be safe. Except that Tait hadn't stood up to the Academy in the first place because they'd been in fear of their life. And now they were still in fear of their life, so hadn't *that* worked out well – except on the other hand, they were in Marek now, and still alive, so maybe they were winning. Sort of.

None of which answered the question: what now? In an ideal world, Tait could practise magic again, could learn Marek-style magic, safe in the knowledge that the cityangel would defend them. But that would require finding out a bit more about the whole setup, and the problem there was to do it without letting on to anyone who might be interested that Tait was here. Marek was, after all, notionally still part of Teren. Tait might be safe from the demon here, but that didn't mean they were safe from the Academy sorcerer who would be binding the demon. Or from anyone else who might report back to the Academy. Tait wasn't stupid enough to think that Teren didn't have spies here. What they didn't know was which part of the Ameten Court those spies might report back to.

Thinking about it, coming to the White Horse might have been a bad idea. Bracken had suggested it, and Bracken knew what Tait was, even if not exactly who Tait was. Tait had smiled and oo-ed through the stories they'd heard at the occasional village tavern of the sorcerer who had raised a demon and run away from Ameten. Untrue stories, but it made sense that that was what was being spread. Thankfully Tait hadn't been described at all – Tait was a lot less impressive than the story-sorcerer – but they were still surprised that no one had even raised an eyebrow. Maybe none of them thought it was likely that a sorcerer on the run would take a job that meant two weeks of trudging up and down bloody mountains, and the risk of needing to use magic if the occasion arose.

The occasion had arisen, and Tait had dealt with it; but there was magic that blood wasn't enough for, or that Tait didn't have enough blood for, and then what would they have done? It had been a stupid bloody risk, not just of themself, but of Captain Anna and Bracken and all the rest of them. But. Tait had got away with it, so maybe best just to put that away and not think about it again. Perhaps nearly bleeding out for their trouble was penance enough.

Tait's next step had to be talking to a sorcerer, and the only reasonable way of doing that was to ask the landlady where to find one, which in turn meant leaving a trail half a mile wide if anyone was looking for them in Marek. Still. Not a lot else to be done.

Tait really wished there had been more options, over the last few weeks. Or before they even got into this hideous mess.

Well then. Dinner, an ewer and soap to scrub themself down a little, asking after sorcerers, a good night's sleep; and then in the morning, they would go find the sorcerers. And just maybe, it would all still work out.

☺ ☺

Marcia was in the library going over her personal accounts – she'd ripped her formal tunic, and she hadn't expected to replace it for a while, which meant moving some money around – when one of the servants appeared around the door.

"A Captain Anna Barcola to see you, please."

Marcia closed the account-book. "Excellent. Show her in here, if you could? And send in an infusion tray, with something from the kitchen, and a decanter of brandy."

Hopefully this expedition had been less hazardous to the health than the last one, but the woman would doubtless nevertheless appreciate something pleasant. The last time Marcia had heard from her was a messenger sent back before they went up into the mountains, confirming that all was well; after that, no one they'd encountered would have had a significant chance of returning to Marek before them. The captain had been unconvinced that messenger birds would survive the trip, and didn't want the inconvenience of carrying them in order to find out. It would be useful, though... maybe another time, if this trip had been successful.

The captain was shown in, and Marcia exhaled in relief as she saw the woman's smile. She was in neat, tidy, uniform, too; she must have stopped at the barracks to change. Unlike the last time, where she'd arrived late, stained and travel-weary, rushing to tell Marcia bad news.

"Fereno-Heir," she said, with a brisk half-bow, like a bird bobbing. "I am pleased to report a very successful trip."

"Excellent news, Captain Barcola," Marcia said. "Do please take a seat and – ah, excellent, refreshments." The servant placed the tray on the table and Marcia gestured her out again. "A mint infusion, or apple brandy, if you prefer?"

"I'll take a brandy, thank you kindly," Captain Barcola said. "Shake the dampness of the swamps out." She shivered in illustration. "It's nice to be back in Marek."

"And we can toast your success," Marcia agreed, pouring the gleaming liquid into small glasses.

The cut crystal sent shards of light into the brandy when she picked the glass up.

"Your very good health, Captain Barcola," Marcia said, meeting the captain's eye as they both took a sip.

"And yours, Fereno-Heir," Captain Barcola replied. Marcia saw the woman's lips continue to move; doubtless saying the customary extra line, *and fair wishes to the cityangel*, which Marekhill preferred not to use and the lower city wouldn't dare to omit. As it happened, Marcia would be perfectly happy to drink fair wishes to Beckett, but she couldn't admit it.

"Anything in particular to report?" she asked instead.

"Well. We sold nearly everything we took with us. Had to go a fair way into Exuria to do it, mind. Nothing to trade just over the mountaintop. Goats and so on. Didn't think we wanted to be trailing goats after us. I did take the liberty of trading for a little in the way of cloth; some very beautiful work and I've not seen it in Marek before. I thought it would do as a sample; if you think it worthwhile, we'd be able to get more another time, fairly close to the pass."

Marcia nodded. "I'll take a look at it."

The closer they could trade to the pass the quicker and thus cheaper it would be, but whether that was worth it depended on what price this mountain goat-cloth would fetch here, or whether it could be traded through the Salinas. If the captain hadn't seen it here before, it might not generally make it out of the Exuria mountains, which meant rarity value.

"A little further down they grow wild mustard, and iyag, and a few other spices I've not encountered before," Captain Barcola continued. "I took a fair bit of mustard and iyag, and a sample of the new spices. I assume they're not worth shipping the long way, but as a luxury good, maybe…"

Wild mustard was a popular spice; iyag was in demand by the Apothecaries, and both were usually expensive, reflecting the shipping distance from the Exurian mountains down to the sea and out by a Salinas ship. Spices and dried plants were light, too, which was good for a challenging trip like this. The Spicers might be interested in the less-common things, or they might not, but it had been sensible to take the samples. Marcia nodded approvingly.

"They weren't entirely convinced by your pens," the captain went on, "but I managed to exchange a couple, in the end, for some scrip from the Guilder cities. Brought most of them back though, I'm afraid."

"Hm. Well, I suppose, we can see whether the samples have engaged interest on another trip." New experiments sometimes took a while to become popular. Madeleine still wouldn't use one of the new pens despite Marcia's encouragement, though they were popular among Marcia's own age-mates. "Do you have the Guilder scrip with you?"

"Delivered to the House Fereno strongbox at the bank," Captain Barcola said. "Together with the stones we got. Everything else the porters took to your warehouse." She pulled a couple of chits, one with the bank's stamp on, and one with a porter's number, out of her belt-purse, and handed them over to Marcia.

The main Marek bank building, a squat, strong stone affair, was on the corner of the wholesale market. All the Houses, and most other merchants, had strongboxes there. Most likely it would have been safe enough for Barcola to bring the scrip here to House Fereno in broad daylight, when she'd already taken it over a mountain and through the swamps. There again, Marcia could well understand her preferring to offload as quickly as possible.

"I've the porters' list here," the captain said, "and I noted the scrip value at the bottom." She handed Marcia a slightly battered leaf of paper, written in her blocky painstaking handwriting.

"I'll check both later this afternoon," Marcia said. "And you'll be due your payment, of course. Where will I find you?"

"We'll be in the barracks for another day or two," Captain Barcola said. "See if there's another job on the horizon."

There was the shadow of a question in her voice.

"I suspect nothing for us again just yet, but I'll check with my mother," Marcia said. "And of course I'll happily give you a recommendation with the pay."

"Greatly appreciate it," Barcola said, ducking her head.

"Anything else of interest that won't wait for the full report?" Marcia asked.

She offered Barcola the plate of cakes and candies again,

and the woman accepted one with a smile. She chewed for a moment, obviously thinking.

"Not so as I can think of. All went very smoothly this time. We had reports of dragon-bears up in the mountains, so I hired a Teren sorcerer to come across the pass with us."

"Dragon-bears?" Marcia said.

"Yes. There was likely enough of us to fight them off with cold steel, but..." she grimaced. "Sorcerer's better at it, with less risk. And indeed we saw a dragon-bear, right near the top of the mountain, so Tait earned their keep. That came out of the extra funds, of course."

"Better that than you and all the goods in the stomach of a dragon-bear," Marcia said. Barcola was right – the troop could most likely have fought off a dragon-bear, but they could just as easily have been unlucky, and they'd never have managed it without losing someone.

"Kept 'em on all the way to Marek, in case of any problems in the swamps. Then they said they were staying. Said I couldn't rearrange their journey back up the river, so we saved that cost. Had to give them the fare from the river to Ameten though."

Marcia's eyebrows went up. "The sorcerer – a Teren sorcerer – came into Marek?"

"Left 'em at the wholesale market," Barcola said, with a shrug.

That was – surprising. Marcia's understanding was that, in the general way of things, Teren sorcerers did not come to Marek. Reb had been from Teren, once, but she'd come here specifically to learn Mareker magic; although she'd never told Marcia why, nor whether she'd done magic in Teren before coming here. Maybe this one wanted the same? But if so... why? Might they, just for example, be fleeing a demon? She tapped her fingers on her leg.

"Did the sorcerer say why?"

Barcola shrugged. "Who can say why sorcerers do things, eh? But," she frowned, "they did seem very keen, if you know what I mean." She looked anxiously over at Marcia. "Is it a problem? Should I not have brought them down the river? They weren't charging much, and I thought, since we had 'em... Though I thought then they'd be heading back upriver, after."

"No, no, it's fine," Marcia said. If it was the same person, there was no way Barcola could have known, and no reason to worry the woman. "Perfectly sensible decision. I was just curious what might bring them here."

Barcola had mentioned the sorcerer's name a moment ago; what was it? She didn't want to ask outright; Marekhill didn't take an interest in sorcery, and she'd already pushed this further than she ought to. Oh, yes; Tait.

"Bracken sent 'em to the White Horse, if there is any problem," Barcola offered.

"Ah, not at all," Marcia said dismissively. "What sorcerers get up to is hardly our business, is it now? Leave them to it." She smiled, and Barcola smiled back in relieved agreement. "So, then, if we do this again, we'll need to allow for dragon-bears."

"The villagers seemed to think it depends on the season," Barcola said. "We saw none the last time."

"But the passage was otherwise easier this time?"

Barcola nodded. "With a sorcerer – a decent sorcerer, which Tait was, give them credit – I'd still rather go this time of year than earlier. I don't much like sorcery, but Tait got that dragon-bear away as neat as you like. And the going other than that was a lot quicker. Safer too."

After a few more minutes of chat, Marcia rose from her chair.

"Thank you for such a prompt report, Captain. I'll go to the bank tomorrow and then come to the barracks afterwards to pay everyone's wages."

"I'll have the full report packet and the accounts for you by then," Barcola promised.

"Until then, you and your team deserve a night out," Marcia said, handing Barcola a couple of golden guilders.

"Thank you kindly," Barcola said, with a wide grin, and gave that bobbing bow again before she left.

Thoughtfully, Marcia seated herself back down at her desk, and tapped her fingers on its surface. A Teren sorcerer, keen to come to Marek? She supposed that there could be lots of reasons... but she couldn't help connecting it with that business Selene had spoken of.

At the very least, it seemed like a good idea to write Selene a note on the matter. A Teren sorcerer at the White Horse. If it wasn't the right person, no harm done. If it was, then that might be good for quite a significant favour at some future point; and Marcia could certainly do with a few favours to call in.

TEN

"What do you mean, you lost them?" Selene demanded.

The unaccustomed Mareker trousers she was wearing felt scratchy against her legs. It didn't help that the fabric was much more coarse than anything she normally wore. But it wouldn't have done for the Lord Lieutenant to be seen out here in this, this *shack* on the outskirts of Marek that called itself an inn; so she had tied her hair under a scarf like some servant, and put on cheap Marek clothes, and gone out the back door of the guesthouse when no one was looking. She didn't have that long, either; it was already nearly sunset, and she had to meet with the sorcerers in an hour or so, and then attend another formal event – she couldn't even remember which, there had been so many of the wretched things – later. She'd received yet another message with a House seal as she was getting changed, and she hadn't even had the time to look at it. She scratched irritably at the back of her neck and glared at her companion.

Hira, the sorcerer who'd been tracking the escapee, fiddled with his beer glass, looking unhappy. Selene had a beer too, but she had no intention of drinking it.

"It's not that I lost them, exactly," he said.

"But you just said…"

"Uh. I mean. We were following them, you understand? I mean, it was following them. The…" he trailed off, not wanting to say 'demon' here where he might be overheard, even though the background noise in the inn was more than enough to cover their conversation. Marekers were unenthusiastic about demons. To be fair, Tereni were too. But Hira was a sorcerer, so he was accustomed to them, and since Selene was apparently responsible for Hira now he'd arrived at Marek, she had to have this conversation, however much she might wish otherwise.

At least the demon wasn't close. Hira had it stashed away somewhere. Selene hadn't asked about the details.

"It was following Tait, yes," Selene said, endeavouring to

sound encouraging rather than furious.

"But we couldn't, like, pin them to a place. Because of them not calling up anything. We were just in the mountains."

Runaway sorcerers weren't unheard of, but the Academy usually managed the problem efficiently and in such a way as to discourage repeats. It seemed deeply unfair that the Academy had chosen this moment to fail, and that this wretched sorcerer had made for Marek and turned this into her problem. She had no desire whatsoever to be associated with this, practically or politically.

"You were in the mountains," she prompted. "So, what, you knew they were in the mountains but not exactly where?"

Hira nodded. "Yeah. Because the connection doesn't, uh, locate itself properly unless," he looked around himself and leaned in. "They'd have had to make their own connection to the spirit plane, see. Then," he brought his hands together, "bang! Link, location, all fine. But they didn't do that."

They probably knew how it worked, and weren't *stupid*, Selene thought.

"But the, uh... it... it didn't have a proper connection, but it had, like, a direction. I knew we were in the right area. So... I got... it... to rile up a dragon-bear. I thought, iffen they had to fight one of those, they'd have to summon *help*, right?" By *help* he clearly meant, *a demon*.

"But they didn't?"

Hira shook his head. "Guess not. I dunno if it didn't find them or what. Maybe someone else dealt with it. Maybe we were in the wrong place. The, uh... it, it said we were close but it's foldy, in the mountains, you know? Even dragon-bears can't actually fly, not properly, not across some ravine or other. And the d– the, uh, it wouldn't be able to tell either."

She could do without all this witless burbling.

"So you followed the trail," Selene prompted.

"Right through the mountains. And over into Exuria."

Selene went cold. "Tell me you didn't take a demon into Exuria."

Hira frowned. "I was following. I was told to follow."

"Tell me no one saw you with a demon in Exuria."

"No." Hira sounded confident. "No chance."

Well, that was a relief. She very sincerely hoped that Hira was right, but there was no point in worrying about that now, and nothing she could do about it in either case. If Hira had sparked a diplomatic incident with Exuria, he would be dealt with back in Ameten, in due course. And it would take a while for word to get to Ameten from Exuria, via official channels. Not her problem.

"Right. Well," she said briskly, moving on. "The trail came back out of Exuria, I'm guessing."

"And down to the river," Hira agreed. "And then along the river, and I figured, I'd do my best to catch up. But we missed the boat by a whisker, and we had to wait for the next one, and I tried to persuade the crew to help her along a bit, with the oars, but they weren't having any of it."

"But you can't have lost the trail on the river," Selene said, grinding her teeth. "The river only goes to one place." Unless the sorcerer had taken off into the swamp proper; but in that case the swamp would deal with them, no further intervention needed. And a sorcerer bright enough to avoid being caught for this long wouldn't be foolish enough to go off into the swamps alone.

"Yes," Hira agreed. "The river comes here, and then people go into Marek."

"So?"

"So now I can't track 'em any more, because they've gone into Marek. Maybe half a day before we got here. Less, even. They've disappeared."

"What do you mean, they've disappeared?"

Hira shrugged. "Marek's under the protection of the cityangel. Don't everyone know that? The... it... it can't feel anything coming out of there." He made a gesture, hands forming a dome. "Like a big cover, over the whole city."

"Then go in," Selene said, impatiently.

Hira looked horrified. "Go in? To Marek? With a... ? You can't. Cityangel won't allow it. Don't you... ?" He met Selene's eyes, and managed to bite back on 'don't you know that'.

"So," Selene said, words clipped. "You followed this rogue sorcerer through Teren, into and out of Exuria – thereby breaking our treaty with Exuria, I might add, though we will hope that they didn't notice – you set a dragon-bear on them, and you've lost them at the Marek gates." She sat back, arms folded. "Wonderful."

Hira hunched his shoulders a little. "I did my best. Tait trained with us. They knew what we'd be looking for. They were prepared!"

Selene inhaled, tongue pressed against her teeth. "And you are supposed to be better trained, and to have been able to solve this problem."

Hira looked a bit like a dog with its tail between its legs, waiting to be beaten.

"Very well," Selene said. "You can stay out here, while I decide what to do next."

Hira brightened up a bit. "There's rooms at this inn, I checked, but I haven't enough left to pay for it…"

"You've been camping out for the last month," Selene said. "I suggest you keep doing that. I saw tents on the far side of the square. You won't stand out. And keep a leash on your… acquaintance. I'll get word to you when I have worked out how we can resolve this situation." She put a vicious spin on the last few words and, with satisfaction, saw Hira wince.

She would be meeting the Mareker sorcerers in an hour. She'd been hoping to hear that she didn't need to talk to them about this; that she could just sound them out about other forms of cooperation. But she had her story planned. The rogue sorcerer, the unbound demon. The same story the Academy would have spread through Teren. That should make these Marek sorcerers amenable to assisting; they wouldn't want a demon running around loose any more than anyone else did.

And she didn't have time to stay any longer here; not that there was anything else to be done. She nodded coldly to Hira – if the *idiot* had just done his *job*, she wouldn't have to be dealing with this – stood up, and began to make her way out of the ugly little inn.

Something crackled in her pocket as she moved, and she remembered the message she'd received earlier and not had time to read. She pulled it out and slid her thumbnail under the seal – *House Fereno*, she thought. As she scanned the brief message, her eyes widened, and she slowed to a stop.

According to Marcia, this sorcerer was indeed in Marek;

and she'd even helpfully given a location.

Perhaps the demon couldn't do anything inside the city, but sorcerers were no more immune than anyone else to a nice prosaic stabbing. She didn't have the resources here that she might in Ameten, but Teren did have... connections, here, that she could draw upon. And potentially she still had these Mareker sorcerers she was supposed to be meeting as a back-up option.

She might yet be able to resolve this quickly and quietly.

Cato scowled down at the tabletop.

"I've changed my mind. Why didn't we just invite the woman to my rooms."

He looked up at Reb just as she rolled her eyes. "You don't even slightly mean that. Stop being annoying."

"Or yours."

"You wouldn't be any happier in my rooms than you are here. And I'm not having that woman know where I live." Her jaw set, suddenly and firmly, and Cato looked speculatively at her, almost distracted from his complaints.

"Anyway," Reb said. "You didn't have to come, if you didn't like the meeting or the venue."

They were in a tediously respectable pub on the Marekhill side of Old Bridge, just off Marek Square. Reb had bespoken a private room, with some nonsense about how the Teren Lieutenant deserved a little privacy. Fine, Cato wouldn't have wanted to have this conversation in public either, but he didn't really hold with hierarchy. The one thing both of them had agreed was that they weren't going to go to Selene, as if Marek's sorcerers were there to be summoned by this dignitary or that. She would have to come to them. Almost annoyingly, she hadn't seemed at all perturbed when Reb had messaged to that effect.

Reb had wondered whether they should be bespeaking dinner rather than merely infusions – or in Cato's case, a beer – but Cato had put his foot down. If he'd wanted to have polite conversation over indigestible food, he'd have stayed in bloody Marekhill.

"Oh, but I am a crucial part of this bloody Group of yours, aren't I?" Cato said. "So I did have to come."

Reb, he could tell, was absolutely desperate to tell him to shove off out of the Group if he wanted to, except that he also knew she didn't want him to do anything of the sort, both because she could hardly claim to have oversight of Marek's magic all by herself; and because Beckett seemed convinced that it needed both of them. Seeing just how far he could push her towards regretting the whole business was entertaining by itself.

Although if he got as far as annoying Beckett, it might be slightly less entertaining.

What, though, had Reb so strangely-tempered about the Teren Lieutenant.

"Oh! I remember! You're Teren, aren't you?" She'd said something about it, years ago, during one of their run-ins back in the day, when he'd done something that had aggravated the Group. "That's why you're irritable about the woman before we've even met her."

Reb eyed him with great and evident dislike. She didn't agree, but she didn't disagree either, which was basically as good as proof.

"When did you come to Marek?" Cato asked. "Why did you come to Marek? I mean, obviously, it's a delightful city and so on, clearly far superior to anywhere in Teren…"

"How would you know? You've never so much as set foot outside the city boundaries," Reb said, with unfortunate accuracy.

"Marek doesn't have boundaries. We have swamp," Cato said. "And the Oval Sea. That's the whole point of Marek, no? In any case. I'm guessing it was magic." Another thought occurred to him, with what felt like blinding insight. "You've practised Teren magic, haven't you. How interesting."

Reb slammed a hand down on the table.

"None of that is any of your damned business, and I am not going to speak to you of it, do you hear me?"

Cato looked at her, carefully, and decided to back off. He raised his hands, considering whether he might go so far as something that sounded a bit like an apology, when there was a knock on the door.

"Your visitor's here, honoured ones," the innkeeper said.

She was obviously uncomfortable to be housing two sorcerers at once. She showed the visitor through with almost excessive haste, and departed again even faster.

The Teren Lord Lieutenant was a short, dark-skinned woman. Her long hair was done up in a complicated plait and wound around her head in a way that spoke of someone used to having a maid assist her. Her dress was richly embroidered. If Cato were inclined to think that way, he might have felt slightly uncomfortable about his own somewhat grubby clothing.

As it was, he smiled widely at her and slouched back in his chair.

"Lord Lieutenant."

Reb had stood up to greet her with a nod of the head. Sorcerers did not shake hands, something which he ought to remember to explain to Jonas.

"Selene will do." She sat down in the other chair, and Reb sat down with her.

"I'm Reb. This is my colleague Cato."

Cato raised a casual hand, and the Lord Lieutenant – Selene – nodded over at him.

"You are the representatives of Marek's sorcerers?"

They *were* Marek's sorcerers – well, if you didn't count Jonas – but he wasn't surprised when Reb just nodded.

"I gather you have a problem that you wished to talk to us about?" Reb said.

"Yes. Well. I will keep it brief. A demon was raised, close to Ameten, a few weeks ago."

"That's a regular part of Teren sorcery, isn't it?" Cato asked.

"Indeed." Selene's voice sounded tight. "However, as a rule, the sorcerer raising the spirit, of whatever type, takes steps to return it to its own plane after their work is completed."

"And this one didn't," Cato guessed. "Oh dear." He couldn't see what the problem was; couldn't someone else just return them?

"There are ways of dealing with that, too," Reb said. She sounded more uncompromising than usual, and when Cato looked over to her, her arms were tightly folded.

"Indeed," Selene said again.

"Which are?" Cato asked.

"Sacrifice the sorcerer," Reb said.

Cato's eyebrows went up. Possibly he should know a little more about Teren sorcery, but it had never seemed particularly relevant. "Kill them?" It seemed... excessive.

"Yes," Selene said, impatiently. "We could not do that in this case."

Cato was definitely regretting not knowing more about Teren sorcery. Both Reb and Selene were several steps ahead of him, and he hated that feeling; but he would hate it even more if he had to ask. He could ask Reb, later, maybe, if he absolutely had to, although doubtless she would gloat over it. Not out loud – quietly, where he couldn't see – but he would know. In any case, he certainly wasn't going to ask here and now. He settled for slouching back a bit further and nodding slightly, to suggest that he knew what they were on about.

"Why not?" Reb asked.

"The sorcerer ran," Selene said. "We have not tracked them down since, despite our best efforts." A muscle in her jaw twitched. She wasn't happy, having to ask for assistance.

"And what of the demon?"

"A group of the Academy's sorcerers trapped it, but they weren't able to return it, and it escaped again. At present, it is roaming – we assume, looking for the original sorcerer."

"Roaming where?" Reb demanded.

"We do not know. There is no word of it."

Reb's eyebrows flickered upwards for a moment. "No word of it? Then it isn't causing any real problems?"

"Perhaps not yet," Selene said, "but I hardly feel..."

"Yes, yes, certainly," Reb said. "However. I understand your concerns, but what do you intend us to do about it?"

"Two things. Firstly – well. Marek has its own spirit." She looked uncomfortable.

"You wondered if the cityangel could help," Reb concluded.

"Why should they?" Cato demanded. He didn't have to know exactly what was being asked to bristle at the idea of Beckett being hassled by Teren. "And, come to that, why should they be able to?"

"The Marek cityangel does not tolerate other beings within the city," Selene said. "That is well known."

That was mostly accurate. There were ways around it – that stupid business Marcia had got herself tangled up in back when they were teenagers – but Beckett had reacted pretty strongly to that, not to mention successfully, via Reb and her then-mentor Zareth. At the cost, of course, of Zareth's life.

It had never occurred to Cato before now to wonder what would have happened if Reb and Zareth hadn't succeeded. But that wasn't something to bring up right now. Instead he nodded, and repeated, "But that's in Marek, not out in Teren. Bluntly, this is your problem, not ours."

"Marek is a part of Teren," Selene said "And it would perhaps be useful to both Marek and Ameten if our sorcerers could work together, rather than apart. I would be very happy to see the bonds between us strengthened."

Beckett couldn't go outside the city's boundaries, which would make collaboration difficult; and Cato didn't particularly want closer bonds with Teren. If anything the opposite. However, he wasn't going to give away the former piece of information, and although getting into the latter argument might be entertaining, it wouldn't get them anywhere useful. He settled for a distant nod.

"Additionally," Selene said, "our information indicates that the sorcerer who raised the thing is moving towards Marek. Seeking, we believe, to hide here. They may, indeed, already be here. Even if you are unwilling or unable to assist with the demon, we would ask for your help in locating the sorcerer."

Reb nodded. "I see."

Cato saw, too. And he didn't like the idea of turning another sorcerer over to be executed, regardless of what they'd done.

"We'll have to consider it," Reb said. "And I can tell you that, so far, I haven't heard of any such person. But we may be able to look for them."

"When do you think you will be able to give me an answer?"

"I will send word as soon as I can," Reb said. "Tomorrow, if possible."

"My thanks." Selene rose. "I won't take any more of your time." She nodded towards both of them. "Sorcerers."

The door shut behind her, and Reb let out an explosive noise.

"A demon in Teren, uncontrolled. Storms and angels."

"Well, it's not up to anything at the moment, apparently," Cato said. "So maybe it's not that much of a problem."

"That it hasn't done anything so far doesn't mean it won't." Reb paused. "How long could you control something like that?"

"A while," Cato said, which was a bit of a lie. "If I worked that way. Which if you recall, I don't. I do *deals*, between planes. I don't bring spirits over here, still less bind them, because that's a stupid idea, not to mention far more work. Honestly. Bloody Teren. Does this really have to be our problem?"

"Well, no, it doesn't." Reb shrugged. "If it does come here, Beckett won't let it in. It might take a fair bit to keep it out, though."

"It could come here?" Cato sat up in a hurry.

"Of course it bloody could," Reb said. "I thought you were supposed to be the expert in spirits?"

"Well, I know it could, but why would it? If it's wandering around Teren, why wouldn't it just stay there?"

Reb shrugged. "Following this sorcerer, for starters. But in any case, we're part of the same land-mass. The swamp's not going to stop a demon."

Cato shuddered. "Well then. Fine, I see why we might want to do something about it, if it does get closer. Where by 'we' I mostly mean 'Beckett'."

"If Beckett will," Reb said. "But there's no point in thinking about it unless and until it happens. Beckett can't act outside the city."

"If it does come here," Cato said, "you can talk to Beckett. They like you better." It was true. Slightly annoying, but true. Beckett made Cato nervous, now that they were actually moving around in Marek as opposed to just... being there, in some kind of abstract hypothetical sense, making magic work. On the whole, Cato had preferred the latter state of affairs; but there was no point in wasting time sighing over that, especially since, arguably, he had been partly responsible for the change.

"Anyway," Reb said. "What Selene asked directly was, are we prepared to track down a Teren sorcerer and hand them over?"

"To be sacrificed," Cato said.

Reb grimaced. "Yes. I didn't think you liked the idea of that, the face on you when she mentioned it."

"I don't," Cato said, fervently. "But it would get rid of the demon, apparently, and I like even less the idea of a demon coming here. I could well do without seeing a fight between spirits ever again. Whoever did this was an idiot. I'd rather they paid for it than me." He swung his feet off the table and onto the floor.

"Are you saying that we do track them down, then?" Reb demanded.

"Ugh. I don't know. Can we leave it for a day or two, see if Teren manages to track them down without us?"

"You're putting off the decision in the hope that you don't have to be responsible for it," Reb said, flatly.

"Yes. Exactly."

"For the love of the angel, Cato. Have you no sense of duty?"

"Uh. No. I haven't. Have you *met* me?"

Reb pressed her lips together, obviously keeping in any one of a number of things she was considering saying. After a moment, she said, tightly, "Very well. When are you willing to revisit that?"

Cato gave an enormous sigh. "Two days from now, I suppose." And once two days came, he could probably put it off for at least a couple more.

"What if something happens? The demon comes here, or we hear of it acting in Teren?"

"Fine, if something happens, I'll think about it again. Happy?"

"Not really," Reb said. "But very well. Two days."

"Are we done now?"

"Yes," Reb said, rolling her eyes again. "Off you go, back to your den of iniquity."

"I quite like that," Cato said, standing up. "Den of iniquity. Sounds good. See you in two days, then, unless Teren manage to sort out their own damn problem before then. Let's hope, eh?"

ELEVEN

Marcia left the bank the next morning in a very cheerful frame of mind; the stones Captain Barcola had brought back were excellent, to her eye. She took a couple of samples to show to the Jewellers' Guild representative she was due to meet with, and withdrew enough money to pay the soldiers, who invariably preferred hard cash to bankers' notes. Hard cash sufficient to pay a dozen soldiers was heavy enough, and worth enough, that she'd brought a couple of the House servants with her. Gen, one of the footmen, carried the bag, and Hetta walked beside him and Marcia, the thick stick swinging in her hand and her stern face hopefully enough to put off the casual footpad.

Once she'd delivered the wages at the barracks – Captain Barcola looked well enough, and had her reports ready, but some of the soldiers Marcia saw slumped over their breakfast looked more than a little green about the edges from their night out – she sent Gen home again. After a moment's thought, she dismissed Hetta too. It wasn't likely that someone in half-formal House dress (she'd even painted her face, just at the cheekbones, enough to emphasise her status during the discussions with the Jewellers Guild, not so much that it wasn't clear that this was a friendly arrangement) would be attacked mid-morning in broad daylight in the middle of Marek Square, and the pocketful of stones she was carrying weren't obvious. If anything, Hetta's presence would make them more so. Hetta evidently thought otherwise, but inclined her head and went with Gen.

The Jewellers' Guildhouse was one of the oldest buildings on Marek Square. It was relatively small compared to some of the newer Guildhouses, and plain on the outside; but inside, niches in the walls held glass-fronted strongboxes with examples of particularly beautiful pieces of mastery-work, and the lavish gold paint highlighting parts of the beautifully painted wallpaper demonstrated the Guild's wealth.

Master Ilana was already waiting for Marcia in the meeting

room that she was shown to, with a steaming infusion pot on the table and biscuits on a plate. The Master's long grey hair was braided back around their narrow face, and their tunic and trousers were a rich deep blue under the silver of their mastery cloak.

"Marcia, how delightful," Ilana said, clasping Marcia's hands with theirs. The two of them had been working on the mountain-pass trading project for a while now; they were past the formalities.

"Ilana. A pleasant afternoon to you too."

Infusions in hand, and pleasantries over with, they both took their seats.

"I think you'll like what the Captain brought back," Marcia told Ilana, taking the small velvet bag out of her pocket. "I brought a sample, for you to check my eye."

Ilana pulled a loupe and a cloth out of their cloak pocket, spread the cloth on the table, and gently tipped the stones out onto it.

"Mm. Yes, indeed," they said, peering at the stones. "Excellent. This is a fair sample?"

"Entirely," Marcia said. "At least, to my knowledge. I can send word to the bank to allow you to inspect the whole batch, if you'd like."

"Mm. Yes, please do," Ilana said. "Excellent though. Well worth what we sent over." They nodded happily. "Very interested in collaborating again."

"I'll keep you informed," Marcia said. "We may be able to fit another trip in before the weather gets too bad, but I'll have to consult with the captain." Though there were many reasons why that hadn't worked out as planned; the season was only one of them.

"Yes, do keep me informed. Delightful working with you." They glanced up at the clock. "Do you have time to stay and talk, or do you need to be away to the Council Opening?"

"I've a little while before that," Marcia said. It wasn't until after noon, though she needed to allow enough time to get into full formal. But while she was here, she wanted to sound Ilana out on the matter of the Council. She sipped at her infusion, and thought over what she wanted to say next.

"Since you mention it," she began, lightly. "I've been thinking about the Council, of late."

"Ah yes," Ilana said, in tones so obviously non-committal that it raised Marcia's interest.

"I…" she paused. "I say this in confidence, you understand." She wished, suddenly, that she could wipe the face paint off. It itched slightly under her eyes.

Ilana looked up, their head tilted slightly on one side in curiosity. "Of course."

"It seems to me," Marcia said, picking her way carefully through this, "that the Council is… unduly unbalanced. The introduction of the Guilds was intended, as I understand it, to recognise the contribution of the Guilds to Marek. To give you a say, as is appropriate for the close involvement between the Houses and the Guilds."

"Yes, that is my understanding also," Ilana said.

It was obvious that they weren't saying everything they were thinking. Marcia rowed onwards.

"I am concerned that perhaps it might not have been working as intended," Marcia said. "I am concerned that the Houses might not be paying enough attention to the Guilds."

Ilana didn't say anything, but their eyebrows had shot upwards.

"It seems to me," Marcia said, "that this is not what is best for Marek."

Ilana's eyes were intent. "Yes?" they said, carefully.

"You are not being given what you were promised," Marcia said, discarding all pretence. "It's not just a question of the uneven vote. The Houses are deliberately excluding you from decisions. I don't think it's right, and, to be blunt, I don't think it's sustainable. I would rather seek to make changes while everyone is still on good terms. It will take time, of course, significant changes always do, but…"

"You may be too late," Ilana said, and it was Marcia's turn to feel her eyebrows rise.

"Too late?"

Ilana pulled a face. "It depends who you ask. Those highest in the Guilds, well, they are still pleased to be included at all. They feel they won a victory, and they do not wish to accept that that victory may have been a hollow one. Those a little younger…" They looked suddenly anxious. "We are speaking between ourselves, yes?"

"Between ourselves," Marcia agreed. She felt a little pulse

of excitement. Was there something here that she could take advantage of?

"Well. Those a little younger would agree with your assessment. I believe they are prepared to wait, a little, until it is possible to make changes. But they are not pleased with the Houses, not at all."

"But what if we could make changes now?" Marcia asked.

"You believe you can?"

Marcia hesitated. "I want to try." That was a different thing, and she could see from Ilana's expression that they knew it.

Ilana shrugged one shoulder. "I do not see the political will for it, myself, not in those who must be won over."

"What would it take, though?" Marcia asked. "In theory. What is it that your peers wish for?"

"The abolition of the Small Council," Ilana said. "Or very stringent limits on its use. Guild agreement, for example, as well as House agreement, that a matter is suitable for Small Council."

Marcia nodded. That was unsurprising.

"And an equal vote. Or more; an extra vote." Marcia winced internally. That would be rather harder to sell. "Thirteen Guild seats. Fourteen, for preference, but most certainly thirteen." Ilana met her eyes.

"You think you can do that?"

Marcia badly wanted to say yes, but she didn't think that lying to Ilana would be good for their fledgling alliance.

"I don't know," she said instead. "I have been... asking questions. Making suggestions, you understand?"

"Not yet making waves?" Ilana said, with a slightly wry smile.

Marcia kept her face still. "I don't think that going in too strongly will help. The Houses can be stubborn, sometimes, and keen on tradition. As I understand it, it was hard enough to get the Guilds in in the first place."

"Yes," Ilana said. "That's my understanding too."

"Were you involved?" Marcia asked.

Ilana shook their head. "Not directly, no. I was a journeyman, at the time. But it's discussed, occasionally, the politics of it." They quirked an eyebrow. "House Fereno was involved."

"I don't think my mother went far enough," Marcia said, bluntly.

"But your mother still has the House vote," Ilana said. "What does she think?"

Marcia opened her mouth to say that she needed to discuss the matter further with Madeleine, then she caught the expression on Ilana's face, and, on impulse, changed her mind. "I believe you can count on House Fereno's vote, when the time comes."

Ilana's eyebrows went up, betraying their surprise.

"I am glad to hear it," they said, and Marcia's stomach lurched. Should she have committed herself like that? Too late now.

"But I should warn you, I fear it will be a while before the votes are there. And you must realise that campaigning too energetically risks moving the matter backwards. The Small Council, on the other hand – that may be more straightforward."

"Without the seats, you'll be facing the same arguments another ten years down the line," Ilana said. "We all know that. You must know it too."

Marcia nodded, slowly. "Yes. But it's a matter of getting the votes."

"Your feeling is that the Houses are against this?" Ilana asked.

"I do not think they have thought it through clearly enough," Marcia said, which they both knew was an evasion. "Of course, in theory, it needs only two votes."

"One more, then," Ilana said. Marcia managed not to react outwardly. She was already regretting that impulsive decision to promise Fereno's vote, but it was too late now.

"Indeed. But in practice…"

"More would be more convincing," Ilana agreed. "But – let us be frank together, as we have been so far. Do you have another vote?"

Their gaze was direct.

"Not yet," Marcia said. "But I have not properly started. Something that would help would be if the Guilds were more willing to take House members on."

"House members are no longer excluded from the Guilds," Ilana said, mildly.

"No. In theory. And yet I am not aware of any who have been approved, and I know of several who have not." Ilana knew that as well as she did. "If that were to change, I think it would help create stronger bonds between the Houses and the Guilds, and that could only improve the situation. Even before any formal changes in Council."

Ilana nodded non-committally. "I will bring the matter up. Informally. Since, you understand, there is no *formal* problem here."

"Of course," Marcia agreed. Well. She'd brought it up, at least. The other thing... She hesitated, then, when Ilana didn't say anything more, added, "Truly, though, on the other matter. I don't think the Guilds threatening their own moves will help."

"That's not your decision," Ilana said. "But I understand your point. I will... pass that on. To the relevant people. Quietly." They smiled slightly. "Both of us need to be able to deny most of this, after all, for now."

"You don't think the Guilds will move yet?"

Ilana shook their head. "Not yet. But I think it's coming. If it can't be resolved first. I think – we have had enough, is perhaps the best way to put it. The Houses cannot survive without the Guilds, and Marek cannot prosper without us. Whatever the Houses may like to think about their importance."

Ilana sat back and sipped at their infusion, and Marcia tried to keep her back straight and to look thoughtful, unmoved, the way her mother had taught her.

"Between us," she said, again. "For now."

Ilana took another sip of their infusion, and nodded. "Between us. But it is good to know that House Fereno supports us."

Storm and angel. At least Madeleine would be pleased that House Fereno was in good odour with the Guilds for now; but if Marcia couldn't talk her mother around in time, their reputation would be in tatters. She had time, though. None of this was going to happen immediately.

"And it is good to know that there is a potential future, here, that does not involve open warfare between the Houses and the Guilds," Ilana concluded.

Marcia winced at the bluntness of it; but she too could see

Ilana's point.

She could avoid that. She had to. Whether or not anyone else saw it, this was Marek's future at risk.

The Council's formal return to session was in the early afternoon. There was a great deal of pomp and circumstance involved, including a welcoming speech delivered by the Lord Lieutenant on behalf of Teren and the Archion. The Houses, in their full formal robes, went directly to the Chamber in litters; the Guilds paraded up Marekhill from the Guildhall with their banners carried by hand-picked journeymen.

It was a waste of time, was what it was, but there you were. Marcia would much rather be, for example, arranging to meet with her acquaintance in the Broderers to see if she could persuade them to consider Aden again for journeyman. But she had to sit through this, and there was no point in complaining about it.

"Excessive nonsense," Madeleine grumbled from where the Heads and Heirs of the Houses were waiting in the foyer of the Chamber. Marcia, looking around at the beautiful carved panelling and the wall-hangings depicting Marek and Teren's history, tried not to remember facing Daril down here, barely two months ago. Across the room, she saw Daril himself, dark hair neatly tied back, his mouth set in a line, standing next to his father. He glanced over and caught her eye, and she knew that they were both thinking about the same thing. To her surprise, the edge of his mouth tipped up, just very slightly, in the echo of a rueful smile. Marcia looked away. What the hell was that supposed to mean?

"What do you mean, Mother?" she asked, to avoid considering it further.

"This nonsense of parades and what-not," Madeleine said. "You don't see the Houses parading around the city, do you?"

"Maybe we should," Marcia suggested with a shrug.

"For what purpose? We do not need people cheering us to know who we are."

Madeleine was making the assumption that people would be cheering. Marcia decided not to point that out. A year or so ago, she wouldn't have noticed the assumption herself. She bit at her lip, then stopped, suppressing a grimace, as the taste reminded her she was wearing facepaint.

One of the Chamber guards came in to inform them that the Guilds were nearly there. The great doors of the Chamber were flung open, and the Houses moved inside, into their appointed places in the three-quarter-circle pews that surrounded the central stage. The Guild representatives filed in through the main doors to follow them in to the newer Guild pews that formed the back and highest – but furthest from the stage – level of the circle.

Down in the centre of the room, Selene sat to one side of the circular stage, next to the Reader's dais and in front of the arms of Teren, painted behind the stage next to those of Marek, with the coats of arms of each of the Houses surrounding them. Once everyone was in and the doors were closed again, the Reader took everyone, one at a time, Heads, Heirs, and the elected Guildwardens, through the process of swearing to their duty.

The stone laid in the Chamber wall that they swore on had, according to the records, been laid there by Rufus Marek when the city was established and the Houses were in their infancy, minor Teren nobility come to make their fortune. Not that the official records put it quite that way. Marcia, taking her turn after Madeleine to swear to do her duty by Marek, city of Teren, noticed, for the first time, the small carving just underneath it. It was, unmistakably, Beckett, despite its rough, stylised outline. She stifled a smile. Apparently the cityangel wasn't quite so much outside of the Chamber and Marek politics as the Houses might like to think.

Marcia returned to her place, and watched the rest of the Heads and Heirs, then the Guildwardens, perform their oaths. Watching Warden Hagadath kneel to place their hands on the stone, she wondered, idly, what the Guilds thought of the cityangel, and how she might usefully find out. Then her gaze moved over to Selene. Selene's expression was intent, watching the oaths being made. Marcia thought, for the first time, about that phrase, 'city of Teren'. She'd said it enough times before, but now she found herself thinking about it in the light of how the Houses treated Selene: as someone to be honoured but not to be included, as a representative of a power that none of them saw as having any say in Marek.

Notionally, Teren had power over Marek; could that power be realised in actuality? Selene hadn't been acting quite the same as the previous Lord Lieutenant. Did she have political goals in mind in Marek, not just in Teren?

The last of the Guildwardens stood up and returned to her seat, and the Reader turned and gestured to Selene to come down.

"Heads, Heirs, Guildwardens," Selene began, once she was at the lectern. She had no notes, which hopefully meant her speech would be short. "As the representative of your country, it is my honour and my duty to be here today."

Your country. Marekers didn't think of it that way.

"I am delighted to see the links renewed now, as every year, between Ameten and Marek, city of Teren," Selene went on. Which was an... interesting read. Selene paused, and looked around the Chamber. "Indeed, I beg to hope that I will see more representatives of the Houses returning to Ameten in the near future. It seems that you no longer take the time to visit us, and it perturbs us that this is the case."

There was murmuring around the room. Selene was right; it was no longer considered desirable for young people to spend a couple of years in Ameten, nor was there a need seen for the Houses to maintain their awareness of Teren politics, and their Teren links, the way Marcia had heard her mother talk about when she was younger. But this was very blunt.

Beside her, Madeleine would never be so crass as to fold her arms in public, but every angle of her body suggested that she would like to.

"In fact, I should like to go further," Selene said, with a pleasant smile. "The Teren Government hereby issues an explicit invitation for one representative from every House to visit Ameten in the coming months, so that we can reinforce the links between this, Teren's furthest-flung city, and our nation's beloved capital and seat of government."

The murmurings were louder now. Quite apart from the way that Selene seemed to be suggesting that she had the right to make such a demand – and it was a demand, for all that it was couched in terms of a request – Marcia couldn't help noticing who was invited, and who was not.

At the back of the room, in the row behind the second row of the Houses, the face of every Guild representative Marcia could see was set like stone. Was Selene doing this deliberately? She couldn't be unaware of what she was saying, and to whom. Marcia had been underestimating Selene, hadn't she, sitting through all those dinners and balls and teas with a pleasant smile. She couldn't have reached her position in Ameten without being politically acute; Marcia had even thought that, the other day, but not followed the thought through any further.

With a sudden shock, Marcia realised who had been talking to the other Houses, about the risks of the Guilds having more power. Did Selene know Marcia – or anyone – had been raising the matter? Marcia hadn't been exactly public about her conversations with other Houses, but she hadn't been hiding them, either. That was the point of trying to raise awareness. If Selene had been paying attention…

At least she couldn't be aware of Marcia's conversation with Ilana earlier.

It didn't entirely matter, she told herself. Now she knew where that had been coming from, she'd be better able to counter it. It would slow things down still further, but… well, Madeleine had said that this would be a slow process, and she was likely right. And, perhaps, if Selene was showing her hand, pushing Teren influence more openly, the Houses would be less willing to listen to her, and more willing to think about their links with other Marekers. With the Guilds. Surely Marcia could use this, if she went at it the right way.

"We do so greatly value," Selene went on, "the work done by our friends in the Houses, liaising between Teren and the wider world. But it is imperative that this liaison remain tightly joined to your country. The Teren Government is distressed that the closeness of our relationship has lapsed somewhat in recent years, and charges you to renew the bond, and work more closely with us, from now on. I look forward to renewing and strengthening our relationship."

She stepped back, and the Speaker stepped forward, and banged their stave on the floor, concluding the ceremony.

There was no scope, in the Opening Ceremony, for anyone

other than the Lord Lieutenant to speak. And as Selene
walked out with the Houses and the Guilds into the
antechamber, there was no scope for private discussion
either. But as Marcia caught Warden Hagadath's eye on the
way out, she realised with a sinking feeling how the Guilds
had seen this: as a challenge, and a further undermining of
their position. She might see opportunities in it, but she
wasn't sure that the Guilds would; and she found herself, as
she stepped out of the Chamber building into the sunny late-
summer day, just a little fearful about the decisions they
might make if they did not.

Marcia and Cato had arranged to meet up late afternoon that
day, at an infusion-salon between Old Bridge and the squats.
Marcia often felt the need to let off steam after the more
pompous sorts of Council sessions; and she could complain
to Cato without him taking any of it seriously.

Today she needed it more than usual; and also more
seriously than usual.

She was there before him, back in casual clothes and with
her face wiped clean, and bespoke a private room. Cato was
shown in half an hour or so later. Marcia had brought a book,
a small pocket edition of a currently-popular romance, to
pass the time; she hadn't been foolish enough to expect him
to be punctual.

"Hello, sister mine. This is fancy, then. Goodness knows
what they'll think of you, letting a ruffian like me in here."

"Oh, do shut up," Marcia said, irritably.

Cato's eyebrows went up, and he sat down on the other end
of the sofa from her. He lifted his feet up to put them on the
sofa, and Marcia pushed them down again.

"Your boots are filthy. Don't be disgusting."

"My socks aren't much better," Cato said.

"Then keep your boots on over them and sit like a decent
human, for the love of the angel."

Cato looked at her thoughtfully for a moment, then
shrugged and left his feet on the floor where they belonged.
Marcia, startled, wondered just how bad she looked.

"What's up, then?" Cato asked. "Council back in action, yes, but I don't see how they can have done anything all that interesting yet."

"It wasn't the Council," Marcia said. "Not exactly. It was the Lord Lieutenant."

"The Lord Lieutenant? Really? But isn't she just a figurehead?" He frowned. "That new one, though…"

"You've met her?"

"You should know. Reb said it was you put her onto us."

Marcia paused, then decided not to pursue that hare any further. "Well. Anyway. She made a speech, in Council. All about linking more closely with Teren, and Marek-city-of-Teren. Inviting us – insisting, almost – to send representatives to Teren." She looked down at her fingers. "Not a word about the Guilds. Just the Houses."

Cato pursed his lips and nodded slowly. "Well, it could be nothing. Hot air. Political point-scoring for her to refer to back home."

"It didn't sound like nothing," Marcia said.

"She can hardly force you all to go."

"Can't she?"

"How? What's she going to do, send an army down the river for us to pick them off as they land?"

"It's not like we have an army to do the picking off," Marcia pointed out. "You going to send the City Guard with their sticks in their hands?" Cudgels, the Guard would say, but a cudgel was still just a glorified stick. "Or all those young House types that fancy themselves down at the salle?"

"You go to the salle," Cato said. "And you own a very nice sword, as I recall."

"And I'm not about to go up against a damn army, even a hypothetical one." She fenced for amusement, and for exercise, and a little bit in case she was out late on her own at night; not that she regularly carried a blade.

"We do have Beckett," Cato said.

"Are you seriously suggesting that Beckett would get involved in a war?"

"I wasn't seriously suggesting that anyone get involved in a war. I didn't think you were seriously suggesting a war." There was just the echo of a question in his voice, but Marcia didn't say anything. He tipped his head backwards and stared at the ceiling. "I see your point. It's a hell of a stretch, though, from encouraging closer links with Teren and issuing invitations, even very pointed ones, to enforcing some kind of, I don't know, occupation with soldiers."

"I'm not sure it's an occupation if we're technically Teren," Marcia said.

"That 'technically' is doing a lot of work there. If being Teren were less of an issue then none of this would matter, would it? You'd all just trot along to Ameten and be done with it. The fact that you're worrying about it suggests to me that you don't think it's that straightforward. I studied Marek history too, remember, back in the schoolroom, with you and Nisha? It was direct rule back in the day, and now it's not, but there's always been a certain tension around the matter. I'd have said that the tension was in both directions and it could, as it were, maintain itself, but if one side starts pulling harder…" He shrugged. "'You don't boss us around and we won't actively contradict you' works just fine until the bossing around starts. Is that what you're concerned about?"

Marcia shrugged. "I don't know. Maybe you're right. All she actually said was about restoring the, uh, in-person links. Like when Mother was younger. And maybe it would be no bad thing for some of the younger House members to be off doing that." She and Cato had discussed that before, although Cato's position on the matter was that he couldn't care less how bored a bunch of over-privileged House-sprigs were; they should count themselves lucky and shut up. "But what's the point? Teren's almost entirely cut off by those mountains. We already have Teren's trade. We should be making better connections with the Crescent, or Exuria, or the islands out beyond Salinas, if we can buy passage there."

"Well then, no wonder Selene and those she represents are pissed off," Cato said. "Might be worth sending some of the young fools off just to keep Teren sweet."

"But now that Selene's said it, will they want to do it? Won't they get their backs up about Marek's independence?" She sighed. "Although… the people in the Chamber, the Heads and the Heirs I mean, they didn't look… as disapproving, as I might have thought they would." She thought about the conversation with Piath, at House Berenaz, and bit her lip.

"Huh," Cato said, slowly. "You know, I'd have thought that showing her hand that clearly was an error... so either she's not very good at this, or she's been laying the groundwork."

"I don't want to assume she's not good at it," Marcia said. "I've got the uncomfortable feeling that I've been underestimating her this far. I think that's exactly what she's been doing." She hesitated. "And I think she's been arguing for the Houses to keep their control over the Guilds."

"You've not had much luck with that, then?"

Marcia shook her head, and sipped at her tea in silence for a moment. "Cato, are you sure you don't want to be involved in any of this? You've the mind for it, you know."

"Sorcerer," Cato said with elaborate patience. "Disowned. You must remember. You were there, and she shouted loud enough." Even now, Cato never used their mother's name.

"I know, but... I said to Reb, you know. Maybe it's time that sorcerers were represented on the Council. Along with the Guilds."

"For the love... No. Absolutely not. That is a fucking terrible idea," Cato said. "What did Reb say?"

"Same as you," Marcia admitted. "I just thought..."

"Well, stop thinking. I won't talk to you about this if you're going to see it as fitting me for up there."

"Very well. I hear you. But – why not?"

"For me? Because I left, and I won't go back." Cato's face was grim. "In the general case, because we've had one go at mixing politics and magic this year, and it didn't end well, did it? And before that? There's a reason for that rule."

"I thought you didn't like rules."

"I don't like baseless rules. Or rules that I don't like. I am quite happy with that one. And so, more to the point, is Beckett."

"Fine, fine," Marcia said. She hesitated. "Reb didn't... I mean, she said she'd mention it to you, as well. That it was a matter for the Group."

Cato raised an eyebrow. "She hasn't yet. But then, we've been talking of other things." He had the look of someone tucking the information away for the future, and Marcia wondered whether she should have mentioned it or not; but then, leaving it as Reb apparently making the decision by herself wouldn't have been right either, would it? Would it?

Cato drained his tea and looked in dissatisfaction at the tray, and Marcia abandoned the train of thought as unproductive. "Nothing proper to drink?" he asked.

"Alcoholic, you mean?" Marcia rolled her eyes, and summoned the waiter, who brought a flask of red wine.

"What of the Guilds, then, since you mentioned them a moment ago?" Cato asked, once the waiter had gone again.

"Well, I don't think they were thrilled with Selene so blatantly ignoring them," Marcia said. "Other than that – well. Mother thinks it would take years, and she won't vote for it either way. I don't have any of the other Houses on board, although I've tried talking to a few, just raising the idea gently, you know? Maybe Mother's right. Maybe I just have to keep bringing it up for years and gradually get people's opinions to shift." If the Guilds would sit still for that. "Nisha's helping, too," she added.

"You realise," Cato said, taking another slug of red wine, "that you're barely scratching the surface?"

Marcia frowned at him. "What do you mean?"

Cato shrugged. "Houses, Guilds… even if the Guilds did get something that looked more like effective voting rights, it's hardly going to affect anything over this side of the river, is it?"

"But the Guilds and the Houses are the ones controlling Marek's prosperity," Marcia said, "and that affects us all."

"They control Marek's prosperity for their own ends," Cato said. "Come on, even you must see that. You've been to the squats, yes?"

"The squats are exactly the sort of thing I mean. Free housing, safe."

"Some of it," Cato said.

"You live near people who don't care for that," Marcia said. "You could move."

"So, you think House Fereno, or the Jewellers' Guild's Master's place, is just the same as, say, Reb's house?"

Marcia's lips tightened. "Of course not, but…"

Cato shrugged. "Then it's not like the wealth and prosperity is coming into everyone's palm, is it?"

"There's nothing wrong with where Reb lives."

"I'm sure it's perfectly charming," Cato said. "You'd know

better than me, sister mine. But I'll bet you anything you like that it doesn't look like House Fereno. Does Reb have servants? She certainly doesn't dress like you."

Marcia felt herself flush. "That doesn't matter."

"Not saying it does. You and Reb, that's between the two of you. I am most certainly not going to get in the way, don't worry. I'm just saying. Why are you fussing about getting Council votes for the Guilds, when they already have wealth and power and control? Why aren't you looking round here for people to give a little power to?"

Nisha and Reb had been saying the same thing, hadn't they? And yet…

Cato sighed. "Never mind. You keep on with fiddling around the edges, eh? Just try not to get yourself into too much trouble, nor yet interfere too much with this much-vaunted Marek prosperity. I wouldn't like to find even less of the House gold trickling down into the squats. That really might put us into trouble."

They talked of other things for the rest of their time, but afterwards Marcia kept coming back to what Cato had said; an uncomfortable lump in the back of her mind that wouldn't quite wear away.

TWELVE

Reb wasn't difficult to find, once Tait started looking. Apparently there had been some plague, a couple of years previously, and most of Marek's sorcerers had died. This Reb was one of those who remained – her, and someone called Cato who lived in the squats, who the barman at the White Horse was clearly a bit dubious about. Tait made themself eat something before they set out, and it sat like an indigestible lump in their stomach as they walked over to the Old Market.

Reb, when she opened the door to Tait, didn't look terribly pleased to be disturbed; though surely she'd be happy enough to see a potential client. Not that Tait was a potential client exactly, but Reb couldn't know that yet. She eyed them narrowly, and folded her arms. "What do you want?"

"Uh. I'm looking for a sorcerer. Can I come in?"

"I suppose so," Reb said, and stood back, allowing them through the door.

Once inside, Tait wasn't quite sure where to start. Or where to go, come to that. The room was small, with two internal doors at the back, both of which were closed, and one of which had a heavy lock. A workroom? To Tait's right was a stove and kitchen equipment; in front and to their left a collection of mismatched chairs and a low table. It was a bare room, but a vase of flowers sat on one windowsill, the only real splash of colour or decoration in the place.

Reb stood, arms still folded, and glared at Tait for a few moments; then she sighed and gestured to the chairs. She stomped across the room and sat down in the battered armchair, and, when Tait didn't immediately follow, gestured again at the wooden chairs by the armchair.

"Well then? Sit down and tell me what you want."

Tait obediently sat, then took a deep breath and went for the bald approach.

"I'm – I'm from Teren. I came…" They stopped, and tried again. "I'm a sorcerer. But I don't want to be, I don't want to work how I was taught in Teren, not any more. Everyone knows about Marek's magic. I want…"

"You want to apprentice here, instead?" Reb said. Her voice was even. Tait couldn't tell what she thought of the idea.

"You've done it," Tait pointed out. It was guesswork – something about Reb's vowels, something about the way she was looking at Tait – but they were prepared to bet on it.

Reb didn't react, though her shoulders tensed, perhaps, ever so slightly. She didn't deny it, either. "Why?" she demanded.

"Well, why did you do it?" Tait asked, and got a glare in response.

"That's none of your business, and you're making a lot of assumptions right now. Why do *you* want to?"

"I don't want to deal in blood, and I don't want to summon demons," Tait said, which was slightly more than they'd meant to say outright.

It had been a hell of a shock, realising what they'd got themself into, that first time back in the Academy in Ameten. As had realising why they'd been trained in the first place. There might have been more sensible reactions to this than to banish the spirit they'd raised and run for it, but Tait hadn't been able to think of any at the time.

But they were safe in Marek now. It might notionally be Teren, but the laws were different, and the magic was different, and the sorcerers were different. And Reb was from Teren, and she'd become a sorcerer here. Maybe this might work out yet.

Reb was still eyeing them. "Have you ever used unwilling blood?"

"No," Tait said, and pushed up their sleeves, showing Reb the tracery of scars right up their arms. Arms were easiest to get at, for blood work. Reb raised an eyebrow, and Tait dropped their sleeves again. Even in Teren they didn't much like showing their arms unless they were working. Here it seemed like a particularly bad idea.

"Have you ever used someone else's willing blood?"

"Ye-es," Tait said. "My tutor. And her other student. And someone who wanted me to perform a spell on them, and I needed it to tie it together."

Reb nodded. "Nothing you paid for?"

"No!" Tait said indignantly. They were aware that some people did that, paid for blood to use in their own spells, rather than use their own, but Tait had always seen it as a bit like cheating. Not as bad as just taking it, of course, but...

Which was why Tait's arms looked the way they did, and some sorcerers seemed to have barely a scar. Of course, the other reason for that was that some sorcerers went directly to summoning-and-binding and Tait had avoided that for a long while, scared for reasons they couldn't quite articulate, until the Academy pushed them into it.

Of course, it turned out that they'd been right to be scared. And right, although they hadn't thought of it quite that way before, to be unsettled about what exactly the Academy was asking for. They wished, now, that they'd run earlier; but then, once they entered the Academy it had already been too late.

Reb was chewing at a thumbnail. "Why have you come here?"

This was the tricky bit. "I told you already. I got fed up with slicing myself open, and I don't like binding spirits," Tait said. Which was true, as far as it went, but they hadn't had the notion of leaving home and coming here until they were already on the run.

"So you've come here."

"I still want to do sorcery," Tait said, and knew that that must sound true because it *was*, desperately and entirely true. "Marek has sorcery, a different sort of sorcery. I wanted... I thought, maybe, someone would teach me."

"And you came to me."

"I was told, there's only two sorcerers left in Marek now," Tait said. "You, and someone that my informant didn't recommend."

"Cato," Reb said. "Hm, well." She didn't elaborate.

"So I came to you," Tait said. "To ask if you'll teach me." She was still looking at them, so Tait chanced another reminder. "And it looks like you did the same yourself, once. If you're Teren. Did you start off with Teren magic, too?"

Reb stared flatly at them, and Tait looked away. "Sorry," they muttered. "I didn't mean to pry."

"No," Reb said, and their tone was absolute.

Tait's stomach plummeted. "No?"

"No, I won't take you on as an apprentice," Reb said. "You're not telling me the whole truth, and I'm not taking on someone who isn't." Her eyes narrowed. "Are you the sorcerer the Teren Lord Lieutenant was talking about?"

"W-what?" Tait managed. Horror pulsed through their skull.

"The one who raised some demon they couldn't control, did a runner, they're still struggling with it back at Ameten."

"No!" Tait said. "I mean, yes, but..."

But they'd got rid of it. They had! Hadn't they?

Too late, they realised that they'd missed their opportunity to deny it, to look casual and unconcerned and maybe faintly surprised. Reb was shaking her head.

"You are," Reb said. "That's you. What on earth are you thinking, coming to Marek, with that thing maybe after you? What on earth were you thinking, just running away from it?" She sounded disgusted. "You have no idea what it could have done. Well, that's not even true, you do have an idea, don't you. That's worse."

"I couldn't... I banished it. I did. Half those scars, the new ones..." Tait felt panic rising. "Surely I couldn't have..."

"You thought you banished it but you didn't check?" Reb said. She sounded scornful. "Well, even if that were true, it doesn't exactly bode well for your careful attitude, does it?"

"Gods, is it free?" Tait demanded. They felt sick.

"Yes," Reb said. "So I'm told. No harm done yet, but who knows what'll happen."

Tait could feel themself shaking. No harm done yet, at least, but...

But they *had* banished it. They were certain of it. They'd seen it disappear, they'd shut everything down...

"I did banish it," they said, but Reb didn't look convinced. "Someone must have raised it again. To look for me."

Reb was shaking her head. "Why on earth would they bother? Just for one sorcerer?"

"The Academy," Tait said. "They don't want, they don't let you go..." But Reb must have been in Marek for years, long before the Academy was established. She wouldn't know. And Tait themself hadn't wanted to think badly of the Academy until the very last minute. They'd ignored so much. They scrabbled for words to explain everything to Reb, but nothing would come together. And they couldn't be *certain*, not any more, that it definitely wasn't their fault...

Reb looked away, obviously giving up on Tait.

"I should hand you straight over to the Teren Lieutenant. Send you back to solve your own damn problem."

Tait stood up, trembling, almost knocking the chair over as they stood.

"I won't," Reb said, with an irritable wave of the hand. "I'm not going to take you on as an apprentice, and I don't want to see you around Marek again. But I won't send you to her."

"But Marek's the only place that's safe," Tait said. They swallowed.

"I said," Reb said, distinctly and slowly, "that I don't want to see you around Marek. Because if I do, I might have to reconsider this decision. Do you understand me?"

Tait nodded, jerkily.

"Now. Get the hell out of here. If you've any morality at all, you'll go back of your own accord and find a way to deal with that thing. Maybe the city sorcerers will let you help without just throwing you to it."

Tait knew how unlikely that was. Reb, presumably, believed what she was saying; but there was no point in trying again to explain. And perhaps it was Tait's own screwup, after all. Maybe they really had messed up the banishing, and just not realised. In which case maybe they ought to sacrifice themself to their own screwup. Gods and angels. What had they done?

Tait couldn't think of anything to say to Reb. Goodbye, thank you – none of it could possibly be right. They just nodded, again, walked across the room, and let themself out the door. They felt Reb's eyes on their back the whole way.

☺ ☺

Tait couldn't afford to let themself think about anything Reb had said as they walked back through the city to the White Horse. They didn't know this place; if they started trying to work out what to do next, or thinking at all about the demon – how could it still be *here*, what had they done? – they would just end up lost, and that wasn't going to help the situation. Time enough to panic, or break down, or whatever, once they were safely back in their room at the inn.

They'd pinned so much on Marek's sorcerers being helpful. They hadn't let themself think about what to do if they weren't. And they hadn't even thought that the demon might be on the loose, again. Still. They'd seen it go back, they'd seen the link to the spirit plane close. They'd seen it, they'd been certain, before they'd run, and now... ? Bile rose in their throat, and they swallowed it back down. It might not have been that, after all. But it didn't really matter, did it? If there was a demon coming to Marek, it was still Tait's fault. They'd raised it; they'd run; they'd run here.

Tait had walked through the market square – this was the Old Market, as opposed to the New Market where they'd entered Marek – more or less without seeing it. The river was in front of them now, with a small passenger ferry loading at a dock to one side, and Tait turned right to walk along the riverside towards Old Bridge. The barman at the White Horse had said that there were quicker ways to get from the Old Bridge to where Reb lived, but sticking to the riverside was the least likely to get Tait lost.

There was another sorcerer. This Cato that Reb had mentioned, and that the barman hadn't thought much of. Reb hadn't sounded like she thought much of – him? them? her? – either. But then Reb didn't think much of Tait, either. Tait swallowed back misery. Cato had sounded potentially dangerous, but... more dangerous than the alternatives? Tait shook their head, trying to dislodge the spiralling loop of thoughts. Best just not to think about any of this until they could sit down quietly and peacefully and work it all out. Otherwise they'd wind up screaming in the middle of the street.

The docks were busy, and Tait tried to distract themself in watching all that was going on. This section of the dock was evidently Salinas, although there were only a couple of their big sleek sea-going ships there at the moment. People did mysterious nautical things with rope and paint on the decks. Tait had never met anyone from Salina. Teren, other than Marek, was land-locked, and the Salinas were devoted to their ships. Smaller boats were loading and unloading crates with various stamps across them. It was fascinating to watch, despite Tait's anxiety. Tait knew about Marek's status as trade-city for Teren, but seeing the reality of it was something else. They loitered for a while, leaning on a rail at the edge of one of the docks, out of the way of the people moving about their business, just watching; then straightened up with a sigh. They were just putting off the moment of deciding what to do next. At least they felt a bit calmer now.

Old Bridge was another five minutes' walk along the riverside. Close to the bridge, the path became a stone embankment for walking, right next to the river, rather than skirting behind the edge of a working dock. It was mirrored on the other side of Old Bridge – the flashier side, Tait had already realised – by a much more elaborate one, with more elaborately-dressed people walking along it. Over here, Marek's poorer citizens might take a few minutes at the middle of the day for a stroll, if they were lucky and had the time and energy; over there were Marek's richer citizens, who could presumably choose to take rather more time for their strolls.

Once Tait reached the White Horse, they found their stomach growling; they'd been too nervous to eat before going to see Reb, and they'd taken their time walking back. Perhaps before going back to the room, they could have something to eat in the taproom.

"Ah, Ser Tait," the barman said – the same one who'd given Tait directions to Reb's. "I trust your errand this morning went well. I'm afraid you've just missed someone asking for you."

Tait's heart warmed slightly. Surely it must be one of the expedition, Bracken perhaps, or, less likely, Captain Anna. Tait hadn't thought either of them had become fond enough of Tait to look them up, but it would be nice to be wrong.

"Or at any rate, he was asking after a Teren sorcerer, just come in," the barman continued.

The warm feeling disappeared. Bracken or Captain Anna would have asked for Tait by name.

"Had a bit of a Teren accent, so I figured him for a countryman of yours, looking for a chin-wag," the barman was saying. "I said you'd doubtless be back later, but he didn't want to leave a name. Just said he'd be back another time. You only just missed him."

Tait's appetite had entirely disappeared. There were no good reasons for someone from Teren to be asking for them. Tait supposed it was just about possible that one of the expedition had mentioned a Teren sorcerer to a Teren friend, and that friend was so desperate for the accents of home that he came looking... but then he'd have Tait's name, wouldn't he? And would have mentioned Bracken or whoever it was?

There weren't many people who knew Tait was here. The expedition. Reb, now. There weren't many people who would have any interest in a Teren sorcerer. But Reb had said that the Teren Lieutenant knew about that wretched demon, and by implication, that she was looking for whoever raised it... That didn't make sense, though. How would they be looking for Tait here in Marek, already? Unless it was sheer luck, that the Lord Lieutenant had heard, somehow, of the presence of a Teren sorcerer here and thought it was worth checking...

The barman was looking at Tait, his eyebrows raised.

"Hmm?"

"I said, Ser, was there something you wanted?"

"Uh. Um, are you serving something for lunch? Could I have some of it sent up to my room?"

"There's fish stew with bread?" the barman offered.

"Yes. Absolutely. Here, let me pay for it – no, I'd rather not put it on my account, thank you."

Tait walked heavily up the stairs to their room, and didn't think to wonder if the Teren enquirer really had gone away and not, say, gone to wait for them, until they'd walked into the room. Thankfully, there was no one there. But it just showed that Tait wasn't thinking clearly.

It could just be coincidence. And even if it wasn't coincidence, maybe if that person did come back, Tait could talk their way out of it. Brazen it out. Would there be a description circulating? It wasn't like anyone else had been around at the time, and the demon was surely unlikely to be co-operating with anyone if it was on the loose... unless it thought it might get fed if it did.

Tait shuddered at the thought.

This was all falling apart. Tait had known that the Academy would look for them – everyone knew what the

Academy did to runaway sorcerers – but they'd figured that if Tait could stay out of sight for long enough, for example, hidden in Marek, under the cityangel's protection, then in due course the Academy would give up. One junior sorcerer; it couldn't be that important, could it? But that had been when Tait believed that the demon was safely back on its own plane. Not when it had yet to be banished, and when everyone knew that the easiest way to do so would be to find Tait and feed them to it. And if they'd gone to the trouble of raising it again just to look for Tait, that was still the story they were putting about, so that was still what Tait had to assume they were planning.

The demon hadn't hurt anyone yet. That didn't mean that it wouldn't. It might mean that it was under control; it might just be luck.

And the other thing Tait had been counting on was Marek's magic. Not just the protection; Marek's magic, to them, sounded almost impossibly wonderful. A long-term, permanent contract with a spirit, that didn't require blood or sacrifices of other sorts or deals or fear or... But Reb had turned them down. No magic. No protection.

Jerkily, Tait started stuffing their things back into their bag. They had to run. Again. But where to, this time? One of those Salinas ships, maybe – did they take passengers? Did they take broke passengers? Tait had their money from the expedition, but they couldn't imagine that it was enough to get them passage anywhere particularly useful. And in any case, where else did sorcery? The idea of a life without magic... but the alternative to just losing their magic was losing their life as well.

Maybe Reb was right, maybe they should go back. But... Tait didn't have the fortitude to go back and voluntarily feed themself to a demon. Even if it was their fault – but it had gone, though, it had *gone* – and certainly not just to feed the Academy's unwillingness to let anyone get away. To let anyone believe they had an alternative, once they'd stepped through those stone doors.

There was a knock at the door, and Tait jerked, horrible visions running through their head, before a bored voice called "Your food!" and Tait cautiously opened the door to take a plate of stew and a small loaf of bread.

The food looked and smelt appetising enough, except that Tait had precisely no appetite at all. They forced themself to sit down and eat at least some of it – they didn't need to start out hungry. They were going to have to leave the White Horse, that was clear, but where to?

As they ate, their mind kept coming back to this Cato. Another sorcerer. Who Reb disliked, and who clearly had a bad reputation. But what other options did Tait have? Maybe the bad reputation would be a help; maybe if Tait made a clean breast of everything that had happened, maybe Cato would find it amusing to help a demon-raiser. A cowardly one, Reb had said, and she wasn't wrong. (But the demon had been banished, it *had*. Tait felt tears start in the corners of their eyes and furiously blinked them away.)

And if not, then presumably Cato would take Tait along to the Teren Lieutenant and hand them over, and maybe that would be what Tait deserved.

It wasn't like there were any good options available. Tait pushed the bowl of stew away, shoved the loaf of bread into their bag for later use, and did a final check of the room for abandoned belongings. They didn't want to leave officially; there were too many people around who were watching, too many people who might be able to tell someone, later, which way Tait had gone.

Tait counted out onto the table enough coins to cover their bill, and a little more, strapped their bag across their chest, took a deep breath, and threw open the window.

THIRTEEN

Marcia had been looking forward to seeing Reb all day. It had been more than a full enough day: the bank, the barracks, and the conversation with Ilana; the expected tediousness of the Council opening interrupted with Selene's weird speech; and then that conversation with Cato, which she was still turning over in her mind.

She took the ferry across the river to the foot of the dock at the Old Market. At this time of day it wasn't that busy; mostly day-servants from houses and shops on Marekhill who lived over in the small terraced houses and flats clustered around the Old Market, and who were paid well enough for the ferry-fare to be worth the saving on their feet compared to walking around by the bridge. The ferry moved so slowly that Marcia had to slap away the mosquitos that caught up with it. As she disembarked and walked across the Old Market, the last stallholders were putting away their barrows, and apprentices were hauling water from the well in the corner to sluice across the cobbles into the gutters, from which a faint smell of rotting vegetables wafted. A couple of children carried a bucket of water between them in front of Marcia up past Reb's house, squabbling about whose turn it was to help their father with the dinner.

Marcia reached Reb's house with a sigh of relief. For now, she could just forget all of this, and ignore Cato's weird ideas. She could spend a pleasant evening with Reb, and relax a bit. She rapped on the door, and smiled when Reb opened it to her, taking in the sight of the taller woman. There were a couple of smudges on the brown skin of Reb's cheek, and her short dark curls looked, as usual, like she'd been running her hands through them.

"Hello you," Reb said, with an answering smile of her own. "Come on in. It's good to see you."

For Reb, that was unusually expressive, and Marcia basked in the warmth of it as she stepped into the house. Once she was indoors and the door had shut behind her, Reb opened her arms, and they embraced. Apparently, Reb felt that it was beneath the dignity of a sorcerer to engage in public displays of affection. To be fair, Marcia wasn't sure how she'd behave if she was over her side of the river, where there was more likelihood of being seen by someone who might report back to her mother. She was gloomily aware that as Fereno-Heir, she shouldn't really be consorting with a sorcerer, even if she wasn't involving herself in any actual sorcery.

Well. There was no point in wasting her time and energy thinking about that right now. Things were what they were, and there was no point in borrowing trouble.

Reb let go of her, and nodded over at the stove.

"I've pan-dumplings cooking, if you want some?"

"That would be lovely," Marcia said. "Can I help?"

"I doubt it," Reb said. "Go and sit down. Or, no, choose an infusion."

Marcia glanced over the row of jars and chose greenherb. By the time the water was boiling and she'd poured it into the cups, Reb had put a dish of pan-dumplings on the table between the chairs. Steam rose from them, scenting the whole room with delightful smells.

"So," Marcia said, once she'd eaten her first dumpling. Reb was a good cook; the minced vegetables were flavoured with something that gave them a pleasant sharpness, and the outer pastry was correctly thin. "Something I thought you might want to know. My expedition over to Exuria returned today, and the captain told me they hired a sorcerer in Teren to help them through the passes. Apparently at this season, you get dragon-bears, and magic is a damn sight easier for dealing with them than brute force, I'm told."

"Yes," Reb said, with an expression that suggested she might know more than Marcia about it. Marcia was once again tempted to ask Reb about her Teren background, but pushed the idea aside. It had never seemed that Reb would be pleased to be asked.

"Wait." Reb frowned over the low table at her. "Sorcerer? A Teren sorcerer?"

"Yes, and the odd thing is – this is what I thought you might want to know about – once they reached Marek, they chose to come into the city, rather than take their paid passage back up the river to Teren."

"A Teren sorcerer in Marek?"

"Yes. Is that likely to be a problem?"

"I've met them," Reb said. She put her fork down and folded her arms. "And yes, they're a problem. I don't know what your expedition were doing, bringing them back."

Irritation swept over Marcia at Reb's tone. "There's no law against folk coming from Teren to Marek, is there? I don't see how the captain could stop them doing what they chose."

Reb snorted. "Well, it's a damn nuisance."

"They came to see you? What did they want?"

"Apprenticing," Reb said.

"That's good, right? Aren't you looking for an apprentice?" Marcia had a sudden pang of worry. If Reb had taken this person on as an apprentice, maybe Marcia shouldn't have told Selene about them.

"Not a Teren one," Reb said. Marcia saw a muscle in her jaw twitch.

"But you're Teren," Marcia said, confused, then regretted it as Reb glared at her.

"I'm a Marek sorcerer," Reb said. "And more to the point, when I came to Marek, I wasn't on the run from raising an uncontrolled demon."

Marcia's stomach lurched. "That *was* this one, then?" She might have told Selene, but she realised now that she'd been hoping that it was a coincidence.

Reb nodded. "Well, they tried to claim that they'd banished it again, but clearly they haven't, if it's been seen in Teren. And the way they froze like a rabbit when I mentioned it, and started babbling about the Academy – they were just trying to cover themself. I've no time for liars."

"So you didn't apprentice them?"

"I most certainly did not. I told them to bugger off and sort out the problem they'd left behind."

"Well," Marcia said, with relief, finishing off the second-to-last dumpling, "that should be done for them, as it happens." If Reb hadn't wanted anything to do with this sorcerer, then it didn't matter what Marcia had said to Selene.

Reb frowned at her. "What do you mean?"

"When Captain Barcola mentioned it, I sent a message to Selene. The Teren Lieutenant?" Marcia added, as Reb's frown deepened.

"I know who Selene is," Reb said. "I met with her yesterday, if you recall. She wanted me – Cato and me – to look out for this sorcerer, if they came into Marek. Cato wasn't keen, but... never mind. What do you mean, you sent her a message?"

"Captain Barcola told me where this sorcerer was staying," Marcia said. "So I messaged Selene, telling her to look at the White Horse for a Teren sorcerer. Though I didn't know at the time it was the right one. But it sounds like it is, which means that she owes me one." Probably not enough of a tie to get Selene to back off as regards the Guilds, unfortunately.

"You handed over a sorcerer?"

"I passed on information," Marcia said, scowling. "Why shouldn't I?"

"She'll take them back and kill them," Reb said. "Feed them to the demon."

"Then maybe they shouldn't have raised it?" Marcia said, though she felt a bit sick. "It's a Teren problem, not mine. And it means Selene owes me one, which is politically useful."

"Sorcerers fall under the jurisdiction of the Group," Reb said.

"But this is a Teren sorcerer, not a Marek one! You just turned them down as an apprentice." Marcia felt annoyance rise. "And anyway, the Group is just you and Cato." She immediately wished she hadn't said that.

"It is what it is," Reb said, her eyes narrowing. "And it has jurisdiction over sorcerers, and sorcery, of all sorts within Marek. It is not down to House Fereno to set Teren onto a sorcerer within Marek."

"So if Teren had encountered them two miles down the road you wouldn't mind what happened?" Marcia said. House Fereno indeed. They were operating on that level, were they now? "Reb, this is absurd. You don't have jurisdiction over all information within Marek that bears on sorcery."

"You set Teren on a sorcerer," Reb said. Her cheeks were flushed dark now with anger. "Without consulting me. Or your brother, come to that."

"Politics is my job, Reb," Marcia said. "You're being unreasonable. As you just said, I am Fereno-Heir, and I act for House Fereno. Of course I didn't consult you. You wouldn't consult me about a matter of sorcery that you thought might affect trade or politics, would you? I don't understand what you expect."

"I expect you to stay out of things you don't understand!" Reb was on her feet now, and Marcia leapt to her own feet.

"You are being ridiculous…"

"What if I had apprenticed them?" Reb demanded, cutting over her. "I'd have an apprentice – someone I was sworn to protect – with the Lord Lieutenant hunting them across Marek. You can't tell me that wouldn't have a political impact, and it would be down to you!"

"Then you might just as well say that you should consult me before taking an apprentice," Marcia retorted. Reb's eyes flashed. "But it doesn't matter, because you didn't apprentice them. It's a Teren sorcerer, it's a Teren matter, and if they resolve it, then we here in Marek don't have to do anything more about it. So I honestly can't see what the problem is!"

"The problem is… Oh, never mind." Reb grabbed the dumpling bowl from the table, turned and stomped across the room to the kitchen bench. "I'm tired. You'd better get the last ferry across the river." She didn't turn round.

Marcia looked at the set line of her back, and clenched her teeth. This wasn't her fault. This was Reb, overreacting to something that didn't need to matter at all. But Marcia was damned if she was going to put in the spadework to resolve this, or be the first to apologise. Reb was being unreasonable, and she could damn well think about it and step down.

"Fine," she said, tightly, and slammed out of the front door. She fumed about Reb's unreasonableness all the way across the river and up the cliff-path to House Fereno; whilst a tiny core of her hoped that the Teren sorcerer had managed to evade Selene's guards. Whether or not they deserved it, fed to a demon didn't sound like something she could wish on anyone.

Asa was lying on Jonas' bed, with the sheets half-covering them, as Jonas stood by the table, pouring a small carafe of wine into two clay cups. He'd fetched the wine up from the pub on the corner before Asa got here, for them to share together, but they'd gotten distracted before he could pour it.

He crossed over to the bed and handed Asa a cup as they sat up a bit against the wall. It had been a warm day, but the air coming through the open window was getting chilly. Jonas picked up the blanket off the floor before joining Asa on the bed, leaning against the wall to face them a little.

"Good health," Asa said, catching his eye as they took a sip of the wine.

"Good health," Jonas responded, remembering not to break eye contact 'til the toast was done.

Asa shifted on the bed, and looked away, their shoulders tensing slightly.

"So," they said. "I was coming along through the docks today, and I saw Tam. And Tam pointed out to me a Salinas ship, called the Lion t'Riseri. I gather it's been in for a day or so now."

Jonas tried not to wince. He hadn't yet mentioned the Lion, or his mother, or the upcoming dinner to Asa. He wasn't sure why. Well, no, he was entirely sure why. He didn't want Asa and his mother to meet, he didn't want to go to the damn dinner himself, and he'd been desperately hoping some alternative would turn up so he didn't have to deal with any of it.

He shouldn't be surprised that this had caught up with him.

"Not being in a hurry," Asa continued, their tone slightly pointed, "I stopped and had a chat with a couple of the crew. Apparently, the captain is here seeking out her son, who's been living in Marek for a while. And she's found him already, and spoken to him."

"Yeah," Jonas said. Couldn't really avoid it any more. "The ship's here, and my mother's here."

"You didn't mention it?" Asa asked.

Jonas couldn't quite read their tone. Were they angry? Tam had known, after all... he should have told Asa.

"I suppose I didn't," he said.

Asa shrugged. "It's up to you, Jonas. But it feels like the sort of thing you might tell your friends."

"Tam only knew because he happened to be there when she came in," Jonas said.

"Whatever. I'm trying not to be hurt, because it's not my business, really."

"It is, though," Jonas protested, without thinking about it.

Asa smiled at him, just a little, looking faintly reassured. "Well, I suppose I'd like for you to have mentioned it. That your mother – that your family, really, aren't the crew that to you? – have come to find you." They shifted round on the bed to face Jonas a bit more. "It sounded like they expect you to go back to Salina with them."

Jonas sighed. "That's what Mother wants."

"Do you want to?" Asa asked. "You said, last month, that you were going to stay. But – " they hesitated. "But perhaps you've changed your mind."

Jonas set his wine cup down on the floor next to the bed, and pushed his hands into his hair. "I want to be here. I want to hang out with you, and I want to learn sorcery from Cato," or mostly he did, anyway. "But – Mother is quite forceful."

"You're an adult," Asa said. "You don't have to do what you're told. It's up to you whether you want to stay here." They took a slug of wine. "Or not, obviously."

Jonas looked down at his hands. "I suppose not. Except…" Except that nothing was ever that simple, was it? "You're right, the crew are my family." Or at least, 'family' was the nearest Marek equivalent to what a Salinas crew were to one another. "I grew up on the Lion, you know. I… miss them."

Except that wasn't quite right, either. It had become steadily harder, as he got older, to be on the Lion. Not the physical work; that he didn't mind. What was harder was realising that his flickers were not quite right, something he had to hide. Something that made him not quite right.

He was hiding those here too, wasn't he? Other than from Cato. Asa didn't know. Nor Tam. Nor Marcia and Reb, although he didn't exactly count them as friends.

Storm and angel, he was tired of hiding things.

"But?" Asa prompted. "It sounded like there was a but, there."

"But I have friends here, too, and a chance to explore something about me that I can't even think of at home," Jonas said. "I don't intend to be dragged back home, if that's what you're asking."

Home, though. Salina was still home. Asa's eyes flickered

slightly, although they didn't say anything. But of course Salina was home. He'd only been here a few months. Whether or not he stayed... it was comfortable here, and he liked it, but...

Asa shrugged, and Jonas pulled himself back to the conversation. The sheet fell off Asa a little more with the shrug, and Jonas tried not to get distracted by the smooth dark brown skin of their chest.

"Obviously I'd prefer you to stay here," Asa said, their eyes affectionate. "But it's your life, Jonas. I just – it would have been nice if you'd mentioned it, that's all. And if you do change your mind, it would be nice if you mentioned that."

"I'm not going to just leave without telling you," Jonas said.

"Well," Asa said. "Good."

"Look," Jonas said, realising that whether or not this was entirely a good idea, it was the best opportunity he'd get, and it was probably too late now to hope that something would happen to cancel the whole thing. "Mother wants me to come to dinner tomorrow, at the embassy, with Kia. Uh, the Ambassador. You know she was on the Lion, too?"

Asa nodded, a pin-scratch frown between their eyebrows.

"She, uh. She wanted you to come along, too."

Asa's eyes widened.

"Hang on. She knows about me?"

"She guessed I was seeing someone," Jonas said. "So she said, I should invite them along."

"Really? Are you sure this is a good idea? Do you want me to come along?"

Jonas nodded with a confidence that he didn't entirely feel. He wasn't even sure how he'd introduce Asa. 'Seeing each other', but... friend? Lover? Salinas relationships tended to be fluid unless and until you had a child together (and often beyond, come to that, but raising a child meant some kind of commitment, even if you never shared a bed again); Mareker relationships, as far as he could tell, tended to be less so, but he and Asa hadn't really discussed it yet.

Now would probably be a good time to do so, but he couldn't even think about trying to deal with that on top of everything else.

"You've left it fairly late to invite me," Asa said.

Jonas pulled a face. "Yeah. Sorry. I was kind of hoping that Marek would slide into the sea and I wouldn't have to go myself, to be honest. But I would like you to be there, if you want to come."

"Well. If you're sure." Asa smiled, looking somewhere between pleased and worried. "What should I wear, though? I haven't even anything Marek formal, never mind Salinas formal." Messengers didn't have enough ready cash to have extra, non-essential, clothes.

"I'd say stick with Marek," Jonas said. "Uh. I could ask Marcia?" Mareker formal wasn't any more gendered than Salinas was, so that could work. He'd been avoiding Marcia for ages. But if Asa was prepared to do this, then he could cope with asking Marcia a favour. He was pretty certain that she still owed him something after everything that happened at New-Year. Mid-Year. Whatever.

Or Cato might have something suitable, which would be a much easier conversation, but he wasn't going to suggest that out loud. Asa was definitely nervous around Cato. He'd ask Cato, and pretend he'd asked Marcia, and it would all be fine.

Asa was looking unsure. "Marcia's a rather different shape from me, up and down. And she's shorter. And Marekhill. I mean…"

"Sure, I didn't mean her stuff, but she'll know how to get hold of something," Jonas said. "Mareker stuff is fairly adjustable anyway, right?" Cato was closer to Asa's shape and size, so that should be fine. "It's my invitation, I'll sort out something for you to wear," he said, more firmly. "Honestly. It's not a problem. I'll skip work tomorrow and get it fixed."

"All right," Asa said, evidently still slightly reluctant. "But… Jonas, are you really sure?"

"Positive. It's fine. I'll sort something out, I promise, and you always look amazing, anyway."

He leant in to kiss Asa, hand trailing down their arm, and Asa smiled and gestured assent as they too moved into the kiss.

He would sort something out. It would all be fine.

FOURTEEN

The trouble with having done what you might term a moonlight flit from the White Horse, albeit in the afternoon and leaving adequate payment behind, was that Tait had no guidance about where to find this Cato, other than 'in the squats'. And then there was the possibility of being followed, or spotted, or…

It ought not to be that much of a risk, not really. You couldn't reliably tell Teren from Marek folk by sight; Tait didn't stand out that way. But if you were looking for someone of Tait's specific description… Tait was taller than average, and they were gloomily aware that they didn't move like a local, and they didn't know their way around the city.

But what they could do was blend in with all Marek's other visitors. It was a cosmopolitan city, and strangers were common. So Tait took a circuitous route over to the squats, wandering around and doing their best to look like any other visitor with no care in the world. They peered in shop windows and stopped in Marek Square to look at the carvings on the Guildhalls, each trying to outdo its neighbour, and at the weird architecture of the Salinas embassy, which was presumably trying to give a Salinas feel to a building that was basically Teren/Marek standard brick, and succeeded only in looking peculiar. They sat on the edge of the fountain in the middle of the Square for a while, trying to look relaxed and instead feeling hideously conspicuous. And finally, they meandered over Old Bridge and up the road to the edge of the squats.

They were slightly formidable buildings, five or six storeys high, and built in a single row with only occasional passageways through into the next parallel street, cut through the buildings with a single-storey height, so more rooms could be fitted in on top of them, and reminding Tait uncomfortably of tunnels.

"You looking for someone, mate?"

The lad who tapped Tait on the shoulder – giving them a

very uncomfortable moment as they spun around, heart in mouth – had a friendly smile, and a red armband around one arm. That meant something, didn't it? A messenger, was that right?

"I – uh – "

"I'm Tam, mate. I don't mean to be rude, but I've not seen you round here before, and you don't look like you're that clear where you're going to. So – can I help? Where is it you're after?"

"I don't know the address," Tait admitted.

"No address? Right. Got a name, then?"

"I'm Tait."

"A name you're looking for," Tam said, patiently.

"Oh! Um." Tait thought for a moment, trying to work out if they should risk asking directly. Then again – what else were they going to do? Wander round in circles waiting for Cato to shoot sparks out of his window? "Cato. The sorcerer."

Tam's eyebrows went up. "You sure, mate?"

Tait swallowed. "Yes. Yes, I'm sure. I need to find him."

"Well." Tam sounded a bit dubious. "I can give you directions, but I'd look out for your stuff, if I were you. Keep your bag close, kind of thing. There's some less friendly folk, up there, and it's coming on to get dark."

"I'll be fine," Tait said, feeling relief. Ordinary foot-pads they could deal with; they'd lived in a couple of very unsavoury parts of Ameten. And one of the things about blood-sorcery was you always had a nice sharp knife about your person.

Tam gave them detailed directions, took them to the right passage, and left them with a friendly wave, refusing the Marek penny Tait offered.

"Nah, I just like to help out where I can, you know? Less'n' you've got a message you want delivered," he shrugged the shoulder of the arm that wore the armband, "I'll happily take for that."

"Sadly not," Tait said, and Tam grinned and turned to jog off back towards Old Bridge.

Tait squared their shoulders, made sure their bag was strapped tight to their chest, and set off towards Cato's house. They only had to dissuade one potential footpad on the way, when they noticed someone coming fake-casually out of a doorway. Putting their hand to their knife and pulling it out, just a little, was enough for the person to hesitate and change direction.

Tait found the correct number on the fifth street away from the river, and went up to the first floor, where a large red painted C decorated the first door on this level. This was the place, then. Tait took a deep breath and knocked on the door.

It swung open.

"Come in, and keep your hands where I can see them," someone called from inside the dimly lit room.

Cautiously, Tait advanced, blinking in the hope that their eyes would adjust faster to the half-dark. It was still daylight outside, but curtains had been pulled across the windows. There were a couple of candles lit by the bed that was opposite the door, and someone lounging on it, propped up with a couple of pillows. As Tait's vision improved, they could see that the figure – Cato, presumably? – had his hands behind his head.

"Oh," Cato said. "You're not – who I expected." He sat up a bit. "Who are you, then?"

At a guess, Cato was a bit shorter than Tait, with dark hair; more than that, Tait couldn't currently see. The candles were slightly behind Cato, no doubt deliberately, throwing his face into shadow.

"I'm Tait." Tait had thought about how to introduce themself; whether to try, as they had with Reb, not to talk about what had happened, or to be entirely honest. They hadn't come to a decision, but here they were, and they had to say something. "I'm from Teren. I'm, uh, a sorcerer."

"A Teren sorcerer," Cato said, slowly. "Really. Are you, by any remote chance, the Teren sorcerer who summoned a demon outside Ameten which is currently causing some concern to, among other people, the Teren Lieutenant?"

Oh, shit.

"I – how did you know?" Tait blurted, then, too late, "But I didn't."

"Well, mostly, I knew because you just told me." Cato sat up and swung his legs onto the floor; stood up and came over to Tait, turning so the candlelight caught both of them.

Close to, the first thing Tait thought was: but he's pretty. From the reputation Cato seemed to have, Tait had half

expected some grizzled scowling sorcerer, like every
storybook illustration of a villainous wizard; despite knowing
fine well that was all nonsense. Cato was maybe in his late
twenties, a little skinny, perhaps, his short dark hair shining a
little red in the candlelight which from this angle now
outlined his sharp, curious features. Tait blinked, and Cato
gave them a little smirk. Tait, to their slight horror, became
aware they were blushing, and hoped like hell that the
candlelight wasn't enough to show it.

"Also," Cato added, "just yesterday evening I was hearing
all about this terrible demon business from the Teren Lord
Lieutenant, and it seemed like an obvious guess."

"Reb took longer," Tait said, without thinking, then cursed
themself again when Cato's eyes narrowed.

"So you've already been to see Reb, have you? Well. How
about you sit down, and tell me all about it. From the
beginning."

Cato sat back down on the edge of the bed, and Tait looked
around, more than a little off-balance now, for a chair. A
stool shot over from the other side of the room, scattering
floor-detritus in its wake. Tait gasped, and Cato smirked
again. That was a lot of power, and applied in a way Tait
didn't even know how to approach. How did Marek magic
even work?

"Sit down. Tell me a story," Cato said.

Tait sat, slowly, and tried to marshal their thoughts.

"We'll take the 'summoned a demon' bit as read for now,"
Cato said, "though I may want to hear more about that later.
How about after that?"

"I banished it," Tait said, gloomily aware that if Reb hadn't
believed them, Cato was hardly any more likely to.

"You banished it?" Cato repeated.

"I thought I did." Tait stared at their hands. "I suppose... I
did, though. I'm sure of it."

"The Lord Lieutenant says it's still running around out
there." Cato sat back, looking thoughtfully at Tait. "If you
thought you banished it, why did you run away?"

"Because they'd make me do it again." Tait might as well
be honest with Cato now, right? There wasn't much to lose.

"Call a spirit?" Cato said. "Was that a surprise to you?"

"No, but..." Tait struggled for words to explain everything

184

that had happened in Ameten. "I didn't expect what they... I didn't think about it enough beforehand," they said in the end, miserably.

"Hmm." Cato scratched at his chin. "Very well, let's leave that for now. But you said you banished it, and the Lord Lieutenant says it's still out there. That's... interesting."

Tait frowned, and risked looking up. Tait couldn't read Cato's expression.

"But you believe the Lord Lieutenant," Tait half-asked.

"Not necessarily," Cato said. "What did you do after you ran off, then?"

"I thought I'd come to Marek," Tait said. "Because you don't use blood, and you don't use spirits, here."

"Well, there is the cityangel. But you're right that it works differently. Go on."

"I mean, I could still use blood-magic, but..." Tait rubbed at their forearms. "But that's limited. So I wanted to come here, but I – the Academy don't like people to leave. I figured they'd be looking for me. So I went to the mountains. I grew up there, and people there – they wouldn't necessarily turn me over. Maybe. I thought I'd stay there a while, let things die down." That had been a very unpleasant few days, hiking at night and sleeping in the day, constantly terrified that they'd wake to find an Academy sorcerer standing over them. "Then when I got up there, there was this bunch of Marekers, looking to go over the pass to Exuria, with a bunch of trading stuff – huge packs, they looked like travellers – but they'd just found out it was dragon-bear season." Tait rolled their eyes. "Dunno how they'd missed that when they were planning it."

"Ah, the Exuria traders," Cato murmured. "Of course."

"And I thought – Marek. And the cityangel. I hadn't thought of it before, but if I was in Marek, the Academy couldn't send anyone after me. No spirits can come into Marek. And maybe even I'd be able to do sorcery again, if a Marek sorcerer would teach me."

"And you were low on other options," Cato agreed. "Yet you didn't go straight there?"

Tait shrugged. "No money, and you can't get passage down the river for free. I'd have been obvious on the road, and you can't get through the swamp less'n you know it proper. But I said to the Marekers, I'll come with you, keep the dragon-bears off, keep the journey down the river after nice and smooth."

"But you couldn't do magic," Cato said. "What if a dragon-bear attacked? You were just going to let them die?" He'd leant forwards a little. A few locks of hair had fallen forwards over his eyes, and he brushed them back impatiently.

"Blood sorcery," Tait said. "Like I said, I wasn't about to summon another spirit. The Academy would find me, if I did that."

"The academy," Cato repeated. "You've mentioned that a couple of times."

"The Academy of the Court," Tait said. "In Ameten. They teach sorcerers."

"Right. Huh. So you went up into the mountains prepared to open a vein if you met any dragon-bears or fell off any cliffs." He sounded a bit mocking.

"Didn't fall off any cliffs," Tait said. "Did meet a dragon-bear." They knew they sounded defensive.

Cato's eyebrows shot up. "You did? What happened?"

"Like you said. Opened a vein. Translocated it."

Cato's eyes widened. "And you were still upright afterwards? That's a hell of a lot of power to pull from your blood."

"I felt a bit off afterwards," Tait said, with serious understatement. "But we got through. I got through." They'd needed a lot of support from Bracken, but after just saving everyone from a dragon-bear support was readily forthcoming. Though it was just as well there hadn't been another one immediately afterwards.

"Lucky thing they don't hunt in pairs," Cato said.

"How do you know?" Tait demanded. "You're from the mountains?"

"Not a scrap of it," Cato said. "Never left Marek in my life. Never wanted to. Only ever seen a picture of a dragon-bear, which was plenty alarming enough for me. I'm making assumptions from the fact that you're not a blood-drained corpse halfway up a mountain somewhere. So. You fought off a dragon-bear, which, well done," he sounded genuine, "you went to Exuria and back with these Marekers, and then downriver. When did you get here, then?"

"Yesterday," Tait said. "Then, this morning, I asked after sorcerers."

"And they sent you to Reb, of course, because everyone makes horrible faces when they talk about me." Cato sounded pleased. "And Reb... ?"

"She said there's a demon roaming Teren looking for me, and kicked me out," Tait said, suddenly desperate for this to be over. They hadn't the first clue what they would do next, but going over all of this, waiting for Cato to kick them out, was becoming too awful. "She said she wouldn't apprentice me. She didn't think I was telling her the truth."

"And were you?"

"Yes!" Tait said. "But... I don't know. I thought I was. Maybe I was wrong." They took a shaky breath. "I'll go. I'm sorry."

"No!" Tait startled a bit at Cato's vehemence. "Sorry. No. Don't go just yet. So Reb sent you off with a flea in your ear."

"She told me to go back and sort my own mess out."

"Is she going to turn you in?" Cato asked. He frowned. "I wouldn't have thought it of Reb, to be honest."

Tait shook their head. "No. She said not, but... I don't know if she told the truth." They were a little reluctant to accuse Reb of lying – it surely wouldn't endear them to her fellow-sorcerer – but Cato seemed to want all the details.

Cato tilted his head slightly, eyebrows drawing together. "Why not?"

"I got back to my room, and there'd been someone looking for me. The Teren sorcerer, staying at the White Horse. And it was a Teren person, the barman said. But then, I didn't tell Reb where I was staying, and I did tell her my name, so... But I don't understand how else anyone could have known."

"If Reb said she wouldn't tell, she wouldn't tell," Cato said, shaking his head. "Reb drives me absolutely up the wall on a regular basis, but she's honest." He grimaced. "Unpleasantly so, at times. Must have been someone else. One of your Marek trading-expedition, maybe? Deliberately or otherwise, mentioning their Teren sorcerer friend?"

"Maybe," Tait said. "I don't know."

"So what did you do?"

"Left money on the table and went out of the window," Tait said.

"And came to find me," Cato said.

"I didn't know what else to do. You're the only other sorcerer in Marek."

"No longer entirely true, even if we don't count your good self, but I take your point. And so, you want to apprentice to me, do you?"

Tait hunched their shoulders. "I guess you won't have me."

"I don't know," Cato said, frankly. "On the one hand, you are clearly in trouble up to your neck, and I am very nervous indeed about how Beckett will feel about this. On the other hand, it would piss Reb off, which is nearly enough reason to do it all by itself. And, unlike Reb, I think you're telling the truth about what you thought happened, whether or not you screwed it up. Although I'd like to know…" He paused, then shook his head. "Anyway. You can't stay here and not learn Mareker magic, and I'm not that keen to send you back to Teren to choose between slicing yourself up and getting eaten by a demon eventually, regardless of what happens with this particular one. I don't mean to be rude – well, not very rude – but it doesn't sound like your spirit work is up to much, and there's a hard limit on blood-work." He paused, then said, lightly, "That is, if you limit it to your own blood."

"Yes," Tait said, with emphasis. "Reb asked me that too. Yes."

"Well then."

Tait's shoulders sagged. "I could just – not do sorcery," they said. "Here, or in Teren. Just – stop."

"Really?"

Tait looked up, but as far as they could see, Cato's expression was just one of curiosity.

"Do you really think you could give it up?" he asked. "Because I sure as hell couldn't." He snorted. "And I am in a position to be moderately certain of that, though that's a story for another time."

"Maybe," Tait said.

"I suspect not," Cato said. "But you can't do your sort of magic here. Beckett won't stand for it. I work with spirits, sometimes, but… well, not the way you do, let's leave it at that for now." He seemed to be thinking of something else, then shook his head briskly. "Anyway. You want to do magic, you want to stay, that means learning our magic."

"Who's Beckett?" Tait asked. "You've mentioned them twice now."

"The cityangel," Cato said.

Tait blinked. "The cityangel has a name?"

"For about the last two months they do, yes. It's – another story for another time, perhaps." Cato chewed on his lip. "I'm loathe to make a decision without some kind of conversation with them, to be honest, but I kind of hate talking to them…"

"Hello," someone said from behind Tait, and Tait screamed.

"Shit," Cato said. "Tait, it's fine. Probably." He put out a hand, and Tait grabbed onto it, white-knuckled, beyond embarrassment at this point. "Beckett, you arse. What do you think you're doing?"

Someone stepped forwards from just behind Tait's right shoulder, and Tait took another gasp. Cato's hand was warm in theirs, and reassuring. Whoever had just walked in – appeared? Tait hadn't heard the door – was tall, taller than Tait, and slightly angular, and their pale head was smooth. Their expression wasn't human.

"You wanted to speak to me." Their voice wasn't human, either.

"Most people knock," Cato said, sourly.

"I am not people."

"Yes, well. Beckett, this is Tait, a sorcerer from Teren who wishes to learn Mareker magic. Tait, this is Beckett, Marek's cityangel."

☺ ☺

Cato was impressed that Tait hadn't just passed out cold when Beckett appeared. They were clearly in a high state of nerves – understandable, in the circumstances – and it hadn't been very considerate.

But then, being considerate wasn't Beckett's style. It wasn't usually Cato's, either, but – well. Tait was easy on the eye, no question, and Cato was shallow. He found himself liking Tait, too, even if they were far too naïve. Whatever Reb might have thought, Cato was confident Tait wasn't lying about the business with the demon. They believed they'd banished it, and Cato couldn't see how you could make a mistake on the matter. Which raised some interesting questions with regard to what exactly was going on, and whether someone else might be lying instead, and if so, who. Plus, Cato would quite like to know what was going on with this Academy in Ameten, and why Tait had left in such a hurry.

But that could wait. Right now, Beckett was standing in Cato's room, and Tait was staring at the cityangel with their mouth open, looking terrified.

"You wanted to talk to me," Beckett said again.

"Right. Well, Tait wants to learn Mareker magic, and since you are, as it were, the source of Mareker magic," not quite true, it was more like Beckett mediated it, but close enough, "I thought, best not agree to such a thing until I'd asked you about it."

"You did not ask about Jonas."

"You knew Jonas already. And you like him. I figured you wouldn't mind."

Beckett blinked, once, slowly. "Why?"

"Why what?" Cato asked, deliberately obtuse. He wanted to buy as much thinking time as possible, plus Beckett's conversational style irritated him and perhaps if he irritated Beckett back, Beckett might change. Unlikely, but one could hope. As long as he didn't irritate Beckett enough to be cut off, which apparently was a threat Beckett was now willing to make.

"Why does this one wish to learn Mareker magic?" Beckett asked, unperturbed.

"You realise that means working with Beckett, right?" Cato asked Tait. "You might want to reconsider."

It was an exaggeration; before this year, Cato had never once encountered Beckett in person, and even in the last month or two, it didn't happen often. Well. Not all that often. Certainly not most times Cato used magic, thankfully. Cato was optimistic that as the effects of Daril's idiocy wore off, it would happen less often. He could quite happily never see Beckett in person again, as long as the cityangel kept doing their damn job.

Tait swallowed, and kept on looking at Beckett. Well, that showed they were a sorcerer, right enough. Cato was more or less inured to it by now – and went to great lengths to resist the effect – but to sorcerer eyes, Beckett was compelling. It wasn't anything as straightforward as a glow, or something you could put your finger on. The cityangel just – was – magic, and it drew you in.

Tait licked their lips. "I summoned a spirit in Teren. A demon. And I thought – I was sure – I banished it, but someone from Teren says I didn't."

Cato shut his eyes. Granted, Beckett was probably going to work the whole business out anyway, sooner or later, but admitting it up-front might not be the best plan.

"I know," Beckett said.

Right, maybe it had been a good idea, then. Getting caught in a lie was almost always an error.

"But I don't want to be summoning, or bleeding myself, anyway. Even without what the Academy wanted me to do," Tait said. And that was the second mention of this academy and their plans. Cato really needed to follow that up. "Marek magic, everyone talks about it like a, a relationship. That sounds better than what I've been doing in Teren." The words were awkward, but Tait's tone was painfully honest.

"You wish to learn Marek magic," Beckett said.

"But if you don't want me to, if… I'll leave," Tait said. "I know you have to protect the city, and… if I'm bringing a demon here, I'll leave."

"No demon can come here," Beckett said.

"If Tait got rid of the demon," Cato put in, "then either there's no demon coming, and that part's a lie; or someone else has summoned it. Either way. Not really Tait's fault."

Tait looked at him in surprised gratitude. Beckett didn't react. After a moment, they tipped their head to one side, a very human gesture. Beckett had definitely picked some things up during their unplanned stay on the human plane, beyond this sodding irritating habit of turning up in person.

"Yes," they said.

"Yes what?" Cato asked.

"Yes, Tait may learn Marek magic," Beckett said. "But you have an apprentice. Reb needs one. Tait should apprentice to

Reb. I will tell her so." They nodded as if they had come to a decision.

"Please don't," Tait said, urgently. "I mean... Reb didn't want me around. I'd much rather learn from Cato." They turned to Cato. "If you don't mind. If you have time."

Beckett frowned at both of them. "Reb would be better."

"Maybe we don't need to manage this right now," Cato said. "If I might make a suggestion?" He didn't wait for an answer. "How about, I keep an eye on Tait for a few days, without any kind of apprenticeship," and without bothering Reb, "while we work out what this demon business is all about. I think something odd is going on. And if I'm right, Reb's objections evaporate, and all is well." And if there wasn't something odd going on, if Tait was just exceptionally good at flat-out lying, then they'd all find that out instead, and that would resolve the problem in another way.

Cato rather hoped that wouldn't happen. He wouldn't like to feel that he was that bad at reading people.

He really ought to tell Reb what he was up to, given this whole Group business and the discussion they'd had with Selene. But Reb had made her decision about Tait without informing him; and if Cato could get more information, it would be rather easier to discuss it with Reb than if he were just relying on his intuition for someone pulling a fast one. The thing was, the more he thought about it, the more he thought that the person who was pulling a fast one might be Selene. He counted quickly in his head. Two days, he'd promised Reb, before revisiting the decision they'd made about helping Selene. Two days would be up tomorrow, dammit. He'd just have to put Reb off for a bit longer, and hope she wasn't counting herself.

Beckett looked stern. "No demon may enter Marek," they said again.

"I know," Cato said. "Look, you know I always use the proper channels and all that, with spirits. The point is, someone is running round Marek claiming that there is one on its way here, and that interests me. It should interest you, as well, if they're right."

"Very well," Beckett said. "You have three days." They took a step backwards, and vanished.

Cato flopped backwards onto the bed. "Ugh. I hate when

they do that. Appear out of bloody nowhere. They never used to do that." He sat back up again. "Well then. Welcome to Marek magic."

Tait, still looking at the place where Beckett had been, didn't reply. Cato ruthlessly suppressed a slight flare of pique.

"Is – Marek magic involves Beckett?"

"Beckett mediates it," Cato said. "The detail is perhaps something to go into another time, say, tomorrow, because it is late now and I have had enough. But as a rule they don't actually show up in person when you're doing magic, if that's what you're worrying about."

"But I won't be doing magic yet, will I?" Tait said.

Cato raised a shoulder. "We-ll. I said I wouldn't apprentice you. I can probably show you a thing or too, though, without too much trouble, since you're not a total beginner. A little taster, as it were."

Tait's eyes went wide, with hope and apprehension. "But won't Beckett disapprove?"

"Well, if Beckett disapproves then they won't help," Cato said. "But Beckett wants Marek magic to expand, so my guess is we'll get away with it." He looked at Tait and felt an unusual urge to reassure them. "It'll be my responsibility, not yours, if Beckett gets in a flap."

Tait was fiddling with the braid that fell down their back. Cato wondered what their hair was like when they let it down. Cato was suddenly glad that he'd avoided the apprentice thing. He was moderately certain that he shouldn't make a pass at his apprentice, whereas if it was someone he was just, kind of, helping out, it was probably all right. Maybe. At the very least, if he saw Tait doing magic, he'd have a clearer idea of whether making a pass at them would be taking advantage, or whether Tait was competent enough to know what they were about. They had fought off a dragon-bear with blood alone, after all.

"So," Cato said. "Tomorrow, we can see how you go with Mareker magic." Cato himself generally stayed up late, but Tait looked done in. Perhaps not surprising.

He rather expected Tait to get up and go, but they hunched their shoulders slightly, and looked awkward.

"Oh. You've nowhere to go, have you? And someone

might be after you."

That would be, was, really, a perfect opportunity to try something on – Cato's bed was large, plenty of room for two, all that business – except that whether or not Tait was generally competent at such things, they quite clearly weren't right now. Cato wasn't in the business of taking advantage of anyone. He strongly preferred enthusiastic agreement from his bed partners. He could, however, flirt a little, see what happened.

"I'd invite you to stay," Tait's eyes flickered over to his, startled, but, as far as Cato could see, not alarmed. Tait licked their lip, then swallowed, and Cato upgraded that to 'possibly slightly interested'. He grinned, and carried on, "but it's been something of a tiring evening for both of us, and you've had what sounds like a tiring time all round. There's no one in the room next door at the moment, and I've a spare blanket. I can set you up in there."

"The room next door?"

"This is the squats," Cato said. "If the room's free, you can stay in there. Free. That's how it works."

In fact, the room next to Cato's was almost always free, because anyone who moved in moved out again very shortly after realising who they were living next to. Cato found this convenient.

"And it's… safe?" Tait asked.

"We're sorcerers," Cato reminded them. "People worry about being safe from us, not the other way around."

Tait didn't look any less worried.

"If you can tackle a dragon-bear, I wouldn't have thought you'd be bothered about the useless lumps round here," Cato said.

"I'd rather not do blood-magic here."

"Best not," Cato agreed. "Beckett isn't keen." Also, it was illegal, inasmuch as that mattered.

"And I don't know who might be after me or what they can do. I'll be asleep. I can hardly knife anyone in my sleep."

Cato made a mental note that Tait obviously felt that they were competent to knife someone whilst awake, which seemed like it ought to be useful information. "Wards?" he asked, and Tait looked baffled. "Right, well, I'll show you how to do that tomorrow, but I can ward your room myself for tonight. Guaranteed no entry for anyone," except Beckett, probably, but Tait would hardly sleep well if Cato mentioned that, "and very unpleasant consequences for someone foolish enough to try. But, um, remember to come in here in the morning, don't just sod off down the stairs, or it'll set the whole thing off."

Cato saw Tait into the next door room, blankets and all, scattered wards-mixture over the threshold on his way out and set the wards in only a slightly excessively dramatic fashion, and retired to his own room with a sense of having done well and acted in an unprecedentedly noble fashion. Marcia would be proud of him. He made a rude face at the ceiling, and settled down to sleep.

FIFTEEN

Marcia was irritable when she got home, and irritable as she tried to sleep, tossing and turning until exhaustion finally overtook her. She woke sandy-eyed. The sense of something being wrong had chased her through her poorly-remembered dreams, leaving behind only a lingering unspecified discomfort.

She shoved her head into the pillow and scowled down into it. This couldn't just be about arguing with Reb. She'd been in the right. Reb was the one who was over-reacting.

However firmly she told herself that, it didn't shift the thick, sticky feeling in her head.

She rang for her morning infusion – rosehip and liquorice. Griya, her maid, brought it up, together with a warm roll with goat's-butter, eyed Marcia, and evidently decided not to say anything. She drew the curtains and slipped back out of the room.

Marcia poked at the roll. Wheat came from Teren, didn't it? Wheat, barley, cow's-butter, though Marekers tended not to eat that. If Selene did have more in mind than just issuing apparently-friendly invitations; if she, or Teren, wanted to put the screws on... Marcia abandoned that unhelpful line of thought in favour of eating the roll.

From the window-seat, she looked out over the river. Watching the boats go in and out of the river-mouth was always soothing; and it was a pretty morning, with a clear blue sky and a handful of small puffy white clouds. Over near the Old Market, she could see the flapping white dots of laundry-lines out in the sunshine on the house-roofs. Reb didn't do her own laundry, she... Marcia cut the thought off. She wasn't going to think about Reb. She was going to watch the river and the sky, and drink her damn infusion.

She was feeling slightly calmer as she finished the last drops, but almost immediately there was a gentle knock at her door.

"Ser Marcia?" Griya came into the room. "I'm afraid –

your mother wants you, downstairs."

"Right now?" Marcia asked.

It was breakfast time, certainly – proper breakfast, not the roll-and-infusion to start the day – but Madeleine rarely summoned her at this hour.

"There's a visitor," Griya said, apologetically. "From House Pedeli."

A visitor at this time of the morning? That had to mean a business call, not social, but even for business it was very early.

"Right," Marcia said. "House casual, then, I suppose, as quick as we can."

With Griya's aid, she was decent, in tunic and trousers with a dab of facepaint, in relatively short order. Arriving in the front parlour, she blinked as her mother looked up from her armchair and Pedeli-Head got up from the couch to greet her. Not just any visitor. Whatever this was, it was serious enough to bring the Head of a House here at this time in the morning. Worry caught at her stomach.

"Marcia. I am pleased you could join us," Madeleine said. Marcia couldn't catch disapproval in her tone, but that didn't necessarily mean it wasn't there.

"Pedeli-Head," Marcia said politely, bowing to them. "A pleasure."

"A pleasure to be here, on this occasion – no, no, I can't say that it is." Pirran, Pedeli-Head was several years older than Madeleine, and would have retired some time ago under the old arrangements. She wore her greying hair in a long plait, and a long robe over an under-dress and very tight trousers (according to Madeleine, the style had been popular in Pirran's youth) in the orange and red of her House.

"Oh dear," Marcia said, taking the seat perpendicular to both Pirran and her mother. "May I ask what has happened?"

"Betrayal," Pirran said. "Traitorous, backstabbing…" She held a news-sheet between two fingers, and waved it at Marcia with evident distaste. Marcia couldn't see what it said from here. She wondered where Pirran had got it from. The Houses, especially the older members of them, hadn't taken to news-sheets, although they were wildly popular in much of the rest of Marek, and Marcia found the trading-sheets useful.

"And this *nonsense* making it worse." Pirran obviously

meant the news-sheet itself this time. "The Guilds need to *control* this, these unrestricted, we cannot simply allow people to print such things, unlicensed, no oversight…"

"Apparently," Madeleine said smoothly, cutting Pirran off (the matter of independent presses was an ongoing discussion, but was evidently a distraction right now), "the Smiths and Cutlers' Guild declined this morning to fulfil a contract with House Pedeli, unless Pirran – as Pedeli-Head, you understand – gives their support to moves to enhance the status of the Guilds in the Council."

Marcia's stomach flipped. The Guilds had chosen to move on their own? Or was it just the Smiths… but surely the Smiths wouldn't act independently.

"Not only the Smiths," Madeleine continued, answering that question. She gestured at the news-sheet. "The Guilds, as a whole, have announced that they will no longer work with the Houses, no longer fulfil House trading contracts, nor engage in further contracting, until there is a more even distribution of power. Four more seats, they want. Four!"

Not just equal power, but increased power. What were the Guilds thinking? And to make such an absolute move, not asking, not politicking, just… leverage, pure and simple. Threats. How could they think that this naked aggression was wise, compared to the slow but more certain gradual approach? How did they expect the Houses to react? Marcia badly wanted to swear.

"Warden Hagadath told me, after that speech yesterday, the Guilds could tolerate this no longer. They said," Pirran was wildly, visibly indignant, "it is *unfair*, that the Guilds generate Marek's prosperity… Of course the Guilds are important, and they are respected, but trade, I told Hagadath, trade is vital, and the Houses are the engines of trade. It is we who negotiate, we who risk our funds, it is we who represent Marek to the wider world. And they *have* Council seats. Is this not sufficient for them?"

"Without the Guilds, we would have nothing to trade," Marcia said, as her stomach churned. "And the Houses regularly ignore and overrule them, in Council." There seemed to be no point in siding with Pirran at this point. She might as well set her own cart out, rather than nodding in pretend agreement to smooth the waters. But what were the

Guilds *thinking*?

And had any of them implicated Marcia herself in this?

"So I understand you to believe, from Berenaz-Head," Pirran said, turning on her.

Oh shit.

Madeleine glared at Marcia, then turned to Pirran. "I assume, Pirran, that you are not suggesting that House Fereno has encouraged any such behaviour as this from the Guilds."

"Encourage the Guilds to breach contracts? I most certainly have not," Marcia said.

"Not that, not that, perhaps not, but you have suggested an increase in their power. Without that, would they have even thought of this?" Pirran's face was dark.

"The Guilds are able to think independently," Marcia said, as calmly as she could. "And if you seek people to blame, I suggest you consider the speech that the Lord Lieutenant made, yesterday. Is it appropriate for Teren to be intervening in Marek affairs?"

"There was no *intervention*," Pirran said. "I cannot see how one could read anything untoward into the Lord Lieutenant's words."

And Marcia couldn't suggest that Selene might have been intervening rather more than that without getting back into what she herself had been doing. She bit the inside of her cheek savagely.

"Of course, we cannot give into this nonsense," Pirran continued. "I trust that, despite your Heir's efforts, Madeleine, House Fereno will act in concert with the rest of the Houses."

"Of course," Madeleine said, and Marcia swore internally. "We cannot bend to such tactics."

If they weren't going to 'bend' to the Guilds' demands, what were they going to do instead? Wait them out? Who could wait longer, between Guilds and Houses? Marcia wasn't at all sure that it was the Houses. If the Salinas didn't get the contracts they wanted from the Houses; well, they might wait for a while, not wishing to embroil themselves in their clients' political struggles, but if it began impacting on their own trade, they wouldn't hesitate to go to the Guilds, would they? Where would the Houses be then?

But there was no point in saying any of that, at this

juncture. She might be able to talk to Madeleine, afterwards, maybe, but not to Pirran right now.

Once Pirran had finally gone, with a final glare at Marcia, Madeleine folded her hands and turned to Marcia, her eyes hard.

"And what is your part in this?" she asked. "When we spoke before, we talked about *patience*, Marcia. This does not look to me like patience. Being embarrassed in front of the other Houses is not acceptable."

"I assure you, this is not my doing," Marcia said, which was true. This wasn't at all how she'd wanted things to pan out. "I have spoken to the Guilds, yes, but I too have been urging patience. I did not expect this."

"The reputation of our House is paramount. I should not need to *say* this to you, Marcia. What did you say to Berenaz-Head?"

"It was Berenaz-Heir," Marcia said. "Piath. I said nothing like this. I broached the idea of the Guilds having more say, and Piath was unconvinced."

"I cannot understand what you intended to *achieve* with this lack of subtlety," Madeleine snapped. "Surely you know better?"

"I was under the impression that Piath would be sympathetic." Marcia paused, frowning. "And I certainly didn't expect them to be gossiping with Pirran."

"If your impressions are that badly out, you should not be embarking on this kind of politics." The words cut.

"Someone else had been talking to Piath," Marcia told her, slightly reluctantly. She wasn't sure how open Madeleine would be to hearing that. "Before I got there."

"Being unaware that someone is acting against you does not improve my opinion of your skills." She paused. "Although – you are correct that if Berenaz and Pedeli are on speaking terms again, it is worth noting."

She eyed Marcia for a long moment, visibly weighing up her options. Then she sighed, and looked away.

"Well. Whether or not this was what you planned, I suggest you speak to your Guild contacts. This could be disastrous for Marek, if we do not resolve it – and I cannot imagine that the other Houses will be inclined to co-operate with such high-handed behaviour."

The *other* Houses? Did that mean that she might be able to persuade Madeleine to co-operate, despite what she'd said to Pirran? Best not ask just yet. If she could talk the Guilds into backing down, into seeking other routes to a solution…

"With your permission, Mother," she said, bowing, and retreated from the room.

⊙ ⊙

In the hall, Marcia hesitated, looking down at herself. Her House tunic would send one message, if she went out in it; but right now, she didn't think that she wanted to be Marcia, Fereno-Heir. Not that Warden Ilana didn't know exactly who she was, but it was a matter of signals.

And if she wanted to give Ilana another indication that she was keen to resolve this problem, she would do better to ask for a meeting, not just arrive on the doorstep of the Jewellers' Guild demanding one. She went to the ironwood table in the hall, its delicate curlicues testament to the patient artistry of the Woodworkers' Guild; ironwood was notoriously difficult to carve. Paper and pen waited on top, the old style of dip pen rather than the new model that Marcia preferred. Marcia wrote a quick note, sealed it with her personal ring rather than her House one, and handed it to the footman who was on duty in the Hall.

"Get a messenger for this, please?"

Upstairs, Griya was still in her room, tidying. She looked tense; everyone in the House would be picking up Madeleine's mood. Marcia changed from House wear into a tunic and trousers in a light rose, with a leaf pattern embroidered around the edges, then went downstairs to her study to await Ilana's reply. A footman intercepted her on her way down the stairs with a reply to her message. That was sufficiently fast that Warden Ilana must have been expecting the request. It said simply that if Marcia were free this morning, Ilana would be at her disposal.

It was still a clear morning, with white puffs of cloud sailing high over the city, but Marcia was not in the mood to appreciate it. Walking down the Hill towards the Jewellers' Guildhouse, she tried to rehearse her arguments, but everything kept jumbling together. She took a long, deep, breath. She knew what she was doing. She knew Ilana. She would just have to play it by ear; and she was more than competent to do so.

She hoped.

This time, she was shown straight in to Warden Ilana's workroom: a well-appointed space with Ilana's worktable by the large window, and two armchairs by the fireplace on the other side of the room. The floor was bare other than a large rug underneath the armchairs; jewellery work didn't mix well with fine furnishings.

Ilana wasn't wearing their cloak, and their shirt and trousers were thick brown linen, with the marks of their profession across them, scars and stains from metalworking.

"Please excuse my appearance," Ilana said, as Marcia entered the room. "Today is a working day for me, you understand, but it seemed that you would prefer to meet now, informally, than to wait for a meeting room and fine clothes."

"Indeed," Marcia said, doing her best to smile. Of course Ilana knew exactly why she was here.

Ilana gestured for her to be seated, and took a kettle off the fire to pour an infusion into two cups. Greenleaf, from the smell of it. They sat down and looked inquiringly at Marcia. Ilana might know why Marcia was there, but she was going to make Marcia start the conversation.

There was no point in beating around the bush. "I thought," *you said*, "the Guilds wouldn't move on their own yet."

Ilana sighed. "Well. The Lord Lieutenant's speech was – not helpful. I was not there, of course, but from the telling of it, the Guilds were excluded entirely. They, we… did not take kindly to that."

Marcia hadn't bitten her fingernails since childhood. She was not about to start again now.

"But such a rapid response?" Marcia said.

Ilana paused, choosing their words. "The problem with having raised the matter, beforehand, you understand, is that the Guilds have begun to… think more clearly, about what we can do. About whether the Houses are, to put it bluntly, needed."

"We have the trade relationships," Marcia said. "We can pack ships efficiently in a way that the Guilds alone would struggle to do. We all do best when we work together, each to their own strengths."

Ilana shrugged one shoulder. "Perhaps. But then, perhaps we could learn these House skills for ourselves, and deal directly with the Salinas."

"The Salinas have relationships with the Houses, and the Houses with the Guilds," Marcia said. "That's far more effective for all involved. The Salinas need to come and go rapidly; would you have them sit around and haggle with each Guild, one by one? Duplicate all of that effort?" By that argument, of course, the Houses too duplicated effort, thirteen of them working separately. Marcia wasn't about to mention that. And there were more Guilds than there were Houses.

"Indeed, I do not downplay the work of the Houses," Ilana said. "But these positive relationships are *mutual*. Without the Guilds, the Houses have little to trade. Teren produce. Some food from Exuria. So if the Houses wish to ignore the Guilds, and to turn instead to Teren... Well. Perhaps the Guilds feel that the Houses should realise what they stand to lose, if they ignore the dissatisfaction of the Guilds."

"The Houses don't wish to turn to Teren," Marcia said. She wished she could say that they didn't wish to ignore the dissatisfaction of the Guilds.

"We did not hear any great clamour against the Lieutenant's speech," Ilana said.

"No, because..." Marcia stopped, frustrated. "Marek is still part of Teren, isn't it?"

Ilana pursed their lips, and didn't say anything. Marcia stared at them. Both of them heard what wasn't being said.

"The Houses are not about to share power with the Guilds," Ilana said. "We both know that."

"I am *trying*..." Marcia started, frustrated beyond bearing, then stopped, and winced.

"You are *trying*," Ilana said, voice calm. "And not succeeding. We both know how little the other Houses are interested. And – I apologise for being blunt – but you are Heir, not Head. You cannot even carry your own House's vote by yourself."

Marcia didn't say anything. There was nothing there she could deny. She felt sick, and the smell coming off the greenleaf infusion wasn't helping. Carefully, she set the little cup down.

"If the Houses wish to make their allegiances clear, then they can do so," Ilana said. Their shoulders had gone back, and they set down their own cup. "Until then – the Guilds' allegiance is to Marek. Not to Teren, and not to the Houses. We are the engine of Marek's prosperity, and we are no longer prepared to sit at the foot of the table and accept scraps." Ilana's normally calm voice had an undercurrent of anger.

"I see," Marcia said. This wasn't just going to blow over, was it? There wasn't anything she could say, any perfect words, to resolve this situation. All her careful planning, all her thoughts about how to move gradually, slowly, encouraging both Guilds and Houses towards a more equal future... all so much scrap.

"I say this informally, you understand, in the light of our strong working relationship," Ilana said, leaning forwards just a little. "Which I would be very sorry to lose. We would far rather continue to work together. We would welcome any positive approach from the Houses. Informal," they made a small gesture between themself and Marcia, "or, in due course, formal."

Marcia seized onto that tiny hope. Could she, Marcia, manage to broker a peace between Guilds and Houses now? Because either someone did that right now, or Marek was going to suffer for it. Ilana gave no indication that the Guilds were about to back down. And Marcia knew all too well how stubborn the Houses could be. Of course, it was in Ilana's interest not to indicate that the Guilds might back down... but when it came down to it, Ilana was right. The Houses had the most to lose.

"Formal, or informal," she said, almost at random. "So if I were wearing House-formal now... ?"

"Then I would be putting this in much more circuitous, perhaps more politic, terms," Ilana said. Marcia's eyebrows went up. That news-sheet had been neither circuitous nor politic. "But the message would be the same. The Houses must make decisions about their own allegiances."

If it came right down to it, if neither Houses nor Guilds would back down, the Guilds would win, in the end.

Eventually. But it would come at a cost to everyone. Houses, Guilds, the rest of Marek. All the people that Cato kept telling her about. Reb's neighbours. Those in the squats.

The Houses wouldn't back down unless someone made them. But if the Guilds were acting together, it would take only two House votes to make the changes they wanted. What would the cost be, if she brokered that? To Marek? To her House? What was the risk of the other Houses going against the outcome of the vote, if it was that close? The Houses acting against a Council vote would be even worse than the current situation.

And where could she get a second vote? Never mind a second vote – her chances of convincing Madeleine about Fereno's vote were slim, when the Guilds were acting this way.

But if she didn't try... what then?

Marcia swallowed. She couldn't think of anything else to say. She took a long breath, and rose from her chair.

"I thank you for your time, Warden Ilana," she said formally, with a fractional bow. "And for receiving me in this thoughtful manner, allowing us to have such a frank exchange of opinions." She meant it, mostly, although she saw Ilana's smile twist, just a little, at the edge of sarcasm that Marcia couldn't quite keep out of her voice. "I will... do my best, to help the Houses and the Guilds resolve this calmly, and quickly."

"I look forward to speaking again," Ilana said.

Marcia walked out of the Guild and into the sunshine without seeing any of the beautiful decor of the Jewellers' Hall.

What the hell was she going to do next?

SIXTEEN

Cato had the vague intention, the morning after Tait's arrival, of showing Tait straight away how to set up a ward. It sounded like protection should be high up their agenda. Not that he had any idea how to go about *teaching* that. Jonas wasn't anywhere close to that stage, so he hadn't thought about it. Maybe Tait wouldn't be capable of it yet either; although maybe their experience with Teren magic would help. Wouldn't it?

Ugh; maybe Beckett made a good point when they suggested that one apprentice was enough to be going on with. He scrubbed his hands over his eyes and wished, quite fervently, that he'd made notes when he was sixteen and learning magic by himself in his room. He remembered the doggedness of trying things, over and again. He remembered ploughing through every book he could get his hands on. Some of his less savoury work contacts, people he still did jobs for from time to time, or who did jobs for him, dated from when he was trying to find ways to teach himself magic that didn't involve apprenticing. No one reputable – sorcerer or otherwise – had been willing to help the teenage scion of House Fereno.

Once he'd been disowned, that had stopped being a problem; but by then he'd been too convinced of his own ability to submit to an apprenticeship. And too much in need of cash, come to that. He'd learnt things from other sorcerers over the years, one way and another. He'd certainly learnt a lot from catastrophically screwing up. But he didn't have much experience of direct teaching as a student, and now he had to work it out as a teacher.

Well. He had plenty of time for Jonas, given how long it was taking Jonas to get past whatever weird hangups he had about magic. As for Tait; well, if Cato had managed, surely Tait could too. They would have an actual sorcerer to copy, standing right in front of them; surely it would be easier than making everything up from scratch.

He rubbed at his eyes, and considered the wisdom of getting up and having something to eat. And an infusion. Something stimulating.

There was a cautious knock on his door, and he sat up. The wards hadn't so much as shivered, which meant it had to be Marcia, Jonas, or Tait. He hadn't heard anyone on the stairs, so it wasn't Jonas, who was amazingly loud when walking for someone who could climb the way he did; and no one was swearing through the door at him yet, so it wasn't Marcia.

Tait. He concentrated and waved a hand, and the door swung open. Tait stood there, blinking at him, and still wearing the same clothes as yesterday, even more rumpled now.

"Come on in."

Cato observed with satisfaction that Tait's gaze fell to his bare chest before coming back up to his face. Tait looked a little pink. Cato and Marcia were both naturally flat-chested, which was a slight annoyance to Marcia and a major relief to Cato. That, together with the apothecary's medicine he took weekly, meant that he hadn't needed any of the more complicated options that some folk used to alter their bodies. He'd tried, once, to use magic, and only succeeded in once again proving that magic couldn't permanently affect matter. Still. He was happy enough with his body; and no one else who'd encountered it close-up seemed to have any issues with it either.

"Good morning," Tait said, and shifted their weight from foot to foot, looking anxious. "Is there… anywhere to wash, here?"

Something clicked over in Cato's brain, and he realised why Tait was still wearing yesterday's clothes. Polite manners would have him find a circuitous way to assess whether he was correct, but polite manners could go jump.

"Do you have any other clean clothes?" Cato asked.

Tait's jaw clenched, then they took a deep breath and put their chin up. "No. I didn't come away with much, and the journey across the mountains was hard on what I did have. I was going to make arrangements at the inn, but…"

"Does what's in your bag need cleaning, or turning into rags?" Cato asked.

"Cleaning," Tait said. Their cheeks were flushed with embarrassment.

"Right," Cato said. "Well then. How about the first order of the day is, we visit the baths. My treat." The warding-lesson could wait, if Cato stuck with Tait to keep an eye on them.

"I can pay my way," Tait said, looking mutinous.

"No doubt," Cato said. "But I said I'd help you out, and I would appreciate it if you'd let that include helping you settle into Marek. Which I imagine will be easier if you feel you and your clothes are clean." He shrugged, offhand. "You'd be doing me a favour, any rate. I prefer company for the baths."

The last was a total lie, but apparently Tait believed it, because the crease between their eyebrows flattened out, and they smiled, just slightly. Cato felt the smile like a personal victory.

"They wash clothes, there, too?"

"Can do," Cato said. "You'll have to leave them there long enough to dry, so you're welcome to borrow something of mine to walk back here in. Won't quite fit," Tait had a good few inches of height on Cato, "but it'll keep you decent." He bit back on the instinct to say that'd be a shame; he didn't want to be making a pass at Tait first thing in the morning. Or at any time when they were so obviously not feeling comfortable.

Which was another good reason to make sure Tait did feel comfortable.

The baths for the squats were a street or two away from where Cato lived, closer to the river than his room was. The baths were right in the middle of the squats area, and used by everyone; there was a semi-official truce in place there, both to deal with grudges, and so that the less law-abiding squat-dwellers didn't harass the more law-abiding. Cato explained a little of this as they walked over.

"Less law-abiding," Tait said. They didn't look surprised.

Cato shrugged. "I'd say, don't wander round here on your own if you don't know where you're going, but you've been seen with me now so you're probably fine." He thought about it. "But maybe still don't wander round on your own if you don't know where you're going."

Tait pursed their lips. "I can cope well enough with

Ameten. I'm sure I'll be fine." They glanced at Cato. "You choose to live in the less law-abiding area, then?"

"Well," Cato said, shrugging a shoulder. "I have been described as having a flexible morality. Personally I think that the flexibility of my morality is less relevant than some of my other flexibilities," ha, Tait was blushing again, excellent, "but I suppose it's true enough. I am motivated largely by whether or not someone will pay me."

And earlier this year that had led him into slightly darker waters than, it turned out, he really wanted to swim, but he wasn't about to tell Tait about that. Cato wasn't normally embarrassed by anything he did, more or less as a point of principle, but on this particular occasion... Well, it had all worked out fine in the end.

"Right," Tait said, looking uncomfortable.

"But in fact at present I'm mostly on the legit side of things," Cato surprised himself by saying. It was true enough, though he hadn't previously thought about it in those terms. *Mostly* true. Semi-legit, at least. "What with one thing and another."

Tait glanced over at him, and Cato saw their eyes narrow slightly. Cato had the unfamiliar experience of someone assessing him, and possibly even seeing through him. Marcia could, sometimes, but all too often she just saw her sibling, not Cato in his entirety.

He tried to tell himself that his heart wasn't beating a little faster because of it.

Tait looked away again. "Well. I suppose I will hope that my guide to Marek and its magic won't be taken away by the Guard any time soon."

"Hah. The Guard don't make it into the squats," Cato scoffed. "And nor would they touch a sorcerer. But I take your point."

They reached the baths, and Cato paid the penny each for entry and a towel. He led Tait along the sunken path at the side of the big main room, to the changing cubicles and the counter where Tait could hand over their clothes.

"To wash, please," Cato said to the attendant. "And these as well." He gave the attendant the small bundle of Tait's other clothes.

"Need another penny for that lot," the attendant said,

sourly. Cato sighed and paid it.

Tait looked uncomfortable as they went back through to the main room, wrapped in a towel. Were they body-conscious? Come to that, Cato didn't know anything about the way that people did these things in Teren.

"I can pay you back," Tait said, abruptly, stopping at the side of the room.

Ah, the money. "Not to worry," Cato said. "As I said before, I'm more than happy to assist a visitor. It all balances out in the end, I find." And favours networks were worth a great deal more than a penny here and there. "Come on. Steam room is this way."

The concrete floor was rough underfoot, but the walls had been whitewashed recently, and the baths looked clean, if basic, which Cato was pleased about. He felt the odd need to show Marek at its best to Tait. They walked between the large warm pool on one side, with a couple of massage tables at the side of it, and the smaller hot and cold pools on the other side.

Cato looked sideways at Tait, and saw a small smile tugging at the edge of their mouth. "Do you like for people to owe you favours, then?"

Cato twitched, then found himself barking a startled laugh. "You see it that way too, then? Well. Yes, I suppose I do."

"Favours can come in useful," Tait said, and flashed him a look that Cato had a hard time not interpreting as flirtatious.

Huh. Well now.

Cato stopped to scrub down under the cold showers – he hated this bit, but it was required, and removing the surface dirt before you started did make sense – and Tait followed suit without apparent concern. Not body-conscious, then; and nor, thought Cato, glancing surreptitiously sideways while Tait wasn't looking, did they need to be, in Cato's considered opinion. Cato ducked out from the shower, opened the door to the steam room, gesturing Tait inside, then sat down next to them on one of the upper benches. Someone lower down leant over to ladle water onto the coals. The steam hissed through the room, and a moment later, the wave of heat hit. Tait sat back and rested their head against the wall, shutting their eyes.

"You have these in Teren, then?"

"Yes, of course," Tait said. "I haven't... it's been a while."

The room wasn't empty, although it wasn't heaving-full either, so Cato didn't enquire further. Cato definitely wanted to hear what Tait had been up to lately; he had a number of questions based on what they'd let slip so far. But people did get excited if they heard you talking about demons, and Tait's story clearly contained at least one of those and possibly more. Another time.

As a rule, Cato liked to talk. But with Tait, he found himself settling into a companionable silence, as they steamed, plunged themselves into the cold pool, and then settled for a soak in the warm pool, getting busier now as mid-morning arrived. It was... nice.

It was possible that Cato needed to watch out for this one. In a good way. Probably.

☺ ☺

Reb had used one of her own sleep charms after Marcia left the night before. It worked well enough, but a sleep charm always left her feeling sluggish the next day. Less, perhaps, than if she'd lain awake all night going over the argument in her head; but enough that she slept late, and then didn't feel much like dealing with orders when she awoke.

It was the aftermath of the sleep charm, definitely, and nothing to do with what she and Marcia had said to one another. Marcia had been in the wrong. That was all there was to it.

Instead of starting work, she took herself over to the infusion-salon a couple of streets east. First, reluctantly, she wrote a note to Cato about the Teren sorcerer, and found a messenger to deliver it. She could hardly criticise him for keeping information from her about Jonas and then do the same to him; and if the Teren had found her, they might very well keep looking and find Cato.

She'd been a Teren sorcerer, once. She'd come here, and Zareth had taken her on, and once he'd made her promise to stop using blood magic, he'd never asked again about her history. Zareth hadn't turned her away.

She hadn't raised a demon and then run away from it. It

wasn't the same at all.

Thinking about Teren reminded her that she and Cato had been supposed to revisit their decision about helping the Lord Lieutenant. She should have arranged to meet to discuss that, in the note. Or go over there, or…

Ugh. She felt exhausted, her feet almost dragging as she walked, just thinking about another argument with Cato. And she'd let the sorcerer go, hadn't she? What did she think they should do? Maybe she should just… let it lie. Cato was hardly going to come chasing her over it, was he? One runaway Teren sorcerer. It wasn't worth hassling anyone about. She just wanted a *rest*.

The bell over the salon door tinkled as she went in, and the owner, Irin, looked up and smiled. She had a jaunty red ribbon bound through her dark plaits today, matching the red flowers of her skirts and her red under-trousers.

"Well now Ser Reb, it's a while since I've seen you. How are you today?"

"Well enough," Reb said, returning the smile as best she could. It wasn't Irin's fault she was in a bad mood.

"Something cheering for you this morning?" Irin suggested. Perhaps the smile hadn't been all that convincing. "Take a seat, take a seat." Irin turned to look over the wall of jars behind the counter.

Only two of the wooden tables were occupied, one by a couple who were talking in low voices, holding hands across the table, the other by a woman reading a news-sheet and eating a pastry. The sea-mural that Irin's daughter had spent weeks painting on the back wall was finally finished now, with cheerful fish swimming around fat underwater corals. Reb sat down in the corner farthest from anyone else, next to a pink octopus.

As she sat down, the large type at the top of the woman's news-sheet caught her eye. GUILD ULTIMATUM, it screamed in two-inch letters. Reb frowned. Guilds… Hadn't Marcia been dealing with the Guilds?

"Here you are," Irin said, placing a large cup on the table in front of her. "Rose and ginseng. Calming and revitalising." She nodded firmly.

"Thank you," Reb said, and hesitated. "Uh. Have you any of the news-sheets in, or just the one she's reading there?"

"I'm done with this one," the woman across the room said, draining her infusion and standing up. "Here, if you like." She tossed it onto the table in front of Reb.

"And I've the Clarion, too, if you prefer something calmer," Irin said, handing her another one, with much more restrained type, from behind the counter.

"Thanks," Reb said, feeling more self-conscious than the interaction warranted. She rarely bothered with news-sheets. She heard news from messengers, and in the Old Market when she shopped there. News-sheets were unreliable, and Reb was certain they intended more to entertain than to inform, but...

But she wanted to know what this business with the Guilds was about, and she didn't want to discuss it with Irin or anyone else until she knew more, because something in her stomach was warning her about it.

She scanned through the news-sheets, both the overexcitable Lantern and the more sedate Clarion. They tackled the story from different angles and with varying approaches to exclamation marks and capitalisation, but the kernel of both was the same: the Guilds were withdrawing all co-operation with the Houses until they had equal Council voting power.

Reb bit her lip. Storm and fire. Surely this was bad news for Marcia. She'd been after improving the Guilds' position, hadn't she? But she'd been talking about it taking a while, about talking people around; and it hadn't been going quite as planned, maybe? For the first time, Reb regretted not paying closer attention to Marcia's political concerns.

The thing was; Reb couldn't see how the Guilds threatening the Houses would help matters any. The Houses were intransigent at the best of times; they'd just dig in their heels. And maybe blame Marcia for stirring things up.

They might even be right to blame her. And it could have disastrous effects for the rest of Marek if neither Guilds nor Houses backed down. Even Reb, who didn't spend much time thinking about politics or trade, could see that. How was Marcia doing – what was she doing – this morning?

Reb scowled down at the table. It wasn't her business, either way. Marcia had been the one who stormed out, last night. It wasn't Reb's problem, and she wasn't going to think about it. She could hardly help a Marekhill problem with sorcery, anyway; and this was, when it came down to it, a Marekhill problem, even if its effects might spread to the rest of the city, not that Guilds nor Houses would likely even notice that. This wasn't Reb's problem to fix.

Her eyes kept going back to the news-sheets. Irritably, she gathered them up and dumped them onto the counter, then went back to sit down and drink her refreshing, cheering, rose and ginseng infusion. It wasn't working.

If she wasn't going to think about Marcia and her problems, and she wasn't going to think about that damn Teren sorcerer, what *was* she going to do today? She had orders, but none of them urgent. She ought to go back to that map and look again for an apprentice. It was the right thing to do, as well as what Beckett wanted. She'd been putting it off for too long.

She was hardly in the mood to encourage someone to apprentice. More likely that she'd scare them off. Better to leave it 'til another day. Tomorrow. Tomorrow would be fine. She found herself nibbling at her thumbnail, and swore under her breath. She'd broken herself of that habit years ago.

She finished off her infusion, and rose to go. She wasn't doing any good sitting here, and she had those orders to get done. They might not be urgent, but they were work, and she should get on with them.

"Ah, Ser Reb," Irin said, sounding nervous. "I wondered... my daughter, you see. She's had the worst of luck lately. I wondered, could you... ?"

"A luck charm?" Reb said. "Of course. I'll have it to you later today."

The flood of relief was overwhelming. Luck charms were reassuringly complicated. She'd have to concentrate properly. No time to think about anything else.

It wasn't an excuse, she told herself as she walked back to her house with a lock of hair from Irin's daughter in her pocket, running mentally through the list of ingredients for the charm. It wasn't an excuse at all.

SEVENTEEN

Daril hadn't expected that being named Heir would reduce the amount of time he spent arguing with his father; which was fortunate, because it hadn't done in the slightest.

"What do you expect me to do, Father?" he demanded.

"I expect you to turn up to things looking respectable, and to keep your mouth shut," Gavin retorted.

"Well, I suppose your expectations are doomed to failure," Daril said.

He stalked over to the window of his father's study, clenching his teeth together in an attempt not to say things he would later regret. It had been an excellent deal, and having Gavin refuse it right in the middle of the final meeting with the apothecaries – except they weren't Apothecaries, that was the whole point of this – was infuriating.

Outside, the river was glittering in the sun. Daril found this unduly annoying.

"I am Heir," he said, without turning round. "I will give my opinion."

"And when it is not requested?"

"I am *Heir*, Father," Daril said. "It is my responsibility to do what I believe is best for the House. Which is not necessarily what you believe is best for the House."

"And I can overrule you," Gavin said.

Daril turned round. "That is true. Alternatively, we could discuss things like adults, rather than sniping at one another in front of trading partners."

"I should never have confirmed you," Gavin muttered. "That wretched Fereno girl."

Daril bit back the impulse to agree with him. He'd wanted this. He had to keep reminding himself of that at intervals.

"The deal would have been good for both us and the Salinas," he said, instead. "And it would avoid the problem with the Guilds." Which, admittedly, had arisen only after Daril had made the deal, but it had been a definite bonus.

Gavin waved an irritable hand. "That won't last. They'll

fold soon enough, when they realise that the Houses won't budge."

Daril was far from certain that Gavin was correct, but he didn't want to be drawn into a side argument. "In any case, there was no need to repudiate it so bluntly if you did not care for it. Or to wait until they were *here* to do so."

"We do not trade in medicines," Gavin said.

"Well, we should. They're profitable. And small."

"We do not have a reputation for that sort of trading."

"Then we can get one."

Gavin didn't mean 'medicines'. He meant recreational substances. Not the banned ones; those were rarely worth it. But there was plenty that weren't banned, or that were banned only in some places. Daril had spent quite some time running the figures and finding the correct captain with the correct route that would make this endeavour both safe and profitable. One had to run the ports in the correct order, to avoid ever having a banned substance in the hold at any given location. It had been an interesting puzzle and it would have been a very profitable one, until Gavin had refused it. In public. Daril's shoulders tensed again in furious resentment.

"Father, you've been happy to trade in wine, in the past," he said instead. Exploding at Gavin wouldn't do any good. It was – just – still possible that he might talk Gavin around, and if he gave the not-apothecaries an extra couple of points on the cargo, to make up for the insult, it could still be worth it. "Consider this in the same light."

Gavin scowled at him. "And if they are confiscated?"

Daril let a little of his irritation show. "As I said. I calculated the route very carefully. At no point would we be trading, at any given port, in something that might be confiscated there."

"We might not. What if the captain decides to, on their own account? Once part of a cargo is confiscated, what of the rest of it? What of the ship?"

"We write that into the contract, Father, if you're concerned," Daril said, trying to keep a rein on his patience. As if any Salinas captain worth their salt would do anything that risky, and it would cost another point to get them to sign a contract that suggested they would. And Gavin had been doing this for *decades*. He knew that as well as Daril did.

"Truly. This is a splendid opportunity."

One which he couldn't access without Gavin's signature. As Heir, he had automatic responsibilities, but no automatic rights. Gavin might choose to give him trading rights under his own seal, but so far Gavin had done no such thing. The limitations chafed.

"No," Gavin said, with finality.

"What?"

"I said, no. I will not sign this deal."

"Father, I've already made the arrangements!"

"Then unmake them. I do not approve, and I will not sign. As I said in the meeting. And another time, perhaps that will teach you not to go so far without consulting me."

"Father…"

"You are dismissed, Leandra-Heir."

The old man turned away, back to the pile of papers on his desk. Daril stood where he was for a moment longer, but Gavin gave no further indication that he was aware of Daril's presence. Daril seriously considered making an almighty scene – that pretty inkwell there would smash most beautifully – but what would that achieve? His father would only believe him even less capable.

Fuming, he turned on his heel and stalked out.

Unwinding the half-finished trade would be embarrassing, and infuriating – the profit margin was significant. More infuriating – more embarrassing, if he admitted it – was that he'd thought his father would be impressed by this. He'd envisaged some kind of rapprochement with the wretched old man.

Well. So much for that. He'd have to take back his word, and if he didn't want to risk being blacklisted altogether by this captain, he'd better find something else to fill the cargo space. Jewellery, probably; nearly anything else would be too bulky. And jewellery made a lousy profit in Exuria, the first and most lucrative stop in Daril's plan, and doubtless even more so now bloody Marcia had been shipping the stuff over the mountains instead of round by sea.

And right now he couldn't even arrange anything with the Jewellers' Guild, because the Guilds weren't speaking to the Houses. He'd been congratulating himself that this trade would be unaffected by the political ructions. All ruined. All of it.

"Demonfire," he said aloud, with force, and startled a squeak from the maid who appeared around the corner with her arms full of sheets.

He reached his own rooms, slammed the door behind him, and threw himself down on the window seat. Bloody Marcia had been doing her own damn deals – that mountain trip – and apparently doing quite well at them. Whereas he was blocked at every turn.

He frowned, tapping his thumb against his chin. Marcia. And the Jewellers' Guild. There was that conversation they'd had the other day, her and Nisha and Adan, about allowing the Guilds more power in the Council. And then the Guilds had taken it into their heads to attempt to insist. Ha. Serve Marcia right for giving them ideas.

Although...

The trouble was, Marcia, and the Guilds, were right. Marek prospered when the Houses and the Guilds worked together. And that ghastly Teren Lieutenant, telling them to align themselves more with Teren. Daril had less than no desire to do anything of the sort. But without the Guilds, what might the Houses be pushed to? Gavin, over breakfast, had been reminiscing about a summer he'd spent in Ameten in his youth. If Daril didn't watch out, he'd be off upriver to Ameten within the week himself, protestations ignored.

But if the Guilds and the Houses came back together – could be shoved back together, maybe – it would put a spoke in Selene's wheel. And Marcia must already be up to her eyebrows in attempts to arrange that. Perhaps he could, after all, contact her again.

At the very least, it would really annoy his father. Right now, that was more than sufficient motivation.

☺ ☺

Daril had been in House Fereno often enough, over the years, for this and that formal function. Yet it still felt odd to walk up the steps; to ask the servant who answered the door whether Fereno-Heir was available for a brief discussion; to be shown into the reception room. Thankfully it was empty, giving him a moment to pull himself together.

He was Daril Leandra-Heir. He did not get emotional over a visit to a House.

It would have been better manners to message Marcia first, but after that meeting with Gavin he couldn't settle, and the idea of *doing* something was just too appealing. It was fine. Marcia could decline if she didn't feel like seeing him.

The reception room was pleasant, decorated in House Fereno's pale blue and grey. Daril considered sitting down on one of the couches towards the far end of the room, but he'd be at a disadvantage if Marcia came straight in, and if she wasn't available, he'd look foolish when he had to stand up and leave. So he stood, instead, by the window, looking out over the corner of Marekhill and down over the edge of the cliff to the river and trying not to be annoyed that Fereno had a better view than Leandra.

"Leandra-Heir."

He swung round to face Marcia.

"Fereno-Heir."

She came towards him, holding out a hand for him to shake. That felt odd too, but he did it anyway and hoped he was carrying it off.

"Perhaps we could stick to Marcia and Daril?" she suggested. "What with one thing and another..."

Formality between them, at this point, did seem a trifle foolish.

"By all means," he said. "Marcia."

"Please, do sit down," she said, leading the way to the pale blue couches.

He pushed away any thoughts of what had happened earlier in the year, and whether that might be contributing to his discomfort. Instead, he sat down on the couch at right angles to hers, and realised that he hadn't actually prepared what he was to say.

"So," she said, after a moment where neither of them spoke. "I assume you're here for a reason?" She sounded cautious, beneath her calm exterior, which was reassuring.

For pity's sake, though. He was acting like a tongue-tied child.

"Your political proposals," he said, abruptly. If he couldn't think of a graceful way to introduce this, he could at least be blunt. (Like his father.)

Marcia's face stilled, then reset in more intent, visibly suspicious, lines. "Yes?"

"I'm in."

Marcia's eyes widened. "Really?" They narrowed again. "Why? You weren't interested, last time we spoke."

"Would you believe that I'd changed my mind?"

"Well, I might," she said, and sat back. "But not when you put it like that. What happened?"

Daril hadn't meant to tell her about it. He hadn't meant to tell her anything much. He wasn't even certain yet what he meant by saying that he was in, and whether he truly intended to stick to it. And yet… "Gavin may have named me Heir, but he isn't acting accordingly," he said, bitterly.

"I know the feeling," Marcia said. "But – Daril." She paused, then made a tiny gesture of irritation. "Look. I'll be blunt. Nothing I've been talking about will make a blind bit of difference to you, do you understand? I'm not talking about hurrying along our own ascendancy. I mean, if that's what you're interested in, sit tight, wait for him to die."

Daril blinked. That was indeed unusually forthright.

He shrugged. "To be honest, I don't really care. I'm fed up with the whole sorry business." The words surprised him as they came out of his mouth; but they felt, now he'd said them, alarmingly true.

Marcia leant back against the arm of the sofa, regarding him with narrowed eyes, and rubbed at her chin with her knuckle. A tiny metal glint was pressed into the middle of one of her neatly-kept nails.

"You're fed up," she repeated. "Daril, I'm not sure why you expect me to take this seriously."

"Since we last spoke, the Guilds have issued their own ultimatum," Daril said. "And that speech from that wretched woman… I'm not interested in 'renewing our links with Teren'. We are not Teren."

"Well, technically we are."

Daril waved an impatient hand. "For now. I don't care, if they stay out of our business. But it seems she doesn't want to, and the Guilds are playing straight into her hands."

"So, what's your suggestion?" Marcia asked, looking at him sharply.

Daril shrugged. "You were proposing very much what the

Guilds want, before."

"Not quite," Marcia said, wrinkling her nose. "They're going rather further than I had thought of."

"Indeed. Which on the one hand makes things more difficult – the angel knows that Gavin is kicking up like mad about betrayal and all that – and on the other hand, perhaps there is scope for, well. Some kind of compromise, that works for both parties."

Marcia didn't say anything. Daril tried not to fidget.

"Can I trust you?" she asked, finally. "Two months ago you were trying to put yourself at the top of the pile. And now, what, you're going to help me limit the power of the Houses?"

"Since I don't have any of the power of the Houses," he said, more bitterly than he intended, "it hardly matters to me."

"It will eventually. And in any case. Wanting to stick it to Gavin isn't the most reliable of motives."

"I spent the best part of a decade consistently motivated by wanting to stick it to my father," Daril pointed out. "As motivations go, it's been fairly reliable."

Marcia stifled a laugh. He felt absurdly cheered.

Time to go on the offensive. "My question is, can you afford to turn away an ally? Most the Houses blame you, and by extension Fereno, for the Guilds' decision. It may be neither fair nor accurate, but that doesn't matter. Your reputation has taken a hit, and I don't see anyone stepping up to defend you. Bluntly, Marcia, do you have anyone else who's prepared to help?"

Marcia looked away. "Is no help worse than unreliable help?"

Daril rolled his eyes. "Well, frankly, yes. Like I say. Can you afford to turn away an ally?"

"I can if I think the alliance will be worse for me, and for the House, than standing alone," Marcia said. "Our Houses hardly have a history of mutual support to fall back on."

"You're prepared to discard enough history. Why not that too?"

Marcia looked like she was thinking more of their own personal history than their House history, and Daril hurried to move on. "This would entirely be in my own interest. I have no interest in Teren, and a divide between the Houses and the Guilds risks pushing the Houses into Teren's arms. But more than that – Marcia, if we pull this off, we'll be powermakers in our own rights." He found his lips pulling back into a grin. "Heir, Head, whatever; we'll be making something happen."

Marcia nodded slowly. "Well. That motivation I can buy. And I can't deny that I need the backing, and Leandra is a strong House." Politely, Daril didn't mention that Leandra was likely stronger than Fereno right now. "Although if you're at odds with your father again…"

"Let me handle that," Daril said, with a confidence that he didn't quite believe.

Marcia, from the tilt of her eyebrow, didn't quite believe it either, but she let it pass.

"Are we willing to do this with no other support?" she asked.

Daril shrugged. "Two votes is enough."

"Numerically, yes," Marcia agreed. "But in practice… what happens if the rest of the Houses push back? Legally, there's nothing they can do, but if they refuse to cooperate… I don't think it's quite as simple as that."

"I'm prepared to go ahead regardless," Daril said. "Like I said. Powermakers. You and I will be making a statement about the strength of our Houses; and at that point we'll be able to work with the Guilds even if the others won't, which would be lucrative to the point that it would be worth it just for that. Fereno is implicated already. Choose to move into that rather than away from it. Show you can turn Marek around even against the will of the other Houses, rather than knuckling under to their preferences."

Marcia's lips compressed, but all she said was, "I'm concerned for the stability of Marek, if the Council is divided."

"The Council *is* divided," Daril pointed out, letting his impatience colour his tone. "You mean, if the Houses are divided. But at least this way, someone is leading. Providing an option that works. The rest of the Houses can be stubborn and hidebound, but they'll have lost the vote. They'll come around, if we and the Guilds keep our nerve." He grinned. "Especially once they see Leandra and Fereno raking it in while they stagnate."

The corners of Marcia's lips twitched upwards. She could play the altruistic card all she wanted, but when it came down to it, she was in this for her own benefit and that of her House just as much as he was. And she liked to take risks a lot more than she was willing to admit out loud. It was just that for once, they happened to be on the same side.

"Well," she said. "Nisha's working on it, too, so we might get another vote. But if not – I think you're right. This is better than failing to act." She took a breath. "I have... a contact, in the Guilds. Who had what we might call a free and frank discussion with me. The Guilds will not back down. The Houses, as a whole, will not back down. But... I am due to speak to the Guilds, tomorrow, in the hope of finding some kind of solution."

Daril sat forwards. "Then we had better think about what you will say." And then afterwards, he would have to work out how he could secure his own House vote, as he had so rashly promised.

He would do it. He'd committed himself, now. And he even believed, as Marcia did, that it was the best course of action.

He just hoped like hell that they were both right.

EIGHTEEN

Cato, when Jonas went to ask him about clothes, was unusually short.

"Of course I don't keep Marek formal around the place. Why the hell would you think I did? And why do you want to borrow Marek formalwear."

"It's not for me. It's for Asa," Jonas hesitated, then said, reluctantly, "My mother invited us to dinner at the embassy."

"Your mother... ?" Cato waved an impatient hand. "Whatever. I don't have time for this. Why don't you try a hire shop instead of hassling me, hmm?"

On his way out, Jonas noticed that one of the other doors on Cato's corridor stood ajar. Had someone risked moving in next to the sorcerer? Jonas doubted they would last long, whoever they were.

He hadn't known that there was such a thing as a shop which hired out fancy clothes – he'd never had occasion to bring a message to one – but once he found one, on the far side of Marek Square, in the district full of home garment-makers and lacemakers and all those who didn't quite have Guild skills but who catered for the locals, the shopkeeper produced an aubergine tunic with adjustable side-fastenings, that would come to mid-thigh on Asa, and fitted trousers. It came with an over-vest, longer than the tunic, with a Marek lacework edging. Jonas, brought up on a trading ship, could see that it wasn't up to the standards that the Lacemakers Guild shipped off to Exuria and the Crescent, but it was nice enough, and perfectly suitable.

It looked good when Asa had it on, too. Jonas dressed in Salinas formal, the heavily-embroidered tunic and loose Salinas trousers that he'd brought with him when he came to Marek, and tried not to feel tremendously conspicuous as they left the squats together. The last time he'd dressed this way, he'd changed up on a roof, but he could hardly expect Asa to do that.

"None of that facepaint stuff?" he asked Asa.

"That's for Marekhill," Asa said, with only a tiny eyeroll. "House stuff. Not for the likes of me, thanks all the same."

He should probably have known that already.

The streets of the squats were dark, as usual; folk here didn't have spare money for torches. Old Bridge was lit, and Marek Square itself had a pair of torches over every door, including the embassy. Jonas squared his shoulders and marched up to the front door.

Xera was polite enough when she opened the door, although she still glared suspiciously at Jonas when she thought he wasn't looking.

"She doesn't like you much," Asa observed, quietly, as Xera led them along the corridor to the dining room.

She also had excellent hearing, Jonas was aware, as her back tensed.

"Mid-Year," he said, with a shrug, and Asa pulled a face.

Shit, he hadn't told Asa not to mention that in front of his mother. Surely they wouldn't anyway. It was hardly suitable for polite conversation, was it? Oh, by the way, Kia let a bunch of idiots use the embassy to try to destabilise Marek, and Jonas helped them, or maybe the other thing, and I hit one of them with a chair. No. It was fine. It would all be fine.

In the dining room, Kia and his mother were already seated, sipping deep blue berith from tumblers.

"Ah, welcome," Kia said. "Please do be seated."

"Mother, Kia," Jonas said, bowing slightly to both of them, before pulling out a chair for Asa. "This is Asa. Asa, this is Kia t'Riseri, ambassador to Marek, and this is my mother, Captain t'Riseri."

"Pleased to meet you," Asa said, sitting down a little awkwardly. "I hope we're not late?"

"Not at all," Kia said.

"Glass of berith? Xera will bring the food in shortly."

"It's quite strong," Captain t'Riseri warned, with a smile that wasn't reaching her eyes.

Asa smiled back, but their smile was forced too. "I'd be delighted to try it. Thank you."

"Berith isn't drunk here?" Jonas' mother asked, watching Asa sip at the tumbler Kia poured. Jonas turned it down; he didn't want to drink more alcohol than he had to.

"Only in the dock bars," Jonas said. And not that often

there, either; it was expensive. But he couldn't draw attention to the expense of Kia's own hospitality by saying as much.

"Marekers are missing out," his mother said. "Wouldn't you agree, Asa?"

"It's nice to get the opportunity to try it," Asa said, with admirable diplomacy. Jonas suspected they didn't particularly want to finish their glass, and wished that he could take it from them without being impolite.

Xera appeared with a tray of a dozen or so dishes, set them on the table, and vanished to fetch more. Salinas meals consisted of a small amount each of a variety of things, most of them cold, although on dry land you could lay them out more tidily than at sea, where large deep dishes served everyone and you didn't bother with a plate.

Asa, paying attention, followed Kia, Jonas, and Jonas' mother in serving themself with the tongs left in every dish, then eating most things with their fingers.

"You're Mareker-born, then, Asa?" Captain t'Riseri asked.

"From the swamp villages," Asa said, their chin going up slightly. "Came into town a few years ago to be a messenger."

"That's the job you're doing, too, Jonas?"

Jonas nodded. He wanted to believe that his mother was just making conversation, but there was an edge to her tone that he didn't like.

"How does it compare, Jonas, to sailing your own ship?"

"Well, I never sailed my own ship," Jonas said.

His mother made an impatient noise. "You were crew, Jonas, it was your ship. It's hardly your own city, here, either."

"Marek's interesting," Jonas said. "I get to wander round it and be paid for it."

"He's good, too," Asa said. "One of the fastest messengers. Pretty good for not being Marek-born."

"That's an important distinction, then? Marek-born or not?"

Asa floundered slightly. "I mean, only that he's had less time to know the city than the rest of us."

"Are there any other messengers who aren't Marek-born?" Captain t'Riseri asked.

Jonas really wished he could say yes. "No," he admitted.

"The Teren folks who come in tend to be craftsfolk," Kia put in.

"And the Salinas?"

"Not so many of them in Marek at all," Kia said cheerfully. Which his mother knew well enough.

"Around the docks there are," Jonas objected, then realised he'd said the wrong thing.

"Sailors," Kia said. "Not so many folk who stay."

He glared at her. This might not be talking about magic, but it was still not helping. Kia bared her teeth at him; she obviously didn't see this as a betrayal of their agreement. His mother, thankfully, missed the interchange; or at least, she didn't give any sign of having seen it, which wasn't quite the same thing.

"Mm," she said instead, tearing a pastry apart and popping half of it into her mouth. Once she'd swallowed it, she said, apparently lightly. "It's interesting, that Salinas don't choose to stay here. Other than you, of course, Kia."

Choice wasn't quite the right word there. Kia smiled tightly.

"Your people don't tend to stay anywhere, much, do they?" Asa said. Which was true; Salinas rarely settled off the islands. Asa sounded slightly defensive, as though they thought Jonas' mother was getting at Marek rather than, as Jonas glumly suspected, Jonas himself.

"I suppose the sea is a strong pull," Captain t'Riseri agreed. "Don't you think, Jonas?"

"The sea's right there just outside the river mouth," Jonas said stubbornly.

"Mm," Captain t'Riseri said again.

Jonas took a bite of one of the wraps. He couldn't taste it.

"So," his mother turned to Asa. "You grew up in the swamp villages. Did you sail, then?"

"Helped my dad with the fishing," Asa said. "He wanted me to take the boat after him, but I wanted to go to Marek proper. It's a hard life, fishing."

"Hard everywhere," Captain t'Riseri agreed. "You don't feel the lure of the sea, then?"

Asa shrugged. "I suppose I didn't feel the lure of the fish, let's put it that way."

"Mm, yes. It's true, one can always tell when one is near a

fishing village."

Jonas winced. The Salinas didn't think much of fishers, or any sailors other than themselves. By the tight smile on their face, Asa too had recognised the insult.

"Yes, it is very noticeable," his mother said, as if to herself.

Jonas just stared miserably at his plate. This was worse than he'd expected. And they still had at least an hour before they could leave. He huddled into himself, and prepared to wait it out.

☉ ☺

Asa stomped across Marek Square; Jonas had to lengthen his stride to keep up with them. Marek Square was busy at this time of the evening, with people passing through on their way to or from their evening's entertainment, and some of them turned to look curiously at Jonas and Asa.

"Well, that was a total clusterfuck, wasn't it?" Asa said grimly.

"It wasn't... that bad?" Jonas tried, knowing as he did that it was a lost cause.

"Jonas. Your mother clearly doesn't think that you should be going anywhere near some Mareker from the squats. And she was hardly subtle about it. The smell of fish villages? Really? Did she already have someone lined up for you at home?"

"No!" Jonas denied, then honesty insisted that he add, "Not to my knowledge. I wouldn't put it past her, I suppose. But she's never said anything, truly."

"Still," Asa said. They'd reached the foot of Old Bridge now. Asa in a hurry could move damn fast. "She made it pretty clear what her opinion is."

"Kia was fine," Jonas said, unable to counter Asa's assessment of his mother but unwilling to concur with it out loud.

"Kia did her best to cover things over to make for a smoother evening, yes, I will give you that. Kia was perfectly polite to me."

"Kia was a bit pissed off that Mother was making things difficult," Jonas said.

"But you didn't say word one," Asa said.

"I did!" Jonas protested, then stopped. "Didn't I?"

"No, Jonas," Asa said. "You didn't. You let her make all those snide little comments, and you contradicted her maybe once. And leaving aside all the business about curious Mareker customs, and the importance of the sea, and all the questions about the squats, leaving all of that aside – she quite clearly thinks she's here to take you home. Doesn't she."

Jonas winced. "Look. How about we stop at the pub, on the way home? Nice soothing beer. Kind of thing."

Possibly Asa would be a little less pissed off if they were in public.

"In this kit?" Asa gestured down at themself, and then at Jonas. "You must be having me on. Quite apart from the attention we'd draw, haven't you to return this tomorrow? Clean?"

"Uh. Do you want to come to my room?"

"Right now what I want is to tell you to fuck right off," Asa said, bluntly. "However. I don't really want to have this discussion in the street, either, and I doubt we'll do better by putting it off. You can come to mine. I have whisky. Right now I really need a whisky."

Jonas wasn't certain that was a great idea, after the tumbler of berith, and the Exurian wine with the meal, but he sure as hell wasn't going to contradict Asa right now either, and it wasn't like they were showing signs of being drunk. Annoyed, yes. Drunk, no.

Meekly, he followed Asa up to their room, where they immediately changed out of the formalwear, putting their customary shirt and trousers back on with a sigh of relief. Jonas supposed that it wouldn't go down well to suggest that they left the whole lot off.

They poured off a wooden tumbler of whisky, and gestured at Jonas with the bottle. Jonas mutely shook his head. Asa didn't have a chair in here; in the absence of other options, Jonas sat on the floor facing the bed, back against the wall. He doubted Asa would welcome him on the bed next to them right now. The floorboards were smooth underneath his fingers.

Asa took a healthy slug of the whisky, sat down on the edge of the bed, and then sighed, running a hand over their face.

"Right. I'm calmer now. So. Your mother doesn't like me; fine. She wants you to come home, and she doesn't want some Mareker encouraging you to stay here, nor, I suppose, does she want you thinking with your dick. I can understand that. But – couldn't you have said something?" They sounded hurt, now, rather than cross, and Jonas felt it like a kick in the stomach.

"I," he started off helplessly, then stopped, not knowing what to say. "I'm not very good at that," he said, eventually, knowing how weak it was as he said it.

"At what? Standing up to your mother? Contradicting her at all?" Asa asked.

"That, basically. Yes. Look, she's not just my mother. She was my captain, for years. And Kia's too."

"I noticed that," Asa said, drily. "And yet Kia still managed the occasional deflection."

"Kia's a diplomat," Jonas said. "I'm not. I know she's being unreasonable, but the way she says things – I can't think of how to contradict her, and if I do she'll ask why, and I can never think of anything to say in time."

Asa was halfway through their whisky already. They set it down, thoughtfully. "I guess I forget how young you are," they said.

"Oh, come on," Jonas said. "There's no need to be like that. I'm only a couple of years younger than you." With Asa looking at him like that, he felt small.

Asa shrugged. "In years, sure. But you were on a ship, with your ma and the rest of the crew looking out for you, until, what, six months ago? I've been making my own living since I was fifteen. Living on my own since a little after that. I'm not meaning anything by it, Jonas, it's just – you've not had long to work out how to stand on your own."

Jonas hunched a shoulder.

"So, fine. You aren't any good at arguing with your ma. Mine can run rings round me, too, it's true, though I'd like to think that if she started on at me about going with a Salinas lad, I'd have something to say."

"If she'd said it like that, so would I!" Jonas said. "But she didn't, did she? It was all about the interest of different cultures, and – she was like you, just now, treating me like a kid."

"Well," Asa said. "I want to say, don't act like a kid. But

that's cos I'm pissed off. So. Moving on. She thinks you're going back, and you didn't contradict her. But that's not what you've been saying to me." Their tone was hard, challenging. "Let's be clear about this, Jonas. It's not that I mind. I mean, sure, I'd miss you if you went back. But we've been friends barely six months, and lovers just a few weeks. I like you, but I'd cope, you know? What I mind is if you're lying to me, straight out."

"I'm not," Jonas said, miserably. "I…" He stopped. The problem was, he didn't know what he wanted. Not enough to say it out loud. He wasn't lying to anyone, he just needed… time. Time to work out what he was doing. Time to work out whether he wanted magic, and those accursed flickers, whether he would ever be able to control it. He opened his mouth, and shut it again. He couldn't find any of the words he needed.

"So it's your ma you're lying to, instead?" Asa said. "Look at me, Jonas. What's going on?"

"I'm not lying to her, either. I'm not agreeing with her. But you saw her, tonight. She's not going to listen to me, if I tell her otherwise, is she?"

"Well, she's certainly not if you never tell her, no," Asa said.

Jonas looked down at the floor between his knees. "She never listened to me before. I don't see her starting now."

Asa took another slug of whisky. "You're a grown man, Jonas. You've moved out, to another country, even. How about you start acting like it?"

Jonas buried his head in his hands. "I don't know what I want to do. I wasn't supposed to stay here. I sure as hell wasn't supposed to become a bloody sorcerer, and angels alone know what Mother would say if she found out anything about that. But how long can I hide it from her?"

Asa sighed. "How long's she staying?"

Jonas shook his head. "It's not that. She can't stay long. She's got cargo to shift. But she'll be back, and if I don't come this time it'll be next time, and she'll want to know whether…" His voice trailed off.

"Whether what?" Asa asked. Jonas didn't reply. His flickers. He didn't want to talk about his flickers.

The silence stretched out.

"Why did you come here, Jonas?" Asa asked.

He heard the bed creak as they sat back a little. He swallowed, and took his hands away from his face. Could he tell Asa now? He glanced hesitantly across at them. They were looking consideringly at him.

"I mean. I know there's something you're not telling me. Known it for a while. And now it seems like there's something your mother thinks you should have done here."

Jonas looked back down at the floor. "I..." Could he tell Asa? Surely he could, if he'd told Cato. And, angels help him, Urso. Asa knew magic. Asa wasn't freaked out by it. And he wanted, so badly, to be able to talk about it.

The moment stretched out. He could feel Asa about to give up. He could say something. He could.

"I see the future," he blurted out, and immediately felt his shoulders go up, waiting for... Asa's reaction.

"You what?"

But they didn't sound angry, or disbelieving, just... surprised?

He was committed now. He might as well go on. "I have these... flickers. Little snippets of the future. Had them since I was a kid. I told my mother, once, and she told me to keep it to myself, ignore it, and it would go away."

"Salinas and magic," Asa said, sounding resigned. "I see."

"But it's not magic, not exactly," Jonas said. "That's the thing. I came here to get rid of it. I hoped, Mother hoped, I'd grow out of it, but when I didn't... I can't join a crew this way."

"Does she think you've gotten rid of it?" Asa asked, then, "Have you?"

"I don't know what she thinks. I haven't, though. No one seemed to know anything about it. And then..." He swallowed. "Urso said he could help. If I helped him."

Asa grimaced. "Right. I see. Well, that explains a lot." Asa had never asked how he'd gotten wound up with Urso and Daril. Asa had just come and helped him. Asa had been on his side.

"But Cato said it was too late. He's tried to help, but... He says, it's not magic but it's related to magic. He said, learn to be a sorcerer and then I can control it, maybe. Except he doesn't bloody know either." Jonas could feel his frustration leaking out. "He keeps asking me about it, he's *nosy*, but then he's telling me I can do magic as well and…"

"And can you?"

"Sometimes. I…" He stopped. He couldn't quite bring himself, even now, to talk about the link between the flickers and magic. "I don't know."

Asa sighed, and got down off the bed to kneel in front of him. "So you don't know if you want rid of your flickers, and you don't know if you want to go back to the sea, and you don't know if you want to be a sorcerer. And your ma's telling you one thing and Cato's telling you another. Am I right?"

"Pretty much," Jonas said. He felt tears pricking at the corners of his eyes.

"So. I guess what you need is to tell Cato and your ma, and me, come to that, to fuck off while you sort it all out."

"I don't want you to fuck off," Jonas said, immediately and honestly. He grabbed at Asa's hands. "Honestly. I'm sorry I haven't been able to talk about it before." He took a shaky breath. "But if you don't want to… I mean, the flickers, they're weird, right…"

Asa shrugged. "Lots of things are weird. It's kind of interesting, to be honest, but I won't be hassling you about it, don't worry."

"I can't tell Cato to fuck off," Jonas said. "He's right. I need to learn to control this thing, if I have it. The sorcery."

"And you can't tell your ma to fuck off, that's clear enough," Asa said. "At least I understand now why you're avoiding her. Look. You have to think this through properly, Jonas. You're too young to commit to anything, but you need to work out what the hell you're doing, and then maybe you need to find the nerve to tell your mother to back off."

Jonas winced.

"Yeah, right enough, but maybe once you've made some decisions it'll be easier. But right now," Asa stood up, still holding his hands, and pulled him upwards, "have a damn brandy, get out of that posh clobber, and come lie down with me."

Their smile had tilted upwards at the side, and Jonas let himself be tugged towards the bed, awash with relief and gratitude that Asa, at least, seemed to understand. Maybe, here, he really was safe.

NINETEEN

Marcia stood in Marek Square in front of the Guildhall – not a specific Guild's hall, but *the* Guildhall, where all the Guilds met – and squared her shoulders. She'd dressed carefully for this; semi-formal, and just enough facepaint to remind them who she was, but not enough to invoke the full power of the Houses. Especially since, on this occasion, she was not, strictly speaking, representing her House. She'd even taken a litter down the Hill, so she wouldn't get rumpled and sweaty on the way down.

Not that she intended to make it clear that she wasn't fully representing her House. It was only as Fereno-Heir (… if then…) that she had any authority at all.

She had to make them understand that what they were doing was only making matters worse, making the Houses less likely to shift. And it was working directly against what she'd been trying to do; but if she talked about that, she'd have to admit how long her method was likely to take. The Guilds wouldn't like that at all.

Even just over the course of yesterday, she was aware that the Houses had been growing more irate. People had been in and out of their reception room all day, mostly talking to Madeleine rather than to Marcia, but Marcia had heard some of the louder discussions through the wall to the smaller reception room next door, and Madeleine had given her a clipped update at dinner. The word 'blackmail' had been thrown around more than once; but from Marcia's perspective, the Houses were becoming uncomfortably aware of how much power the Guilds hold here. Unfortunately, they were using this as a reason to resist the Guilds' demands; arguing that they couldn't possibly 'give in'. Marcia couldn't help but see Selene's hand in it. Encouraging the Houses to 'stand firm'; driving a wedge between them and the Guilds; pulling them back towards Teren.

Whatever Selene was saying, whatever hot air the Heads of the Houses were spewing, Marcia was sick-sure that Marek would fall apart unless the Houses and the Guilds came back together. She had to find a way to bridge the gap.

Now that she came to the moment of entering the Guildhall, it was more intimidating than she'd expected. They might just send her away with a flea in her ear. But standing around out here wasn't going to improve anything. She took a deep breath, and walked up the steps to the big carved main doors.

A very tidy-looking apprentice with a Weavers' Guild mark on her shoulder showed Marcia into the meeting room where three of the Guildmasters waited. Marcia knew all three of them by sight: Warden Ceril of the Vintners, Warden Hagadath of the Smiths and Cutlers, and Warden Bradley of the Broderers. All of them were wearing robes, making Marcia glad that she was formally dressed too. Warden Hagadath had one of the Guild Council seats, but neither of the others did. She wished Warden Ilana was here. Not that Ilana had been particularly encouraging when they'd spoken the day before, but at least they had an on-going working relationship.

All three rose to greet her, and there was a couple of minutes of fussing around before they were all seated again. The room was comfortable, with armchairs rather than a meeting-table, and the apprentice hurried to offer Marcia an infusion. The Guildwardens already had theirs.

"And how is your mother, Fereno-Heir?" Warden Ceril enquired. She was a little older than Madeleine, and Marcia knew she had been heavily involved with the campaign to add Guild representation to the Council.

"Doing well, thank you, Warden Ceril," Marcia said. She wasn't about to say that her mother knew nothing of this current visit, nor of Marcia's agenda for it. "And your own family?" She'd played with Ceril's grand-daughter, when they were both children; the Guilds tended to marry younger than the Houses.

"Ah yes, all well too," Ceril nodded. Warden Bradley coughed, a little stagily, and Warden Ceril stopped what she had been about to say, and moved on. "So, what is it that brings you to us today?"

As if they didn't all know.

Marcia took a deep breath and waded in. "I am here

seeking to broker some kind of agreement between you and the Houses, with regard to your current – complaints."

"You're speaking for the Houses, are you, Fereno-Heir?" Warden Bradley asked, directly.

Marcia kept her face controlled. "In honesty, Warden Bradley? No, I am not."

All three of the Guildwardens crossed their arms, in unison, all looking somewhere between disapproving and annoyed. Marcia bit back a bubble of wholly inappropriate laughter. The gesture was so neatly synchronised it could have been staged.

She forged on. "I am not, because if I were here speaking on behalf of the Houses, we would not get anywhere for protocol and long speeches. As well you know. My aim is to liaise between you and the Houses."

"So what do you have authority to offer?" Warden Ceril asked.

"I agree with you that we need a more equal spread of responsibility between the Houses and the Guilds," Marcia said, evading the question of 'authority'. "The Small Council has been woefully over-used; and three seats is too many for the Guilds and the Houses to differ in Great Council."

"So what difference would you see as appropriate?" Warden Bradley demanded. "Two seats? One?"

"Twelve Guild seats," Marcia said. Thirteen was fair, of course, but knowing from Ilana that the Guilds wanted fourteen, she could hardly start negotiating there.

Warden Ceril shook her head. "And the Houses still outvote us? No."

"The Houses rarely stand so firmly together as to all vote as a block," Marcia argued. It was even true.

"And yet, if it comes to outvoting us, I fear that they will find it in themselves to do so," Ceril said.

"Twelve seats and no more use of the Inner Council, other than for matters that affect strictly and only the Houses," Marcia said.

"And who defines that latter?" Warden Ceril asked. "Come, come, why would we abandon our current position just for that? Fourteen Guild seats, and the abolishment of the Inner Council."

"Warden Ceril!" Marcia protested. "How do you expect the

Houses to agree to that?"

"And yet the Guilds were expected to agree to a mere ten seats to the Houses' thirteen. We have now withdrawn our agreement."

"The Teren Lord Lieutenant..."

"Is organising against us," Warden Bradley said. "Indeed. Are you telling me that the Houses will return to the embrace of Teren rather than negotiate with their fellow Marekers?" His eyebrows were raised.

Marcia rubbed her fingers across her lips. She wanted to say that no, they would not; but that removed what little negotiating power she had. And on yesterday's evidence, she feared that it would be untrue. Should she offer thirteen seats now, to see if that shifted things?

Warden Ceril's eyebrows had gone up now too. "So the Houses might indeed prefer Teren to the Guilds? Well. Fereno-Heir, I fear that this information does little for your case, since it indicates in what little esteem the Houses hold us."

Desperation gnawed at Marcia's insides. This was falling apart around her. Why had she thought she'd be able to convince them of anything?

Warden Ceril sat back. "In any case. Before we bother to discuss this any further, on what basis are you able to negotiate? Are you promising us that what we agree here will go through the Council? Despite the interference of the Lord Lieutenant?"

Marcia, of course, couldn't promise any such thing. Not without hearing from Daril. She hadn't even talked Madeleine around yet. She hesitated; and they all saw it.

"I am in discussions," she said, trying for an assured tone and grimly aware that she wasn't making it. "In order to have those discussions usefully, I wanted to negotiate first with you." None of them were convinced. They read her as ineffectual, trying to offer something she had no control over. They weren't wrong.

Warden Hagadath leant forwards. They were tall, and broad, with close-cropped hair and a scar on one cheek. "I am not sure the Guilds should trust you at all," they said, their voice quiet but clear. "You are here without backing, you have no real interest in meeting our needs. Why should we negotiate with you?"

"Because no one else is even trying," Marcia snapped.

Warden Hagadath shrugged. "We believe we can outlast you. The Guilds have other options. The Houses have been useful so far; but perhaps we have outgrown them."

"Even if the Guilds can outlast the Houses," Marcia said. "It will cost everyone, to change the way things are done. You believe the Guilds will suffer less; but you have no experience in making deals, no experience with putting together a cargo for a ship. Even if you, or agents working for you, can learn those skills, it can't happen overnight. The cost will be immense."

"But worth paying, if there is no other way for us to be heard," Warden Bradley said, quiet but implacable.

The Wardens were looking at one another, shifting in their seats; Marcia could feel that they were about to close the meeting, and she hadn't got anywhere.

"Thirteen seats." She couldn't leave without offering it. She should have offered it earlier, before they realised how weak her backing was.

And yet... all three Wardens looked back at her, and their expressions had changed.

Warden Hagadath raised a single eyebrow. "Leaving aside the matter of whether you can deliver this... Thirteen seats? And then what if there is a tie?"

"Two options," Marcia said, thinking on her feet. "Either we agree that in the case of a tie, nothing has been agreed; that anything must have at least some support from either side to pass the Council; or the Reader is given the right to vote on a tie-break."

"The Reader belongs to the Houses," Warden Bradley said.

This was true; the Reader was customarily a junior House member.

"But the Reader has demonstrated their impartiality over the last ten years," Warden Ceril said. She was looking thoughtful, tapping against her upper lip with one finger.

"This one has," Warden Hagadath said. "Another might not."

"We could negotiate for a change in Readers," Warden Ceril said.

"You could accept junior House members into the Guilds,"

Marcia said. She hadn't been sure she'd be able to wind that matter into these negotiations; she'd assumed that any suggestion she needed the Guilds help to get enough House votes would destroy the whole fragile discussion. But from this angle, she could introduce it without showing her hand.

"Junior House members are permitted to be Guildmembers," Warden Bradley said.

"In name only, and we all know it," Marcia said, folding her arms. She felt like she might have solid ground under her feet again. "Change that. It benefits you immediately – surely you are losing talent at present – and it benefits us. It benefits both of us, in fact, by strengthening bonds between Houses and Guilds. And it solves the Reader problem. It's a problem for the future, correct, since the current Reader is acceptable? So. Accept junior House members into the Guilds now, and then in due course, the next Reader can be selected from one of those." And Aden and people like him would have more options for their futures. Options that would strengthen Marek as a whole.

"Well now," Warden Ceril said. "This is... an interesting proposal." She smiled slightly at Marcia. "But not one that is, exactly, in your purview at this time. However, on that ground, I am prepared to withdraw my criticism with regard to the Reader. Which returns us to the question – can your proposal get the backing of the Houses?"

"Does it have the backing of the Guilds?" Marcia asked. In an ideal world, the Guilds would commit to the matter of House members joining them; but she didn't have the leverage to insist. Frustratingly, that would make it harder to get further House votes on this; but she could hardly admit that to the Guilds.

"We cannot confirm that for certain," Warden Hagadath said. "As I am sure you know."

"But... I think I can say that, as a proposal, this would be one that we could consider," Warden Ceril said.

"I can say that to the Houses?" Marcia pressed. "As I said. I have been in discussions. I believe there are other Houses who could support this." House, singular, but...

"If you feel it will help. With appropriate caveats." Warden Ceril was smiling, but her eyes were still cold. "I hope and trust that the Houses will see the wisdom of collaborating with us, rather than with Teren." She paused. "Unless, of course, you all wish to return to Teren. I am sure we could get on quite well without you."

"I'm sure you wouldn't want to lose our long trading relationships with the Salinas," Marcia said, more or less by rote. Warden Ceril made an agreeing noise, but the calculating look in her eyes didn't shift.

Marcia needed to get out of here before this fragile moment of agreement broke. She stood up, and bowed to all three in turn.

"Honoured Guildwardens, I thank you for your time. I am sure we all agree that it would be best for Marek if we can resolve this situation to the satisfaction of Houses and Guilds alike. I will undertake to do my best in this regard."

Politely, the Guildwardens rose and bowed back to her.

"Indeed," Warden Ceril said. "We look forward to hearing from you again."

Marcia walked out of the room. She should feel pleased – she had wrested some kind of agreement out of this – but she was mostly just terrified. Could she really get the votes for this? Especially without a commitment from the Guilds on House members. Or were she and Daril wildly overestimating their abilities?

Madeleine first. If she couldn't convince Madeleine, she might as well just give up.

Asa was already gone when Jonas woke up the next morning. He pulled a face at his formal Salinas wear, folded neatly over the back of Asa's chair together with the stuff he'd hired. He didn't want to be walking through the streets first thing in that, but he had to wear something. After a moment, he pulled the trousers on anyway, and took a spare shirt of Asa's from the press to wear over the trousers on his way back to his own room. Asa wouldn't mind, but he'd better return it later; wasn't like any of them were awash in spare clothes. He picked up his formal tunic along with the clothes to return, and headed for home.

Once he was dressed in his Mareker working kit, with his

Salinas clothes safely put away in the press, he knew he ought to find something to eat, ought to return the borrowed clothes, ought to get working, ought to...

He didn't want to do any of it.

Instead, he climbed out of the window, up to the roof, and sat there, hugging his knees and staring out across the river towards the Old Bridge and Marekhill beyond it. A pigeon landed in front of him, cooing curiously, then settled itself into the lee of the chimney when he ignored it. He had a sneaking and uncomfortable feeling that pigeons – and possibly birds in general, a seagull had spent half an hour peering in his window the other day – had become slightly more interested in him since that absurd summoning spell. Maybe he was just imagining it.

Magic. Magic and flickers.

Cato had said he could get rid of the flickers, if Jonas wanted that. If the two things were linked, then that meant he could get rid of the magic, too.

Cato had also said it would hurt like hell, and that there might be other consequences. Cato had been worried enough about that to talk about his own past, and his own family, and Cato never did that.

Or, instead of getting rid of them, he could just choose not to use it; well, choose not to use the magic, anyway. The flickers came on their own timetable.

Except that now they came when he used magic, didn't they? The idea that he might, after all, be able to control them rose up in a dizzying alluring rush. Could using his magic mean he would control his flickers? Or was being able to induce them not the same as being able to prevent them?

He'd come here to get rid of his flickers, like his mother wanted. He'd never imagined, or wanted, the magic. Cato said getting rid of them would hurt; it might do, but then it would be over, and they'd be gone.

And he'd be denying a part of himself.

Asa had said, last night: what do you want? That was the trouble, wasn't it? He didn't know.

Or – a more difficult thought – he did know, but he was avoiding admitting it.

The sun was warm on the side of his face, and the city was spread out in front of him. Fondness rose inside him as he looked it over: Old Bridge down towards his feet; the tiny Salinas embassy across in Marek Square with its dots of flags outside it; New Bridge away to the west; the Houses over on Marekhill with the sun glinting off their brightly painted roofs. He looked down at the ships at the Salinas docks. He couldn't make out the banners from here, but he knew the Lion by her shape. He knew every inch of her, every board. He saw the islands in his mind's eye, the Lion tying up at home, and his heart ached with fondness for ship and islands both.

What he *wanted*, if he let himself admit it, was all of it. He wanted to explore his magic; he wanted to understand how his flickers worked; and he wanted to go back to sea again.

But those things were mutually exclusive.

Which left him with choices. Embrace the magic, reject the sea. Reject – stifle – the magic, and return to the sea.

Or challenge the whole either/or system.

What if his flickers, or his magic, could be useful to his people? They never had been, before, but he'd been suppressing them as hard as he could. What if he tried to get to grips with them, to have more understanding of how to interpret them? What if he really could in some way make his flickers and the magic work together?

He felt something delicate rising, unfurling, inside him. Something like hope.

What would it feel like to open himself to a flicker, instead of pushing it away? To invite it?

He'd never tried. He wasn't sure he had any real idea how to do it. But, riding on that tiny, delicate feeling under his ribs, he lay back on the roof, and stared into the sky, and tried to control his mind. He thought of how a flicker felt, and nudged himself towards that feeling. He tried to spread his mind out, to let it pour outwards, out of his skull, receptive to anything that might be out there.

Slowly, gradually, something began to grow inside him, filling up his chest, expanding into his throat. A tingling began in his fingertips.

... The Lion t'Riseri, seen from the top of Marekhill, her banners flying, sailing out of the mouth of the river and away, and a feeling of regret and satisfaction and pride all mixed together...

It hadn't hurt, this time. That was the first thing Jonas noticed. It wasn't much of a flicker, it wasn't an important one, but it told him something. It told him that he was staying here, that he was doing this.

Magic and flickers, linked.

He could still feel that tingling, the tightness; the aftermath of the roaring in his head. He remembered how it had felt when he summoned the pigeons; that same tightness, that feeling of focus. He didn't have the frustration now but he could feel the edge of how it had been, could bring it towards him and collect it inside his head...

He stretched out his hand, the way Cato had taught him. He didn't have any focuses, for any of the more complicated spells; but Cato said you could do a light just with your own self. He cupped his hand, and thought about light; and there, barely visible in the sunlight, was a tiny ball of fire, cupped in his palm.

He felt buoyant, joyous. He stretched out the other hand, and another one joined it.

Remembering a former shipmate, who'd taught him to juggle once, long ago, when they were becalmed, he threw the light gently into the air. Then the other; and another one to join them; and then he was juggling three tiny magical balls of light, feeling the grin spread across his face, as a semi-circle of curious pigeons gathered on the rooftop in front of him, cooing and bobbing their heads like any audience watching one of the Marek Square street-performers.

This was where he was. Here and now, this was what he wanted. And maybe, if he made it work, he could talk his mother, his people, into making use of it too.

Jonas spent the rest of the day determinedly running as many messages as he could, in an attempt to bulk up his sadly-reduced purse. He didn't mind constantly being on the edge of penury – most of his friends were too, relying on their ability to make a bit more money with a few more hours with their armband tied, and on the closely-knit messenger network to support anyone who was ill or otherwise laid up for a while – but after his mother's pointed questions, he would feel better with a little more to hand.

He'd always known that, unlike some of his friends, he had help if he needed it from the embassy. He'd never wanted to use that, never yet needed to, and he really didn't want to right now.

Running messages, too, gave him space to think. He wanted both his heritage and his magic, and he didn't see, any more, why he shouldn't have both. Maybe not now; but sometime.

That meant staying in Marek; which in turn meant deciding what to tell his mother.

He didn't even slightly want to tell his mother about his magic. But that was the whole problem, wasn't it? He'd been avoiding being honest with anyone – with himself – about who he was and what he wanted. Sure, he could fend his mother off for a while longer, maybe even until she got fed up and sailed off again. The Lion couldn't stay in port much longer, not without putting a serious dent in trading relationships and profits.

He could put it off until she left; but then he'd only be having the same conversations all over again whenever she was next in port. He'd be hiding. Again. Still.

He thought about it, as he ran messages. And, once he was done thinking about it, towards the end of the day, he made his way to the dockside, bearing goats-cheese pastries with him as a peace-offering.

The crew member on deck gave him a friendly wave as he came up the side of the ship and over the coaming. "Alright there Jonas. You coming back with us, then?"

"Not just now," Jonas said. "You away soon then?"

"Been loading up today, bit more tomorrow at first light," she said. "Away on tomorrow's noon tide."

He needed to get this done.

"M'mother's below?" he asked.

"Saw Fett taking a drink in to her a few minutes back."

Fett was the ship's steward. Someone else that Jonas had grown up with. At least that meant that his mother would have her coca, which might improve the situation.

He squared his shoulders, slid down the ladder, and went

forward to his mother's cabin.

"Come!" she called after his knock.

He went in and shut the door carefully behind him. He could smell the aroma of the coca, and his mouth watered slightly. Marekers didn't drink the stuff, and much though he liked Marek-style infusions, it wasn't quite the same. He looked around the cabin. He'd grown up here, spent half his childhood here, spent the other half down with the rest of the crew in the main part of the ship. He belonged here, too; except that here, he had to hide part of himself.

And didn't he in Marek, too? In Marek he wasn't at sea, wasn't with people who understood everything he'd grown up with.

But that wasn't *hiding*, not in the same way. And if he had to decide between the two...

"Jonas!" His mother sounded delighted, and he felt a stab of guilt. "I was going to send to you. We've to be away tomorrow, so you need to be on board tomorrow midday."

"I'm not coming."

He hadn't meant to say it that bluntly. Too late now.

His mother's expression changed to irritated disapproval.

"Jonas. This is ridiculous. You need to come back with us. It's past time. Have you even resolved the matter of..." She waved a hand, obviously not wanting to refer even obliquely to his flickers.

"I haven't," Jonas said.

"Jonas..."

"And I'm not going to."

His mother folded her arms. "You're not going to resolve it."

"You don't mean 'resolve'. You mean get rid of."

"And then what?" she said, ignoring him. "Find excuses to duck below with a headache every time one of them comes on? Risk being seen as your crew's source of ill-luck if anyone finds out? You'll never make captain that way."

"You're assuming that I want to make captain," he said.

His mother looked baffled. "But since you were tiny, that's been..."

He shut his eyes, and tried again. "Yes. Fine. I always wanted to be a ship-captain. Of course I did, growing up on board, with you. I still do. But, Mother. Not at the cost of, of hiding myself." His voice shook, and he clenched his teeth.

"Of course not." She sounded impatient. "That's why you came to get rid of them."

Jonas shook his head. "That's just another form of hiding." He went on before she could interrupt. "I don't want to pretend part of me doesn't exist. Why should I get rid of something that isn't a problem for me just because it is for you. No one *here*, in Marek, cares, you know."

"You've told people?" Her eyes widened with horror.

And that, there, was why he'd told hardly anyone.

"Not many," he admitted, reluctantly. "But the people I have told... Mother, they've been interested. They haven't treated me like I've got the blue plague. It's just... something I can do."

"Well, these Marekers and their magic." She shrugged dismissively. "There's no need to take *their* approach to it."

"But I want to," Jonas said. The point of no return was coming up. He had to keep going. He couldn't stop now. "Mother, it's not just the flickers. I. I can do magic. Mareker magic. I'm apprenticed to a sorcerer."

His mother's mouth opened, and shut again. Her face was pale.

"Magic?" she said, finally. Her voice cracked.

Too late to take it back. The only way was forward.

"My flickers are magic," Jonas said. "A different sort from what they do here, but... I guess it's part of the same, I don't know, talent, or whatever."

"And you want to... pursue this."

Jonas swallowed, hard, against the lost look on her face. "Yes. I do. But I don't want it to be that or the sea, Mama." He reverted to the baby name. "I don't see why it has to be. My flickers – they could be useful. Magic could be useful. To us. Don't you see?"

"Mareker style magic is only useful in Marek."

"True, but... it's helping me get a better handle on my flickers," Jonas said. "So they're less disabling, less... It's better. Mama, this is part of me. It's something that – it feels right, to find out more about it. Maybe I'll stay here for a bit, and then I'll come back aboard and never use it again. But I want the chance."

"You'll come back aboard still having those... things?" He

could see her torn, between wanting him back on the sea and her dislike for the flickers. It hurt, still, knowing how she thought of them; but it hurt a bit less, now he knew people who didn't react that way.

"I don't want to have to choose," he said again. "I want to be able to use all of me."

"You don't have to," she said, after a moment. "I know I said you have to get rid of it, but... You don't have to. You can just not use it, aboard ship. If that's better. If that means you'll come away with us. Come back to the sea, Jonas."

Jonas shook his head. He hated doing this, but he couldn't go back. Not now. "I need to use it, Mother. At the least, I need to understand what it is, and how I can use it. Maybe after that I'll decide not to, and maybe then I'll come back. But for now, I need to stay here."

There was silence in the cabin. Steam was rising from his mother's coca cup, but she didn't reach towards it.

"Is there anything I can say to dissuade you?" she asked, finally.

"No," Jonas said. "I'm an adult now, remember? I need to make my own decisions, and not let you talk me out of things."

She smiled, just a little, but it helped his heart. "That's true enough. I shouldn't complain, should I, if you're finding your own path? I always swore that I wouldn't do that to you." She closed her eyes for a moment, then opened them again. "Very well. I can't say I'm happy about this, Jonas. But you're right. You're grown, and you have to make your own choices. I thought – well, I thought that getting rid of this, this thing of yours, was the right solution, and I can't see how you can have it and still sail, but... well. I suppose I have to let you work this out."

She sighed, and then opened her arms. "Come here, then, before you go."

Jonas went to her, and they held onto one another for a bit.

Finally, she released him. "I love you, little fish. Remember that, yes?"

"Do you know when you'll be back?" Jonas asked.

"Four, maybe five months," she said. "We might have a side trip over in the Crescent, depends on... well, anyway." She smiled at him. "I'd say, stay tonight for dinner, but..."

"I think it'll be easier not to," Jonas said, honestly. "I do miss the sea, you know. I just... I need to do this."

Her lips pressed together, and he realised with a shock that she was trying not to cry.

"Mama. I'm happy, honestly. It's hard, but... so it is on a ship, ne?"

She rubbed at her eyes. "I know. But at least you have your people, your family, here. In Marek..."

"I've got people in Marek, Mam. I've got Asa. I've got," he swallowed, but she had to hear it, "other sorcerers. I've even got Kia, if I can make her promise not to report back without telling me."

"I suppose you have, at that," she said, then looked thoughtful. "Kia... You know, if you insist on staying in Marek..."

"*Mother*. Leave off."

She looked at him, and sighed. "Sorry. Force of habit, thinking through the options. It's not my life, is it? It's yours. Well. Go safely, and I'll hope for you to come back when you're ready."

"I'll make sure I catch you whenever you're here," Jonas promised.

She caught him in another embrace, tightly, and he hugged her back. "Miss you, Mama."

"I miss you too, little fish," she said. "Go safely, now, you promise?"

"Sail well," he said, "and may the winds be your friends."

"Follow your heart, little fish," his mother said, "and may the currents treat you well."

It was all Jonas could do to leave the cabin, to shut the door and climb back up the ladder and go back over the side of the ship to dockside. Tears were pricking at the corners of his eyes. Half of him wanted, with a painful desire, to turn back; to sail away from Marek and leave all this, magic and flickers, behind. But 'all this' was part of him. He couldn't leave himself behind, and it was foolish to think he could. Maybe, hopefully, once he'd figured out how to work with it, he could return to the sea, sometime. Eventually.

As he walked away from the docks, the feel of Marek enveloped him, and he took a long, slow, breath. This was the right decision.

TWENTY

"Perhaps," Madeleine said, looking up from the notes she was jotting with a fine-nibbed dip pen, "it would be good for you to go to Teren for the autumn."

Marcia looked at her in horror.

"Mother! What brought this on?"

They were supposed to be discussing their forthcoming trading commitments, the state of their connections with other Houses, with the Guilds, and with various captains, and identifying the spaces that needed to be filled. It had been in both of their appointment books for a month, a routine discussion for this time of year when the Salinas ships began to return. Marcia had been bracing herself to discuss the matter of the Guilds; but she hadn't expected this. They weren't even past the easy part yet, dealing with goods already in the warehouses or being loaded onto ships.

"Selene made an excellent point," Madeleine said. "In my youth, we had closer links to Teren. Perhaps it is time to renew those."

Marcia sat back and eyed her sourly. "Selene has an agenda of her own. You know that. We discussed it, last week."

"Everyone has their own agenda," Madeleine said. "The question is whether it is helpful or otherwise to our own."

"She wants what's best for Teren, not what's best for Marek," Marcia said.

"Those two things can march in step."

"But she's antagonised the Guilds."

"The Guilds," Madeleine said, sounding a little scornful. "Yes, well. If the Guilds have become unreliable, perhaps it is time to look more to our other relationships."

"Mother." Marcia tried to control her exasperation. "Be reasonable. Are you seriously suggesting that Teren goods could replace the contribution of the Guilds to Marek's success?"

"You sound like them," Madeleine said.

"That's because they're right. Teren is one country. One

small country whose only real link to the rest of the world is through Marek. Marek is successful because it trades with many countries, and cities –"

"Then we should strengthen our links elsewhere, too. I wholly agree."

"And because of the extra value the Guilds provide," Marcia forged on, ignoring the interruption. "Trading Teren wood and wool for Exurian berries and Crescent rice is all well and good, but the profit lies in what the Guilds can do with wood and wool and steel. And you know that, Mother."

Madeleine's mouth pursed, and she looked away.

"As a matter of fact," Marcia hesitated, but she had to raise this, and there was no point in waiting for a better opportunity. Either she could talk Madeleine around to this or she couldn't, and she might as well find it out now. "As a matter of fact, I wanted to talk to you about supporting the Guilds."

"*Supporting* them? You want to give them what they want?" Madeleine sat back and folded her arms, glaring at her daughter. "Marcia, we cannot allow ourselves to be held to ransom like this. We cannot *give in*."

"The Guilds have the power," Marcia said, bluntly.

"Nonsense." Madeleine sounded at once shocked and disbelieving.

"We have power too," Marcia said, trying to soften her initial words. "Of course we do. We have the connections – overseas, and with the captains. We have the power to put together the most lucrative cargo, taken as a whole."

"We take on the risk," Madeleine said, "whilst the Guilds rake in the money. From us."

"We take the risk, and we make more than they do. That's the whole point of the arrangement, isn't it? Without their goods, we would have less to trade, and much less than is truly profitable. Without us, they would have a much harder time realising that potential profit. It is a mutually beneficial arrangement, do you see?"

Two months ago Madeleine had been happy to antagonise the Salinas. Now she was happy to antagonise another part of the trading web. Marcia was struggling to see what her mother was thinking. She seemed caught in the idea of the superiority of the Houses, convinced that their success was down to their own efforts, rather than part of a mutually beneficial system. Surely she hadn't always been like this? House Fereno had an excellent reputation for making solid deals, for working smoothly with captains and Guilds alike. They had trading relationships going back decades. Why had Madeleine stopped seeing the importance of that, and how had Marcia not seen that it was happening?

"We can rebuild without them," Madeleine said, brushing Marcia's words away, but Marcia saw something change, just a little, in her eyes.

"We can, I suppose," Marcia said. "Although I don't much fancy competing with the Guilds for ship-space. It's bad enough competing with other Houses. How can it make sense to make our lives more complicated?"

"To show them that they cannot dictate to us," Madeleine said.

"I don't want to treat this as a win-lose game," Marcia said. "It's not castles, Mother. It's baracal."

The goal in baracal was to maximise your joint score. Cato had always been better at it than her. If Cato hadn't chosen magic, he would have made a better Heir than her. He'd be more able to talk Madeleine round; except that he would choose to needle her into losing her temper instead, because he would find it amusing.

Marcia was close to losing her own temper, but she wasn't finding it amusing in the least.

"I will not be party to an arrangement that puts the Guilds over the Houses," Madeleine said with finality. "Whatever the cost."

With relief, Marcia recognised the opening.

"I wholly agree, Mother," she said, with conviction.

"You do? Then what are we arguing about, Marcia?"

"We could put neither Houses nor Guilds in charge of the Council," Marcia said. Madeleine frowned and opened her mouth. "Hear me out, Mother. I understand the Guilds' concerns, especially in light of Selene's comments. And I am of House Fereno, remember? One day I will be Fereno-Head, where you are now, responsible for the well-being and the honour of the House. I assure you, Mother, I do not take that lightly. And it is that future I wish to look to. A future in which the Houses and the Guilds and the sea-captains all prosper, together." She took a deep breath. For a wonder, Madeleine didn't interrupt. That slight frown was still there between her neatly-painted eyebrows, but she was listening. "I wish a solution that works for us and for the Guilds, rather than pushing us deeper into conflict."

"And that solution is?" Madeleine asked, her voice ostentatiously neutral.

"Thirteen seats for us. Thirteen for the Guilds."

"And a tie every time there is a problem," Madeleine said. "Marcia, surely..."

"One might argue that if neither a single House nor a single Guildwarden can be convinced of the other's position then perhaps there is a real problem," Marcia said, then held up a hand. "But no. The Reader has no vote, at present. In the event of a tie, if it persists – give them the casting vote."

Madeleine's eyes narrowed. "The Reader... Yes. I can see how that might work."

Her tone was reluctant, but at least she was engaging with the problem. She was, Marcia suspected, making the same calculation that the Guildwardens had – that the Reader belonged to the Houses. If she didn't point out the problem – not that it was a problem from Madeleine's point of view – then Marcia wasn't going to either. Agreement in principle was what she wanted. Details could be... managed, later.

"So you would agree to that?" Marcia pressed.

Madeleine grimaced, just a little. "I can see the advantages, I suppose. And I take your point that it would be better to find a solution with the Guilds rather than to try to rebuild our trade in other ways, and squeeze the Guilds out again if they try to trade directly. But I mislike the idea of giving in to their, their *threats*. And you must see, Marcia, that I must support the Houses."

"You supported including the Guilds ten years ago," Marcia argued.

"Yes. Ten years ago. More reason for me not to be the one undercutting the Houses now. Can you not see that?"

Marcia's heart sank; then an idea came to her. "So don't support it."

"Then what is the point of us discussing this?"

"Don't support it," Marcia said again. "Let me carry the vote. Let me support it. And then complain, afterwards, about ungrateful children."

"No," Madeleine said. "I will not make House Fereno appear divided. I am concerned with the Houses, but I am concerned most nearly with our own House. And so ought you to be." She sighed, and was silent for a moment. "But – you will be Head, eventually. I cannot continue to enforce my opinion over yours, every time. And your arguments, with regard to the Guilds... I see their force, even if I am distressed that it has come to this."

"But it has," Marcia said. "You can't push the river back upstream. And the Guilds are determined. I do not believe that they will back down easily, and fighting them – it will weaken us all, Mother. Surely you see that."

"You've spoken to them," Madeleine said. It wasn't a question, so Marcia didn't answer.

After a moment, Marcia tried again. "We could lead on this, Mother. You say you wish to support the Houses. We can support the Houses by leading them out of this quagmire, back to profit for everyone. And House Fereno will be seen still to have the vision, and the wisdom, that we have shown before. The alternative is that all the Houses suffer, and in due course, I truly believe that we will be forced to give in. That will leave us far weaker than if we move *now*, if we take control of the situation. The other Houses may complain, but as Marek prospers further with closer relationships between Houses and Guilds, they will look back and be grateful to us for taking the lead." She tried for a small smile. "Even if they never admit it openly."

Madeleine smiled too, a tiny rueful twist of her lips, and Marcia's hopes leapt. Madeleine looked down at her fingers, sighed, and looked back up at Marcia.

"If I agree – *if* – then I have a requirement, in exchange."

"A requirement?" Marcia said, cautiously.

"You will be Head, in due course, Marcia. You are responsible for the future of the House."

"Mother..."

"You need an heir," Madeleine continued. "I do not insist that you do this thing immediately. I want you to consider it, fully, and to be prepared to discuss it with me."

Marcia's heart sank. She should have guessed that this was coming. Madeleine had brought it up before, but Marcia had always put her off before, and Madeleine hadn't pushed.

"I assume you have some unsuitable lover," Madeleine said. "To be honest, Marcia, I couldn't give a rat's arse about that."

Marcia's mouth fell open in shock; not so much at the sentiment but the language, coming from her well-spoken, impeccably-mannered mother.

"Have the child however you like. By full-contract, by child-contract, with no contract at all. But if you tell me that you are concerned with the future of the House, if you wish to carry our vote and to lead the House, it is high time that you take that seriously."

"My Heir needn't be of my body," Marcia objected.

"Indeed not. You might well prefer to adopt."

"I could look among the cousins."

Madeleine grimaced. "You could, but you can scarcely offer to name one of your age-mates as Heir, and by the time we know what the next generation looks like it will be getting late for you to raise a child yourself. One child is hardly enough, in all honesty; not everyone is suited to this job."

"Mother…"

Madeleine took a long breath, and shut her eyes. When she opened them again, there was an ache and an honesty in them which stopped Marcia in her tracks. "The House needs someone to be Heir after you. You get to choose how that happens, Marcia. But as your mother, I would wish for you at least to think of a child, of your body or otherwise. I would wish a grandchild, not only someone to be named once you are Head."

It wasn't even that Marcia hadn't thought of the matter herself, before. She knew how this worked as well as Madeleine did. It was just… she wasn't ready, yet, to think about that future. But – when would she be ready? If she had to do this thing anyway…

"What do you want me to say?" she asked, slowly.

"I am not asking you for a decision this moment. I ask that by, let us say, next Mid-year, you take steps towards having a child."

"And in exchange, I can carry our vote tomorrow, and vote to give the Guilds their extra seats."

Madeleine nodded.

She'd have to do this, sooner or later, anyway. She might as well get something out of it.

"Very well, Mother," she agreed.

Storms and the angel, what was Reb going to say?

Surely this wouldn't come as a surprise to Reb. They both knew who Marcia was, and what that meant. And it needn't affect what she and Reb had together. Except in that who Marcia was, and who Reb was, did affect their future, and they both knew it, and neither of them wanted to speak about it.

They'd only been together for a couple of months. She was taking this all too seriously.

Her mother was smiling at her, relief clear in her expression. "I will support your vote whole-heartedly," she said. "I will give it to be understood that you have convinced me, and that I believe you to be correct."

Marcia swallowed. "Do you, though? Believe me to be correct?"

"I... have concerns. But you make valid points, and you will be Head, in due course. You care for our House as much as I do. I will be telling the truth."

Having her mother's support – having bought her mother's support – felt like more of a relief than she wanted it to.

Marcia quirked an eyebrow at her. "Well, this is politics, Mother. Haven't you always told me that truth is a thing to be used?"

Her mother smiled at her fondly. "I'm glad to see that you listen to me some of the time," she said, and patted Marcia's cheek.

Daril glared at the message in his hand. It bore Marcia's seal, and it said:

One. And you? Will lay it tomorrow, if you confirm. M.

So Marcia had found one of their needed votes. Her own, most likely. (He certainly hoped so. She could move the motion regardless, but it would look weak if Fereno moved it but didn't vote for it. If Nisha had talked her own Head around, they might not, in that case, stay talked around.) And he hadn't got around Gavin yet. This was… unsatisfactory.

He couldn't put it off. They didn't have to lay the motion as soon as tomorrow, but if the Houses didn't shift, and soon, there was a real risk that the Guilds would try making their own cargo negotiations. Once that happened, the Houses would be even more set in their position; whilst the Guilds would be developing the means of moving on without them. The Houses were right in the middle of making themselves irrelevant, with great self-congratulation. Daril had to get on with his part of this.

He'd got into this with the idea of annoying Gavin; but shortly after his meeting with Marcia he'd realised that whilst annoying Gavin might be satisfying now, convincing Gavin to agree with him would be – well, a shame, in one sense, but a better long-term tactical move.

Ideally, he'd like to carry the vote himself. He could use the boost. But Gavin's agreement would suffice. It would be easy enough to subtly spread the word that it was Daril's work.

So. Gavin might be stubborn, and hidebound; but he was also a sharp operator, with an eye to the reputation of the House, and to Marek's future. Daril just – 'just' – needed to convince him that both would be served by this change. And if that didn't work – well. There were alternatives.

He chose his moment carefully. Gavin was always more compliant immediately after dinner; and Daril had spoken to the cook beforehand. He sat at the table with his father, being as polite and affable as was feasible, without tipping over, he hoped, into being suspicious. Gavin was observant, drat the old buzzard.

"Well then, my boy," Gavin said, pushing back his plate and sitting back in his chair. "What is it?"

"Excuse me?" Daril said. Dammit.

"M'favourite food, you at your best – you can be charming, boy, when you put your mind to it, never been in doubt. Out with it. What do you want?"

Fine, perhaps he hadn't quite been subtle enough. But Gavin sounded amused, rather than irritable, so it had worked.

"This business with the Guilds, Father."

Gavin scowled. "Wretched upstarts. Don't know what they

think they're playing at."

Daril let the first part of that slide. "What they're playing at, Father, is messing with our bottom line. Not to put too fine a point on it. That rearrangement of cargo we discussed the other week? We need small things, fairly light, easy to pack, if we're not to breach our contract."

"Jewellers, maybe the Broderers, the Spicers," Gavin said, almost automatically. "The Haberdashers, some of them work in small goods more than cloth."

"Indeed. If only any of them were prepared to talk to me." Daril's bitterness wasn't feigned. He'd been frustrated and angry to have to make the change, but it was even more frustrating not to be able to. "The ship has to go in two days, to make her schedule. We're going to have to pay for the use of the space, plus a fine for change of cargo, and with no profit out of any of it."

Gavin looked like he'd bitten into a pickle. "And what? You want me to go back on my decision about these medicines?"

"That wasn't my suggestion," Daril said, then added, "Although, if you would care to do so... the providers aren't Guilded, so they'd not be affected."

Gavin scowled. "No, I stick by what I said. I don't believe it's safe, or wise."

By the angel, when he was Head, he was going to trade the damn stuff by the shipload.

"Then we need another solution."

"More unguilded goods," Gavin looked away.

"Father. You know as well as I do that there's next to none of that. No one in a Guilded occupation is going to trade in their goods, regardless of whether they're a member or not." The Guilds all had roughly the same rules on that. There were, for example, embroiderers not in the Broderers Guild who made stuff for sale in Marek, mostly to the lower classes. The Guild permitted that, but not trading it outside of Marek; not that it was good enough to trade well anyway. Anyone breaching that agreement would lose suppliers, under Guild pressure; for a House to even consider it would be a wholly shocking suggestion in normal circumstances.

"I suspect that my medicine people will be wrapped into the Apothecaries at some point," Daril added, "but they can get away with it until that happens. No one else will risk it."

"They won't last," Gavin said. "The Guilds. They'll learn that they need our acumen. Our experience. We just have to outlast them."

"They might learn that, or they might not," Daril said. "The question might come down to whether the Houses or the Guilds have the best-stocked coffers, and I'm not sure I want to gamble on that. Father, there's nothing *stopping* them from trading on their own behalf. Rules, custom, yes, but they've broken those already. Why stop there?"

"They haven't the skill," Gavin scoffed. "The Salinas will skin them alive."

"And then they'll learn, and improve," Daril said. "Meanwhile, the Guilds are making money, even if less than they'd make with us; the Salinas are making money; and the whole Oval Sea is learning to get by without whatever the Guilds can't manage to trade on their own behalf. The only people really suffering will be us, Father."

"The Guilds won't trade much on their own," Gavin said. He seemed infuriatingly incapable of grasping anything that deviated from his own established opinion. Surely he hadn't always been this bad? "Once it's resolved, there'll be a backlog in demand right across the Oval Sea. Premium prices. We'll make it all up then, if we hold our nerve."

"Or they'll have found other goods, other suppliers, and they won't care to pay 'premium prices' for ours," Daril said. "If the Crescent Alliance were to stop sending us rice and silk, the wheat and potato and fine woollen folks would step into the breach. There might still be a market for rice and silk when it came back, but it would have shrunk, and you know it. The same applies to everything we trade out from here. Father, this is a gamble."

"We're traders, Daril. Gambling is what we do."

"Not when it's not necessary. And not when we don't have the dice weighted."

Gavin scowled again, his face creasing up into folds. "And what's your answer, then, boy?"

"Support them," Daril said, bluntly.

"What? Support these... manufacturers?"

"Support them, in exchange for preferential treatment for our next cargos," Daril said.

Gavin's eyes narrowed; calculating the weight of his different concerns. Daril pressed the point.

"Every other House is burning their bridges. Why are we burning ours along with them when instead we could profit from the situation?"

"The other Houses won't have anything to do with us should we move. We need allies in the Council."

"If we've supported the Guilds, we'll *have* allies in the Council. The Guilds will support us while the other Houses are angry. In due course, it will lose relevance. We have a great deal to gain here, Father."

"Us alone? Won't fly."

"No. House Fereno will vote with the Guilds." Or someone would, but Daril couldn't afford to seem uncertain at this point.

"Will they now. How interesting." Gavin looked sharply at Daril. "What's going on between you and that Fereno girl, then? You're both Heirs now. There can't be anything formal."

"With Marcia?" Daril couldn't suppress the horror in his voice. "Hells, no."

"She drags you back in here after whatever that was at Mid-Year, you're plotting with her now... You were together once, I remember it."

"That was ten years ago, Father," Daril said. "I assure you, Marcia and I do not feel like that about one another."

"Always been at odds with House Fereno," Gavin said, scowling again. "And now you want us to stand with them to back a bunch of grubby-handed makers and labourers?"

Calling the Guildwardens either grubby-handed or labourers was a hell of a stretch, but Gavin could tend his absurd prejudices if he wanted. What mattered was the vote.

"I won't pass up an opportunity, Father, a profitable opportunity, just because of some hereditary enmity," Daril said. "Didn't you work with her mother a couple of months back?"

"Would have been a shame to pass up on the opportunity," Gavin said, then realised he was echoing Daril's words and frowned.

"Exactly. *Exactly*. So. House Fereno and House Leandra, working with the Guilds, and putting one over thereby on every other House too busy posturing to make the most of the situation. And," Daril leant forwards, "we will be seen to be leading Marek. Power-brokers, Father. You know how valuable that is."

"Hmm." Gavin's eyes narrowed, and for a moment, Daril thought he'd won.

Then the old man sat back, and shook his head. "No. Enough. I won't have it. We must stand with the Houses, and the Houses must remain in control. I won't fall to these threats."

"Father…"

"I said, *enough*. I've given you a fair hearing. I won't have it, and that's an end of it."

Daril's jaw clenched.

"Very well, Father."

He would have to move on to his second plan. Which, unfortunately, meant that he was about to have an uncomfortable evening.

He slipped his hand into his pocket to reassure himself that the antidote to the emetic was still there. His medicine-makers had been very helpful. Not that he could take it right now; it would look suspicious if only one of them were ill. He hadn't eaten as much of that syllabub as Gavin had, but it would be enough. If Gavin had agreed, he'd have given both of them the antidote in the port; as it was, he'd just have to wait it out and take it once he'd been ill enough to allay suspicion.

He poured port for both of them, anyway, and made polite conversation with Gavin while he got through his glass. Finally, he was able to retire without it looking like he was doing so through anger. Gavin needed to believe that all was well between them.

"I find myself tired, I'm afraid," he said, apologetically, as Gavin gestured towards the decanter. "I think I'm for my bed."

"Very well boy, very well. I must say, it's good to see you taking disagreement gracefully," Gavin said. "I'll see you for the Council meeting tomorrow, then."

No you won't, Daril thought.

It was a high-risk strategy, to be sure; if Gavin could prove it, he could disinherit Daril, which was why he too had to be visibly unwell tonight. Unwell; but well enough, with his younger constitution (and the help of the antidote, once he'd been conspicuously sick once or twice), to carry the House vote tomorrow.

Of course, Gavin would be furious once he recovered. But what option would he have? Their public feud over the Heirship had done enough damage to their House's reputation. Daril's vote tomorrow would set House Leandra up as a power-broker; Gavin could accept that, or he could destroy it by setting himself against his Heir. Gavin would be furious, but he'd knuckle under rather than make the House a laughing-stock. Daril was greatly looking forward to that interview.

Marcia wouldn't like any of this in the slightest, were she to find out about it; but then, it was none of Marcia's business. He was in this for himself, and his House, and he was about to do very well by both of them.

TWENTY-ONE

Marcia woke early, and restless in a way that could only be resolved by exercise. There was no doubt in her mind about why she was restless, any more than there was about why she'd slept badly and woken early. She'd had a message from Daril, late in the evening, saying only,

Two.

Which meant she would be laying the motion at the Council this afternoon. They couldn't delay any further. The Heads weren't going to get any more amenable with time; they'd spent the last two days talking themselves deeper and more securely into their existing positions. The Guilds must know that too; and the longer she delayed, the more likely it was that the Guilds would decide to make their own move, and the gulf would grow wider.

Even with Madeleine's backing, she was anxious. But there was nothing she could do about anything this morning. She had to get out of the house.

She wanted more than just a walk in Marek Park, inviting though the autumn breeze was when she opened her bedroom window. Instead she went down to the salle on 4th Street and spent a deeply enjoyable hour in swordplay. She stopped briefly at the baths on the way back, then went back up to the House, feeling significantly better.

The feeling didn't last. There was a message waiting for her on the shelf in the hall. She opened it there and then, standing in the hallway; and her heart fell. It was terse, it requested (in language that strongly suggested 'demanding') her presence at her earliest convenience, and it was from Selene.

She glanced over at the clock that stood in the corner of the hall and grimaced. She wished, now, she'd spent a little longer at the saal; as it stood, with a couple of hours of the morning still left before she needed to get ready for Council, it would be difficult to argue that 'at her earliest convenience' wasn't 'now'. And when it came right down to it, diplomatic niceties notwithstanding, the Teren Lieutenant had the authority to make this request. Still, Marcia lingered for a moment, hoping that something would mysteriously arise that prevented her from going.

Nothing did; and she sighed, penned a swift message to Selene, and went upstairs to change into full House formal. The message had that kind of tone; and if she was about to get into it with the Teren Lieutenant, she wanted as much of the pomp of her position behind her as she could muster. Also then she needn't change again before Council.

It seemed impossible that this could be about anything other than the Guilds. But even if Selene were willing to interfere openly and directly in the matter, could she, *how* could she, have found out about what Marcia was planning? The Guildwardens wouldn't have spoken of it beyond other Guildwardens; they had more sense than that. Nisha wouldn't betray a confidence.

Daril, now – well. It was more than possible. Daril wouldn't hesitate to betray her if it suited him; but on this occasion, she didn't think it would. She didn't think he'd been lying, or even dissembling, when they'd spoken; she thought he genuinely agreed with her on what was best. And he'd sent that message last night. He couldn't have told Selene.

Of course, everyone knew that Marcia had been talking to the Guilds. They just didn't know that she'd talked Madeleine round, or any other House, nor that she was planning to lay a motion on the matter today.

She felt her shoulders tense, and deliberately relaxed them. It was imperative that no one knew that until it happened. Her best chance was in surprise, so the Houses had no time to react.

Selene couldn't know anything. She was fishing, or it was about something else. There was no point in worrying through what would happen *if* Selene knew and *if* she chose to reveal it to the rest of the Houses, unless and until that was really happening.

"Excuse me," the footman stationed in the hall said. "I fear it is raining. Shall I have the chair brought round."

Marcia sighed. "Yes, please do."

When wearing a floor-length tunic with full House

embroidery on it, if she arrived damp around the edges she would look exceptionally foolish.

Selene's rooms, when Marcia was shown up to them by the owner of the guesthouse, were very pleasant. Well furnished; perhaps not quite as well as, say, her own drawing room, but very comfortably and all Mareker-make. The room's most appealing feature was the huge window that looked out over the cliff and down the river; a view similar to that from House Fereno, albeit lower.

Selene was standing by the window, which put Marcia at a slight but immediate disadvantage. Selene would be able to see her well, despite the rainy overcast outside, but she couldn't see Selene's expression at all. She bowed, formally, as befit what she was wearing and the tone of Selene's message, and Selene bowed slightly in return. Selene was pulling out all the stops to intimidate her. She was claiming the rights of the Teren Lord Lieutenant, rights which in theory elevated her above Marcia.

In theory. What would happen if Selene pushed too hard on those rights? Marcia didn't know, and she wasn't keen to find out.

Marcia moved slightly to the left, to encourage Selene to move round herself and lose a little of the advantage of the light.

"Lord Lieutenant," she said. Keep it formal. "I was surprised to receive your message."

"I am concerned," Selene said, "with this declaration of the Guilds." She hadn't moved. Drat.

"Yes?" Marcia wasn't about to offer information.

"Teren desires a closer relationship with Marek, with the Houses. But I understand the importance of the Guilds in Marek's trading engagements with the rest of the world. The Guilds enhance Teren goods, after all, and that is beneficial for us." She wasn't wrong; many, though not all, of the raw materials that the Guilds used were from Teren. "We have been able to talk usefully before. I was hoping that we might be able to again now."

Which all very well; but why then had she been flinging her position around?

"I have tried to speak to the Guilds," Marcia said, which was entirely true. "They are… intransigent. I hope to speak to them again." She hesitated. Maybe it was worth at least testing the waters here. "I did however wonder whether discussing their demands further might be useful. Perhaps we could find a middle position that might satisfy both Houses and Guilds."

Selene frowned. "The Houses run Marek," she said. "I am surprised that you would even consider wishing it otherwise."

"The relationship between the Houses and the Guilds is, as you rightly say, important," Marcia said. "The foundation of our prosperity, even. As such…"

She nearly missed the very faint flicker of satisfaction in Selene's eyes, at 'foundation of our prosperity'.

"I understand that you were attempting to undermine exactly that prosperity, even before the Guilds began to throw their weight around," Selene said. "How has that worked out for House Fereno?"

Marcia smiled sweetly at her. "House Fereno is, as ever, concerned with what is best for Marek. I stand by my position that if the Guilds are unhappy, Marek will suffer for it, and I regret if my fellow Heirs and Heads have seen that differently. I am as distressed as anyone else that the Guilds have acted so intemperately to resolve these problems."

"My sympathies that your concerns have been taken so badly," Selene said.

Marcia didn't believe in her 'sympathies' for a single second.

"Intemperate is indeed the word. And intemperate behaviour, surely, should not be rewarded." Selene's tone did, at least, suggest that she didn't know what Marcia would be proposing later in Council. "I urge the Houses to hold fast. Teren will support you, if you need, for example, a better deal on goods, while the Guilds are holding out. I feel certain that the power of the Houses is sufficient to win through this challenge." She smiled, briefly. "The Guilds will, I am certain, blink first."

"That is certainly the view of my mother, and of the other Heads," Marcia said, her mind running fast. So that was Selene's angle. Strengthening the bond between Teren and Marek; making the Houses dependent on Teren goods. They could carry on trading raw materials without the Guilds, and that would surely be good for Teren. But it wouldn't be good for Marek. Was that the only thing Selene wanted? Or was it more than that; did she see the Houses weakening, and calling on Teren for aid. What sort of aid? If the Guilds and the Houses were in conflict...

A sudden chill ran through Marcia. If the Houses asked Teren aid in quelling the Guilds... surely that couldn't be what Selene was playing for. It would destroy Marek. And it would put the Houses, and therefore Marek, in Teren's grasp. Surely the Houses wouldn't be that stupid. Would they?

"Of your mother, but not of yourself?" Selene prompted, and Marcia dragged herself back to the conversation at hand.

"It is my mother who holds the vote," Marcia evaded. "I would simply prefer to see an end to this that doesn't involve the Houses and the Guilds starving one another out."

"Well, I wish you luck in convincing the Guilds to back down," Selene said, then shifted her weight. "I called you here primarily for another reason, though, as it happens."

Marcia blinked, startled by the sudden change of subject.

"I am grateful to you for introducing me to those Marek sorcerers," Selene said. She sounded like she was holding the word 'sorcerer' with tongs. "Unfortunately, they are not co-operating. I have reason to believe that the Teren runaway has come here; but I have heard no word from, who were they? Reb, and Cato."

"Maybe the sorcerer hasn't come to them?" Marcia suggested.

"Surely they should know, if another sorcerer is wandering around the city? Otherwise what is the point of this Group? Our Academy would certainly know if the situation were reversed."

Marcia hadn't known there was such a thing in Ameten. She stashed the information away for future reference, and for Reb's benefit.

"I must insist you find another sorcerer for me," Selene continued. "I am aware that there are fewer than there were, but there must be someone more competent."

Marcia's eyebrows flicked upwards for a moment before she got them under control. Reb and Cato must have deliberately chosen to present the impression of being two of many, and she had no intention of treading on either of their toes.

"I'm sorry," she said politely. "The Group is the only way in which I can reasonably put you in touch with sorcerers. It would be – most inappropriate, for me to do anything else."

"And what if the Houses were to hear of your relationship with this Reb?" Selene said.

Marcia didn't manage to control her jerk of shock. "My *what*?"

"You are spending a great deal of time with the sorcerer," Selene said. "Overnight, even." It was impossible to miss her insinuation; more so as it was true. "I understood that the Houses are not permitted to engage with sorcery."

"You've been *spying* on me?"

Selene shrugged.

"The Houses will not tolerate such behaviour from Teren towards one of our own," Marcia said, coldly furious. How dare Selene do this?

"A sorcerer brother, and a sorcerer lover," Selene mused. "Are you certain that they won't be grateful to me for exposing you?"

"The ban is on using sorcery," Marcia said, in tones as frigid and as assured as she could muster. "Not on knowing sorcerers. Say whatever you like, to whomever you like. I regret that I cannot assist you. Now, if you will excuse me."

She bowed, barely and dismissively, and turned to leave the room.

"Do let me know if you change your mind," Selene said, behind her.

☺ ☺

Jonas sat on the Guildhall roof and looked down on the late-morning Marek Square crowds below. Clouds raced across the sun, casting strange scudding shadows over the red roof-slates. A juggler was performing by the fountain; if Jonas wasn't mistaken, there was a pickpocket moving through the watching crowd, either working with the juggler or merely taking advantage of the distraction she offered. Being up here in the daylight was perhaps a little risky; but in his experience nearly no-one ever looked up in this city.

He'd come up here to be certain that he'd be alone for a

while. He'd woken up with the feeling that there was something that he was missing; something important. Eventually, he'd remembered the flicker he'd had, before, the one he'd ignored. The one that spoke of danger.

The thing was, seeing danger was all very well, but it hadn't been particularly informative. Unspecified danger, to unspecified people. Which was part of why he'd ignored it. That and the fact that he didn't want to have to deal with it.

He wasn't feeling comfortable about that decision any more. And he kept thinking that there must have been something that he'd missed.

He needed specifics, so he could make a more informed decision. And that meant trying to see it again, deliberately.

The wind was picking up. Jonas shivered and wished he'd brought his jacket up with him. He'd been warm earlier, but he'd been on the move then. Then he rolled his eyes at himself. Wasn't he supposed to be a sorcerer now? Cato had tried to teach him a warming charm the other day, telling him it was useful in winter for those who lived in the squats and were occasionally low on cash, and also useful if one wanted to be able to help out one's neighbours once in a while. He'd looked almost furtive when he said that last. Cato was an odd bloke; he went to great pains over his careless, callous reputation, but Jonas had begun to suspect it was, if not exactly an act, an overstatement. Sure, Cato's morals weren't up to, say, those of his sister, and he cared not even slightly for a number of social mores that were important to many of his neighbours. But he was basically kind; and he had a deep and abiding care for Marek and its people. At least, for those who weren't rich and who hadn't annoyed him lately.

Jonas reached into his pocket and brought out the little bag with the remnants of the base for the warming charm; then hesitated. He hadn't been able to do this when Cato showed it to him; and whilst Cato hadn't exactly forbidden him from trying magic on his own, he had strongly suggested that it was best, for now, to practise with him on hand in case of emergencies. (Like, for example, every pigeon in the city arriving.) But the instructions for this were easy, and Jonas *felt* like he'd be more able to do it now. He'd brought a flicker on by himself. He'd told his mother he was a sorcerer (nearly). He wasn't scared of the idea of magic any more.

And maybe it would be easier doing this on his own, out from under Cato's cool gaze. And if it wasn't, well, no one had to know.

Plus, he was cold.

He took out a pinch of the mixture, and scattered it at five points around him, as Cato had shown him. He reached out for that feeling that was Beckett noticing his request. As he concentrated, there was a feeling like something bursting gently at the base of his skull, the pinches of the mixture shivered and scattered away in all directions, and warmth spread through his body.

It had worked. It had just... worked, exactly as he'd wanted it to. Maybe he really was, finally, getting the hang of this.

Now for the flicker. He'd managed to bring one on before. Feeling that warmth in his bones, he wondered suddenly if this time, instead of just trying to induce it, he could do something with Marek-magic to enhance it. Even if the flickers themselves weren't Marek-magic.

He picked at a fingernail, hesitating. Really, if he was going to try that, he ought to go to Cato, to get his support. He had no idea what he was doing, after all. Doing a warmth spell in exactly the way he'd been shown was one thing; making something up all by himself was rather another.

But then, Cato didn't know anything about his flickers or where they came from. He wouldn't know how to go about this either.

He'd help, if Jonas asked. But that would mean explaining why he was keen to direct them, and that would mean explaining the danger-flicker to Cato. And he really wasn't keen to do that unless and until he had more information.

So. He could give up, and wait to see if anything more happened on its own; or he could give it a try. What did he have to lose?

He looked round the roof, and considered his own position, perched on the ridge. Perhaps trying out a brand new piece of magic, in particular attempting to trigger a flicker, would be better done closer to the ground. Or at least somewhere slightly less precarious. A ridge-pole was safe enough in the ordinary way of things, but not if he lost his balance.

There was a flat piece of roof between two chimney-pots, in a place where two rooftops sloped downwards to meet it.

That would do nicely, and would avoid him having to go all the way down to the ground, where there was far too high a risk that someone would see and interfere.

He squatted in the small space and considered his next steps. He was still warm from the previous spell. But he didn't have any other spell-makings on him. He chewed at his lip, considering the problem. What, after all, was the purpose of the spell-makings, the powders and the crushed this and that? They focussed the mind, maybe; they called up a particular energy. But the energy that he wanted to call up was all in himself, wasn't it? And what he wanted was, in effect, to ask Beckett's help to sharpen his own vision. Beckett, who belonged to Marek; and here he was, on the roof of one of the symbols of Marek. Perhaps the roof of the Council Chamber would have been even better; there again, the Council didn't hold with magic, did they? The Guilds probably did.

He pulled his pocketknife out and scraped at the edge of the chimney until he had a fair amount of soot; then pulled gently at his eyelashes until one came away, and added that to the little pile of soot in the palm of his left hand. Something for Marek, something to symbolise his own sight. Was there anything else he could add?

In the corner where the roofs came together, he spotted a feather. A crow feather. The crows circled over the city; they watched people and things. And the birds liked him, he was increasingly sure of that. He picked it up, and used it to swirl the soot and the eyelash gently around in his hand, watching them closely, watching the little barbs of the strands that made up the feather, watching the soot coat them and the eyelash stick to them, letting his awareness reach slowly outwards, seeking that feeling of being balanced between here and there, opening himself up to the awareness of Beckett…

There was a flash of light across his eyes, a confused welter of images, and then he cracked his head as he fell sideways, and everything went dark.

TWENTY-TWO

Marcia was early to Council. Not her normal approach, but she wanted to lay the motion before anyone else arrived. She was relieved to see that the only other person in the foyer was the Reader's Clerk in her long grey robe, a dour woman with short-cropped hair who had held the job for as long as Marcia could remember. Marcia greeted the Clerk politely and handed over the sheet of paper with the motion on. The Clerk read it over without so much as twitching a facial muscle; stamped it; and pinned it up on the board next to her small desk.

Marcia hadn't signed it. People usually did, but one didn't have to; and she didn't want to have to field attacks on it before she'd even stepped through into the Chamber. Presumably it would be assumed that it had been placed by the Guilds; what no one would know for certain would be whether or not the Guilds expected any House support.

Her palms were sweating. She wished she could go through now and sit down, but that would look peculiar. A fair fraction of the business of the Chamber happened out here, unofficially; one didn't deliberately absent oneself from it.

It was another few minutes before other Heads began to trickle in; then the Guildwardens arrived in a solid phalanx. Daril came in just after them, not looking even slightly anxious, the rotten shit. He swanned through the foyer without even looking at her, going straight to talk to Haran-Head. From the gestures, it looked like Haran-Head was asking after Gavin. She was faintly curious as to why Daril was here instead of Gavin, but not curious enough to ask. She might not like the answer.

No one had gone to read the motions-board yet. She wished they would; even without the signature tying it immediately to her, she was tense waiting for the first reactions.

Athitol-Head came up to her, and she stopped trying not to glare at Daril – and trying not to worry that he was going to back down at the last moment – and transferred her attention to the other woman.

"Your mother is not here today?"

"Mother and I agreed that I would begin carrying our vote some of the time, this year," Marcia said, which was a slight exaggeration.

"Well. That's an interesting reaction to your recent behaviour." Her tone was cutting.

Marcia kept a smile on her face. There really wasn't anything she could say to that. To assure Athitol-Head that she and her mother were not at odds would just make her more likely to believe that they were, and were trying to cover it up.

Athitol-Head looked faintly thwarted not to have got a rise out of Marcia. "I see you're not the only Heir carrying your vote today," she said, nodding across the foyer. "Young Daril tells me that Gavin is not well today." Unwell, was he? Huh. Athitol-Head sniffed. "I trust it will be a while longer before your generation takes over *entirely*."

Well, it would, because Athitol-Head's generation – and Madeleine's, and Gavin's – had made sure of that. But that wasn't an argument Marcia wanted to get into either.

"Mm," she said, instead, through her pleasant smile, and, after another moment, Athitol-Head sniffed, and turned, and swept away. Wretched woman.

Athitol-Head was on her way to the motions-board. Marcia's stomach flipped. Athitol-Head's shoulders twitched – surprise? disapproval? both? – before she began to turn, and Marcia hastily looked away. She didn't want to allow Athitol-Head to catch her eye. Out of the corner of her eye, she saw Athitol-Head go over to where Daril was still speaking to Haran-Head. Marcia bit the end of her tongue, and stayed where she was. Daril would say what he would say, truthful or otherwise, and she had to let that happen.

Several Guildwardens were clustered around the board now; and Marcia could see the news beginning to percolate around the room. She was grimly aware that however much she might be trying to avoid it, someone was going to talk to her, sooner or later. Everyone knew what she'd been up to. After the Guildwardens, she was the next likely candidate to have laid the thing. And it wasn't like she wouldn't have to speak up once she was in the Chamber. She might as well speak in favour now as then. She'd only left it unsigned to buy as much time as possible before she was challenged.

She'd heard nothing from Nisha about a third vote. Two would be enough, but... Maybe she'd be able to say something during the discussion to persuade someone else. She hadn't wanted to go into it this way; wouldn't be doing it at all just yet if it weren't so clear that in a few more days the rift between Houses and Guilds would be unbridgeable...

"Marcia!"

She turned round. "Nisha? What are you doing here?"

"Message for you," Nisha said. "Really I suppose I should wear a nice red armband, no? I need a moment in privacy." She jerked her head at one of the small alcoves off the main foyer, and Marcia, a little reluctantly, followed her in there, feeling eyes on her back.

"I got you another vote," Nisha said, her voice low, once they'd closed the curtain behind them.

"What? Who?"

"Kilzan, of course." Nisha looked smug. "I found out some very interesting information about Kilzan-Heir."

Marcia's eyebrows shot up. "Blackmail? Nisha..."

Nisha shook her head. "Not exactly. More that – you know the old man's been wanting rid of Yttra for ages, and who can blame him. That's what happens, though, when you name someone you barely know as Heir, right? Anyway. All he had was suspicion. I managed to establish that Yttra's been defrauding the House. Hard evidence, you understand, not speculation." She looked pleased with herself. "She's about to be accused of serious assault, to boot. Kilzan-Head will be disowning her immediately."

Marcia looked at the curl of Nisha's smile, and made a deductive leap. "And bestowing the Heirship on you instead?"

Nisha bobbed a dainty and self-satisfied curtsey. "And in the process I talked him into voting with you, should the issue arise, and I suggested that it might do soon. He's not particularly impressed with House Fereno at the moment, but I think I convinced him that perhaps you were seeing a bit further than the rest of them were. I... have some links with the Guilds myself, which may have helped." She meant, Marcia was fairly certain, that she'd offered Kilzan-Head some particularly good contracts. But that, too, was something Marcia didn't intend to enquire into. The vote itself would suffice.

"Nisha, you're a star," Marcia said fervently. "By the way – did you hear anything from Aden?"

Nisha shook her head. "Not a thing. It was always a bit of a long shot, that. But this is good enough, right?"

"Yes," Marcia said, as convincingly as she could. It was, technically. Three votes. More than enough. But she could have wished for more.

The rustle outside indicated everyone was going into the Chamber. Marcia nodded to Nisha, ducked out, and went into the Chamber to take her place.

Selene was sitting in the same place as when she'd opened the Council session. Marcia's stomach lurched uncomfortably. She hadn't seen Selene go in. She hadn't expected her to be here at all. The Teren Lieutenant *could* attend, most certainly, there was no question of that. But the previous one never had.

Selene could attend. And... Marcia's stomach lurched, and for a moment she thought she was going to be sick. She had a vote, didn't she? The Lord Lieutenant could vote, if they wanted. They never did; it was unheard of, for centuries. But... it was there.

She felt almost outside her body as she took her seat, counting through the votes. Ten Guild members. Thirteen Houses. Three voting with the Guilds. Thirteen-ten, so even if Selene did vote, it wouldn't matter. *If* everyone kept their word. It didn't help to shake the feeling of doom pressing on her shoulders.

She sat down, and took up the pencil and paper that was left by each seat, to send a note to the Reader's Clerk, quietly sitting now by the door through to the Chamber, to check whether she was right about Selene's vote.

Technically, yes. However no Lord Lieutenant has exercised it in modern times, the note she got in return read. Marcia folded it into halves, quarters, eighths, and put it down.

No Lord Lieutenant has. That didn't mean Selene wouldn't.

But either way; there was no point in delaying this further. She felt sick enough as it was; she wanted to get it over with.

As soon as the Reader began the session, she stood up and moved the motion.

"That the Chamber increase the Guild votes to thirteen," she proposed. She'd decided to leave out the casting vote for now; if someone else wanted to put it in, they could. Marcia herself rather liked the idea that any measure that couldn't gain some support from one side or the other was doomed. If anyone else didn't, it was up to them to suggest alternatives.

Athitol-Head was already on her feet, the frown-lines on her face deep. "I move that this be discussed in Small Chamber."

"I oppose," Marcia said, stomach tight with anxiety. She'd anticipated that this might happen, and there was no counter she could think of. With the motion to the Small Chamber both proposed and opposed, it was up to the Reader to decide whether it was suitable to move it.

To her surprise, Jyrithi-Head got to their feet. The subdued browns and deep blues of their Council-formal gown swirled around them. "Before the Reader makes their decision," they said, slowly. "I urge them to consider this carefully. Of late, we have moved a great many decisions to the Small Chamber. Of course, there is an argument that as we know which way the Guilds will vote, this is a matter for the Houses to decide. But equally, I feel there is more weight to the point that as this concerns the Guilds so closely, it would be a miscarriage of our governmental system were we not to allow them the right to decide on this matter." Jyrithi-Head looked around. "I urge the Reader, and my fellow Heads, to consider most carefully what is best for Marek in this matter."

The Reader was frowning as they banged their staff on the floor. "Motion is dismissed. This will be discussed here, in full Council."

There was a rustle of discontent among the House benches, but Marcia breathed a sigh of relief.

And wondered whether what Jyrithi-Head had said indicated that they might have one more vote than she had counted on. House Jyrithi had a tendency to keep itself to itself; but Marcia had always seen Jyrithi-Head as among those who wished to cling as hard as might be to their House privileges. But then... Jyrithi had voted with her mother when the Guilds were included, hadn't they? She stared at Jyrithi-Head, wondering, and they turned their head, caught her eye, and gave her a bland smile that told her nothing.

She had three votes in any case, which carried the vote; but that didn't mean that the Houses would fall neatly in line, that the rest might not try to push back. An extra vote could make all the difference in how functional this change would be; on whether it resolved the divisions in Marek, or deepened them.

☺ ☺

Marcia barely remembered what she'd said to propose the motion, afterwards. She knew she'd spoken well; she'd practised debate since she was a child, part of her education first as potential Heir, then as likely Heir, then as confirmed Heir. She'd made notes, beforehand, and she knew she'd spoken to the notes. The importance of a strong relationship between the Houses and Guilds in Marek. Her regret that the Houses had failed to listen to the Guilds, and thus that the Guilds had reached the point that they'd been forced to express themselves quite this strongly. (She had to say something about that. She couldn't directly address the matter of 'giving in', of being 'held to ransom', as Madeleine had put it, but she could do her best to reframe the Guilds' ultimatum.) Her desire for the Houses and Guilds to move forwards together, strengthening Marek and increasing its prosperity and its sway in the world.

She said all of those things, but even as she heard her own voice in her ears, it felt pointless. Surely everyone in the room had already made their minds up. And until Daril cast House Leandra's vote, the Houses would assume – clearly were assuming, from the impatient looks cast around the Chamber – that it would go their way.

The trouble would come when the vote passed. What the resolution said, and what might in reality happen next, were different things. Marcia wished she could be certain that they would coincide.

Warden Hagadath spoke next, after Marcia had sat down and allowed her legs to shake under her gown. Their speech went nearly exactly as Marcia would have expected. It was clear that it, too, wasn't going to sway anyone's vote: there was nothing there that hadn't been in the calmer of the news-sheets about the matter, although Hagadath at least refrained from any of the more flowery or aggressive statements that they might have made. Throughout the speech, there were frowns and rustles from among the Heads. Those Heirs who were present, Marcia thought, looking around, were perhaps more on the side of the Guilds, or at least more open to persuasion; there were more thoughtful looks among them, and more deliberately neutral expressions. Not that they would, with the exception of her and Daril, get to vote.

Daril, across the room from her, sat back at his ease, a small, borderline smug smile on his face. Marcia was gloomily aware that Daril must have worked out a way in which this was going to be a good financial deal for House Leandra. He'd been right about the status impact, showing Leandra as power-brokers, but that would never have been enough by itself for him to take the risk. And certainly not for Gavin to agree. There was another angle on this for Daril, or Leandra, or both.

Marcia was so busy worrying about what might happen next, and telling over the ideas she'd come up with to sway the mood of the Chamber, afterwards, if that were necessary, that it was a complete surprise to her when Selene stood up and indicated to the Reader that she wished to speak.

The Reader frowned. This was not within the expectations of the Chamber. A speech at the Opening, yes. For the Lieutenant to attend, perhaps. But a speech in the normal way of business? They hesitated for a few moments, while Selene looked more and more impatient, and then gestured to give her the floor. She was, after all, entitled to it, just as she was entitled to vote. And Marcia was gut-wrenchingly sure, now, that she would do so.

It shouldn't matter. But would it?

"I am surprised," Selene said, her voice carrying forcefully around the Chamber, "that the Guilds would forget themselves in this manner; and still more surprised to see House Fereno supporting this absurdity. House Fereno, it seems, forgets the position of the Marek Houses. Forgets the important role you hold, linking Marek to Teren and maintaining Marek's, and thereby Teren's, position in the trading community."

Selene didn't appear to notice, but Marcia did: the Heads and Heirs shifting their weight as she spoke, beginning to frown in a different way. Was Selene about to stab herself in the foot? Was there a way she, Marcia, could draw attention to that? And what would the implications of that, itself, be for Marek's future? She caught Daril's eye across the Chamber. He had one thoughtful eyebrow raised.

"The Guilds do valuable work, of course," Selene was saying, her tone faintly dismissive. "But it is the Houses which hold Marek, and which create it in all its strength. I urge you to consider this carefully when you vote. I am sure you will wish to maintain the power of your position, rather than to dilute it by sharing it with a set of people whose oaths and motivations may be very different from your own, as nobles of Teren."

There was an audible intake of breath at that last statement; but Selene didn't seem aware of it. She sat down with a self-satisfied smile.

It took a moment for the Reader's eyebrows to come down, then they banged their staff on the floor to quell the rustlings and murmurings around the Chamber.

Selene had been dripping that version of the Houses and Marek into people's ears since she arrived; Marcia was certain of it now, even though she herself hadn't heard much of it. She thought she'd convinced the Houses, or enough of them, that Teren was their future, instead of just their distant past. She wanted to pull Marek backwards. But Marcia, looking around the Chamber, felt the hairs on the back of her neck stand up. Selene, she thought, just might have finally and publicly overplayed her hand.

"Further to speak?" the Reader demanded, and Marcia found herself on her feet again.

"You have heard the words of the Teren Lieutenant," she said, finding the words just in time to say them, and hoping they wouldn't dry up in the middle. And that she was judging the mood of the Chamber correctly. "The Heads and Heirs of the Marek Houses are Teren nobles, she says. True, that is part of our history; but is it, now, today, our most important truth? Our most important loyalty? Are we not Marekers, above all? The Lieutenant wishes us to see ourselves as Teren first; she wishes us to draw away from the Guildwardens, our fellow Marekers. Are we certain that she has the best interests of Marek at heart? It seems to me that the Teren Lieutenant," she gestured at Selene, "has another agenda. It seems to me that Marek, as we have been until these last few days of argument, is strong, and prosperous, and powerful. It seems to me that Marek rejoices in links throughout the Oval Sea that Teren does not have. It seems to me that by driving a wedge between the Houses and the Guilds, Teren might seek to limit our power…"

"Not so!" Selene protested.

The Reader banged their staff. "I will have quiet while Fereno-Heir speaks!"

"I invite the Houses to consider this most carefully," Marcia said. "Do we wish to align ourselves with our own city, our own citizens? Do we wish to move our city forwards, together? Or do we wish to allow Teren to increase its control now that we have so nearly shaken it off altogether. Do we wish to acquiesce meekly to Teren preferences? We may be Teren, but we are Marekers first, and we must look to our responsibilities as Marekers before our links to Teren." She shrugged. "I for one care much more for my House here than I do for lands I have never seen in Teren. And I am suspicious of the attempts of the Teren Lieutenant to convince me otherwise. I do not know what she has in mind, but it seems to me that whatever it is, it concerns Teren rather more than Marek."

She sat down. She couldn't tell whether she'd swayed anyone. Selene stood to answer, but the Reader waved her to sit again. She hesitated for a moment, and the Reader waved at her again, more forcefully. She sat with visible ill grace.

"We proceed to the vote," the Reader said.

The Reader called for the ayes. The Guilds, of course, all ten. She stood, herself, and opposite her, Daril got to his feet. Shocked murmurs ran around the hall. Kilzan-Head, to her left, didn't move, and Marcia swore under her breath. If Selene voted, they would be even. And the default, in the case of a tie, was the status quo.

Just as the Reader was about to gesture them to sit down, Jyrithi-Head stood, slowly but with their shoulders set. The murmurs intensified. Jyrithi-Head was staring across at Selene, their eyes just a little narrowed, and Marcia noted it for future reference. Then, hesitantly, not meeting anyone's eyes, Tigero-Head rose. He didn't quite straighten all the way up, his shoulders hunched against the whispers from the rest of the House benches, but he was standing. Had Aden had come through, after all? Or was Andreas finally starting to think for himself? He'd be dealing with Marcia for a lot longer than he would be dealing with the current Heads, wouldn't he. She should make sure she met with him, as soon as possible after this.

Four votes. She hadn't begun to think of four votes. A wild elation began to bubble up inside her. Daril, opposite, was smirking more widely now. The annoying arse.

The Reader waved them down, and called for the Nays. Eight Heads, and Kilzan-Head still seated. The Reader waved a hand towards him, and Kilzan-Head slashed his hand sideways, gesturing abstention. Well. That was at least better than voting against. Fourteen, eight, one. It was a victory, but was it enough of one?

Selene hadn't stood. Her face was set like granite. But she too could count. Marcia would have bet every penny in her pocket that Selene had been planning to vote no. Marcia wished that she had voted anyway; that she had demonstrated her contempt for Marek's customs more clearly, that the Nays were taken first. But Selene wasn't that stupid.

The Heads sat, and the Reader said, "Fourteen ayes. Eight nays. One abstention. The ayes have it."

A babble of voices rose through the Chamber. Marcia couldn't quite make out the overall tone.

The vote might have passed; but would it hold? Athitol-Head was the only one that Marcia thought might have the strength to spearhead any resistance. Standing against the Council's sworn decision – it had happened in the past, Marcia knew, but it was costly for everyone involved. She could only hope that Athitol-Head – and the rest – would not see it as worthwhile to challenge the Council, however unhappy they might be.

Surely, at this point, they must know that they couldn't risk further antagonising the Guilds. Mustn't they?

The Reader, barely audible over the uproar, made the

formal declaration of no further motions and dismissed the session. Slowly, Marcia got to her feet, looking around her, trying to read faces.

Kilzan-Head walked briskly across the Chamber floor towards Warden Hagadath, and showily shook their hand, nodding to the other Wardens. Marcia watched, tense. Athitol-Head followed. She looked furious, but she shook Warden Hagadath's hand anyway, and Marcia let out a breath. That was enough. That would swing it. Six Houses openly acquiescing. The other seven could stand against, but only at heavy commercial and political cost, especially given that the Ayes hadn't cut along the traditional block lines. Fereno and Leandra had voted together, to start with; and neither Athitol nor Tigero were connected with either of them.

Pedeli-Head turned round from the seat in front. "I am far from sure, Fereno-Heir," she said, icily, "that this is a wise move. Nor one that your mother would approve."

"I think it is wise," Marcia said, politely, choosing to ignore the second part of that. It wasn't for her to affirm that House Fereno stood together; that would only look weak. "I think we strengthen Marek this way, that we will open new doors to new ideas that will make our city stronger."

"Well. Well. We shall see, I suppose. In any case – I cannot but agree with you about Teren." They frowned. "Our independence, here... well. Yes. She went much too far." They nodded, and moved away towards the door.

Marcia watched them go, unsure of how to feel.

"How dare you."

Marcia spun round to see Selene behind her, face flushed with anger.

"I beg your pardon?"

"Deliberately breaking the bonds between Marek and Teren? You will regret it, I guarantee it. When Teren magic comes here, when I find that sorcerer... You will regret it."

She swept away, and Marcia watched her go, cold dread suddenly pooling in the pit of her stomach. It might just be hot air, Selene furious and saying things to scare her. But there was something in what she'd said, something that tugged at a strand in Marcia's memory...

She had to go talk to Reb. Right now.

TWENTY-THREE

Jonas opened his eyes, blinking up at the sky above him, dark clouds piling up against afternoon-blue, and for a moment had no idea where he was. Cold roof-tiles under his head. His feet wedged against – more tiles? Warmer than he ought to be for the chill in the air. He sat up and rubbed at the sore place on his head, then looked around and recognised the tall peak of the main Guildhall roof. Everything clicked back into place like a series of dominoes falling. On the Guildhall roof. Chasing flickers, because he was a damn idiot. Thank goodness he'd been smart enough to move down here. He could have come off far worse for it.

He'd been floored by flickers before, but never that badly. He shut his eyes again, still rubbing at his head, and reached for the memory of it before it could escape. A tall figure, someone Jonas didn't recognise, but they had long hair braided right down their back. What overwhelmed the flicker, what had Jonas shivering just as he experienced the memory again, was the shadow that fell across them, growing as he watched. Usually Jonas' flickers were fairly concrete – he saw real people, doing real things. This might be like that, too; but it felt like something else. The feel of the shadow was larger than its look, as though it were falling not just over this one person but across the whole of the city. And though there was, unusually, no background to the flicker, he was certain that it was Marek.

What was the shadow? It was the one he'd seen before, in that flicker of catastrophic dread from Marek Square. His image of it was still shapeless, yet it felt like it had more arms than it should, and more teeth. He shivered.

So, on the bright side, the experiment had worked. Kind of. Fine, he might have nearly knocked himself out. But he'd taken an existing flicker, and he'd obtained more information about it, through the same means as he used for sorcery. Not as much as he might have liked – he still didn't know what that shadow was – but he would know the person he'd seen,

289

if he saw them again. At least, from that angle.

He rubbed his hands over his face. He had to tell Cato. This was important. He couldn't doubt that any more; couldn't push it away again. He had to tell someone. And Cato took him seriously, albeit in his own special way. Cato would listen.

Jonas held his hand out to be sure it had stopped shaking, then climbed back out of his protective roof-dip, back up to the roof-ridge of the Guildhall. How long had he been out for? The sun had dipped from its noon height, though he wasn't sure quite how far. Still mid-afternoon, sometime. He couldn't read the Guildhall clock from up here, owing as how it was underneath him. It couldn't have been all that long, surely. He hoped. He shivered again. His warmth charm was wearing off, but he didn't know how long it was supposed to have lasted.

It didn't matter. He just needed to go and find Cato, whatever the time was. If he was going to do this, he should get on with it.

It didn't take him long to get over to Cato's. Through the door, up the stairs, and he paused just outside Cato's door with its red C, frowning a little. He could hear voices inside. If Cato had a client, he'd likely not be thrilled to be interrupted. But then, nor would he be thrilled to find Jonas skulking outside the door when the client left, and some of Cato's clients might take that particularly badly. He rubbed his tongue against his teeth a couple of times, and knocked.

The door swung open with no one behind it. Jonas had been intimidated by that trick the first time he'd come here. Now he just stepped forwards. Cato was lounging on the bed; a tall figure was behind him, outlined against the light from the window, looking out at the city. Presumably this was the client.

"Jonas? What are you here for? I wasn't expecting you today." Cato was frowning at him.

"Yeah, well." Jonas took a deep breath. "I had…" Now he was here, the words were hard to get out, and he didn't want to talk about this in front of some stranger, either. "I needed to talk to you about something. Urgently."

The figure in the window turned round and moved slightly away from the window, and Jonas got a good look at them.

What he had thought was short hair was long, with a braid thrown forwards over their shoulder, and that face...

Jonas took a step backwards. He couldn't think properly. Whoever it was stood now next to the window, the window's edge throwing its shadow across them, just like his flicker. But that shadow had been bigger, darker, more significant...

"Oh, right," Cato said. "This is Tait. They're from Teren. Also a sorcerer, but here to find out a bit more about Mareker magic."

A friend of Cato's? From Teren? The shadow moved again, across Tait, and Jonas bit back on a scream. He was being completely irrational, but he couldn't think of what he could say next.

"Jonas?" Cato asked, frowning. "Is something wrong?"

"I think it's me," Tait said. Their voice was soft, and their whole demeanour was unthreatening, but that shadow that wasn't there, that had nothing to do with the sunlight and the window, it was looming over them, getting darker...

"You're bringing danger," Jonas blurted out. "I... I saw it."

A number of expressions flickered across Cato's face, too fast for Jonas to read, before Cato leant forward, his face serious. "A flicker?"

Jonas nodded. His legs felt wobbly, and he couldn't look at Tait any more. His head throbbed.

"Let him sit down," Tait said, and moved towards Jonas, who shied away without even meaning to. Tait stopped dead.

"Honestly, Jonas," Cato said, exasperated. "I don't know what you've seen, and I don't know how reliable it is anyway, but Tait isn't a threat to you, for fuck's sake."

Tait moved back again, hands spread open, unthreatening, their eyes on Jonas. "Whatever's going on here, he's distraught and scared. Get him sitting down."

Cato, scowling, gestured the stool across to Jonas, before throwing himself back on the bed.

"Right. You've seen something, and Tait was in it? I don't think..."

"It could be true," Tait said, quietly. "Couldn't it."

Cato bit his lip and stopped talking.

Jonas swallowed. "Normally I get something – specific. A place, a moment, even if I don't recognise it 'til I get there. This was – like that; Tait in the shadow there. But it was more than that, too. The shadow grew, it wasn't just a shadow, it was something… It was over Marek, the whole of Marek. It's bigger than one person, but." He stopped, made himself look at Tait, quickly, before he looked away again. "But it's attached to you. It's not your shadow, it's the wrong shape, and it has…" teeth, it had teeth, but he couldn't say it. "It's attached to you," he said again, instead.

Out of the corner of his eye, he could see Tait hunching into themself.

"No one person can risk the whole of Marek," Cato said, bracingly, then turned to look at Tait, and blinked. "Tait?"

"It's the demon," Tait said. Jonas glanced at them again. Their arms were wrapped around themself, and they were staring at the floor.

"You banished it," Cato said. "It's gone."

"But maybe I didn't," Tait said, miserably. "The Lieutenant said… maybe she's right."

"I didn't trust her," Cato said.

"The Academy…" Tait said, then stopped.

"Right," Cato said. "The Academy. How about you tell me about the Academy, then. Inasmuch as I thought about Teren sorcerers at all, I thought they worked alone."

"It's new," Tait said. "They've been… recruiting. Students." He looked at Cato. "That's new. It used to be, you'd have to go seek someone out, if you wanted to learn. And not that many people did. But they came into the university and the colleges, and they looked for people."

"They recruited you?" Cato asked.

Tait shrugged a shoulder. "They made it sound good. And they paid. I was running out of money anyway, I was going to have to leave the university. They housed you and they paid and they said you'd learn to do magic, for the good of Teren."

"Mmm," Cato said, his tone very neutral.

"Blood magic, fine," Tait said. "They were a bit unhappy that I wouldn't use animals. But even with my own blood, I'm strong. They told me that, too. And then, there was the demon."

"Just the one?" Cato asked.

"You train a lot before you do it," Tait said. "And I didn't… well, anyway. You summon it and you bind it."

"It's a lot easier to negotiate with a spirit, you know," Cato said. "Why didn't you try that first?"

"Negotiate?" Tait said blankly. "You... you have to bind it, to keep it safe."

"No you don't. But fine, that's what you were told. And then what?"

"They wanted me to use it."

"Ye-es?"

"On people. There was... a demonstration. Students. I knew some of them. I... I said I wouldn't, and they said I would, and I banished the demon before they could make me. And then I ran away." Tait's voice broke. "I banished it! I did!"

"Right," Cato said. "Your so-called tutors at the Academy wanted you to bind a demon and use it against your fellow citizens. Well, fuck them, then. You did the right thing. You banished it, end of story."

"But there's something attached to them," Jonas said. He felt that Cato was perhaps missing the point.

"See?" Tait said. "I must have made a mistake. Like the Lieutenant said."

"Or something else has happened," Cato said. He was chewing at a fingernail. Cato didn't normally have tells. "Jonas isn't seeing a demon. He's seeing a shadow. That could mean quite a lot of things, and none of them necessarily your fault. Right? Teren is definitely after you in some way. Maybe the shadow... it needn't be the demon, Tait. It could just be Teren putting the screws on Marek over this matter. The shadow of the Academy, kind of thing."

"But if there's someone chasing me... if the Academy are bringing danger, and it's down to me... I should go," Tait said.

Cato shook his head. "No you shouldn't. You're in Marek, now, remember? I don't care what the Academy are up to. Their power is in binding spirits, right? Which means you're safe. Other spirits are not welcome, here. We have our own."

There was a crack in the air, and Beckett stepped into the room, from nowhere. All three of them swore. Jonas nearly fell off his stool as he cringed backwards; Tait was pressed against the wall. Beckett's thin face was blazing with rage.

"Who has brought this thing to my city? Who?"

A wash of relief overwhelmed Jonas' shock and fear. A

shadow, a demon; whatever it was and whether or not it was Tait's fault, regardless of any fast words Cato might bring to this, Beckett wasn't going to tolerate someone putting Marek at risk. And if Beckett got rid of the shadow, Jonas didn't much care how he did it.

⊙ ⊙

"Right. Hang on. Let's all slow down a bit here," Cato said, attempting to regain some control of the situation.

He felt out of his depth, which was both an uncommon, and a deeply uncomfortable, experience for him. This was *his* room. He was supposed to be in charge. He was supposed to know what was going on.

He had a horrible feeling that he did know what was going on. He just didn't like it.

Beckett, over by the door, was nearly shooting sparks out of their fingertips; and at the best of times Beckett took up more space and light in a room than they should. Cato really hated Beckett's new-found habit of just *appearing* out of *nowhere*, but there was sod all he could do about it.

Jonas was clearly scared out of his wits, and Cato felt obliged to take Jonas' flickers seriously. And given what Tait had said, and what that Teren woman Selene had said, he was coming to some uncomfortable conclusions, which Beckett's arrival merely underlined.

Tait was hunched into themselves, next to the window, with their back against the wall. Cato fought a strong urge to get them to sit down next to him and be reassured. It didn't look like reassurance was on the cards right now.

"How about everyone just calm down a bit, and let's start this from the top," Cato said, doing his best to be soothing, with no idea whether he was succeeding. Soothing was hardly his forte. "Jonas, you've seen – foreseen – something alarming involving Tait here and Marek. Beckett, you say there's something – a demon, I'm going to assume – coming to Marek? How can that even happen?"

"Because I summoned it," Tait said, wearily.

"Because they summoned it." Beckett's voice had risen. Threads of magic pulled and twisted through the air, moving towards Beckett.

"That's the shadow I saw, then," Jonas said. He sounded either resigned, or so far past scared that he'd run out of emotions.

"You didn't summon it in Marek," Cato corrected, speaking clearly and with as much conviction as he could muster. "Because that wouldn't work." Or, Beckett would have known a lot more immediately than that, and reacted a lot more strongly. Not that the cityangel wasn't quite pissed off right now.

"Reb said you summon spirits," Jonas said.

"I don't *summon* them as such, and also I am not in Marek, technically, when I do it," Cato said, casting a nervous glance over at Beckett, who didn't react. "We are straying from the point. Tait summoned and bound a demon, in Teren, yes, fine. But they banished it." He turned back to Tait. "That's what you remember, isn't it?"

"Obviously I didn't actually do it." Tait's voice was a tiny thread of sound.

Cato shook his head. "No. I don't buy that. You're not stupid, Tait. And you're evidently a strong sorcerer. The demon-bear, remember? You wouldn't have just... not noticed a failed banishing."

"You don't know anything about Teren magic," Tait said. "How would you know?"

Cato fought back the impulse to scream. Did Tait have some kind of death-wish?

"No, indeed, I don't go around binding spirits," he agreed affably. "As previously discussed. I negotiate with them instead. And from time to time, I have made an agreement." Not often, because it was easier just to store power, but he had done it when the need arose. "Which is, I believe, analogous to a binding, just agreed rather than imposed. I know the drag of an active agreement. You can *feel* the thing, all the time. I can't believe a forced binding would be any less obvious. You would know." He paused. "Also, by your own account, you were trotting up and down the damn mountains a fortnight or more before you came here. If you'd just bungled the banishment, you'd be eaten by now."

"And yet it is here," Beckett said. Tait, who had been looking a little bit reassured, sagged again.

"Hang on, wait. Here, as in, here in Marek?" Cato asked, startled. More than startled. Beckett had said coming to, he was sure of it. If this spirit had found its way past Beckett's boundaries… but surely Beckett wasn't furious enough for that…

"Not in Marek," Beckett said, almost impatient, and Cato's stomach somersaulted in relief. "Outside. But I cannot dismiss it. Or overcome it. It is attached to this plane."

"Just because it's attached to this plane doesn't mean it's attached to Tait," Cato said, then turned to Tait. "Because I'll tell you what my working theory is, and that's that the Academy want you back, and failing that, they want you dead."

"Why?" Tait said. "Why would they bother?"

Cato shrugged. "You're middling strong, which might make it worth it, depending on who else they have available. But in all honesty, given what you've said about what they're up to and why you ran away, I think this is more about demonstrating that you can't run. Do you think you're the only one who wouldn't have wanted to use a demon on your fellow citizens? What about the other students?"

"Some of them wouldn't care," Tait said. "Some of them would be happy to. But… some wouldn't, if they thought there was another option."

"But there isn't an option?" Cato said.

"Once you're in, you stay, or you fail," Tait said. Cato had a sneaking suspicion that 'failing' in this context didn't mean you got a cheery handshake and booted out of the back door. He kicked himself for not having followed up on Tait's initial references to the Academy until just now; he'd meant to, and then he'd forgotten about it. If he'd known all of this, he might have thought a bit more seriously about this business of the Teren Lieutenant and her claims – her lies – about demons, and what the implications of those lies might be.

"So if you'd banished the demon and then said, no thanks, I want out?"

Tait shook their head with utter conviction. "No. You can't just leave. You can't just stop. That's why I ran."

"Right," Cato said. "So. You ran away. If they let you run, what happens? Everyone will be at it. But if they drag you back and feed you to a demon… it shows their power. It shows there isn't an option. Or, I suppose, they could feed you to a demon down here and report it back, but it would work better if it's more public."

Tait swallowed. "Punishment is... usually in public, yes."

"The demon is here," Beckett said impatiently. "Trying to get in. I want it to go. Why are we talking about this?"

"To find out how to achieve that," Cato said patiently. "Look. If Tait raised it and didn't banish it, and we feed them to it, then fine, it goes away. But if someone else raised it again, bound it, and set it on Tait – which I am pretty sure is what has happened here – then we wouldn't achieve anything."

"It would have what it wants and it would go away," Beckett said.

"I am not feeding anyone to a demon just to get rid of it unless there is absolutely no fucking alternative," Cato said. "End of story. And it's hardly Tait's fault that they're being chased." He looked over at Tait and winced. "There will be an alternative. I'm not falling for that wretched story that Teren woman fed me." Except he had fallen for it, when Selene had spun him the yarn, which was perhaps part of why he was so angry. He took a breath. "Do we have to care, if it just hangs around outside Marek?

"It won't," Jonas said. His face was pale, and he was fiddling with his hair. "It wants in."

Beckett was scowling. "I am not invulnerable. My power is not unlimited."

"Your power is the whole life-force of Marek," Cato said. "That might not be unlimited, but it's surely bigger than any other spirit can call on while they're here." Cato knew spirits could do a great deal while in their own plane – he'd rather counted on that, in fact, when working with them – but were rather weaker, though still more than strong enough for human purposes, while they were wholly over here. Of course, mostly Beckett wasn't over here either; mostly, Beckett stayed spirit-side, and handled their peculiar connection to Marek from there. Or something like that. Cato would be the first to admit that he wasn't... entirely clear on the matter, because before this year it had never bloody *mattered*.

"You misunderstand," Beckett said. "I will not accept this continued threat of intrusion. I will not accept this draw on my power. We must break the link, and the link is through that one." They nodded at Tait.

"Well, if you're certain the link is through Tait, I suppose that confirms that it's them it's after." Cato looked over at Tait. "Still doesn't make it your fault."

"Even if I didn't summon it," Tait said, their voice shaking a little, "if it wants me… killing me will get rid of it, won't it? It'll protect Marek." They straightened up, set their shoulders.

"Very well," Beckett said, and raised their hands.

"No!" Cato yelped.

Beckett turned and scowled at him. "This is not endurable."

"I can't believe that there's no way other than Tait dying to break this link of yours. Especially since Tait didn't damn well summon the thing. Not this time, anyway. I will not give in to sodding Teren on this." Especially not when he'd been *lied* to. He rubbed at his forehead. There had to be another solution. "Let's go through this again. You summoned it, you didn't do anything much with it, you sent it back again, someone else raised it and set it on you. Giving it some kind of link to you, which we need to break."

"There is a simple solution," Beckett said, in what they probably thought was a quiet voice.

"No! For pity's sake Beckett, have some patience."

"Marek's in danger," Jonas said, tension thrumming through his voice. "We may not have much time for patience."

"Look. We can always just kill Tait, any time," Cato said, through his teeth. "Especially since they've just expressed their intention not to resist. Let's take a few minutes to see if we actually have to, all right? We have three sorcerers here, even if Tait knows a different form of magic. Are we all entirely useless?"

"It might be linked to me, but it's not bound to me the way I recognise," Tait said. Which at least suggested they'd accepted Cato's argument about the banishing. "I can't feel anywhere to push. I can't feel that it's *there* at all." Their voice wobbled.

"Wait!" Cato said. "Hang on. It's not bound to you, but Beckett says it's linked. So. Talk me through how this stuff works for you, in Teren. If you summon a demon, and bind it, do you just bind it to the sorcerer, or to the job that you want it to do?"

"Both, usually," Tait said.

"Usually. Right. And this one is outside Marek, in this plane, and it's linked to you. You're not the sorcerer that bound it – which means there must be someone out there who did, but I don't think that's relevant right now – you're the job."

"That's right," Tait said. They were frowning at Cato. "Or – not necessarily. But probably, if there's a link."

"There is a link," Beckett said again.

Cato ground his teeth and just about managed not to tell the cityangel to shut up; restraint made easier by the fact that he could feel his fingers beginning to tingle with rising glee. He could feel the edge of a *solution*. "So… if we have strength, and we have a link… who's to say that we can't just break it."

Tait's expression hadn't changed. If anything, they just looked more bemused. "But you can't give me your strength."

"No," Cato agreed. "But Beckett can. And Beckett can take our strength. Right?"

Beckett still looked sulky, but marginally less so. "I may not be able to link to this one. They are not Mareker."

"Try it and find out?" Cato suggested. "If Tait doesn't mind?"

Tait shrugged. "It's this or get eaten by a demon. Or whatever else the Academy can think up. Try whatever you want."

Beckett's expression grew concentrated, then they looked over at Tait. Tait flinched, then their eyes widened, and they stared at Beckett. Beckett, suddenly, looked slightly less grim. Cato could feel his own victorious grin. Then Beckett blinked, and Tait flinched again, and rubbed at their arms.

"It will work," Beckett said, unnecessarily.

"Well then," Cato said. He'd realised what they were missing, although he didn't much like it. "We need as much power as possible, which means we're currently short one sorcerer. Let's go find Reb."

He was not looking forward to this conversation. But Reb was a soft touch. Sort of. She'd be up for this.

☺ ☺

Beckett had disappeared into nowhere, and would doubtless reappear from nowhere again at Reb's place. As they made their way across Marek, Cato was bracing himself to not be incredibly pissed off at this. He realised that Jonas was hovering with intent, as much as one could hover whilst walking.

"What's up?" Cato asked.

"Do we have to… I mean, can we…" He was looking shifty. "I'd rather not tell Reb about my flickers, just yet. Can't we just let Beckett be the one who says about it all?"

Cato considered the matter. Jonas was right; given that Beckett was making such an almighty fuss, the whole thing where Jonas was prophesying doom could probably be left out. It might even make for a somewhat smoother explanation, with fewer awkward moments and unnecessary side-tracks centring around the question of why Cato had not previously informed Reb about these flickers.

"Fine," he conceded. "Unless she won't be convinced, in which case we might need it."

Jonas scowled, but nodded.

"Did you hear that, Tait?" Cato asked. Tait was walking on his other side, shoulders hunched.

"Eh? What?"

"Leave out Jonas' whole 'foreseeing the future' thing, yeah?"

"Oh. Of course." Tait's good manners resurfaced, and they attempted a polite smile. Jonas didn't look convinced.

It was late afternoon now, the sun beginning to cast long shadows; there were dark clouds off in the distance, coming in towards the city. Just their luck if they had to go out to the city boundaries and chase off a demon in the rain.

It didn't take long to reach Reb's. Cato could have wished, in fact, that it had taken a little longer.

"What the hell are you doing here?" Reb demanded, on opening the door. Then her gaze switched to Tait. "And you!" She glared viciously at Cato. "What is going on?"

"How about, you let us in and we'll explain," Cato said.

Reb's eyes narrowed, and he thought she was about to refuse.

Then Beckett, from behind her, said, "Let them in."

Reb actually jumped, which pleased Cato greatly, although he tried not to show it.

"I told you not to do that," Reb said, through her teeth, but she stepped back into the room and let them all in anyway.

To Cato's immense surprise, Marcia was there too, wearing what he recognised as the tunic that belonged under her full Council formal robe, and a deeply anxious look.

"So," Cato said, brightly. "Turns out there's a demon on the doorstep – Marek's doorstep, that is – which appears to be after Tait here. A bit like Selene said, except it wasn't Tait's fault." He wasn't sure Reb accepted that part, from the expression on her face, but he kept going. "Beckett can't get rid of it on their own, but I think that together, using the link it's made to Tait, we could manage it. Without feeding Tait to it. Are you in?"

"No," Reb said, flatly.

Over her, Marcia said, "It's Selene. Selene summoned it."

"Selene isn't a sorcerer," Cato said.

"Then someone summoned it on her behalf," Reb said, impatiently. "And I said. No."

Cato blinked. "The alternative is to feed Tait to it," he said again, in case Reb had missed that part.

Reb shrugged. "Why do I care?"

"What the hell?" Cato demanded. "Aren't you supposed to be all moral and stuff? Fuck knows you keep bloody lecturing me about my decisions."

"I don't like demons," Reb said. "And I don't like sorcerers that run away from their mistakes." She glared at Tait, then back at Cato. "I thought I warned you."

"You sent a message," Cato agreed. It had been a bit too late by the time he'd got it, of course, but she *had* sent a message. "Yes indeed. But I think you were then, and apparently are still, under the impression that Tait failed to banish this thing. Not so. I am moderately certain that someone else dragged it back onto this plane and set it onto him, to avoid him getting away from their demons-as-guard-dogs setup."

"Cato. Stop. What in the hells are you going on about?"

At least he'd got her attention now. Cato, as briefly as he could – which was more briefly than it might otherwise have been, given Beckett's deep scowl and Tait's look of being about to collapse inwards on themself – explained the whole situation with the Academy and Teren, as he understood it.

"Setting demons on people?" Reb asked. She turned to stare at Tait, who nodded miserably. "You're certain?"

"Absolutely certain," Tait said. "There wasn't – I didn't misunderstand. That was what they wanted."

Cato forebode to point out that not two minutes ago, Reb had been happy to have a demon set on a person. To be fair, she'd thought this situation was Tait's fault; but still.

"Tait ran away rather than comply," Cato said, in case Reb had missed that part. "Seems understandable to me. Moral, even." He gave the word a bit of a spin.

Reb turned to Tait. "You didn't tell me that." She sounded annoyed. Possibly with Tait; possibly with herself. Possibly with Cato himself, come to that.

Tait shrugged. "You didn't seem like you wanted to believe me." They were pulling at their fingers. "I don't think I believed me, not really."

"I still don't really want to believe you," Reb admitted. "But…" She sighed. "I don't want to believe Selene either, I suppose."

"I didn't think much of Selene," Cato muttered. Reb ignored him.

"The demon is close to Marek," Beckett said, apparently under the impression that any of them might be forgetting that part.

"Does that mean it'll do anything here, though?" Reb asked. "Must we barge out there and deal with it, which I assume is the aim given you're all on my doorstep like this? Can't we just wait for it to go away?"

"Assuming it does go away," Marcia said. "If you think this is Selene's doing somehow – she's really pissed off. And she wanted Tait back."

"She can't get Tait while they're in Marek," Cato said. "So she can want whatever she likes. She isn't getting it."

Just as he finished speaking, he felt a shiver in the air. Beckett swayed slightly.

Reb looked sharply over at Beckett. Marcia hadn't reacted.

"Uh," Cato said. "Who just felt that?"

"Felt what?" Marcia demanded, at the same time as Reb

and Jonas both nodded.

"It is trying to get into Marek," Beckett said, sounding much calmer than Cato felt they ought to.

"But it can't, right?" Cato demanded.

"I will not permit it," Beckett said.

The shiver came again. Was it stronger?

Cato licked his lips. "Uh. I ask this merely hypothetically, you understand, but... what happens if it keeps trying?"

"I have the strength of Marek," Beckett said. "I am stronger than any of my kind can possibly be." Their voice held, perhaps, just a shade of nervousness.

"How much of the strength of Marek are you using, though?" Cato asked.

Beckett didn't answer. Cato exchanged glances with Reb. He was fairly certain that Reb was drawing the same tentative conclusions as him. He turned his hand up, and made the gesture for a witchlight. The first trick he'd ever learnt as a baby sorcerer, still hiding out in his room in House Fereno and trying to work out what he was doing. Something he could do without effort or thought or concentration.

There was a tiny, faint, flash above his fingertips. That was it.

Reb, watching him, looked alarmed. She reached into her pocket for a pinch of something, tossed it into the air, and blew. The tiny pieces fluttered, without a twitch, to the ground.

"Well, shit," Reb said. "Beckett, you're using *all* of Marek's strength for this? There's nothing left over?"

"I will prevail," Beckett said.

"But what if you don't?" Cato muttered under his breath, then, louder. "Or, we could deal with it ourselves, directly, right now. Get rid of the thing rather than waiting it out. Fine, Beckett can hold it off forever, or maybe it'll tire out eventually," it rather depended on the power source, and Cato wasn't sure that Beckett could hold it off forever, but he didn't want to head down that track, "but I'd really rather not find out how *long* that will take by destruction testing it. And Beckett said before that they didn't want to have to keep doing this."

"The shadow's coming closer," Jonas said, quietly. He was shivering, and his eyes looked distant. It was unnerving.

Also, at this rate Jonas wasn't going to be able to keep his damn secret that much longer. Reb wasn't *unobservant*.

Reb glared round at all of them, then threw her hands in the air. "Fine. Let's go face down a sodding demon, then, and risk all of our lives instead of just one."

Cato winced. "I wasn't planning on risking any lives."

"The demon is," Jonas said.

Once again, Cato exercised massive restraint in not just telling someone to shut up.

"The Group of Marek should be stronger," Beckett said.

It was Reb's turn to wince. "I know. I should have built things back up sooner," she said.

"Well," Cato said. "You and I are strong. We have Beckett. And Jonas and Tait both have at least some ability." He gestured at Tait. "Did Tait tell you that they opened a vein and sent off a dragon-bear? By themself?"

"They're hardly versed in Marek sorcery," Reb said.

"But Beckett will be right there," Cato pointed out. "And will have to connect with Tait for any of this to work. It could hardly be easier to practise Marek sorcery, in the circumstances."

"Very well," Reb said. "I suppose…" The air shivered again, and her lips tightened. "Well. There's no time like the present. Let's go."

"Finally," Beckett said, and strode out of the door. The rest of them followed him like a set of magical ducklings.

Cato managed to catch at Tait's hand, as they went out of the door behind Reb, and smiled at them.

"It's going to be all right," he said.

Tait smiled wanly back, and Cato really, seriously, hoped he was telling the truth.

TWENTY-FOUR

Cato shivered. The sun had disappeared entirely while they were in Reb's house, covered over now with towering dark clouds. It ought just to be weather – it was autumn, it rained – except it didn't feel like that at all. The streets were oddly empty. Cato decided against asking Beckett about that.

They were passing the north end of Old Bridge, but Beckett didn't turn. Cato was fairly sure he knew where they were going. Out to the wholesale market, where the carts brought goods in from Teren. The market itself was within Marek. At some point, out beyond that, where the road and the river went off towards Teren, it wasn't Marek any more. What Cato didn't know was where the boundary was. In the river dockyard? Further? Nearer?

Next to him, Tait was shaking, very slightly. Cato hesitated, then reached out and took their hand again. Tait didn't stop shaking, but they did turn a grateful face to Cato. Cato did his best to give them a reassuring smile, although he wasn't at all sure how good his best might be. Tait didn't look any worse for it, so that was something.

Beckett was going on foot, rather than telling them where to go and meeting them there. Cato added that to the mental list of things he didn't want to ask about. He strongly suspected that it was for the same reason his light spell had failed; that the demon's attempt to get into Marek was taking all of Beckett's energy. Which raised the alarming question of what the hell they were going to do when they actually got there.

Another alarming question was: the demon was outside the city, because Beckett wouldn't let it in. But could Beckett *leave* Marek? And if they couldn't, what happened then? There was a point where Marek ended, but if Beckett couldn't go past that point, could Beckett's power? If Cato stepped over that line, would he still be able to do magic? One couldn't do Marek magic in Teren. Was it an absolute cut-off point, or a gradual change? Cato cursed the fact that it had never previously occurred to him to test this. Of course, he'd never intended to leave Marek – he still didn't intend to leave Marek, come to that – so it hadn't seemed remotely interesting or important.

Ugh. Why was he even here? Following dutifully after Beckett towards some *demon* bent on attacking the city; instead of, say, hunkering down and waiting for it all to pass. Except that he wouldn't be able to do much in the way of sorcery until Beckett got rid of this thing. That was a reasonable reason.

The less reasonable reason was that he wanted Tait to think well of him. Which was absurd, not to mention foolish.

Tait was still holding his hand. Or Cato was still holding Tait's. One of those. Cato probably ought to let go.

Of course, everything they were doing right now was predicated on the assumption that Beckett *could* get rid of this thing. One thing that had been categorically established during the summer's 'exciting' events was that being immortal didn't make spirits immune to damage from other spirits. What if the demon turned out to be stronger than Beckett? Cato really didn't want to think about what might happen if they needed to find a replacement for Beckett. That had hardly gone well before either.

He tried to tell himself that they were all going to be fine, that Beckett was going to snap this demon into kindling. He didn't find himself very convincing.

He glanced beyond Tait at Jonas, who was a nasty pale green now and only on his feet, as far as Cato could tell, because Reb was helping him. At this rate Jonas would be no use to them at all, especially given how erratic his magic had been at the best of times. But they could hardly just have left him behind at Reb's.

Beckett led them to a spot just past the middle of the square by the docks where the barges and distance-carts unloaded. The square was empty, not only of people but also of the pigeons and crows and seagulls that Cato would have expected to be here, bickering over scraps; he could certainly see the scraps, and smell them, but there wasn't a living being here other than themselves. Under the smell of dock and river and rotting vegetable matter, the air smelt like a storm was coming, and the hairs had risen up on Cato's arms.

Tait dropped his hand to scrub at their own arms; not just him, then. The clouds were towering ever higher, and the sky to the west was grey-black, with swirling purple clouds that were far too close to the ground.

"Where is everyone?" Marcia asked. Not being a sorcerer, arguably Marcia really should have stayed behind, but making that suggestion absolutely wouldn't have been worth the argument that would've ensued. Cato knew his sister.

"I sent them away," Beckett said.

"What, you showed up and told them?" Marcia was visibly shocked.

"No. I made them go away," Beckett said.

Cato and Reb exchanged glances. Cato reckoned Reb was just about as horrified by this new information about Beckett's abilities as he was, but there wasn't time to deal with that right now. The strange feeling in the air was thickening.

"It's coming," Jonas said, hoarsely, and suddenly Reb was struggling with him, his body a dead weight.

"He's fainted," she said, unnecessarily, and lowered him to the ground, frowning down at him in concern.

"If it's just a faint, he'll be fine," Cato said. "Also we have rather more urgent things to be worried about. Look."

On the road leading out of the square, past the barge-docks and winding along beside the river towards Teren, there were two figures, still a fair few yards away; and the purple clouds were boiling down towards them. Cato looked up, and saw more purple clouds, directly overhead.

"Where's the boundary?" he demanded, with a jolt of horror. "The city boundary. Between here and there, obviously. But where exactly?"

Beckett paced towards the road and the figures. If they'd been human, Cato would have described their body as tense. He wasn't sure if that really translated in spirit terms.

The purple clouds around the two figures coalesced, suddenly, and there was a third figure there, outlined in that unnatural purple, together with a feeling like Cato's ears had popped, but located in his sense of magic.

Jonas, on the ground, jerked and woke up, his eyes wide and pupils blown. "It's here," he said, somewhat unnecessarily in Cato's view.

Jonas scrambled unsteadily to his feet. Tait was damp with sweat around their hairline, their eyes terrified.

Beckett had stopped a few metres from where the road left the square, just by the edge of one of the barge-docks. Cato swallowed and made himself walk towards them, doing his best to retain his usual nonchalance. It was hard to do that, walking closer towards that purple shape on the road.

"Here," Beckett said, without turning round. "Here is the boundary."

The purple shape, and the two humans with it, were moving towards them.

Reb swore, and Cato echoed her. They caught each other's eye. Without needing to say more, hastily both began to spread rosemary and salt around their little group. Two rosemary-and-salt circles, one inside the other; that was more than double the protection that Cato usually worked with, when he bothered with protection at all, and yet he had the horrible sinking feeling that it wouldn't be enough.

"Someone must be outside the boundary," Beckett said. "Or we cannot reach the demon. One of you. I cannot go further."

Cato stopped for a moment and looked around. He really, really didn't like this. "Right. So. You're standing exactly on the boundary? Just the Marek side of it?"

Beckett nodded without looking away from the purple outline of the approaching demon.

"Use Beckett as the centre of the circles," Reb said, curtly, and Cato gestured agreement.

Which meant he would have to go outside the boundary of the city himself in order to complete the circle. He really, *really* didn't want to do that. He didn't see that he had much option. He gritted his teeth, and glanced over at Reb. He was slightly heartened to see that she too was visibly bracing herself.

"Go," Cato said, and they both stepped out over that invisible boundary at the same time, scattering salt and rosemary.

The sudden change in pressure nearly knocked Cato off his feet, and he saw, out of the corner of his eye, the purple shape speed up. But in barely a second more, he'd met Reb, and between them they had a full circle. The pressure didn't go away, but it reduced, enough that he felt he could take a breath. He and Reb exchanged another glance and continued around. Once they were done, they'd each made a full circle, and were back inside Marek. Cato stumbled as he stopped, then pretended he hadn't.

"It won't hold," Beckett said.

"It will if you put some bloody effort into it," Reb said through her teeth. "I thought you were the cityangel. You're on your home ground here, and that thing is not."

Beckett looked a bit startled. Cato tried not to cheer out loud. Then Beckett scowled down at the ground, and there was a sudden flare of magic that nearly had Cato falling into Tait. (Well, it was an ill wind, and all that...) The air changed smell, just a little, and the hair on Cato's arms tingled again.

"Thank you," Reb said.

She looked around at them. "How are we going to do this?"

"Someone needs to be in that side of the circle," Cato said. "Outside Marek. Tait's the one with the link, so they should stay inside Marek's protection or risk losing it. Beckett has to be there and no further. Marcia at the back, she's got no powers at all. But stay inside the circle, you hear, Marcia? And stay behind Beckett." He scowled, not liking where this was going.

"You and me in front," Reb said. She didn't look any happier than he did, that was the only consolation.

"And me," Jonas said. He still looked like hell.

Reb and Cato looked at each other. "He's an apprentice," Reb said.

"I won't be if we don't fix this, will I?" Jonas said. After a moment, Reb, reluctantly, nodded. Jonas stepped forward to stand with her and Cato, and the three of them waited as those three shapes on the road drew nearer to them, Cato's heart thrumming in his chest.

Reb squinted at the three figures closing on them in the dusk-dark light, the sun wholly invisible behind the dark clouds boiling overhead. Her heart was hammering. She had no idea what to expect here, and two rosemary-and-salt circles didn't feel like remotely enough protection, even with the cityangel at her back. The figures were still indistinct, the purple of the demon wisping and clouding around them. Was that...

Marcia, behind her, swore. "Selene."

Marcia had been right, then, however ridiculous it might sound that the Teren Lord Lieutenant would be attacking Marek with a demon. There must be something more to all of this – and whatever was going on, it couldn't possibly be in anyone's best interests for Teren and Marek to be at odds – but politics wasn't Reb's strong point at the best of times, and right now it wasn't important. Once they'd – if they – dealt with this, Marcia could take on that side of things. Surely it could be resolved.

She reached out to Cato, and, after a moment of hesitation, he took her hand, and reached out to take Jonas' on his other side.

"Is this necessary?" Cato asked. "We're in a circle, that ought to be enough." Cato never had been much of one for working with other sorcerers. He'd never ever apprenticed. She wondered, suddenly, feeling the tenseness of his hand in hers, if he felt he'd missed out.

"Skin contact helps," Reb said. "And I think we need all we can get, here."

"Do we need – herbs, or anything?" Jonas asked. His voice shook, just a little. Cato couldn't blame him.

"Something to strengthen the Marek bond," Cato said. "And something to strengthen us. Soot, and floor sweepings, for Marek."

"I have those," Reb said, using her free hand to reach into the herb-bags at her belt.

"I have ginger," Cato said, dropping her hand and digging into his own pocket.

Together, they threw a pinch of each into the circle at Beckett's feet. The ingredients began to swirl in their own little dust spout, and Reb took Cato's hand again.

"You need me too," Marcia said. "The Marek bond."

"Marcia..." Reb said.

"This is my fight too," Marcia said. "I can't do magic, but I am of House Fereno. I am of Marek."

"Yes, and being of the Houses is exactly why you

shouldn't be doing magic," Reb pointed out. "Again."

"I'm not doing magic," Marcia said. "I am supporting the defence of our city. And I am *damned* if I'm going to put the House absurdity about magic over the safety of Marek. Or – well. Never mind that now."

Cato was looking over his shoulder at Marcia, and Reb couldn't quite read his expression. Of course, Marcia had spent the last ten years interpreting Marekhill strictures about sorcerers as loosely as possible so she could stay in contact with her brother, and she'd been getting away with it just fine. Then Marcia met Reb's eyes, and Reb wondered... but she couldn't think about that right now.

Marcia moved next to Tait and laid one hand on Reb's shoulder and the other on Cato's. Reb's back tingled at the touch. She smelt Marcia's lemon soap; she felt Marcia's hand on her shoulder linking her down into the ground, and a taste of Marekhill in the back of her throat. There was a rush of energy through Cato's hand into hers: Marekhill again, more distant this time; three different overlaid sets of feelings about the city; a sense of connectedness; the calls of seagulls in her ears and the smell of the sea – Jonas?

Selene, and the person who must be the Teren sorcerer controlling the demon, and the demon, cloudy deep purple and oozing a power that Reb could feel even through the barrier, stopped in front of them.

"Selene," Marcia said.

"Fereno-Heir. Is this really your business? Sorcery?"

"You've brought a demon to Marek. It most certainly is my business," Marcia sounded furious. "And if you don't back off right now and send that thing back where it belongs, I will tell the Council all about it. I thought you wanted closer links between Marek and Teren? This is hardly the way to go about it."

"You've been undermining that since I got here," Selene said. "Guilds and the prosperity of Marek and all that nonsense. You'll talk to the Council, though, will you? Really? You're prepared to instigate civil war between Marek and Teren for the sake of some Teren sorcerer? And out yourself as using magic? Are you sure?" She gestured to Tait, standing next to Beckett. "Alternatively, you could hand that one there over and we would be all done here. No more trouble."

"I'm not using magic," Marcia said.

Selene's eyebrows went up. "You are standing immediately next to someone who is. Are you certain you can defend yourself from the accusation?"

"I am *certain* that you should keep your nose out of Mareker matters which do not concern you," Marcia snapped. "It is not for you to decide what using magic does or does not look like. And I'm *certain* that I'm not going to hand someone over for you to feed to a demon."

"No one is doing that," Reb said. Whatever she might have said before, right here and now, she finally knew she couldn't consider doing anything of the sort. She felt a wriggle of regret and self-recrimination that she'd sent Tait away in the first place. Not that taking them in would have helped avoid this, and Cato had stepped up where she'd failed, but...

But she should have known better. Cato doing a better job than her was a hard thing to swallow.

Selene shrugged. "It's their demon in the first place."

"I banished it," Tait said, their voice shaking.

"True," the demon said, in a voice that scraped glass across the nerves. "And then this one brought me back to search for you."

"Ha!" Cato said. He glanced over at Reb. "Told you so."

Then why? Why did tracking down one sorcerer matter this much; so much that Selene was prepared to antagonise Marek for it? Or was she assuming that no one else would know about this, that she'd win?

Reb glanced over her shoulder and saw Marcia biting her lip, lines of concentration folded between her eyebrows. Marcia was the one who knew politics. This wasn't her problem. Her problem was the magic here; and if the demon was giving things away, maybe that was a sign that it wasn't as predictable as Selene thought.

Of course, that didn't mean it was any less powerful; but it might make it possible to scare it away. Spirits didn't normally try to bother Beckett. Reb didn't believe that this one would be trying this of its own accord. Gently, a tiny movement, she squeezed Cato's hand, and he squeezed back, just as small a movement. Marcia's hand tightened on her shoulder.

Selene scowled at the demon. "Quiet!" She turned to the

sorcerer, a quiet person in a dark hooded robe. "I thought you were in control here?"

"This isn't easy, you know," the sorcerer said through clenched teeth. They gestured, and the demon, evidently about to say something else, bulged at the corners of its shape and howled instead. It reached out towards Tait, and bounced off the rosemary-and-salt circle.

The circle was suddenly almost visible in the air around them, a dome of protective power that Reb could see with a sense that wasn't sight. The demon dented it inwards, pushing as hard as it could, before it rebounded off again.

But as it pushed, Reb felt, attenuated by the circle, a change in the atmosphere around them, as if in trying to breach the protective circle, the demon had taken its attention away from its attempt to break into Marek as a whole.

Now.

Beckett's voice echoed in Reb's mind, and without hesitation, Reb opened her magic up, and felt Beckett grabbing fiercely at her attention. It was nothing like linking up with Zareth had been. It was terrifying, an out-of-control feeling like nothing she'd ever done before, and it took all she had not to close herself back down again, yank herself out of it.

Through Beckett she felt again a faint echo of Cato, and the sea-tinged feel of Jonas, unsure and untrained but with something behind his sorcery that she couldn't identify at all. Beckett linked them all through to Tait, and Reb could feel them too, Tait's worry and ambivalence and a willingness, now, to do whatever it took to solve this problem. Behind that, echoing back through her shoulder and Cato's into Beckett, without any tinge of sorcery, Marcia and the Houses and Marekhill, a deep and unbreakable linkage to the city that rooted all of them into the ground, tendrils spreading out underneath them.

The banked power swirled around them, and Beckett hit out with it; but it didn't touch the demon.

The demon howled gleefully, and surged upwards, deep and purple and terrifying. Reb felt its malice and its hatred at its binding focussed in on them. The circle dented in again, more and harder this time, and Reb felt the protection grow thin at the same time as she felt Beckett trying to pull more from all of them. Her knees shook.

"Tait!" Cato said, his voice higher than normal in worry.

Beckett couldn't do this. It had to be Tait. Tait might not have summoned it this time, but they had summoned it before, and it was them it was hunting. Tait had to use that link.

Beckett hit out again, with no effect other than to send Reb light-headed for a moment.

"Beckett, you can't, remember? Let Tait do it," Cato growled.

Reb looked over her shoulder. Tait stood behind Beckett with their eyes shut, an expression of deep concentration on their face.

"I can't reach it," Tait said, panting, without opening their eyes. "I'm trying, but…"

"Whatever you're trying to do, it won't work," Selene said. Her voice was scornful, dismissive. "This is more powerful than you." She paused, and when she spoke again, she sounded calm, convincing, generous, even. "Give me the sorcerer, and all this will go away. No need for any dramatic gestures. No need to damage Marek. They're Teren anyway, after all. They're ours to bother with. No concern of yours."

"No," Reb said, echoed by Cato and Marcia, and Beckett underneath, a bass note that shook them all. Even the demon juddered.

But it wasn't going anywhere.

"I can't link to it," Tait whispered. "It's there, but it's the wrong direction, I can't push it back… Give me up. You'll have to." They sounded agonised.

"Absolutely *not*," Cato said, through his teeth, and Reb felt him pushing harder, with every ounce of his strength, could feel his power shaking through Beckett and out again – into Tait.

Reb gritted her teeth and copied him, pouring her magic-sense through Beckett and into Tait. She thought, just maybe, that she too could feel the link now. A tiny, tenuous one, a faint feel of the demon who was still outside Marek, outside Beckett's power, but if they could just reach it… but it wasn't there, it wasn't happening, and Reb knew she was running out of energy altogether. Marcia's hand clenched on her shoulder, fingertips digging into the muscle, and Reb tried to push Tait onwards, but she didn't have anything left, she couldn't, and beside her Cato took a sobbing breath...

Jonas, beyond Cato, impossibly distant across the few feet of the circle, turned his face to the sky, and screamed. That sea-tinge intensified, and for a fraction of a second it felt like Marek was convulsing under them without moving, and then from every corner of the sky birds appeared, pigeons and seagulls and crows, as if materialising from nowhere, a terrifying storm of feathers and beaks and claws. Tait fell forwards, flinging their arms around Jonas, and screamed in their turn, and every single bird descended, as a mass, upon the purple demon.

All the power they'd accumulated, all of them, shot through Beckett, to Tait, and outwards down to the demon, in a rush that blurred Reb's vision.

The link built, and surged, and broke; and the demon disappeared.

TWENTY-FIVE

Jonas lay on the floor, blinking up at the sky, with no idea where he was or how he'd got there. Somewhere in the open? The sky was full of racing grey clouds, but he had the vague impression that it had looked different, not very long ago. Black and purple and swirls above him.

The shadow, though. The shadow, over Marek, across him… it had gone. He drew in a long breath, and even with the smells of water and mud and rotting vegetables around him, the air felt clear.

"Shit," he heard from somewhere above him.

Cato. That was Cato. Where was he, then? Slowly, Jonas levered himself up, and looked around. Tait was sitting on the ground next to him, slumped forwards, their head in their hands. Cato had just knelt down beside Tait and had a hand on their shoulder, leaning forwards intently to say something. Reb and Marcia were both standing nearby, leaning in on one another, and just past their feet, he could see the remains of a circle in white and green powder.

Salt and rosemary. He remembered now. Some of it, anyway. He wasn't sure how hard he wanted to try to remember in detail.

Further away… there were empty carts, their traces propped on the ground, over to one side, and sturdy plank docks away to his left. But not *the* docks… He didn't think he knew this place. The river was here, though.

Marcia straightened her shoulders and walked away, towards two figures Jonas didn't want to look at. Reb turned towards him, and bent down.

"Jonas? Are you all right?"

"What's happened? Where am I?" He was aware as he said it what a terrible cliché it was, and winced. Reb didn't seem to notice.

"What's the last thing you remember?" she asked, briskly.

"In your house?" Jonas said, slowly. He only had a few snippets of recollection of that, even. "Was Beckett there? I

317

was at Cato's, and I told him... and then we went to your house." He looked around. "Did we come here? Where is this?"

"Beckett brought us to the edge of the city," Reb said. "This is the river docks, where the caravans and the barges unload, though it's normally rather busier than this. Beckett," she wrinkled her nose up, "appears to have... made it clear. Which I suppose is for the best, given what's happened, but I won't pretend it's not a bit worrying to think of."

"The demon," Jonas said, but the sudden spike of automatic worry didn't have any real power to it. He knew with bone-deep certainty that the demon, the shadow, was gone.

"Gone," Reb said. "Disappeared or back to its own plane or... I don't know where, and I don't much care. Beckett went immediately after."

"Didn't even say goodbye," Cato drawled.

Jonas twisted to look up at him.

"Is he all right, then?" Cato asked Reb.

"He's fine," Reb said. "Lost a bit of memory."

Cato crouched down to meet Jonas' eyes. "You did well," he said, sounding genuinely sincere. "We couldn't have done it without you. I thought we weren't going to."

"Me?" Jonas asked. "I didn't... ?"

Cato looked a little bothered, and like he was trying to hide it. "You really are quite strong when you're playing to your strengths. Seagulls. Birds..." He trailed off, looking thoughtful. "Well now. I might give that some thought, when you're well enough to be working again."

Jonas rubbed at his head, and then at his arms.

"He's shivering," Reb said. "We should get him back indoors."

"Tait, too," Cato said. "I think the link snapping was pretty hard on them." He looked over at where Marcia was. "Not as hard as it was on the sorcerer controlling that thing, mind." His tone was viciously pleased.

Tait still had their head in their hands, their shoulders hunched up around their ears. They said something unintelligible.

"Tait, no," Cato began, but Reb interrupted.

"What did they say?" she demanded.

Tait raised their head. "I should leave Marek," they said. "I'll stay here. Wait for people to come back, or the next barges to come in, or something. That's the way I came in."

"Why leave now?" Reb asked. "The problem you brought to our door is resolved." She looked over to where Marcia was talking to the other woman Jonas had seen. He couldn't hear what they were saying, but Marcia's back didn't look happy. "Also, if you leave now, I strongly suspect that Selene there, or her colleague, will pick you straight back up again. I rather thought that was what you were trying to avoid."

"I'm hardly welcome here though, am I?" Tait's face was drawn.

"Do you want to learn Marek magic?" Cato asked, more gently than Jonas was used to hearing from him. "That's what you said. Did you mean it?"

Tait hesitated, then, slowly, nodded. "I don't want to go back to Teren." He glanced over at Marcia and Selene and the Teren sorcerer, and shuddered.

Cato shrugged. "Then stay, and learn. Fuck knows we need more sorcerers." He gestured around. "Marek used to be full of us. Now, this is it. You want to come, you can stay." He looked up at Reb, his chin raised. "Right, Reb?"

Reb sighed, and shut her eyes for a moment, looking pained. "I'm hardly in a position to criticise someone coming from Teren magic to Marek, am I now?"

Jonas looked at her in surprise. "You... ?"

"It's a long time ago," Reb said. "But yes."

"You said I should leave," Tait said.

"And if you had done, we wouldn't have had to solve the problem this way," Reb said. "Which would have been an improvement from my point of view, although not so much from yours. However. It's done now. And in all honesty, having told that woman she couldn't have you, I'd rather you didn't go ahead and undo all of our work. Stay." Jonas wouldn't have said that she sounded hugely enthusiastic, but she did sound sincere.

"I can take them on as an apprentice," Cato said.

"You're barely finding the time to work with me," Jonas objected.

"Jonas is right," Reb said, crisply. "Something you should resolve, Cato, while I'm on the subject. Also, if I'm not mistaken," she looked at Cato, his arm around Tait, who was leaning against him, "it would be highly unethical for the two of you to work together." She sighed again. "I'll do it."

Cato looked as though he was considering being offended, then shrugged. "Fine. I can see the advantage of doing it your way, in any case." He looked across at Tait. Tait flushed.

Marcia stomped back towards them, looking frustrated. The other two people were walking away, towards the road they'd come in on. One of them was limping slightly, their arms round themself. The other was straight-backed, their walk almost... jaunty? Couldn't be. Those two had *lost*, right?

"Let's go," Marcia said, tersely.

Reb bent down to help Jonas up. His legs were still a bit wobbly, but he managed to start walking. Back towards the centre of Marek, surrounded – he looked around – by the sorcerers of Marek.

He was a sorcerer of Marek, apprentice or no. The realisation hit him hard in the middle of the chest, and he stumbled. Reb caught him.

"Jonas?" Cato, arm still around Tait, sounded worried.

"I'm fine," he said, finding his feet again. He felt, all of a sudden, more stable. "I'm fine, honestly."

He belonged here. Maybe not for ever; but for now, he truly did belong here.

☺ ☺

Marcia's conversation with Selene had been short, and extremely frustrating.

"So," Selene said. "Do you intend, then, to instigate civil war?"

Her arms were folded, and her expression cool and secure. She didn't look like someone who had just lost her demon, and the sorcerer she'd been chasing. She looked like she was in control.

Her sorcerer, on the other hand, the one who'd been managing the demon, had just thrown up on the ground, and was shuddering in a heap on his knees. Selene ignored him.

Marcia looked at Selene's bland expression and clenched her teeth.

"You realise," Selene said, "that this is only a taste of what we can do. We have a great many more sorcerers, now. A great many more demons, if we wish. Declare war on us and you will have a demon army marching on your city. Your *cityangel* cannot stand against us." She sounded faintly contemptuous. "Not to mention the question of how seriously you will be taken were I to tell them my side of the story. You, and your sorcerer brother, and your sorcerer lover, threatening the Teren Lord Lieutenant with magic? Your word against mine. Who do you think they would believe?"

"I am Fereno-Heir," Marcia said, coldly, but she felt the worm of doubt inside her. She might have more witnesses than Selene, but they were all sorcerers; relying on them might cause more harm than good.

"Then by all means, let us try it. If you're right, you will be secure, but Teren and Marek will be outwardly and publicly at odds. Think carefully about the cost of that. If you're wrong, I will have demonstrated that the Council should have listened to me this afternoon, rather than to you." She smiled, without any warmth at all. "Of course, in due course I am sure that decision will be revisited. But for now – we can simply continue as we are. No need for Marek to challenge Teren, and face the costs of that. No need for *you* to face the costs of it. So. Are you certain you wish to force a confrontation? Or are you going to be sensible?"

She stared at Marcia, coolly mocking.

Marcia desperately wanted to say that yes, she would denounce Selene, would tell the Houses what she had done, would make the truth public and take the consequences.

The problem was, Selene was right. She couldn't put Marek openly into opposition with Teren. They didn't have the strength. She'd just managed to pull the city out of one catastrophic disruption. She couldn't plunge it immediately into the middle of a second one, one with potentially much bigger consequences.

And, more ignobly, she wasn't sure she could withstand the scrutiny that Selene would, in return, throw onto her. Everyone knew about Cato, and accepted that Marcia met with her brother, even if no one mentioned it to her in public. But Reb, that might be a different thing. The events of the summer – only Daril truly knew about them, granted, but there had been mutterings afterwards. The gossips had assumed something political was going on and never thought of the magical, but if anyone thought to really look into it... And now, here she was, again, at the centre of a magical attack on Marek. Resisting the magical attack, of course; but that wouldn't necessarily matter, to the Houses. And this time, she hadn't just stood on the sidelines. She'd taken part. Only as a link back to the city, perhaps, but still; she'd broken the law, no question about it, and Selene knew. Even if she managed to explain it to the Council and wasn't expelled from her House on the spot; even then, the pressure on Madeleine to disinherit her would be intense.

Madeleine had disinherited Cato without so much as a glance behind her afterwards.

Maybe this wasn't quite the same. Maybe.

And if Selene did win the argument, if Marcia was disinherited for sorcery, Marek would be even worse prepared to withstand whatever it was Teren was planning, and even more primed to believe Selene in the future.

Selene watched Marcia fail to say anything, and a tiny smirk of a smile appeared at the corners of her mouth.

"I have another two days in Marek, before I return," she said. "I'm sure I will see you at another of these balls or meals or however else the Houses choose to entertain me."

She bowed, very slightly, and turned to walk away; then turned back. "Oh. And if I were you, I would look to your squats and your own poor. What we've seen in Teren will come here, too. Read a news-sheet, if you can lower yourself that far." She sounded vicious. "And in due course you'll realise why you should have taken this opportunity to align yourself with Teren again, and you'll come crawling back to us begging to come under our wing."

She turned again and walked away; shakily, the sorcerer rose to his feet and followed her. For a moment, he too turned back, and his hood slipped a little so Marcia could see his eyes. But he wasn't looking at Marcia; he was looking, with longing, at Tait.

No, not at Tait, Marcia realised. At what Tait represented. At Tait, in Marek.

Then he turned back and hurried after Selene; and, sick at heart, Marcia turned to her own people.

TWENTY-SIX

It seemed a lot further, walking back from the edge of the city, than it had seemed getting there; although in fact Cato and Tait were only going to the squats, so it was objectively less far. Cato's feet, and his all-over bodily ache, didn't agree with objective fact. There were still a few grey clouds around, but the wind was blowing them away, and the setting sun had appeared again underneath them, casting red fingers across the streets. People were back in the streets, too. Back doing all their usual things, running messages, fetching water, standing idly around chatting… Nothing had changed, for anyone else.

He should be used to that. Magic happened off at an angle from everyone else. But he felt, as he walked through Marek, like he was lagging an inch or two behind his body. Like his skin itched slightly. He wanted to tell people to *pay more attention*, except that was both stupid and pointless. He wanted…

He wanted a *bath*, was what he wanted. And quite a lot of wine.

They reached the outskirts of the squats. Cato nodded at Reb and Marcia. They looked roughly like he felt.

"I'm going this way," he said, unnecessarily. "Jonas? Tait?"

Tait hadn't said anything since they left the river-docks, and didn't seem to want to now. But they followed after Cato. Jonas turned up the street towards the squats, too. He was looking better than he had when he'd been having those flickers – Cato really did need to follow up on those – but still not what you'd call full of the joys of life. And he was Cato's apprentice. Cato should probably… look out for him, or something.

He had no idea how to do that.

"Uh. Jonas. How're you doing?" he tried. "You should maybe… go and have a lie down. Or something."

He sounded like an idiot, didn't he? Jonas glanced over at

him and rolled his eyes. Cato chose to read that as affectionate.

"I'm going to go find Asa," Jonas said. "I'm fine." He jerked his head to one side. "In fact, I'm going that way." He turned left. Presumably he lived that way. Or he was just really desperate to get away from Cato's attempts at master-apprentice bonding.

"Come by tomorrow afternoon! Lesson!" Cato called after him, and Jonas raised a hand in acknowledgement without turning round.

Which left him and Tait.

"I think," Cato said, thoughtfully, "that what I really need right now is a lovely long soak in the hottest water the baths have to offer." He paused. "And some wine. Definitely some wine. Like, right now."

He glanced sideways at Tait, who looked like that was a very appealing thought, and also like they didn't think they were included in the idea.

"Yes? Coming with?" Cato asked.

Tait's face brightened a little, then dropped again. "My money's back in the room, and I don't know, I shouldn't just…" Their shoulders were hunched in embarrassment.

"Don't worry about the money," Cato said, then, more sternly, "really, don't worry. Hang onto your demon-bear payment, and you can owe me one for some future time when you are a rich Mareker sorcerer. Also, you need to pick up those clothes you left for cleaning, so you might as well."

"Oh! But I don't have the token… ?"

"You're with me," Cato said. "They'll remember which are ours, trust me." They'd have washed them and kept them separately, because people were annoyingly superstitious about some things in this city. Not that it wasn't handy enough.

Tait looked like they really, really wanted to agree. Gently, giving them plenty of room to back away, Cato put a hand on their arm.

They didn't back away, and Cato's heart – no, no, he refused to engage with any notions of his heart. Something else – leapt.

"Come on," Cato said firmly. "Come and soak with me."

They didn't talk much in the baths, but Cato surreptitiously watched the tension soak out of Tait as they scrubbed themself off, steamed for a while, and then soaked next to Cato in the warm pool. The enormous tumblers of cheap red that Cato had bought for both of them were probably helping, too.

"Reb'll do right by you," Cato said at one point, though the words stuck a little in his craw. "She's bloody annoying, and terribly ethical, but she's a good sorcerer."

"Whereas no one ever finds you annoying, I'm sure," Tait said.

"I don't know what you could possibly mean," Cato said loftily, and rejoiced in the indication that Tait might be beginning to bounce back from the afternoon's events. It would take longer than this, of course. But if Cato could help, a little...

They both swapped their dirty clothes in for their clean ones, dressed, and walked up the road together, then up the stairs to the landing where both of their doors stood. Tait hesitated, for a second, and Cato took a breath.

"So," he said. "Are you up to anything this evening?"

Tait looked at him. "Not that I can think of."

Cato grinned, and leaned on the doorway of his room. "Want to come in?"

Tait grinned back. "Sounds like an interesting plan."

They were already kissing as the door shut behind them.

☉ ☉

Marcia watched Cato, Tait, and Jonas head off towards the squats, and raised an eyebrow at Reb. "Am I seeing what I think I'm seeing, there? Cato and Tait?"

"No idea how long it'll last," Reb said. "He's your brother, you know what he's like. But better I apprentice Tait, either way."

Marcia was still looking thoughtfully after Cato. "He was being surprisingly... nice. Though it's not like I've ever got to meet any of his, ah, friends, before. I don't get the impression they last all that long." Cato hardly ever mentioned lovers to her, though she was confident that he had them, even if only ever temporarily.

Reb shrugged. "As long as they can get on politely afterwards I honestly don't care. Tait seems nice enough, when they're not bringing demons to Marek, so I'm not sure it's the best of matches."

"Hey," Marcia said, automatically. "Cato's nice… enough…" She stopped. "He's my brother. Be kind."

"Of course," Reb said, and smiled sideways at Marcia.

"Was the demon Tait's fault, though, in the end?" Marcia asked. "I had the impression it wasn't, but that part all went by a bit fast for me." She waved a hand. "Magic and stuff. You know."

"They raised it in the first place," Reb said, "but they say they banished it, and the demon confirmed it, inasmuch as you can trust that. That other sorcerer must have raised it and used the old link to hunt Tait, I suppose. So – yes, not their fault." She frowned. "What with everything else Tait said about Teren sorcery, I'm a bit… I need to talk to Tait, once they've had a rest."

"Selene talked about a demon army," Marcia said.

Reb blinked. "She what?"

"She threatened us – sort of – with a demon army. If I told the Council what she'd been up to. She said, it would be civil war, and did I really want that." Marcia chewed on her lip. "Which – I don't see that I can say anything, now." She decided not to mention Selene's other threat. It seemed like it would be hard to talk about that without also getting into the matter of where she and Reb were going. They'd have to discuss it, eventually. But… not right now.

"Storm and fire," Reb said. "I really do need to speak to Tait." She sighed. "But there won't be any demon army right away. It can wait a while."

"Maybe you need a rest, too?" Marcia suggested.

"I was about to say the same to you," Reb said.

They were close to Reb's house now, and Reb stopped on the street corner.

"Are you going back across the river, or," she paused, "uh, I know I've been a bit of a shit lately, but would you like to come back to mine?"

"I'd like to come back," Marcia said "I mean, I've been a bit of a shit too."

Reb started walked again, and Marcia walked with her.

"I should apologise," Reb said, at the next street corner.

Marcia looked over at her. "Really? I figured it was me that ought to, as it happens."

"I may have my responsibilities, but you've got yours too. I don't like politics, but it's your job, and I accept that. I've no right to dictate how you manage that, and I shouldn't have tried. I'm sorry."

Marcia laughed. "Funny. That was more or less exactly what I was going to say, but the other way around."

Her responsibilities. Like, for example, the promise she'd made to her mother. Which she really did have to tell Reb about. Just... later. Another time. Right now, they were in charity with each other, and she was tired, and all she wanted was to go to bed with Reb and forget about everything else, just for a while.

Nothing was happening right away. There was no decision that she had to make immediately. She could just... leave it, for now.

Reb put out a hand, and Marcia took it. "Maybe we both need to make allowances?" Reb suggested.

"And a bit more time for each other?"

Surely they could work something out, between them, if they both wanted to. They'd solved far harder problems, right? If they both wanted to... She'd tell Reb, and they'd talk about it, and they'd find a solution. Both to the business of Marekhill and magic, and regarding Marcia's heir. It needn't be a problem for Reb, right?

Another day. Another day, she'd tell Reb all about it, and they'd sort it out together. For now, she was just going to enjoy Reb's company.

They'd reached Reb's door, and Reb opened it, and smiled at her. "More time, huh? I'm free this evening. How about you?"

"No plans," Marcia said.

"I can think of some," Reb said, and pulled Marcia a little closer as she shut the door behind them.

"I was hoping for dinner first," Marcia said, plaintively, then gave the lie to her statement by kissing Reb.

"How about dinner after?" Reb said.

"Oh," Marcia murmured into her mouth. "I imagine that could be arranged."

※ ※ ※ ※ ※ ※ ※ ※ ※

ACKNOWLEDGEMENTS

A book is simultaneously a thing you create whilst spending a lot of time all by yourself in a room, and a thing contributed to and supported by many other people.

Shoutout to Jo Ladziński, Lore Graham, and Ian Llywelyn Brown for reading an earlier version of this book and giving me patient and helpful feedback; and to the folks on the writing Slack for cheerleading, problem-solving, and making 'sitting at a desk staring at a computer screen' feel like a slightly less solitary endeavour. Thanks to Aliette de Bodard for kind words and fountain pen enabling!

Peter and Alison at Elsewhen continue to be both excellent publishers and lovely people to chat to. My thanks too go to Sofia for her sterling editing work.

Everyone who's said to me anything along the lines of "oh, there's going to be another book? Cool!" — it really does help to hear that when toiling in the word-mines. Thank you!

And finally, love and gratitude as ever to doop, Pete, and Leon, for putting up with me.

Juliet, November 2019

Elsewhen Press

delivering outstanding new talents in speculative fiction

Visit the Elsewhen Press website at elsewhen.press for the latest information on all of our titles, authors and events; to read our blog; find out where to buy our books and ebooks; or to place an order.

Sign up for the Elsewhen Press InFlight Newsletter at elsewhen.press/newsletter

THE DEEP AND SHINING DARK

BOOK 1 OF THE MAREK SERIES

JULIET KEMP

"A rich and memorable tale of political ambition, family and magic, set in an imagined city that feels as vibrant as the characters inhabiting it."

Aliette de Bodard

Nebula-award winning author of *The Tea Master and the Detective*

You know something's wrong when the cityangel turns up at your door

Magic within the city-state of Marek works without the need for bloodletting, unlike elsewhere in Teren, thanks to an agreement three hundred years ago between an angel and the founding fathers. It also ensures that political stability is protected from magical influence. Now, though, most sophisticates no longer even believe in magic *or* the cityangel.

But magic has suddenly stopped working, discovers Reb, one of the two sorcerers who survived a plague that wiped out virtually all of the rest. Soon she is forced to acknowledge that someone has deposed the cityangel without being able to replace it. Marcia, Heir to House Fereno, and one of the few in high society who is well-aware that magic still exists, stumbles across that same truth. But it is just one part of a much more ambitious plan to seize control of Marek.

Meanwhile, city Council members connive and conspire, unaware that they are being manipulated in a dangerous political game. A game that threatens the peace and security not just of the city, but all the states around the Oval Sea, including the shipboard traders of Salina upon whom Marek relies.

To stop the impending disaster, Reb and Marcia, despite their difference in status, must work together alongside the deposed cityangel and Jonas, a messenger from Salina. But first they must discover who is behind the plot, and each of them must try to decide who they can really trust.

Book 1 of Juliet Kemp's gripping series

With "absolutely gorgeous" cover artwork by renowned artist Tony Allcock

ISBN: 9781911409342 (epub, kindle) / ISBN: 9781911409243 (272pp paperback)
Visit bit.ly/DeepShiningDark

Thorns of a Black Rose

David Craig

Revenge and responsibility, confrontation and consequences.

A hot desert land of diverse peoples dealing with demons, mages, natural disasters … and the Black Rose assassins.

On a quest for vengeance, Shukara arrives in the city of Mask having already endured two years of hardship and loss. Her pouch is stolen by Tamira, a young street-smart thief, who throws away some of the rarer reagents that Shukara needs for her magick. Tracking down the thief, and being unfamiliar with Mask, Shukara shows mercy to Tamira in exchange for her help in replacing what has been lost. Together they brave the intrigues of Mask, and soon discover that they have a mutual enemy in the Black Rose, an almost legendary band of merciless assassins. But this is just the start of their journeys…

Although set in an imaginary land, the scenery and peoples of *Thorns of a Black Rose* were inspired by Egypt, Morocco and the Sahara. Mask is a living, breathing city, from the prosperous Merchant Quarter whose residents struggle for wealth and power, to the Poor Quarter whose residents struggle just to survive. It is a coming of age tale for the young thief, Tamira, as well as a tale of vengeance and discovery. There is also a moral ambiguity in the story, with both the protagonists and antagonists learning that whatever their intentions or justification, actions have consequences.

ISBN: 9781911409557 (epub, kindle) / 9781911409458 (256pp paperback)
Visit bit.ly/ThornsOfABlackRose

QUAESTOR

DAVID M ALLAN

When you're searching, you don't always find what you expect

In Carrhen some people have a magic power – they may be telekinetic, clairvoyant, stealthy, or able to manipulate the elements. Anarya is a Sponger, she can absorb and use anyone else's magic without them even being aware, but she has to keep it a secret as it provokes jealousy and hostility especially among those with no magic powers at all.

When Anarya sees Yisyena, a Sitrelker refugee, being assaulted by three drunken men, she helps her to escape. Anarya is trying to establish herself as an investigator, a quaestor, in the city of Carregis. Yisyena is a clairvoyant, a skill that would be a useful asset for a quaestor, so Anarya offers her a place to stay and suggests they become business partners. Before long they are also lovers.

But business is still hard to find, so when an opportunity arises to work for Count Graumedel who rules over the city, they can't afford to turn it down, even though the outcome may not be to their liking.

Soon they are embroiled in state secrets and the personal vendettas of a murdered champion, a cabal, a puppet king, and a false god looking for one who has defied him.

ISBN: 9781911409571 (epub, kindle) / ISBN: 9781911409472 (304pp paperback)
Visit bit.ly/Quaestor-Allan

The Unwritten Words series by Christopher Nuttall

The Golden City has fallen, the Empire is no more, ancient magic threatens the land. In *The Unwritten Words*, Christopher Nuttall's story-telling mastery weaves a new epic which follows on from his bestselling *Bookworm* series and is set in that same world.

I – The Promised Lie

Five years have passed since the earth-shattering events of *Bookworm IV*. The Golden City has fallen. The Grand Sorcerer and Court Wizards are dead. The Empire they ruled is nothing more than a memory, a golden age lost in the civil wars as kings and princes battle for supremacy. And only a handful of trained magicians remain alive.

Isabella Majuro, Lady Sorceress, is little more than a mercenary, fighting for money in a desperate bid to escape her past. But when Prince Reginald of Andalusia plots the invasion of the Summer Isle, Isabella finds herself dragged into a war against strange magics from before recorded history …

… And an ancient mystery that may spell the end of the human race.

ISBN: 9781908168311 (epub, kindle) / 9781908168212 (416pp, paperback)
Visit bit.ly/ThePromisedLie
Available as an audiobook from Tantor

II – The Ancient Lie

After the campaign in the Summer Isle, Isabella rides out the winter storms by studying the godly magic under Mother Lembu, in the process learning about the origins of the old gods.

Crown Prince Reginald receives word that his father the King, is ill while his sister Princess Sofia, acting as regent, is imposing a regime that is strangely similar to what had been happening on the Summer Isle – nobles killed, temples smashed, enforced public worship of old gods. Concerned that his family, and indeed his homeland, are in danger, Reginald is determined to return home. But the storms are still raging with what appears to be unnatural force, making any attempt to return to Andalusia too risky for the Prince and his men…. unless Isabella can somehow use the new rituals she has learnt to placate the powers behind the storms and navigate the fleet safely home to face whatever has taken control of the kingdom.

ISBN: 9781908168397 (epub, kindle) / 9781908168292 (352pp, paperback)
Visit bit.ly/TheAncientLie

III – The Truthful Lie

The story concludes.
ISBN: 9781908168502 (epub, kindle) / 9781908168403 (paperback)

ABOUT JULIET KEMP

Juliet Kemp lives by the river in London, with their partners, child, dog, and too many fountain pens. They have had stories published in several anthologies and online magazines. Their employment history variously includes working as a cycle instructor, sysadmin, life model, researcher, permaculture designer, and journalist. When not writing or parenting, Juliet goes climbing, knits, reads way too much, and drinks a lot of tea.